THE SHADOW OF DOUBT

*To Geraldine,
with best wishes*

Joan Brittaine

Joan Brittaine

To Laurie
for his ongoing encouragement
and support

Joan Brittaine

THE SHADOW OF DOUBT
Copyright © Joan Brittaine 2006

All rights reserved.

No part of this book may be reproduced in any form by
photocopying or any electronic or mechanical means,
including information storage or retrieval systems,
without permission in writing from both the copyright
owner and the publisher of the book.

ISBN 978-184426-402-5

First Published 2006 by
UPFRONT PUBLISHING LTD
Peterborough, England.

Printed by Print-on-Demand Worldwide Ltd.

Joan Brittaine

Author's note

Very little information exists about Madeleine's behaviour, thoughts and emotions during her earlier life, as are the years leading up to her arrest, her confinement in jail and during the trial – and for the purpose of this memoir this has been fictionalised. The dialogue used, minor characters involved and the various situations described therefore are entirely coincidental and have no resemblance to actual events, locales or persons living or dead. Details of the trial however are authentic, as are the letters written by Madeleine Smith and Emile L'Angelier.

THE SHADOW OF DOUBT

Was Madeleine Smith guilty?
You be the judge

JOAN BRITTAINE

Joan Brittaine

Chapter One

James Smith flung wide the door of his study for his daughter to pass and in a voice edging on irritation demanded, 'You must leave us now Madeleine. We have work to do!' The men he had called to a business meeting that morning shifted about uncomfortably in the immediate silence, one of them decidedly embarrassed.

Madeleine's cheeks burned hot as she rose to leave, but the lingering blush was not for her father's glare. One young man, taking her fancy that morning had praised her slim ankles when she'd revealed her white silk stockings, and the others had joined the teasing when she'd giggled, tossing her dark ringlets that had taken forever to arrange.

She smoothed a gloved hand over the blue silk dress she had chosen to wear, inclining her head provocatively towards the men who watched her every move. And as the clock ticking became louder in the embarrassing hush she hesitated briefly before sweeping past her father with a polite nod – and turning with a provocative smile, she murmured, 'Good-day gentlemen.'

* * *

'Your behaviour in this house is both perplexing and distressing,' her father declared as Madeleine faced him the following day. She had expected him to send for her. It was not the first time he'd caught her flaunting herself and with her hands folded submissively in her lap, she wondered what would happen this time.

'Do you have any idea what I am speaking of?' he went on irritably.

Of course, she did – but how could she say! 'Perhaps I do father,' she answered meekly.

'And what may be your idea I wonder? Tell me.'

Her parents' silent stares and reprimands had become more frequent of late and there was the time she had lost her temper when they remonstrated about her arguing and rushed from the room with her father following to scold. On the other hand, could it be something to do with the children she wondered, grasping at excuses. She had to say something. Anything! She couldn't admit to the sin of enjoying the company of men!

'It seems you and Mama disapprove of me for some reason father,' she said at last. 'Perhaps how I deal with the younger children?' Her eyes widened, 'Maybe I am too strict?'

She felt her throat restrict as his eyes bore into hers – until unable to stand the feminine weakness of tears when he saw her mouth starting to quiver, he snorted, 'You really have no idea do you?'

She brushed a hand across her eyes watching him strut away, arms held rigid behind his back with clasped hands – and flinching back as he suddenly wheeled round and flung at her, 'then just dress a little more suitably when my clients arrive Madeleine if you have to be there. And what's more,' he went on, flicking an outstretched hand, 'you are far too young to indulge in... er, these fancy hairstyles.'

Quickly recovering, she rose indignantly, 'Mama always tells me to look well turned out when I receive your business associates father. I try to look presentable.'

'And why should you be doing this so often may I ask?' he hurled. 'This is your mother's responsibility. Entirely hers.'

'She asks me father,' she answered with determination, and her resentment showed. 'When she is unwell she asks me. You know how often she is...'

'I know, I know,' he interrupted, strutting irritably again ... *only too well he knew. Drat it! How could he escape from the incompetence of women – and now a daughter flirting with his clients, in his own study of all places! Behaving like a tart and rapidly getting out of hand!*

* * *

Calmer and in more control back in her room, Madeleine studied her reflection in the mirror, glancing first one way then another. Her father's angry outburst had brought an attractive flush to her cheeks and her eyes still burned bright with indignation. She leaned closer to the glass and moistening her fingertips smoothed the long curved lashes up into dark fringes as she widened her challenging grey eyes, then shaking the ringlets shining like ebony that had so annoyed her father, she suddenly laughed out loud making her face come alive.

Slowly brushing her hands down her slender figure, breathing deeply as she turned to admire her slim waist and full bust, she shivered. New sensations were surging throughout her body. Feelings she did not fully understand but found she enjoyed. She knew the effect she had on men. She knew they found her attractive – like the men had in her father's study yesterday. She enjoyed the way they looked at her. The way they teased, *and why was this so wrong?* A quiet tapping at the door suddenly interrupted her thoughts and spinning round she heard her mother's voice outside, just above a whisper and sounding agitated.

'Your father has spoken to me Madeleine,' she muttered, hurrying into the room and fussing nervously as she closed the door. 'He is very annoyed.' She hovered uncertainly, her sunken eyes bright with pleading and Madeleine felt unsure what to say. How could she reveal her true feelings and bring further torment to her mother who already suffered so much.

She tried to sound reassuring as she took her mother's hand, cold and shrunken it felt as she warmed it between her own. 'He has talked to me too, Mama. Don't be distressed.' She desperately wanted to take her in her arms and hug her but they had never embraced and she slowly released her mother's hand and moved away, feeling awkward. There had always been this embarrassing distance with her parents and she could never remember when the childish cosseting ended and restrained custody began as she grew older. 'Everything will be all right, Mama,' she said gently, turning to face her again. 'You must not worry. Father will be kind and I'm sure he means well.'

Such a beautiful child she'd been, Elizabeth Smith mused, regarding her with a pang of regret. *But why? Why had she changed so much? What have we done? She was still beautiful – a joy to behold and kindness itself now she depended on her so much, but her forceful ways, the temper tantrums – and all the arguments. So unbecoming and so unlike her mild-mannered friends,* **and so like her father!**

Madeleine had inherited many of her father's traits, with flares of defiance and temper tantrums thrown in for good measure – and this overshadowed all efforts by her parents to instruct her in the social graces demanded in a strict Victorian household. At first they had reasoned this to be part of growing up, particularly her mother who always argued in Madeleine's favour but as time passed even she began wondering and they discussed endlessly how best to deal with her.

Unsurprisingly, James Smith failed to recognise his own shortcomings in his daughter's behaviour, although he would never have admitted it even had he done so! He bellowed pompously whenever challenged by

Madeleine's behaviour as his wife cringed in horror, but nearer the truth, he was utterly hopeless about putting Madeleine in her place. Despite these upheavals in their otherwise complacent family life however, Mrs. Smith found her daughter indispensable. From the age of eleven – and as expected of the eldest daughter in the family at the time – Madeleine had cared for her younger siblings and by the time she'd turned sixteen she had also taken over many of the household duties as her mother's frequent pregnancies took a toll on her health. And making her position in the home even more worthy as her mother's strength weakened, she had now embarked on managing a cook and scullery maid hired by Mr. Smith as his family increased.

Apparently oblivious to the tedium of household matters, Mr Smith's business was never affected in any way and he even felt grateful at times that his eldest daughter could deal with domestic matters now becoming difficult for his ailing wife, particularly handling the two servants he detested having anything to do with! All the same, as Madeleine adopted more authority in running the home, he felt increasingly undermined by her bossy attitude clashing with his role of supremacy – *and I have to put a stop to this outrageous flirting with my clients!* – so with a hint of urgency following a further exasperating outburst of arrogance from Madeleine, plans that had been festering in his mind for some while now began taking shape.

He chose the time well to discuss his plans with his wife, knowing how much she depended on her daughter, and equally carefully, he chose his words. It had been a good day – the children well behaved all day and now preparing for bed, and Madeleine safely occupied elsewhere in the house. More importantly, when his wife Elizabeth joined him in the lounge after dinner, she had lost her irritating care-worn expression and appeared to be more relaxed when she wandered in with a contented smile. All this instantly changed however, when he aired his intention about sending their daughter away to a finishing school in London and she suddenly burst into tears. Although this reaction was not totally unexpected – or her stunned expression which gave way to an emotional outburst about Madeleine being away from their influence and vulnerable to picking up bad habits – he considered it wise to remain silent and allowed a suitable pause for her to recover. And when no further comments were forthcoming as she snivelled quietly, he went on to outline the advantages of his plan.

'If she goes to a school where tutors are concerned with purity of mind and body with strict discipline for the structure of her development,' he said gently, 'this can be of great benefit my dear.'

Elizabeth dithered trying to put her thoughts in order, then bravely aired her views once more about Madeleine being away from her influence and picking up unsociable habits, and when the menacing silence lengthened as her husband paced the floor, she suddenly flared. 'Surely her behaviour is part of growing up James! She is only sixteen. And what about her place in society? She could pick up common talk. Anything! Especially in a place like London!' *I need my daughter! Oh God how I need her. I can't bear the thought of her being sent away. Whatever would I do!*

With his patience already wearing thin despite his resolve to stand firm, he wheeled round, 'Nonsense woman! The school is first class. I have had excellent reports. There will be continual guidance,' and lowering his voice as he leaned towards her he mouthed, 'and certainly there will be no opportunity to flirt!'

Elizabeth shrank back in horror. She knew about this but always put it from her mind and she dare not admit she had been aware of it. He'd be furious!

'She flirts with my friends, my clients and any men who come to the house for that matter,' he bellowed. 'People are beginning to talk Elizabeth! Surely, you must be aware how she flaunts herself? She behaves like a tart!

'James, don't! How can you suggest that about your own daughter?'

'Don't tell me you didn't know?' he breathed with contempt, leaning close again. When his wife timorously repeated her excuse about the problems of growing up he suddenly lost patience and yelled, 'Growing up, be damned woman! 'We've been saying that for years!'

Elizabeth twirled the girdle at her waist nervously, winding it tight, making her fingers hurt. 'Perhaps somewhere nearer then,' she ventured. She knew the hopelessness of arguing when he was in this mood but in desperation dared to add, 'Where we could visit and still retain our influence James.'

'There is nowhere within miles except these puny little schools where teachers are too weak or frightened!' he raged, strutting away in exasperation and as she watched his retreating back fearfully she flinched away when he suddenly spun round and came striding towards her with outstretched hands. 'The school in London is the best place. You must understand. They teach Godliness and good manners. Fine teaching,' he emphasised, and when he noticed the fear in his wife's eyes his voice softened. 'They are strict there Elizabeth where the aim is to turn young girls into young ladies and instil the principles of refinement and gentility. It's exactly what our daughter needs.'

Elizabeth notched another twist in the girdle, squeezing her fingers and hurting them more as she flicked her eyes nervously at her husband then quickly looked away. She would try again later she thought. It was pointless going on. He generally had his way and she satisfied herself by believing there might be a chance of being able to keep her daughter at home. *If only she could think of something! Somehow, there must be a way. There must be!*

Contenting herself that given time she would be able to think of something to persuade her husband to change his mind, Elizabeth endeavoured a smile. 'I understand James,' she said with her voice slowly trailing away, and with her heart beating so fiercely she feared it would burst from her chest, she added meekly, 'Anything you say dear. I understand how you feel. Anything you say.'

Chapter Two

When they arrived at the school resembling a prison rather than a place of learning for girls, neither father nor daughter felt disillusioned. Her father placed his trust in the sombre surroundings for influencing his daughter in the way he intended her to be subdued and she was too excited to care! Nothing had dampened Madeleine's spirits from the time she had left Glasgow that morning. It had been like setting out on a picnic as the train sped towards London! She yearned to be free – sick of the grumbling, the criticism and bitterly resentful of all the stupid restrictions constantly holding her back – *and was that too much to expect at her age?*

She had glanced at her father several times on the journey, wondering whether she dared to talk. His sour expression had never lifted and so far, no conversation passed between them. She hadn't minded leaving her home, indeed welcomed it! She was on the threshold of a new life! But why was she being sent so far away? Did her parents not love her? Was she such a disappointment they no longer regarded her as part of the family? And why hadn't her father spoken since they'd set out?

As the train clattered noisily through a clearing, she raised her voice and ventured, 'Are you angry with me father?'

He looked surprised at the intrusion, glaring like a stranger and fidgeting in his seat before turning to face her.

'Angry?' he blustered. 'You have the privilege of attending a finishing school my girl. Surely, you realise that. Why should I be angry? It's for your own good.' He cleared his throat noisily as he shifted in his seat again. 'And there is much you have to learn Madeleine. As you know.'

'But I have learned in the Glasgow school father,' she interrupted gently. 'Were my school reports not satisfactory?' *Is this why he is angry?*

His rapid response startled her and she edged away. 'There are more accomplishments necessary in this life than reading, singing and playing the piano Madeleine. And this is a place where you can acquire other attributes I hope.' As his jaw snapped shut, she continued to hold his gaze. He sounded annoyed she thought and watching his face darken she waited for him to go on.

'There is appreciation of discipline for one thing and observing protocol for another,' he went on pompously. 'And showing respect,' he emphasised. 'Also knowing how to behave in a dignified manner – which has been, humph, somewhat lacking of late,' he rapped out, *this high-spirited slip of a girl! His own daughter! She had to be taught a lesson. Showing contempt – even now! Too ready with her repartee and flippant behaviour she was. Too full of herself and only sixteen years old! Time indeed for her to be taken in hand.* Irritatingly embarrassed as he struggled to stay calm in her continued glare, he clenched his lips and turned away. Still not looking her way, and with his voice softening, he went on, 'It's a finishing school Madeleine. And as I say – it will turn you into a lady, which is everything your mother and I desire.'

She turned to the window, watching stretches of green flash by with trees suddenly looming and disappearing in an instant and others in the distance giving way to farms and buildings every now and then. She thought of her mother who had said very little when she'd left that morning and how she'd turned away when the train was ready to leave, dabbing her eyes Madeleine noticed when she'd turned back to look.

She glanced again at her father who had settled back in his seat, his mouth once more straightened into a firm line. And she knew there was nothing further to be said.

★ ★ ★

'It will be a delight to have your daughter with us at this school,' Miss Gorton said with a stiff smile and James Smith bowed graciously at the prim headmistress into whose hands he was entrusting his offspring. 'We pride ourselves on our girls' achievements here as you know,' she continued, with a gesture towards certificates lining the walls, and noticing Madeleine squinting to read one, peered over her spectacles and announced, 'And that is where your name will be one day young lady. I'm sure.'

Smiling demurely, Madeleine had taken her place sedately on a chair beside her father. On the way in, she had noticed girls peering through the banisters on the upper floor stifling giggles – and knew this would be where she could have fun. Savouring the thought, she remained quietly submissive listening patiently while her father and the surly headmistress continued discussing the fine attributes of the school.

★ ★ ★

Bidding his daughter goodbye that day however was a mix of relief and regret for James Smith – relief for the welcome peace when he returned home and regret for not having accomplished his rightful authority over an unruly daughter – and Madeleine's sparkling eyes meeting his look of disdain at that moment offered little encouragement! *She even looks delighted instead of snivelling as a normal girl would at a time like this!*

He turned to the headmistress with another gracious bow as they exchanged pleasantries. 'I shall look forward to receiving reports of my daughter's progress,' he said amiably, and as Madeleine waited hopefully for a show of affection as they walked to the gloomy reception area outside, her father gave her a curt nod as he strolled past her – and brandishing his cane elaborately, continued in a dignified manner to a carriage waiting outside.

Chapter Three

It took Madeleine only a short time to get a measure of the school despite the headmistress explaining soberly the procedures and principles to be strictly adhered to as she met her new pupil's lively expression with a severe glare. She announced that a mistress waiting outside would familiarise her with the layout of the school and then show her to her room. 'And I sincerely hope your name will be on one of these documents as a result of your stay with us,' she added icily, indicating the certificates inspected by Madeleine earlier – and with the suggestion of a smile she was introduced to the mistress waiting to take over her new pupil and with a swish of her stiff taffeta skirt, Miss Gorton returned to her office and closed the door.

Still in high spirits, Madeleine pranced along a labyrinth of corridors reeking of disinfectant and polish, continually questioning and hanging back every so often to peer into classrooms and inspect areas of the school where she would spend the next two years. 'We like our girls to proceed quietly and sedately,' she was reprimanded at one point and, apologising profusely, she immediately fell into step again forcing herself into a sombre mood.

Overall, the building looked drab with many layers of paint barely disguising the plain brickwork walls. Huge fireplaces faced rows of desks in many of the rooms with blackboards resting on easels set at an angle. In one room several tables held an array of bowls, some weighing scales and trays of cooking implements, and in another, shadowy with heavily curtained windows, tall bookcases were lined up across the room with chairs and desks scattered around and books placed neatly on shelves around the walls.

Brushing a casual wave as they passed a large room with stools arranged at tables, the mistress announced offhandedly, 'That is where you will have your meals.' And hesitating briefly as she faced Madeleine, added grimly, 'There is no talking on those occasions you must remember and all girls are expected to be at table a good ten minutes before meals are served. And remember also,' she emphasised, 'you must be upstanding as soon as Miss Gorton enters the room to say Grace.'

At the top of the building, Madeleine entered a drab room sparsely furnished with an insipid counterpane flattened onto an iron bedstead. A plain jug and bowl stood on a dark-brown washstand, a chest of drawers matching the drab linoleum was crammed at an angle into a corner and a window so small it was almost unnoticeable mostly shrouded the room in shadow. But this was Utopia! – and as soon as the door closed and retreating footsteps faded into the distance Madeleine flung herself onto the bed and kicked her legs in the air. This was where she could enjoy the freedom she had yearned! She could be her own person and not restricted to how everyone expected her to behave. Nobody knows me here she thought wildly – and like taking on a role in a play she considered all the different parts she could portray – or conceal! 'I could even become an entirely different person!' she told herself.

A loud rap at the door brought Madeleine down to earth with a start and she leapt off the bed, almost tripping. Two girls stood in the gloom outside, both wearing the obligatory uniform of a blue striped dress overlaid with a white pinafore and for a second they all exchanged glances sizing one another up, Madeleine admiring their fashionable hairstyles held high either side with elaborate combs and they admiring her smart travelling outfit. Then they all began talking at once and immediately collapsed into giggles.

'Our rooms are just alongside.' It was the taller of the two girls who introduced herself as Emily, a serious-looking girl with delicate features. 'We just wanted to say welcome,' she said, grinning widely and stepping back indicated her friend Alice, a ruddy-faced country-looking girl with piercing brown eyes. 'We've been here a few months,' she went on, 'and thought you might like to know what happens here.' Lowering her voice behind a cupped hand she glanced around guardedly, 'Like who to avoid and who to trust,' and with a mischievous wink at Alice, 'and what there is to do in this wicked, wicked city!' Both girls collapsed into giggles again and flinging wide the door Madeleine welcomed them into her room where they all sprawled on the bed.

★ ★ ★

Emily Perry and Alice Ford came from families whose parents had moved overseas at short notice and Miss Gorton had agreed to take them into her school in the middle of a term. Like Madeleine, they had lively minds and a spirit of adventure and with a head start in finding their way around were only too pleased to instruct Madeleine in the fine art of enjoying life to the full. They also had a penchant for making up stories whenever anything stood in their way of getting out and about and lost no time in making this known. Emily came across as the more self-assured of the two and pulled no punches, giving Madeleine her first lesson on how to survive in an environment bordering on a convent. Facing her with a serious expression she maintained stoically that anything could be done outside the rules and regulations, 'as long as you sound convincing,' she emphasised. 'And really believe what you tell the mistresses yourself,' she said shaking a finger. 'Always remember that. They fall for it every time. It's amazing!'

'Act it out beforehand,' Alice chipped in with a delightful lisp Madeleine failed to notice earlier. 'We alwayth plan well ahead when there is something we want to do. Think how to go about it though and what you intend thaying. You get to believe it yourthelf in the end!'

Both girls obviously had a flair for telling lies and recounted cunning methods they had devised in the past to do all manner of things. Although having developed her own devious techniques back home Madeline needed no lessons in that direction – and could even have taught her new friends something new! Even so, comparing their lives with her mundane existence so far, she put a spark in her voice and risked a confidence. 'I've heard and read about life here of course, and what goes on! But never having been here I'll be relying on you to show me around.'

When the girls glanced at each other with widening eyes Madeleine feared she might have offended but with her choice piece of information to impress them decided to continue as she covered her cheek in mock horror. 'I used to eavesdrop you see, outside the door when the men retired to another room after dinner to smoke their cigars. It was terrible the things I heard. They talked about it all the time!'

Emily looked thoughtful although she hadn't the slightest idea what this new girl was really talking about, but wanting to preserve her authoritative position, flourished a hand, 'Oh yes we know all about that,' she said, 'but we don't get involved in such things. And neither will you!' she cautioned with a severe look.

The Shadow of Doubt

For a split second, Madeleine's earlier strait-laced family restrictions loomed as Alice joined in with a warning finger. But when Emily's eyes glazed over almost immediately and she began talking about what they could do that very evening if they could manage it, she brightened.

'Supper's at seven sharp,' Emily said, studying the clock. 'And if we're lucky, by eight we could be finished.' Closing her eyes in concentration, she continued in a slow drawl, 'You could explain to Miss Gorton before we go into supper about an uncle of yours being in town. Your father knew he would be in London and you'd been invited to meet both of them at a local hotel – that's if you could be allowed to go.'

Madeleine stared in astonishment, 'What! Whatever are you saying?' She had told them about arriving with her father that morning but a plan such as this was madness! 'I never said any such thing about an uncle,' she went on. 'My father is already on his way home, long ago.' but her words hung in the air as Emily closed her eyes again, flapping a hand to silence Madeleine's protests.

'This uncle of yours,' she went on dreamily. 'Your nearest and dearest relative by the way,' she added, staring Madeleine full in the face. 'He's going abroad for a long time. So this is your only chance of saying goodbye.'

'And you are his favourite niethe,' Alice chipped in.

Madeleine listened patiently as the girls became carried away. She welcomed the friendship of these two and decided not to interrupt until her commonsense suddenly got the better of her and she realised she had to stop it. 'I can't say anything like that!' she said gently. 'You have to admit it would have been mentioned to Miss Gorton this morning if my father intended such a meeting. She would never believe it. It's quite outrageous.'

Emily sounded annoyed. 'You assumed he would have said something,' she corrected emphatically. 'But with all the arrangements and discussions going on about you starting here, well, it must have slipped his mind!'

Alice slid from the bed, shushing them into silence as she aired another plan. 'Like I said, you must thound convincing Madeleine,' she lisped as she stood resolutely before them. And stroking her chin thoughtfully went on, 'Now! The nearest hotel to this place is The Royal,' – and with great aplomb she explained knowing someone who worked there who would be only too pleased to support them if any questions were asked.

'That's brilliant Alice,' Emily shrieked, jumping up. 'In case Miss Gorton gets in touch to check. You could even recommend us as chaperones! Tell her we've promised to look after you as you are new to the city.'

Despite this growing excitement, the concocted plans stretched even Madeleine's fertile imagination to ridiculous lengths and with a strong feeling of not wanting to offend still tormenting, she felt torn. She was an intelligent girl with sensible reasoning and despite her own limited ventures outside the dictates of Victorian decorum, the idea of being allowed out in a busy city shortly after arriving at a new school was too ridiculous to contemplate, particularly trying to convince someone of Miss Gorton's calibre, she realised.

'All the same, I don't think it would work,' she said at last. 'I really feel I can't go along with it. It would be too...' but without allowing her to finish, both girls were already at the door and mortified by their swift reaction Madeleine reached out, pleading for them not to go. 'Don't leave. Please,' she said urgently. 'But you must see it from my point of view.'

Emily tossed her head with a look of scorn and

snapped, 'We thought you were one of us. What a disappointment.' Again Madeleine stretched a hand, 'Please wait,' she persisted. 'If you really think it would work...'

'Of courthe it will,' Alice interrupted as she flounced back. 'Fanthy asking! It's a reasonable request. How can anyone refuthe, and if it's not allowed, well it isn't the end of the world,' she added.

Madeleine struggled with her conscience as they glowered with contempt. Even with her expertise for telling lies, she knew she could never outwit the sharp-witted, rigid headmistress they expected her to deceive and, lost for anything further to say as she shook her head, watched helplessly as they both swept from her room and walking briskly along the corridor disappeared into their own rooms.

On the verge of tears, Madeleine persuaded herself into concluding that she really did welcome the companionship of these lively girls and tried justifying this ridiculous plan in a new light at the same time as battling between commonsense and a preposterous idea beyond sensible reasoning. Then swinging in favour of an ability to convince people to her own way of thinking, as she had so many times at home in the past, she wrestled between practicality and nonsense which still mingled with her overbearing desire to make an impression on these girls. 'I'll give it a try,' she muttered to herself at last and ignoring all sense of reason and the persistent waves of apprehension that kept flooding back, she put on a brave front and made her way down to confront Miss Gorton with her proposition.

★ ★ ★

Peering over her spectacles as Madeleine remembered earlier that day, Miss Gorton now came over as quite a different person. 'I can't understand your father not saying anything about this Madeleine,' she said with a sour expression. 'This is most irregular. He surely would have mentioned it,' she sniffed as she shuffled papers around. 'And we do like our new girls to settle in on their first evening in order to get to know everyone and become familiar with the routine.' With the interview terminated in her estimation at that point, she glanced up at the clock and as she prepared to rise glared in disbelief as Madeleine continued to stand her ground.

'I can only apologise on my father's behalf,' she persisted politely. 'Quite clearly he overlooked this,' and biting her lip as she leaned forward in a confidential manner, went on with a smile, 'we met my uncle only briefly Miss Gorton. Just prior to coming here. My father knew he would be in town and hoped we may be able to meet for dinner this evening at The Royal Hotel – which I understand is not far from here?' she added brightly. 'It was only half expected of course that I could join them when my uncle suggested this,' she emphasised, 'but I know he particularly wanted to see me before he left.' Her face lit up with growing confidence as she straightened and believing she was making a good impression despite Miss Gorton's devastating scowl, rushed on, 'He is travelling overseas you see and expects to be away for several years.' Lowering her voice at this point, she tried to sound dejected and forcing the hint of a sob continued, 'I may not even see him again.'

Outwardly unmoved by this brash impudence, Miss Gorton's steely gaze never faltered and in the growing silence, Madeleine stumbled on.

'I understand the rule about chaperoning ma'am – so perhaps I may be accompanied by the two friendly girls in the adjoining rooms to mine who have been so kind since I arrived?' She attempted another smile but the rigid expression opposite was dousing her confidence and she began struggling. 'I know my father would welcome this meeting ma'am and both he and my uncle would quite understand I'm sure if we returned here immediately after seeing them, if only just briefly and, and not staying for dinner.' With her voice fading to a tremble, Madeleine could feel her nerve giving way as she drained her imagination for further ideas. And when nothing tangible surfaced, and the face opposite remained sour, she suddenly burst into tears hoping this might bring a sympathetic reaction, at the same time as cursing Emily and Alice and her stupidity going along with their ridiculous plan.

Well used to such emotional behaviour, Miss Gorton sat quietly waiting for the composure she knew would follow – and fighting for control as the silence lengthened, Madeleine eventually brushed her knuckles across her eyes, straightened in her chair, and glanced miserably across the desk.

Still without comment, Miss Gorton rose elegantly from her chair, walked to the window where she hesitated briefly as though noticing something of more importance outside, then slowly turned to look down at Madeleine.

'I have had little chance of getting to know you Madeleine,' she said in an acid tone. 'Or for you to realise that I will not stand for any nonsense. And as far as the latter is concerned you will learn that I expect all young ladies in my care to follow certain rules of conduct whilst at this school.' *Madeleine's confidence plunged as the austere figure of Miss Gorton brought back memories of her parents admonishing her about what she could and couldn't do!*

'I fully understand and sympathise with your desire to be with your relative at this time,' she went on frostily. 'If indeed that is the case,' she continued with a doubtful glare to emphasise the point. 'But nothing will persuade me to allow this. London at night is not a place for a young girl new to the city – as you will learn. And furthermore I do not consider Miss Perry or Miss Ford to be suitable chaperones in these circumstances.' Nearer the truth, she considered them positively inappropriate as chaperones – or even friends of this new girl! She also wondered with growing dismay, with such a plan so quickly worked out between the three of them, whether she had yet another troublesome pupil on her hands.

'Dinner will be served at seven o'clock Madeleine,' she went on loftily. 'I shall expect to see you there where I shall introduce you to the other girls,' and looking down her nose as she held the door wide, she afforded her a curt nod as Madeleine slid past.

★ ★ ★

What Madeleine had seen only hours earlier as a sanctuary for her future freedom, her room now felt like a cage and she murmured words under her breath she would never have dared utter aloud. In the distance she could hear girls talking and laughing – preparing for supper she supposed, which made her feel more isolated and desperately lonely than she'd ever felt in her life. She stretched out on the bed staring unseeingly into the gloom for what seemed an eternity, hating Emily and Alice for dreaming up this wretched plan and hating herself for being so stupid by going along with it. Only a while ago they had been in here and she sat up suddenly, looking around – *sitting on this bed laughing together we were and so friendly* – and she began wondering where they were now and whether she should tell them what had happened.

There were no sounds coming from the adjoining rooms – *probably downstairs enjoying themselves and telling the other girls what they'd done at her expense,* she thought bitterly and with rage building until she could no longer stand it, she jumped off the bed. *She would tell them. Let them know what a fool they'd made of her.* Rushing along the corridor she rapped first on one door, then the other, and when no one answered pushed at each in turn and barged in. But neither of them were there and the empty rooms further mocked her frustration. Worse, when she sidled into the dining room later when sheer hunger compelled, they were nowhere to be seen there either! They had vanished into thin air, and glancing at the sea of unfamiliar faces when Miss Gorton stood up to 'introduce our new girl to the school,' she felt so desperately alone she wished the ground would swallow her up.

Miserably sleepless that night in her hard bed she asked herself repeatedly why? Her first day promising so much was ruined and she felt completely at a loss to understand such a change in heart after the girls' friendliness and enthusiasm. Was it mischief? Playing tricks maybe, because she was new – and taking advantage of her for this reason. They had certainly succeeded if that were so, she thought, and suddenly she went icy cold, *if it was that. If they had really been that mean, just because she was new and they wanted to play a trick. Should this be a warning?*

Chapter Four

Despite that unfortunate venture on her first day at school, Madeleine settled in quickly. She excelled in her studies, turned out to be a popular student and her parents congratulated her on the good reports they received during the term. Her private life also opened up interestingly and with no further mention of their mischievous involvement on her first day – and Madeleine thinking it wise not to enquire – Alice and Emily had become bosom friends and all three enjoyed jaunts into the city where Madeleine was pitched into the social scene.

One rule high on the list of strictly forbidden pursuits outside the school however was not mixing with the opposite sex – which most of the students did anyway and always hotly denied if questioned! Madeleine and her friends got round this by mixing in a large group which provided ample opportunity for an intermix of the sexes – and whenever the hovering chaperone happened to be distracted, Madeleine threw caution to the wind and flirted outrageously, until Emily and Alice felt it their duty to heed discretion on one occasion! She'd already caught disapproving glances in her direction on one occasion when chatting and laughing with one young man in particular and having picked up 'fast', 'easy virtue' and 'common' from their mumbled conversation, faced criticism from Emily when they all returned later that evening.

'What are you doing making such an exhibition of yourself?' Emily sneered – and Madeleine made matters worse by picking up her skirts and twirling round the room with taunts about jealousy, which resulted in a fiery spat between the two of them. Something in Emily's tone nevertheless warned she should be less flippant in future, although despite this scrutiny of her behaviour Madeleine had no hesitation in accepting an invitation from the handsome young man she had flirted with. His name was Neville and he stood out from the crowd, a good head-and-shoulders above the rest and as a popular young man about town with a sparkling personality to match her own; there had been an immediate attraction. He had tickets for a theatre he told her and with a polite bow asked if she would be able to accompany him. 'When I've asked my mistresses for permission of course, which is a strict requirement at the school,' she added coyly after having immediately agreed. And although having no such idea in her head to do so, she immediately began planning how best to make her escape!

★ ★ ★

'What about a chaperone? You know how things are here!' Emily asked sulkily when Madeleine burst into her room later that evening with the news. Mortified by the unfriendly attitude she stood biting her lip as Emily continued to glower. 'Where are you going anyway?' she went on, moderately changing her tone – and stupidly Madeleine could not say! She was utterly lost for words! She had never been to a theatre in her life. She didn't know a thing about them, and momentarily, after a shift of gazes, had to admit she had no idea. 'I didn't ask,' she said, cringing at the thought that she had not even asked Neville either!

With criticism coming easy to Emily, she ignored this stupid ignorance and sniffed, 'If it's a music hall, they are sources of low morality for people with Bohemian life styles or for those of the working class.' Then crushing what remained of Madeleine's confidence, she feigned a yawn and making excuses about being tired began hustling Madeleine out of her room. Determined not to be put off however, Madeleine pulled a wry face after shutting the door with a thud and noticing a light across the landing beneath the door of Penelope, an older girl who'd taken her under her wing recently, wondered whether she dared knock. It was late she knew but took a chance, tapping hesitantly, and as the door opened a crack, she whispered, 'I'm sorry it's so late. I noticed your light and wondered...' and as the door widened, she heaved a sigh of relief and sidled in.

Cigarette smoke hung in the air and Madeleine felt an instant welcome in the comfortable glow of candles, plumped cushions scattered on the bed and pictures hanging from ribbons on the walls. Penelope was nearing the end of her final year and on numerous occasions before had indulged Madeleine's heartfelt outpourings when she had a problem. 'From the look of you, it must be important. Bet it's about a man!' she said huskily, and allowing her non-stop talk without interruption as Madeleine blurted out the events of the evening, Penelope relit the cigarette she had hastily abandoned before opening the door.

With a catch in her voice, Madeleine repeated Emily's caustic comments about rowdy music halls and owned up to her stupidity not knowing anything about it. 'I completely forgot to ask in my excitement,' she added hurriedly. 'It could be drama at a theatre. Anything I suppose! I've never ever been to either so I know very little about any of that,' and wary of another rebuff went on guardedly about her foolish ignorance until Penelope suddenly scoffed, 'So what! I would have accepted straight away too. Never turn down an invite whatever it is! Always ask questions afterwards,' and with Madeleine's confidence immediately restored, her fears were swept away with some lengthy, down-to-earth advice rapped out through a haze of smoke.

'There's to be no escaping from the school unnoticed though,' Penelope said, as she took a last puff and with great concentration stubbed out what remained of the cigarette into a tin box. 'You should know that for a start!' Having educated Madeleine on many other occasions in the fine art of compliance with careful manipulation, she emphasised strongly she should ask for permission first – 'with perhaps just a little embellishment of the truth regarding your invitation!' she said, with a glint in her eye. With a quick stride over to the washstand, she reached for a bottle of lavender water and sprinkled it liberally around the room. 'Have to get rid of the evidence,' she said with a grin. 'Then we can talk about making final arrangements about what you should wear as you're not sure where you are going,' she went on, 'and choosing a suitable chaperone of course,' she said curling up against a cushion. 'But get approval from your class mistress first remember,' she said, shaking a finger. And heeding this advice when Madeleine faced her class mistress the following day with a contrived story about the invitation having come from a young man whose parents had strong connections with her own family, the unsuspecting mistress agreed that everything would be in order – 'As long as you know this young man well Madeleine,' she told her.

★ ★ ★

Madeleine had much to learn when preparations got underway the night of her visit to the theatre – and the strict rule about keeping rooms tidy at all times went by the wayside when Penelope strolled into her room. The place was in utter chaos with clothes laid out on the bed, shoes and boots kicked into a corner, brushes, combs and slides used for a new hairstyle scattered over the chest of drawers and hats brought from home by Madeleine, with some loaned by friends if she wanted, piled in another corner awaiting a last minute decision. Then the question of cosmetics was discussed, about which Madeleine was totally ignorant. Up to now she had never used any beauty aids. She knew nothing about such things. Her mother certainly had no use for such risqué embellishments and she had always followed her guidance. 'Just pinching your cheeks and biting your lips to add colour is quite sufficient if you want to improve your appearance,' Elizabeth Smith always advised her daughter prior to preparing for a party. So when Madeleine talked about brightening her cheeks with some colour her adroit friend looked totally astounded and told her firmly, 'Surely you know that whitening the complexion is more fashionable now? Not colour!'

Madeleine stood open-mouthed wondering what to say as Penelope suddenly dodged out of the room, returning minutes later and looking long and hard at Madeleine as she closed the door. Speaking in subdued tones, she warned that no one in the school should ever know anything of what she was about to do and stared at her intently for a few seconds as though weighing up whether or not to go ahead. 'Particularly here,' she emphasised quickly. 'Never ever mention this to anyone. Never say anything,' she repeated as she continued to hold Madeleine's startled expression. After promising faithfully not to do so, and feeling somewhat alarmed, Madeleine stared wide-eyed as Penelope opened a paper packet with care and stirred a white powder into a bowl of water.

'Dab this liquid carefully on your face and along your

arms,' she mumbled, shifting aside as she handed Madeleine a sponge. 'And as long as you use it with care and avoid your eyes,' she said, 'there is absolutely no risk I can assure you.'

Madeleine began dabbing cautiously in what looked like an apparently innocent liquid, straightening after a while and glancing up at her friend. 'But what is it?' she asked – and with what sounded like a tinge of exasperation she learned about arsenic being the latest aid to beauty, at which Madeleine immediately threw down the sponge with a look of horror as liquid dripped all over the floor. 'That's a poison. I can't use that!'

'Oh for goodness sake – where have you been? Fancy you not knowing about arsenic. Wonderful stuff. Everyone's raving about it.'

Madeleine remembered how her father used arsenic in the garden for killing rats and felt uncertain – *and to actually bathe in it! It didn't seem right!*

She looked at her arms suspiciously, half expecting the skin to hurt or sting and supposed it was all right. Then with a quick look at her friend's gleaming arms – and secretly honoured to be sharing this secret with someone whose lily-white skin she had always admired, picked up the sponge and began splashing her skin more vigorously.

★ ★ ★

Madeleine's visit to the theatre was something beyond her wildest dreams and after the dull regimentation and routine of school life, it was like being plunged into another world as madrigals, acrobats and comic turns took the stage. She laughed at jokes she could not understand, because everybody else did and she felt out of place not doing the same. She marvelled at the hissing flares, flickering gas jets, the band, the never-ending shouts and jeering from the audience and cheering at the end of the show and the clapping that went on forever and stung her hands until they hurt. Apart from all this was the devoted attention of Neville who charmingly ushered her to their seats and presented a beautifully wrapped box of chocolates when they settled. But most of all, and the best part of the evening when she thought about it later, was the daring late night kiss after she'd dismissed her chaperone at the gates of the school building. 'I'll be fine now and thank you for your care,' she'd told her with confidence – and strolling up to the main entrance she had hidden in shadows of the building with Neville, talking in whispers until he was about to leave. She had turned away in alarm at first when he moved closer, murmuring breathlessly, 'No, no!' repeatedly. Then ignoring her protests he'd touched her cheek gently, persuading her round to face him as his lips brushed across hers softly, and lingering there a while as he took her in his arms, he held her tight against him as he kissed her firmly on her mouth.

Creeping softly up to her room later, and grateful for the lateness of the hour with no prying eyes, Madeleine noticed a light beneath the door of Emily's room and rushed in to confide. She had to tell someone. There could be no sleep until she had! Marvellous ... wonderful ... exciting ... the words tumbled out endlessly and as she listened without comment or change of expression, Emily eventually stopped her with a toss of her head. 'Oh I've done all that Madeleine. Don't go on so! Operas, variety shows and the music halls – I've been to most of them,' she told her flatly. And when Madeleine thrust out her hands to interrupt and tell her how they had huddled together in the porch after escaping from the chaperone, Emily's face suddenly hardened, and after hearing about the kiss she straightened and moved to the door announcing tartly it was late and that she wished to go to bed.

Madeleine resisted an immediate urge to lash out as everything about her wonderful evening suddenly spewed to the ground as meaningless tripe. 'How can you be so damned disinterested?' she said narrowing her eyes. 'You can't bear to hear about anyone else having fun can you? Particularly with a man! Are you jealous? Is that it?' She spun on her heel making to leave, and then wheeled round again. 'Are men not interested in you Emily and you resent it when they turn to me?'

Clearly, Emily was straining to keep her temper under control, but the glint in her eyes piercing like daggers was a betrayal. 'Keep your voice down,' she hissed. 'Don't you know the time? Do you want the whole school to know what you've been up to?'

'Up to! How dare you! You're a fine one to talk, telling lies and encouraging me as you did once to be involved in something underhand when I first arrived here.' A brief silence followed as they hedged guardedly – both aware that raised voices would mean trouble and in hushed hostility, the sparks flew as they gave vent to their feelings.

'Think what you like Madeleine,' Emily finally announced, opening the door to make sure of a safe retreat. 'I have no interest in what you do – and certainly not your gadding about with whoever takes your fancy. There's nothing more to say.' And jerking her head to the corridor outside mouthed, 'Get out!'

In spite of this heated spat, Madeleine felt determined not to let her evening be spoiled. Stupid to have confided in Emily anyway she thought remembering what happened once before and, back in her room, she crossed to the window raising it quietly allowing the cool air to flow over her hot cheeks. Never had she felt so cross and never met such spite. Then glancing down to where she had been kissed only a short time ago – and knowing that Neville was all that really mattered at that moment – her temper gradually cooled. She was in love! For the first time, she was in love she realised. A man had held her and kissed her, with passion. She had heard and read about this. Talked about it with her friends and now it had happened to her and on a tide of emotion the resentment from Emily gradually became meaningless as she spent a restless night savouring the delights of her first romance, and revelling in the passionate dreams it brought.

★ ★ ★

Madeleine managed to escape with Neville from their group of friends whenever an opportunity arose, even under the watchful eye of Emily and Alice – and the chaperone at times when her interest centred elsewhere. He introduced her to all the aspects of London life and she delighted in the bustle and noise, the horses, barrel organs, street sellers and the carts and carriages that jostled for space and the crossing sweepers who swept a path for her over a dirty street. Even the drizzle and fog fascinated when horses loomed suddenly through the mist – and when Neville teased by pretending to stumble uncertainly in a thick fog, she loved the chance of being able to cling closer!

He was studying Law he told her – with crime in particular, and gave her newssheets filled with lurid stories about brothels, public house brawls and murders to take back and read. They talked about things she'd never heard about and he once offered to take her to a public hanging. 'Quite a spectacle,' he explained, getting carried away, 'the only thing is getting too absorbed when they drop and swing. That's when to look out for pick-pockets,' he added. But she couldn't be persuaded, particularly when he described young children being taken to a hanging as an example of how they would be punished if they persisted with bad behaviour!

They talked about the use of arsenic and the cases of murder he had been studying – which immediately took her interest having secretly used this as a cosmetic, but he dwelt only on the more sordid side. 'There is no evidence of a murder being committed sometimes by people using arsenic they have said they've bought from a chemist for killing rats in the garden! Some women have actually killed their husbands Madeleine – and got away with it when it's believed they have died from cholera or gastric fever, or even dysentery which has the same symptoms as arsenic poisoning.'

'But can't anything be done?' she interrupted, 'I can't bear to think about it. It sounds awful.'

'Doctors don't always know; that's the problem. As I said it's difficult to detect,' and he went on describing cases he'd worked on, embellishing the grisly details and agony suffered by the victim, until he noticed Madeleine's agonised expression and decided to change the sordid side of arsenic to the more acceptable use such as a stimulant or beauty aid.

Madeleine immediately pricked up her ears. 'A beauty aid,' she said, trying to sound innocent. 'But surely it could be dangerous if it's a poison!' Penelope had not fully enlightened her about using arsenic, and not daring to divulge having used it, wanted to know more!

'In the right proportions, it's fine. Women use it all the time. But there are other less drastic uses, although care is always needed.'

'What about it being a stimulant as you said? Why use this even if it could kill? What does it do?'

Neville loved her innocence – and to spare her blushes explained how it enhanced a feeling of well-being rather than dwelling on its use as an aphrodisiac. He let her prattle on endlessly. She knew so little about life he realised, although feeling surprised. Madeleine too became suddenly aware of her limited knowledge as she took in this different side of life. In the docile surroundings of her home she had been sheltered from the sordid side of life and as Neville closed his hand over hers when he noticed her anxious expression she felt thankful for his caring. Despite the many threats and challenges however, she was learning fast – and not only about the sordid side of life and how people here lived and died as he described. In the school, she had certainly met some strange behaviour as well as changeable personalities – much to my humiliation she recalled – although I've toughened up since those early days she contented herself. Nevertheless, and thinking ahead to whatever else life could throw at her in the future, she knew this was not enough. She would have to grow stronger. Learn how to survive whatever lay ahead in this mysterious world with so many challenges, and without betraying her feelings if she could – which she knew would not be easy.

★ ★ ★

The first anonymous note, written in a clumsy hand and left in the headmistress's office stated that Madeleine Smith was secretly involved in an unsavoury friendship with a young man not considered suitable for a young girl. How it arrived remained a mystery and although it was not something to be ignored, Miss Gorton chose to keep this information to herself for the time being. Malicious behaviour and tale-telling among the girls happened from time to time – if it happened to be someone within the school – she considered. Up until now, there had been no concern about Madeleine's behaviour, despite that unfortunate business on her first day. She had been a fine pupil. She worked well. She was bright and as far as she knew, got on well with her mistresses and the rest of the girls. She knew she was headstrong and often argued with her elders, and with telling lies a further unfortunate trait just coming to light, she realised there was no point trying to extract any information from Madeleine herself at this stage!

Meanwhile, back in Glasgow, Mr. and Mrs. Smith felt considerably more settled in their life without the constant upsets with Madeleine. Her father was in total command of the family once more and when she returned home for the holidays, they noticed a remarkable change for the better. On these occasions, her mother welcomed her daughter's help about the house again and when her husband was in an agreeable mood even timorously suggested she should stay for good. Unsurprisingly, he overruled this in his usual pompous fashion and when Madeleine returned with great enthusiasm for the new term in her second year, James Smith felt he had chosen well for his daughter. So when a letter arrived one day asking them to contact Miss Gorton with some urgency concerning Madeleine's behaviour, they were shocked into disbelief and all their earlier fears returned.

Chapter Five

When more anonymous notes arrived in quick succession concerning Madeleine's involvement with this yet unidentified young man, the headmistress realised something had to be done. Still of the opinion it could be handled without too much fuss however, she entrusted a member of staff to investigate Madeleine's evenings out, but elbowing through crowds in dubious areas with eyes darting in all directions failed to reveal anything suspicious.

'The girl's as slippery as she is mysterious,' Miss Gorton declared at a meeting she had decided to hold with the mistresses to discuss the problem. They'd all reported that Madeleine's conduct was excellent, similarly her achievement in studies, so there was little further to be done for the time being, until the next anonymous note arrived, in the post this time, making serious allegations about Madeleine and indicating that advice should be sought from a doctor.

★ ★ ★

The prospect of a girl in her school becoming pregnant was Miss Gorton's greatest fear and this was the thought uppermost in her mind when the latest letter arrived. Up to now none of her girls had given cause to suspect anything other than their virtuous behaviour and she considered they all conformed to the Victorian value of preserving their virginity at all cost – and felt convinced Madeleine also fell into this worthy mould. With this latest letter however, doubts began to fester. She realised it would be catastrophic for the future of the school if a pregnancy was reported, which could well lead to its closure, and this was something to be avoided at all cost.

Much as she detested the undercover practices she had already resorted to, she instigated a further investigation by one of her trustworthy staff to secretly examine Madeleine's clothing and monitor her future requests for sanitary protection – and with great relief received the welcome confirmation that menstruation was continuing normally. Despite this temporary reassurance nevertheless, the atmosphere at the school changed. The mistresses were advised to be on the lookout for any sign of a problem and with them constantly on tenterhooks, a gnawing cloud of suspicion pervaded throughout the school. Miss Gorton hedged her bets into believing the situation could never be as serious as the threat of a pregnancy – and even clung to the thought it could possibly go away! But it didn't. In fact things took a turn for the worse when a further letter arrived indicating that arsenic had been discovered in Madeleine's possession.

'Arsenic of all things!' Miss Gorton declared in exasperation at another hastily convened meeting, and in shock and disbelief she let slip her refined composure for once and exploded, 'What the hell is the girl doing with arsenic? Where has it come from? And more to the point why does she have it?' And with growing horror, she turned over in her mind how on earth she intended using it!

Where the letters came from remained a mystery, apart from it now appearing to be someone within the school, and possibly someone who also had access to Madeleine's room. So with this supposition, all the domestic staff was interrogated, but with no reasonable outcome in that direction, Miss Gorton was again thrown into total confusion. All along, she had held the opinion this was a mischievous hoax by one of the girls, but with the situation gradually worsening now began wondering. Then unbelievably Madeleine solved the mystery herself the following day when she had slipped back to her room to fetch a book she had forgotten and urgently needed in class.

★ ★ ★

Cursing for having to rush all the way upstairs to her room, and knowing there would be trouble should she be declared missing from class, Madeleine hesitated abruptly in her haste when she discovered her door slightly ajar. Someone was moving around, shifting things about and, after glimpsing through a crack of the door, she burst in just as Emily was in the act of upending the contents of a drawer onto the bed.

'What the devil are you doing?'

Emily made a rush for the door with her face flaring crimson, but before she could escape Madeleine grabbed her blouse, ripping buttons that flew in all directions.

'What are you doing?' she screamed again.

Emily struggled to keep her balance. 'I've lost something,' she murmured. 'I w-w-wondered whether...'

Madeleine thrust her away, watching her stumble and fall. 'Lost something? Belonging to you? In my room?' As Emily struggled to her feet, Madeleine towered over her shrieking, 'I thought someone had been meddling with my things, and you of all people! What were you doing?'

Always being the one to boss Madeleine about in the past, Emily's puffy face now twitched uncharacteristically as she stammered excuses. 'Look, I w-want to help. Really I do. I was told to...'

'Told! Told! What do you mean told? Told to do what?'

On her feet now, Emily made another lunge at the door and Madeleine grabbed her, slapping her full in the face.

'Don't you knock me about. I'll report...'

'I'll do more than that you interfering bitch.'

Suddenly the door flung wide pitching Madeleine off balance as both girls stumbled back into the room, and dowsing the atmosphere like a blast of ice on an inferno Miss Gorton marched into the room with a mistress following close behind.

'What on earth is going on here?' she demanded.

Madeleine swung round, her eyes blazing. 'This... this person has been snooping in my room,' she sneered, and moving across to the bed jabbed a finger at the jumble of clothes tipped in a heap. 'She said she was told to do this and I want to know who told her. And why!'

Totally ignoring the outburst, Miss Gorton turned to Emily, her face white with anger. 'What has happened to your blouse girl?'

Clutching her chest, Emily flicked her eyes towards Madeleine.

'Answer me!'

'It was me,' Madeleine screamed defiantly. 'It ripped when I grabbed her. And I slapped her face for good measure! What about that!'

'How dare you!'

Visibly trembling, Emily quickly sidled out when ordered to her room. 'And stay there until I come,' Miss Gorton commanded.

Madeleine turned away, her stomach churning and now irritatingly close to tears as she moved across to the window. Her once friendly room became a cage as it had on a previous occasion she remembered, but now she felt hostility tearing away her confidence.

'Face me girl,' the headmistress ordered and

Madeleine spun round unsteadily, propping against the wall to regain her balance. 'Clear this mess,' she went on with a look of disgust at the jumble piled on the bed. 'And when everything is straight, I want you in my office.'

Huddling miserably in the shadow of the wall Madeleine felt the glower from Miss Gorton like a hawk after its prey, shuddering as she uttered tartly, 'You should be thoroughly ashamed of yourself girl,' before wheeling round and stalking out of the room.

★ ★ ★

Miss Gorton always assured parents of her school's excellent integrity when placing their daughters in her care. Equally, this assurance extended to their daughters receiving fair consideration at all times – who would certainly have reported to their parents if anything had happened to the contrary! So with this in mind she decided to allocate a mistress to assist Madeleine in her room before she took on the task of chastising the girl about her appalling outburst, and knowing the excellent counselling qualities of this particular mistress, she counted on some information coming to light about the unsavoury situation that had been developing. Contrary to the expectations of her superiors however, Madeleine failed to respond. At seventeen, and fast developing the wiles of an older woman, she also had the ability of twisting minds to suit her own purpose. So her first reaction when Miss Collins – who had huge sympathetic tendencies towards girls in distress – entered her room, was an outburst of indignation about intrusion and spying, which nevertheless gave way to emotion and tears as they worked together sorting, straightening, folding and replacing everything back tidily in the drawer.

Miss Collins talked all the while as she smoothed the

bed and plumped pillows and picking her words carefully in a sympathetic manner explained how baffling circumstances had led to this unfortunate scene. 'I feared it may come to this,' she said with an air of resignation. 'But there was nothing I could do Madeleine. Nothing like this has ever happened here before and it was a mystery how the letters arrived.' The words were out before she realised and clapped a hand over her mouth as her cheeks flamed.

'Letters? What letters?'

Reacting quickly she grabbed Madeleine's hand, clasping it between hers. 'You don't know of course,' she said quietly. 'I'm sorry. I shouldn't have said.'

'But you did! And I want to know,' she said tearing herself away. 'What letters? Tell me.'

The mistress stifled an urge to reveal all to this unfortunate girl at the mercy of some serious mischief making, but doubts about her own credibility held her back despite Madeleine's continuing insistence.

'Why wasn't I told?' she persisted in quiet disbelief. 'If it concerned me surely I should have been told. I don't understand.'

'You must trust me Madeleine – and this must be between us. Please. I want to help you.' Desperately Miss Collins struggled to retrieve the situation berating herself all the while for blurting out about the letters so stupidly. 'I haven't seen the letters myself Madeleine,' she said. 'I only knew they were arriving. That's all. It is all very distressing.'

'Does Miss Gorton know?'

'They were addressed to her!'

Madeleine had never felt so angry and frustrated as tears began stinging again and when Miss Collins' next question followed after a long silence fear clutched as her confidence plummeted further.

'Is there a man you have been friendly with Madeleine?' she asked quietly. 'Have you been walking out with anyone, alone, without a chaperone perhaps?' She had taken a chance changing the subject and as the tense atmosphere transformed instantly, Madeleine's immediately flushing face provided the answer.

Shrugging defensively, she turned away to hide her face. 'How could I possibly?' Madeleine said and her voice was unsteady. 'I know the rules about chaperones and have always observed them.' *What else can I say?* she thought desperately, hating this woman's penetrating look as she glanced back, praying she hadn't given herself away.

'But is there anyone Madeleine?' she persisted. 'Honestly? It can remain a secret between us, I promise, and I may be able to help.' Miss Collins' voice was quietly persuasive.

Unnerved by this goading to confide and puzzled by her insistence, Madeleine hesitated, knowing she had to be careful. 'Why? Why do you ask?'

She knew well she should not be speaking about another student in this manner, but Madeleine's tormented appearance as she hunched miserably on the bed compelled the mistress to step outside the restriction of conformity. 'Something happened a while back,' she said softly, 'when Emily returned to the school early one evening. I believe you had all been out together. She appeared to be upset and it seemed she'd been crying and when she realised I had seen her she fled to her room, and I followed.' She hesitated here, expecting a reaction from Madeleine when she mentioned the girl she had fought with earlier, but with no response went on, 'She said something about treachery.'

'Treachery?' Madeleine rose from the bed thoughtfully, recalling in an instant Emily's attitude when she had confided about Neville, and a picture began to form. 'I don't understand what is meant by treachery,' she said with an air of innocence, *but she did know and had to be careful. She knew Emily also liked Neville but she dare not divulge they had been associating with men outside the school, and above all, she must not betray Neville with whom she was now so involved!* She edged across to the window, thinking quickly. There was too much at stake here if she talked, even with this friendly mistress. 'I really have no idea what's going on,' she said at last and contriving a look of bewilderment shook her head convincingly, 'and I certainly have no idea what could be meant by treachery.'

Miss Collins knew she was lying but with Madeleine in this mood there was little more she could do and having failed to gain her co-operation, which she hoped may have gone some way to sorting out this unfortunate situation, it seemed pointless to pursue the question of arsenic being discovered in her room as she'd intended. 'I'll leave you to get ready for supper then,' she said, smiling patiently as she prepared to leave, and in a sharper tone, 'Remember you have to see Miss Gorton later, as she requested.'

And into the lion's mouth young lady, she thought as she closed the door. *Certainly facing Miss Gorton would not be such a friendly discussion as this one!*

Chapter Six

Miss Gorton's boarding school in London had been modelled on a genteel middle-class family life and had an excellent reputation far and wide. With this distinction of esteem therefore, her responsibility for girls removed from the protection of their homes was profound and she depended on well-chosen mistresses to enhance her integrity and to influence their students likewise. Aside from this, she also had a responsibility to the trustees of the school who had recently taken over what had been a privately owned school when funding for its continuation had been in jeopardy. So with the authority for upholding the strict principles of the school now shared with a board of governors and trustees, Miss Gorton's thoughts dwelt carefully on how to proceed with the delicate matter she now faced. With arsenic having been discovered on the premises, and suspicion about Madeleine's association with the opposite sex, there was no question about this information having to be reported – and not only to the authorities she realised. The parents also had to be informed.

Madeleine had also thought long and hard about her disastrous circumstances, particularly how to deal with being associated with a man outside the school, should this be discovered. Approaching Miss Gorton's office later that day, the dreary gas-lit gloom helped little to lift her spirits. She sat ramrod straight when invited to do so, and with her head held high and hands clenched tight in her lap to give herself courage, she faced Miss Gorton with as much calm as she could muster and an expression she hoped would not betray her feelings.

The questions came thick and fast with little time allowed for an answer. 'What did she do in her spare time, particularly outside the school? Who did she know outside the school? Had she been in the company of any men without a chaperone?'

Miss Gorton thundered on endlessly still of the opinion that the girl was involved in an illicit affair with someone of the opposite sex. She had been relieved to discover she was not pregnant. Nevertheless, she felt determined to find out exactly how her time had been spent outside the school, which might also throw some light on these anonymous letters. 'Answer me girl!' she commanded. Already Madeleine's prolonged silence was trying her patience.

Taking a grip on her skittering thoughts, Madeleine decided a wise course of action was to own up to having visited a theatre with a young man. Having earlier confided this to friends, she realised they could also face the same piercing scrutiny of Miss Gorton if it came to them being interrogated – and she announced this event somewhat timidly.

'So you disobeyed my rule about not associating with men?'

With a huge effort to stay calm Madeleine widened her eyes innocently, 'I was accompanied by a chaperone all the while I was away,' and after a momentary pause questioned whether this arrangement had been in order.

Well used to this persuasive twisting of what the girls felt they should or should not do when questioned on behaviour Miss Gorton refrained to comment. She turned instead to Madeleine's outrageous behaviour earlier that day, dwelling on the virtue of restraint, however irksome a situation may be. 'And certainly not to indulge in a disgracefully common display of temper as you did,' she said with contempt.

Unable to stand the persistent discerning stare, Madeleine lowered her eyes and taking advantage of this humble demeanour Miss Gorton watched carefully for a reaction as she suddenly declared, 'It appears that sachets of arsenic have also been discovered in your room Madeleine. What have you to say about that?'

Her blood drained. Her heart thumped. It was like waking in the middle of a nightmare and she fought for control.

'Well?'

She had to say something and struggled to put her thoughts in order.

'This is a serious matter Madeleine. Answer me.'

Straightening, Madeleine took a long shuddering breath as the headmistress leaned forward, her eyes piercing like daggers.

'Why did you have this substance in your room Madeleine?' she said, uttering each word slowly. 'I want to know.'

Back on guard Madeleine remembered Neville giving her a thimbleful for her to use as a face wash when she pleaded for some. She had wrapped it in paper. Tucked well out of sight – and felt certain no one would ever discover it. *And she couldn't betray him! She must not!* 'I... I didn't know it was there,' she lied, meeting the frosty gaze. 'And never would I dream of asking or accepting if it were offered. I really wouldn't.'

Miss Gorton reached for her diary, flipping the pages and spreading them open. Clearly, the girl was lying and there was only one course of action as she ran a finger down a page.

'This matter will have to be investigated,' she said pursing her lips – and almost to herself as she continued to concentrate on the diary, 'And that means a consultation with the Governors and contacting the

Health department of the school.'

'So you don't believe me!'

Miss Gorton looked up instantly at this incredible outburst but without comment returned to scanning the diary. 'It's a school policy in a matter such as this Madeleine,' she announced at last and placing her arms on the desk as she leaned forward, said measurably, 'Can't you understand the seriousness of this matter girl? The possession and use of arsenic anywhere is scandalous in the extreme and in an institution such as this it is outrageously disgraceful and must be fully investigated.' With that she shut the diary with a thud and began tidying her desk. 'And it's not a matter entirely in my hands unfortunately,' she continued with an air of resignation. 'As well as contacting the outside authorities I mentioned, it has also been necessary to advise your parents.'

'No! You can't!'

Miss Gorton's eyebrows lifted in surprise. 'I beg your pardon?'

Madeleine wondered whether she had done right to deny all knowledge of having the arsenic. She should have admitted to accepting a scrap for cosmetic purposes. She should have told the truth. Surely, there would have been no harm in having it. It was in general use. Penelope had told her – but without having a chance to speak, Miss Gorton was talking again.

'Your father and mother are travelling down next week and in the meantime I shall be arranging for you to see our medical adviser.' As she rose from her chair, Miss Gorton dismissed Madeleine's further protests with a wave of her hand and walked stiffly across the room, waiting for her to stand as she opened the door. 'Needless to say,' she said icily, 'you will be confined to the school until all this has been resolved.'

★ ★ ★

Although no arsenic had been discovered in Madeleine's room when a thorough search subsequently took place, the insinuation in the anonymous letter demanded a thorough investigation and it was agreed a doctor should determine whether any of the substance had been used either for ingestion or been secretly concealed on her person. Both Miss Collins and Miss Gorton were required to accompany Madeleine to the examination room and they sat quietly in the background as Madeleine walked uncertainly to face the doctor, a hook-nosed man with grey whiskers and decidedly brusque in his speech and manner. He was abrupt with his questions as Madeleine sat timidly before him and she replied quietly to everything until asked whether she had received any arsenic and kept it in her room. The silence became ominous as she hesitated. *She could hear girls talking and laughing in the distance – as she had been herself until this nightmare started,* she thought miserably, and desperately yearned for some merciful release from this torment. She watched the doctor's hand shift impatiently on the desk and saw his fat stubby fingers beginning to drum.

'Well?'

'Just a wee bit,' she faltered. 'To try as a face wash on one occasion,' and endeavouring a smile, 'I had been told it acted as an aid to beauty.'

A sharp intake of breath came from Miss Gorton listening in the background registering her disgust as she remembered Madeleine's pronounced lie when she had posed the same question earlier.

The doctor turned to her at once, glancing over his spectacles. 'Do you know otherwise madam?'

Madeleine threw up her hands before anyone could

intervene, jumping up from her chair to face Miss Gorton as the words tumbled out.

'I'm so sorry. In the awfulness at that time when we talked, I regret I forgot all about it when you asked ma'am. It was such a tiny amount – just to try,' she said spacing her fingers, and with a nervous laugh, 'In fact it was so small, I actually mislaid it and never got to use it anyway.' She dropped her hands to her sides and with a pained expression went on, 'I do apologise most sincerely for what was unmistakably a mistruth ma'am,' and with what she hoped might satisfy everyone else in that room, sank back onto her chair feeling utterly miserable. This was not to be however.

'It will be necessary to carry out further investigations here madam,' the doctor said with an air of irritation as he turned to Miss Gorton. 'I am not entirely satisfied and with the seriousness of this situation. I must be absolutely certain.' With relief the headmistress felt thankful for having shared the responsibility of this distasteful affair with a higher authority, and when two women wearing nursing attire were summoned by the doctor to replace their chaperone duties, she and the mistress took their leave.

* * *

When Madeleine's parents arrived at the school later that week, they had clearly been in some disagreement when Madeleine arrived in Miss Gorton's office. Mr. Smith sat tight-lipped, barely acknowledging his daughter as she entered. His wife sat upright beside him with her chin thrust out in grim determination, and with thumbs tucked into the lapels of his frock coat, the doctor stood quietly in the background with a slightly amused expression. Despite the headmistress endeavouring to establish a degree of calm however, the atmosphere immediately became electric when Madeleine appeared.

'My daughter has never been involved with anything like you are implying and is totally innocent,' Elizabeth Smith announced in a shrill voice as she rose from her chair. Rushing across to Madeleine, she placed a hand on her shoulder – and to no one in particular protested, 'I cannot believe that she would become involved in anything so outrageous.' She ignored her husband's restraining hand as she turned away, and continued in her high voice, 'Nothing like this has ever occurred within our respectable family or in our immediate social surroundings.'

'But this is London madam,' the doctor interrupted with a wry look.

'Nonsense! London or anywhere else! My daughter has grown up in genteel circumstances with a God-fearing family and has more than likely never even heard about arsenic, let alone have it in her room! And to have actually used it! It's... it's ridiculous to suppose!'

Clearly embarrassed by this extraordinary outburst from his wife, Mr. Smith cleared his throat noisily and quickly changed the subject. 'Regrettably my wife is of the opinion that Madeleine should return home to where she will be in more...' and fumbling for words he hoped would not offend, blurted, 'Shall we say, in more cultured company.'

Miss Gorton bristled immediately. 'Which is where she has been I can assure you sir,' she protested, 'ever since she joined us a year or so ago.'

'I do beg your pardon madam,' Mr. Smith said, shifting uncomfortably. 'I apologise for my unfortunate choice of words, and of course I respect your sincere dedication to my daughter's education and care.'

'Which is more than I do,' Elizabeth interrupted jumping to her feet again. 'Otherwise we wouldn't be here discussing this dreadful affair.'

To everyone's amazement, Elizabeth then appeared to shrivel after this further attack and, as they watched anxiously, she sank back onto the chair as her voice slowly faded and she blinked through a fog of tears. To relieve the awkward silence, Mr. Smith again cleared his throat and returning quickly to the question of Madeleine returning home he looked squarely at his daughter as he announced, 'Personally I regret removing her from this school having achieved so well since being here.' He nodded politely in Miss Gorton's direction and attempted a smile, 'She has done well here madam. Very well indeed, I must say. But in the circumstances,' he went on slowly, 'perhaps this may be the best thing for all concerned.'

As Miss Gorton continued her praise concerning the excellent reputation of the school and pointing out at great length that the girls under her supervision were subject to strict control at all times, Madeleine switched off and became lost in her own thoughts. She knew her father expected her to react about returning home when he had glared in her direction and she hoped her face did not betray her feelings. Going back home would be a complete disaster after the freedom she had enjoyed. Returning home meant not seeing Neville again – her beloved Neville with whom she was now hopelessly in love and enjoying all the pleasures this brought. Going back meant strict control once more. Petty grievances, not being able to leave her home unchaperoned, and more than anything, back to the boring ritual of family life after the excitement of London and all it had to offer!

'That is until they leave this building on the few occasions they are allowed out for social recreation...' Miss Gorton was still stressing the fine attributes of the school as Madeleine forced back her attention '...which is then entrusted to the chaperones I insist should always accompany the girls,' she continued as she faced Mrs. Smith with a scorching look.

'Forgive me. I have no wish for our decision to be a criticism of your excellent school madam.' Mr. Smith spoke hurriedly, trying to mollify the threatened tension he suspected was about to rise again. 'I realise everything is done within your power to protect the girls madam, even outside the school of course,' he said, bowing his head in her direction. Whereupon Madeleine's mother sprang to life once more and jumping from her chair wheeled round to face the doctor.

'And this is when they fall into bad company,' she said with spite. 'As you pointed out so clearly, this is London! And from what I hear it is no better than a den of iniquity!'

Chapter Seven

Madeleine climbed into bed that night cold, miserable and utterly exhausted. Never had she witnessed her mother in such a ferocious mood and her father so compliant. Facing her parents had been a horrendous experience in itself and despite their concern for her welfare, she felt trapped. She had been stupid and entirely responsible for everything that had happened. Going out alone with Neville had been a mistake and trying arsenic was foolish, albeit using it innocently as a cosmetic. It was no use denying anything in view of what was likely to happen now, she thought, and forced into returning home – along with all the threatened restrictions – she mouthed bitterly, 'Oh God, I can't go back. I can't! Never seeing Neville. All those dreadful social occasions. Meeting boring people – and forever being under scrutiny! And not even being able to talk to my father's clients!

Her small dark room offered no comfort as it had on other occasions recently and as tears streamed she pondered on everything leading to this horrendous situation – discovering Emily meddling in her room, learning about the letters and that interrogation with the headmistress. The disgrace of her parents being there hearing about everything that had happened, and that doctor! *Oh God. That dreadful doctor, and those awful women!* Even now her face burned hot just thinking about it and how he'd forced information out of her with his constant questions, getting more short-tempered when she failed to answer quickly.

'Was she taking arsenic as a stimulant?' he had persisted and, with barely time to expect an answer, 'Why was none found in your room then when it had been discovered there originally?'

Her lips had remained clenched.

'Have you secreted it on your person?'

All she could do was to shake her head and grip her hands tight to stop the trembling as he continued relentlessly despite her silence, following up with intimate questions and insisting she tell him about things she would never have discussed with anyone, however well she knew them. He kept digging on and on, his voice growing louder as he demanded answers and when she'd eventually turned away covering her burning face, he'd summoned the two women standing quietly in the background.

'We have to be certain that there is no hiding of anything young lady,' he had told her resignedly in a loud voice and with a wave of his hand the two women stepped forward and took her forcibly behind the screens and stripped her.

Recalling the humility of that search Madeleine's whole body flushed with embarrassment and, stiffening in her bed as she breathed slowly, she tried to calm herself. She failed to understand – even having turned it over repeatedly in her mind so many times – why there had been such a personal examination. It was unbelievable and she clutched at the bedcovers pulling them over her head, trying to shut the memory out as she lived through the agony of it again. She could not make out what was happening at first, puzzled by the two women forcibly restraining her as she had resisted. Yet despite their constant whispered apologies and her growing indignation as they removed her underclothes, they had just carried on!

'We have been told to be thorough,' one of them said quietly in a sympathetic manner. And all the while, as they undid buttons and loosened tapes, they begged her pardon. They searched through her clothes thoroughly first before dropping them to the floor – then as one of them held her firmly when she struggled, the other one examined her intimately.

'For goodness sake does he really expect me to put it there!' she had exploded in horror, but to no avail. They totally ignored her embarrassment and protests, and continuing to excuse themselves, they still carried on. It had all been so degrading and disgusting, and all the time that doctor had been at his desk listening and waiting for them to finish. And then he smiled at her smugly when she eventually emerged from behind the screens to sit before him again with her cheeks blazing hot.

★ ★ ★

The headmistress never knew the extent of Madeleine's medical interrogation. The fact that there were female attendants with her throughout this process satisfied her that all had been well, and content with the way arrangements were proceeding, she returned to her office where she concentrated on the leaving formalities for her errant pupil. In Madeleine's favour she offered support by providing excellent reports, having already told her parents at that disastrous meeting how she felt proud having had her as one of their pupils. 'She is particularly bright and has always been wholeheartedly dedicated to her studies,' she had said. At which they had looked impressed, although still standing by their decision that their daughter should leave the school at the end of the current term.

In the meantime, Emily had mysteriously disappeared from the school and with her room now cleared of everything she owned, none of the other girls knew what had happened. It was as though she had never existed. As it turned out, an interrogation had taken place when a staff member discovered her entering the head mistress's office one night – and investigations at her previous school revealed that she had been involved in a similar situation which resulted in blackmail – which was clearly the intention for Madeleine had the matter not come to a head sooner. It was with some relief to Miss Gorton therefore to be arranging for the two girls to leave her school – albeit the earlier hasty dismissal of Emily and the more drawn out leaving procedure for Madeleine.

★ ★ ★

As Madeleine faced the prospect of returning to Scotland with impending gloom, her parents' anticipation of her living at home again brought a mixed reaction. Her father arranged for her final year at a small private school in Glasgow, whose aims he wholeheartedly endorsed in glowing terms to his wife. 'The curriculum emphasises that they encourage the development of cultured Christian homemakers able to preside at their future husband's dinner tables with grace and reasonable intelligence,' he told her with a satisfied expression – which went some way to meet her mother's approval despite her personal requirements for her daughter being focussed in a different direction. Although memories of the difficult days prior to leaving home for the London school had not entirely vanished, Mrs. Smith nevertheless cherished the thought of having her daughter under her influence once more – and that was not all. With Madeleine now approaching marriageable age, she also looked forward to seeking suitable young men she could welcome to the house who might ask for her hand. All this speculation was for an unknown future however; as it was for Madeleine who now passed her remaining days in London uneventfully until the time came for her to leave and when the day arrived, she sat in the reception hall calmly waiting for her father with no outward appearance of emotion.

Miss Gorton, Miss Collins and several of the girls turned out to wish her well and all were genuinely sorry to see her leave. She had been an intelligent, dedicated pupil with a likeable personality and some of the tutors, who were also there to see her off, were disappointed she was unable to go on to higher education at one of the new ladies colleges.

Mr. Smith had arrived alone at the school having left his wife organising a welcome home party – and despite any secret misgivings either may have had, their joy was matched for the time being in rejoicing that their family would be complete once more with the approach of the Christmas season. 'Things can never be as trying as they were before,' Mr. Smith had soothed when his wife expressed doubts should the old problems return. 'She has matured considerably while she's been away my dear despite what has been reported. You have seen for yourself – and now on the brink of womanhood, things will be different. You mark my words. All that nonsense is behind us I'm sure Elizabeth. And as you said yourself, quite rightly at the time I remember,' he added in a patronising tone, 'her behaviour was probably all part of growing up.'

When they reached home after the long, tedious journey, James Smith hesitated by the carriage as Madeleine sprang down and ran to greet her mother. He watched them thoughtfully as she welcomed her with open arms, his wife's eyes bright with excitement – or were they tears he wondered as the two walked into the house with arms entwined. His enthusiasm for this grand welcome home however did not match with his wife on this occasion. The information he had received just prior to leaving the school still rankled and he had done some serious thinking on the journey back to Scotland. He would have to remain silent nevertheless for the time being he realised.

Madeleine had been bidding farewell to Alice and Penelope and a collection of the other girls and the teachers – and Miss Gorton had looked decidedly cheerful for once, he thought! Why the doctor had been there however when they were about to leave he could not fathom at the time. He'd recognised and acknowledged him with a brief smile as he made his way to the carriage, noticing how he distanced himself from the other people, then at the last minute, just as they were preparing to go, he sidled up to him.

'Just a minute,' he said stepping forward with an outstretched hand. 'A word in your ear sir,' and as Mr. Smith offered his hand in return as the doctor approached and raised a cupped hand to his mouth, he said quietly, 'I thought you ought to know, and it is with much regret to have to tell you sir, that your daughter is no longer a virgin.'

Chapter Eight

After a month at home, life quickly settled down to what became a routine of monotony for Madeleine. When she first arrived, everyone behaved politely in a reserved manner – although this quickly gave way to the usual hustle and bustle of a comfortable family relationship. There were days when Madeleine's niggling hostility rankled and there were problems, but for the time being all boded well. Until her restlessness got the better of her.

Many organisations had sprung up in the area while she had been away and with her lively enquiring mind, she began questioning her father about joining one of them. There were the feminist campaigners, the reform movements and a growing number of lectures were opening up with the opportunity for women to attend. She also talked about entering some kind of profession at which her father fairly exploded telling her in his bombastic way that, 'Only poor girls work when their fathers are unable to support them my girl,' and with an indignant scowl dictated that none of his daughters would ever be expected to work.

As far as marriage was concerned, Elizabeth had all but given up on the question of finding a suitor for her daughter. Countless young men had been invited to house parties and family picnics, but for whatever reason Madeleine had so far shown no inclination to further an association with any of them.

'What the girl says or does in their company is absolutely beyond me,' she complained to her husband when yet another young man declared he would love to come again but then never did. 'Perhaps these visits should not be family occasions,' she suggested. 'Maybe what we are doing is not right. Nowadays, young people welcome the chance to be on their own for some of the time and perhaps we should stay in the background occasionally and leave them alone together.' But with his dark secret still festering at the back of his mind, Mr. Smith immediately cast this preposterous idea aside. At all cost he was determined to keep a strict control on Madeleine's activities – and to leave her alone with a young man as his wife suggested was unthinkable.

★ ★ ★

The school chosen for the remaining months of Madeleine's education did little to stimulate her interest. After being in London, even after all the problems she encountered there, it was boring and with it being situated well outside the city, the surrounding area was dull and dreary. The subjects were uninteresting and tedious and with education for girls still not considered to be of any significance, there were endless hours of religious subjects, music, painting and countless lectures on moral values. Particularly boring was the ritual of cutting out and sewing basic garments for charities to donate to the poor.

'We have to sew horrible coarse cotton,' Madeleine groaned to her mother one day. 'It smells foul and has black threads poking out and we have to join long stretches of the wretched stuff together for making baggy chemises. It's boringly dull and I'm not learning anything useful now as I did in London.' And after a further dreary account of further useless pursuits throughout the day she said, 'I may just as well stay at home and do something more useful here.'

Always sympathetic to Madeleine's stream of

complaints her mother listened patiently and with her worsening health problems she felt justified in suggesting this idea to her husband. Unsurprisingly it met with his usual pompous scorn, until a more worthwhile opportunity arose one day, which he viewed as a commendable alternative.

'Certainly Madeleine must be involved in this gracious gesture,' he told his wife as details were explained – although in truth his more urgent desire was for his daughter's time to be totally accounted for to prevent any possible furtive behaviour! Furthermore, as an eminent philanthropist in the locality, he endorsed this new scheme which was being organised through the Poor Law for educated young ladies to visit children in their homes to help them read and write. Many parents were already beginning to take advantage of this opportunity, even though it often meant them having to forego the pittance earned by their children in factories, on farms or in the coalmines, so the thought of his daughter spending her time with these poor unfortunates met with his full approval.

Madeleine on the other hand had her own reasons for grasping this opportunity. Just being able to leave the house where she'd felt imprisoned under watchful eyes for far too long, offered an iota of freedom – and, with a bit of luck, it could even mean the chance of having a little free time to do what she wanted!

★ ★ ★

Although marginally younger than Madeleine, James Smith decided that his younger daughter Bessie should accompany her sister on many of the forays to visit the children, *and she would never dare stray from propriety in the presence of an impressionable younger sibling,* he reasoned! So either taking the carriage, or walking when the weather allowed, they visited what often turned out to be hovels where doleful children awaited their arrival. One little boy chosen by the authorities eventually took most of Madeleine's time, the only boy in a family of six girls. The mother had received limited education before falling pregnant and being hastened into marriage when she was sixteen and although still unable to read or write herself, she had ambitions for her son. 'I want better for my boy than I ever 'ad,' she said when the girls arrived. 'Someone to learn 'im to read and write,' she told Madeleine as she suckled the latest addition to the family at her ample breast.

His name was Charlie and on the days Madeleine called he was always sitting quietly at a scrubbed table ready for his lesson in a cramped kitchen with damp clothes and bits of rag draped from a length of string stretched across the ceiling. He had done his best to remove the grime from his face and hands when he rushed home from where he worked for a few hours nearby, and eager for his lesson he smiled his welcome.

This work was something Madeleine thoroughly enjoyed, despite the appalling conditions and strange wafting odours, and Charlie warmed to her gentle coaxing and encouragement. And to add a little zest to her laudable work, after bidding her little charge goodbye at the end of his lesson, she also welcomed the chance of freedom as she and Bessie strolled back home.

Something Madeleine discovered on these journeys however was that during her absence at the London school, Bessie had become as much of a flirt as herself and with her sister's insistence that they took a longer walk on their return journey home, she was in for a surprise. This route back home meant strolling along the fashionable Sauchiehall Street where well-to-do residents of Glasgow arrived in carriages or on foot to shop at haberdashers, stationers, hosiers, jewellers and confectioners and where people stopped to pass the time of day with friends and acquaintances, and where women with doubtful characters often hovered suspiciously! Shocked to catch Bessie swaying her hips and fluttering eyelashes when young men passed by however, she saw fit to admonish her on many of these jaunts. 'What do you think you're doing,' she cautioned under her breath. 'Remember your place in society,' and flaunting the superiority she had already established over her siblings, dictated how her young sister should behave on such occasions. This nevertheless provoked a feisty reaction from Bessie.

'What about when you told me about sneaking out of school in London to meet men,' she reminded. 'All I ever do is to look and if men happen to glance my way and I smile, I see no wrong.'

Cursing for having confided about her escapades in London, Madeleine bit her lip but decided to stand her ground. 'At least when you are out with me then, you should behave with decorum,' she declared. She was nonetheless aware of the continuing admiring glances as they drifted along and trusted Bessie would heed her example when she decided to ignore any glances or simply nodded politely as she passed.

One such walk through the town however was impossible to ignore when a young man stepped before them and put on a show of recognition. He introduced himself as Robert Baker, then immediately made faltering apologies when Madeleine challenged him.

Looking embarrassed as he excused himself, he bowed courteously. 'Please forgive me Miss,' he said, 'but I believe you to be the daughter of Mr. Smith, with whom my father is well acquainted. Of course you may not know,' he hurried on defensively and with a forced smile continued, 'although I must admit I have not yet had the pleasure of your acquaintance.'

Madeleine looked at him hard, with a momentary glance at the elegant young man standing alongside who had already caught her eye. It was true she did not know all her father's acquaintances and her brief hesitation as she pondered offered encouragement for this Robert Baker to continue.

'Perhaps I may introduce my good friend Pierre Emile L'Angelier,' he said, standing aside. 'He's just returned from France,' and flashing a quick smile at Emile, 'He's newly discharged from hospital this week, from injuries sustained in the war.'

Emile extended a gloved hand and as Madeleine shyly accepted, he made his acquaintance in an exaggerated accent. At a distance she'd noticed this handsome gentleman, fascinated by his dandified appearance as he approached but she screened her intrigue well and with the suggestion of a smile simpered, 'Delighted.' And as he closed his hand over hers, holding it far longer than socially acceptable, he promptly apologised when she felt it appropriate to draw away.

Having already noticed this attractive young lady walking in the town on previous occasions, L'Angelier had briefed his friend well and while Robert engaged Bessie in polite conversation, Emile did likewise with Madeleine after further apologies for having intercepted them so abruptly. Secretly delighted, she listened with as cool an expression as she could manage as he enthused about the peaceful surroundings in Scotland after his recent horrors on the battlefield. Until suddenly aware they were attracting glances from passers-by, and fearing they may be mistaken for common street women, Madeleine fabricated an excuse and placing a firm hand on Bessie's arm, made a polite departure and proceeded sedately in the direction of their home.

Wrapped in their own thoughts and personal fantasies, neither girl spoke on the way until they were in sight of the house. Madeleine had adored Emile's accent and impeccable manners and savoured the sweet way he bowed and apologised so enchantingly when he feared he'd offended by their abrupt intrusion. She nevertheless thought it wise to keep these feelings private for the time being. To divulge such awareness to Bessie would be wrong at this stage. There was an example to be set. Her sister was only sixteen after all. So when Bessie, who was unable to contain her excitement any longer, also praised the virtues of this charming Frenchman with his adorable accent and grand manners, Madeleine quickly brought her to heel and insisted she abandon such ridiculous thoughts at her age – which nevertheless brought a further swift reaction.

'If Monsieur L'Angelier finds me attractive, I'll do no such thing,' she remonstrated, and seeing it as a distinct claim on choice added, 'Remember it was my idea to walk home by this route in the first place. We would never have met him otherwise, especially as it was me who glanced at him encouragingly before they stopped to speak.'

'You did what?' Madeleine came to a halt abruptly, glaring at her sister's face set with determination. 'Have you no respect Bessie when you are out walking in public?' Clearly, influencing her young sibling was her responsibility she considered as they proceeded after a heated exchange, and continuing to admonish Bessie's persistent silly talk Madeleine finally flared at her as they reached the house, 'Oh do stop this nonsense Bessie. Just shut up will you!' And more to protect her own interests as they hesitated outside the door she added sternly, 'And just remember, there must never be a word about this to either mother or father – particularly if we do happen to see those men again,' she added guardedly. 'So be warned!'

★ ★ ★

As an outrageous philanderer, Emile L'Angelier used devious plans to ensnare girls he wished to get to know and with his charm and extravagant stories he'd made many conquests, and deflowered several on the way! With Madeleine however, things were different he realised, but with the introduction now made – and hopefully a future affair in sight – this new encounter had to be handled carefully. His friend did know the Smith family well as it happened and through this useful contact L'Angelier had gained much useful knowledge about Madeleine and her excellent social standing. Girls he'd met so far had been from the village in Jersey where he grew up, so an introduction to a girl like Madeleine was a tremendous boost for his ego considering his humble background. Since arriving in Scotland, where he had hoped to improve himself, he never divulged his simple start in life to people he wished to impress and this introduction to a well-heeled young lady fitted in very nicely with his ambitions.

Apart from this devious scheming to improve his lot, Emile L'Angelier also excelled at deception. He was not the dashing French man he led people to believe. He had not even been born in France! It was his father who was of French origin. Emile had been born in St. Helier, Jersey where his parents scratched a living running a small market garden business, and with a talent for mimicking his father's accent, together with a flair for haughty behaviour, he had acquired characteristics to convince people otherwise when necessary.

As the eldest son, and brighter by far than any of his

siblings, Emile had also won favouritism with his parents, which together with his assumed self-importance and vain streak, served well in encouraging his extravagant ambitions. So having endured an impoverished childhood and his teenage years in a mundane family existence, he now set his sights on mixing with the upper strata of society and began seeking friends far above his own station in life. More than this, he warmed to the idea of marrying into the higher echelons of society. And having been introduced to Madeleine, this now looked distinctly possible. 'What more could a chap want!' he congratulated himself. Particularly a girl like that – with stunning looks into the bargain!

Chapter Nine

Mr. and Mrs. Smith were more than delighted when Madeleine became increasingly involved helping underprivileged children with their education. It dealt with her earlier restlessness and with her interesting accounts about the little boy she worked with and his appalling home and family life and how he was making progress with his reading, she became more settled.

Madeleine and Bessie in the meantime continued their strolls along Sauchiehall Street when the weather was fine, each secretly hoping they might encounter Robert Baker and Emile L'Angelier once more but neither of them voicing such a suggestion. This never happened however and both girls wondered why. Equally, Emile – who was now in full-time employment and unable to pursue his flirtatious advances so freely – felt increasingly uneasy about the loss of a future lucrative courtship. Never one to miss an opportunity however, and with St. Valentine's day on the horizon, Emile risked sending Madeleine a brief note and a single red rose anonymously to the address supplied by his friend. And when a special delivery man turned into the Smith's drive, where in keeping with other young girls on this special day both the sisters were hopefully positioned behind lace curtains, Bessie tore off to the front door with Madeleine in hot pursuit protesting about her behaviour.

Allowing her sister to tear open the note, Bessie peered over her shoulder and read:

Mademoiselle, I so enjoyed meeting you recently.

May I have the pleasure of seeing you again? I shall be in Sauchiehall Street next Saturday – in the bookshop at 2pm. May I have the pleasure?
My humble good wishes.

Madeleine knew immediately who it came from and ignoring Bessie's protests and grabbing fingers, snatched it up and hastened to her room, slamming the door behind her. Her heart pounded as she crushed the bloom to her face and closing her eyes relished the memory of this fascinating stranger. She held the rose at a distance then placed it tenderly on her table in a shaft of sunlight from the window, a token of love she told herself, although it had to be a secret she immediately decided and planned to plead ignorance should her parents ask any questions. Bessie too had already guessed who had sent it and burst into her room ready for a quarrel. Prepared for this outburst, without a flicker of emotion however, Madeleine simply reminded Bessie about not revealing their earlier encounter with the two men to their parents. 'Who undoubtedly wonder this very minute what is going on with your snivelling behaviour!' she added.

'But why assume it is yours? It could easily have been for me. It's unfair and I've a mind to tell mama and papa.'

With the first seeds of hatred for her sister sown as Bessie continued to wail, Madeleine decided to placate her by suggesting they visit the bookshop together on Saturday. 'I'm sure he would be delighted to see us both,' she said, and for the time being, the tension eased. Madeleine knew, however, that she was the one on the brink of a romance.

★ ★ ★

Blissfully unaware of his two daughters' exciting

prospect of meeting a man they both fancied, Mr. Smith assumed he had full control over his family once more. Grave concern for Madeleine's future still rankled nevertheless and in their mutual efforts to get Madeleine safely wed, both he and his wife decided she should be included in all their future social calls to affluent friends wherever he considered the prospects looked favourable. Elizabeth Smith, who was still blissfully unaware of her daughter's fallen virtue, felt increasingly proud of Madeleine and when well enough to attend one of these arranged functions herself, portrayed her lovely daughter as a credit to the family and a worthy example to her younger brothers and sisters. Justifiably, she had excellent reasons to sing her daughter's praises with her own health failing so miserably and having to take to her bed more often with various health problems, real or otherwise. So with Madeleine entirely responsible on many occasions for running the home with her fine achievement of control, as well as keeping a wary eye on the expenditure in the house, ordering meals and overseeing the servant's duties, all augured well for the time being.

Madeleine's demure behaviour at the social functions arranged by her parents, and their glowing attribute about her being a paragon of virtue in the family home, nevertheless clashed strikingly with her conduct when she met Emile for the first time on her own. Protocol had dictated her refined conduct on the first occasion in Sauchiehall Street when Robert Baker had introduced the two girls to his friend, and similarly there had been polite restraint when she and Bessie met him in the bookshop as later arranged. But her Victorian respectability waned abysmally when they met on a secretly planned date in the local park when Madeleine had contrived a situation to be away from the house on her own. She failed to pick him out at first in a crowd milling around a band playing lively tunes. Then feeling a touch on her arm he was suddenly there and she immediately grasped his hand and without a moment's hesitation accepted his invitation to take a stroll. Despite this boldness however, it immediately deserted her and suddenly she could think of nothing to say – and when he held her gaze as she glanced up she felt embarrassingly shy. *How delightfully his soft dark eyes regarded her, how handsome his elegant moustache, and hair smoothed and parted so fashionably. Was there ever a man like this!* Then flustered again she started talking quickly, too quickly, about the weather, the band, the music and the crowds and with hardly time to draw breath found herself talking about her family and describing the children. He drew her arm through his as she chattered non-stop and as she gradually calmed he quietly steered her into a comfortable conversation, easing closer as he enlightened her about himself and she formed a picture of someone rather like her as his life history unfolded. His family held him in great esteem he told her and when explaining about instilling a rigid code of good behaviour on his siblings for whom he felt responsible, she realised how much they had in common. He said nothing about his parents' market garden business – concerned that this may sound a trifle common. However, with his penchant for impressing people about his military achievements he endorsed in glowing terms his many adventures in the army during the Revolution, his bravery on the battlefields and the terrible injuries sustained as he fought for the honour of France, as wide-eyed Madeleine took it all in! Then thinking fit to dwell on the finer attributes of life, he talked about his religious beliefs and regular attendance at church, the fine people he knew and the excellent career awaiting him when he arrived in Scotland – although he never expanded on this and felt grateful for no forthcoming questions – and this was just as well. In truth, Emile L'Angelier was a scoundrel and an atrocious flirt who frequented beer shops in dubious districts. More so, he had to accept the only work available in the severely depressed area of Glasgow when his money began running out and for the niggardly sum of ten shillings, worked all week as a packing clerk in a Seed Merchant's business!

A more sinister side to L'Angelier's life, and one that accounted for his dwindling funds, was a constant need for surreptitious doses of arsenic to which his more well-to-do friends had introduced him. Also, as a hypochondriac, he habitually swallowed drugs for whatever malady he believed he was suffering from at the time and whenever he passed a druggist's shop could never resist the temptation to buy a 'pick-up' to enhance his health or indulge in any remedy claimed to do wonders for his well-being. This alleged 'bad health' he never discussed with people he wished to impress however, and certainly not with any young women who had taken his eye. It was only older women, particularly landladies where he'd rented a room, who indulged his many health complaints and maladies he believed he was suffering from and he eagerly wallowed in their overbearing mothering and sympathy.

Yet another odd side of L'Angelier's personality was excluding himself from people he worked with. He seldom talked and when he did have anything to say his voice was falteringly dull. His colleagues thus regarded him as a quiet conscientious man as he went about his work industriously. Although no one really got to know anything about him and at the end of the week when he queued up with everyone else to receive his wages, people assumed he returned to his wife and family as a dutiful husband.

In her ignorance about all this, Madeleine was nonetheless impressed as they strolled through the park. She was utterly mesmerised by this handsome man in abundantly high spirits and in awe of his tales of dangerous exploits on the battlefields, she found it all wildly exciting. She even dared to consider introducing him to her parents, or at least discussing him with them and thought earnestly how she could bring this about, although she realised having to admit walking out with him, without their permission, and more so without a chaperone, was out of the question. As it turned out however, there was no need to dwell too long on this when the introduction of Emile to her father took place, quite unexpectedly one afternoon. Which bordered on disaster!

Chapter Ten

Madeleine's father still clung to his own reasons for launching his daughter onto the marriage market and his endeavours in finding a suitor to make an honest woman of her were second to none. Nevertheless, as time passed he became increasingly concerned about her not having received a proposal of marriage despite the number of men who had shown interest.

'The most promising young men still fail to return even when they appear to be infatuated,' Elizabeth sighed after yet another unproductive house party. 'She appears to turn every eye when she puts in an appearance, so I fail to understand why.'

There had been no need for his wife to explain their daughter's attraction to the opposite sex. James Smith had already been aware of the effect she had on men! She never failed to turn heads with her fine aptitude for dressing attractively and her looks that were more striking than beautiful – and whenever a situation dictated a charming shy reserve, her cunning ability never wavered. 'She is yet only eighteen,' he said, more to convince himself than any encouragement for his wife. 'There is time yet. She seems content for some reason so we must be patient.' And certainly Madeleine had her own reasons for not encouraging any other young men to share her life at present!

Mr. Smith's prophecy for his daughter's romantic future however was soon to be put to the test when he suddenly encountered Madeleine and Emile strolling hand in hand as he turned a corner in the town and the confrontation was as traumatic as it was surprising. It was when Madeleine had promised to visit a local family on her mother's behalf – and on this occasion was allowed to make the journey on her own. Equally shocked as they stumbled in front of her father, Madeleine justified being with Emile as a friend apparently known to one of his business colleagues and, introducing him briefly, immediately launched into a string of lies about her fruitless visit. 'It's been a complete waste of time calling on that family,' she announced peevishly. 'This visit was arranged weeks ago by mama – and for their benefit!' she said, throwing up her hands in despair. 'How could they not be there, wasting my time,' and, turning to Emile with a soft smile, added in a faltering voice, 'Fortunately this gentleman has made my wasted journey more pleasant however by offering to accompany me home.'

Mr. Smith declined Emile's extended hand, simply nodding briefly in his direction and after an awkward silence, Madeleine went on hurriedly to introduce Emile. When no conversation followed this repartee however, and she fought with ideas on how to continue, she passed quickly to describing his military achievements as she remembered them – until her father, looking totally unimpressed and leaning heavily on his cane with an air of boredom, cleared his throat noisily.

'You must let your mother know about this – er – family you went to see,' he said, fluttering a hand. 'She will know what to do. It can't be left.' A further stunned silence followed which had them all shifting about as if contemplating a fight and as Madeleine's father fixed him with a glare, Emile tweaked his moustache nervously wondering what to do. He had to impress this man he realised and suddenly blurted out, 'Your daughter failed to mention my regiment when she told you about my military career,' he said, with a hint of a smile. 'Perhaps I should explain that I was an Imperial Guardsman, and proud for the privilege of defending my Monarch.' He thrust out an arm as his smile broadened, turning back a sleeve to display a scarcely visible scar. 'Proud to have defended him so meaningfully too,' he went on with a swagger, and still with no reaction from Madeleine's father, he launched into explaining about the medal he expected to receive when he returned to France.

It was blatantly clear that Mr. Smith was not impressed. *Something about this chap didn't ring true. Too sure of himself. Cocky! More so were his appalling manners. Not once had he addressed him as Sir! And messing with his moustache in public was repugnant!*

He turned to his daughter, his lips compressed in distaste. 'You should get back home Madeleine,' he said shifting away. 'Talk to your mother about these people you went to see. The carriage is just up the road.'

Madeleine turned to Emile urging him forward. 'And mother I'm sure would be delighted to meet Emile,' she said, at which her father immediately swung round.

'No,' he flustered, turning to back away then edging round again he allowed Emile a cursory glance as he hesitated. 'No. Not on this occasion. You understand,' he mumbled in his direction and placing a firm hand on his daughter's arm, he began urging her away. 'These can be delicate matters,' he added hoarsely. And he was gone, marching off with long strides with Madeleine following hesitantly at his bidding, looking back every now and then to see Emile standing isolated and confused, wondering what to do.

Not a word passed in the carriage. The tense atmosphere trapped them in isolation and Madeleine knew well not to talk when her father was in this mood. She sat bolt upright, hands clenched in her lap and her thoughts in disarray. Memories surfaced of previous confrontations such as this, the vicious quarrel with

The Shadow of Doubt

Emily at the school in London, the probing into her affairs, that dreadful doctor she remembered with a shudder, the restrictions and not being able to see Neville. And with a sly glance at her father she knew it would be the same all over again after this. She had persuaded herself she had fallen in love again with this exciting Frenchman – different this time of course to how it had been in London with Neville, she told herself – and this tore at her heart. Her parents wanted her wed for heaven's sake, which made her father's behaviour towards Emile quite inconsiderate, unjustified and rude she decided as she flashed him another sly look.

When they arrived at the house, it was worse. As her father climbed down and held the door for her to alight, he announced forcefully, 'I forbid you to have anything further to do with that man.' And without waiting for a reply or any reaction he stalked up to the house.

'Why?' she screamed, following quickly, but he had disappeared into the house either not hearing or choosing not to. Then almost immediately, he lurched out again just as she had reached the door and flinching back, she was terrified he would strike her.

'I said I forbid you to see that man again,' he thundered. 'That's the end of it!' Thrusting his face into hers he added with bitter contempt, 'Now go to your mother and tell her what has happened – and make sure she hears the truth.'

★ ★ ★

'Common little Frenchman!' she heard as she approached her mother's room and she hung back. Her father had gone straight up to his wife's bedroom where she languished with another attack of some malady, alarming her by suddenly bursting into the room with a face black as thunder.

'I won't have my daughter associating with someone like that,' he went on, pacing the floor. 'Walking along brazenly holding her hand and she behaving like a cheap little tart.'

With her husband in this state Elizabeth chose to bide her time and unable to carry on an argument in her present state of health anyway, shrunk back into the covers. Then the thought suddenly occurred that her husband's criticism of their daughter may have some reflection on her authority as a mother and she braved leaning forward to make a point.

'You've no idea how difficult things have been,' she started timorously as her husband strutted across to the bed and walked away again. 'She's always been wilful as you know and used to getting her way. But...' *dare she suggest it she thought as she plucked at the blanket.* 'Surely James,' she continued in a firmer voice addressed to her husband's retreating back, 'Surely it's time she found a suitor. Perhaps this man would be suitable?'

'Not one like that if that's what you're suggesting,' he stormed, spinning round. 'I won't have it. I have my position to maintain and I suspect this... this so-called soldier does not have a penny to his name. Do you not want a respectable husband for your daughter woman? One that is able to provide a good home for her?'

Elizabeth shrunk into her pillows defenceless against the striding monster that was her husband, yet somehow she again found the strength to pursue and in a tiny voice ventured, 'But you know nothing about him James. At least we could meet him. Or perhaps allow me the opportunity to...'

'I have met him,' he roared. 'Did you not hear me? And I won't have him in the house. I've forbidden the girl to ever see him again. And there is nothing further to say on the matter.'

Angrier than Elizabeth had ever seen her husband, she knew further protests were useless and as she withdrew into her pillows she watched fearfully as her husband stormed out and slammed the door.

Madeleine had already fled back to her room where within minutes of leaving his terrified wife her father now confronted her in a fit of rage. From her earlier experiences, Madeleine had learned how to exploit such situations to her advantage however and with a supreme effort managed to stay calm as he burst in. She sat demurely with her hands in her lap trying to make sense of what was happening and what he was saying as he gave vent to his anger, and even managed a tear to fall at the appropriate moment as he began spinning out reasons for her not seeing that 'common little Frenchman' again.

'He is not of the same calibre as you,' he exploded, thumping a fist. 'Don't you see that? I will not have this exploitation. Surely you realise what he's up to? And more to the point, how dare you walk out with a man unknown to me and your mother without a formal introduction!'

Madeleine continued to sit quietly, her feelings disguised behind a fixed expression as she regarded her father. This was the man she loved dearly as a child. The man who teased her and played games with her as a child. Brought home presents for her as a surprise, and had always treated her fairly. Now he was unrecognisable, a demon, totally without reason and insulting. Her thoughts flashed back to the memory of Emile standing abandoned when she'd been hastened away without a polite departure. More than that, although the threat never again to see the man she loved was bad enough, to regard him as common and not worthy of her affection was more than she could bear.

She summoned courage. 'Then what do you suggest I

do father?' she said evenly. 'I suggested Emile accompanied us home to meet mama in the assumption that you both appear to have a desire for my betrothal?'

'Do!' he roared. 'Haven't you been listening?'

'I've heard every word father,' she answered, struggling as fluttering nerves began clutching. 'But forgive me. I fail to understand why you resent my choice when you and mama are so anxious to see me wed and that the first man I feel comfortable with is not even given a chance to meet with us socially.'

Incensed by the reaction of her cool manner and more so by her making him feel inadequate, he towered over her with a raised hand. 'If you were one of the boys Madeleine,' he said between clenched teeth, 'I would make sure you understand why.' And with his voice rising, went on threateningly, 'Furthermore, do you not understand that this is my house?' he roared. 'And it is I who invite people into my house?'

Madeleine ducked beneath her father's outstretched hand, quickly making for the door, drained of colour and trembling now as she turned back to face him.

'Very well then father,' she said in a soft voice. 'I will do as you bid. I shall tell Emile L'Angelier he is not welcome at *your* house,' and she shot from the room, picking up her skirts as she hastened down the corridor with her father's voice following like a howling storm as he roared, 'You are not to see him again girl. To tell him anything! Didn't you hear me?'

★ ★ ★

Elizabeth dragged herself out of bed and shuffled to the bedroom door, holding it ajar for Madeleine when she heard her rushing upstairs and, placing a finger to her lips, she quickly turned the key after hustling her inside. Never had either of them seen Mr. Smith in such a temper and never in her life before had Madeleine feared her father would strike her.

'You must get back into bed,' she told her mother, taking her hand. 'I'm sorry. I did not wish for this.'

'Do as your father bids, Madeleine,' she pleaded breathlessly as she crept beneath the blankets. 'Don't cross him over this Madeleine. Please – for my sake.'

With plans already crowding her mind, her mother's pleas fell on deaf ears as she soothed and watched her hands flutter against the quilt. She contemplated running away. Meeting Emile, and disappearing somewhere. Making plans to go away together – even getting married without her parents knowing. They could do this she thought and live well away from them – and they would not be able to do anything. She smiled down at the face she loved and placed a comforting hand on her cheek, wet with tears now and twisted in misery. Her mother needed her so badly, particularly now. She was unwell so often nowadays and with a quick glance at the clock suddenly remembered the younger children downstairs who would soon want their tea – and then off to bed. She took a deep breath, standing quietly a moment longer until her mother settled and she herself felt calmer. She must be strong, as much for her mother's sake as her own she told herself. 'Rest quietly,' she said, plumping pillows and tidying the bed as her mother's eyes followed her anxiously. Opening the door a crack she listened for sounds in the house, but all was quiet now, apart from the children's voices as they played. The storm had passed.

★ ★ ★

For the rest of the day, and until the family retired for the night, it was as though nothing had happened. To support her daughter, Elizabeth had made an effort to leave her sick bed and join the family for tea whilst her husband took up his usual formidable stance at the fireplace, gazing glumly at his family as they satisfied their appetites. Madeleine talked amiably to Bessie and her brother Jack as she helped the younger children to sandwiches she had prepared earlier, joking with them and calling them to order when she saw fit. Madeleine's feelings were in chaos however, whatever normality showed outside. Come what may she had decided, she would carry on as usual helping with the children and running the home, if only for her mother's sake, but with growing resentment she was also determined to see Emile again. The only problem was how – and when and where. From now on she knew she would be under the constant stern eye of her father, which meant facing the prospect of interminable questions whenever she wanted to leave the house! More than that, there would undoubtedly be a new chaperone in tow whenever she planned an outing. So somehow, by some means she'd not yet devised, there had to be another way, and determined to find one she vowed that nothing whatsoever would stand in her way!

Chapter Eleven

Since the disastrous outburst in her room, Madeleine had studiously avoided her father and many sleepless nights of hope and despair followed. She clung to the possibility of being able to persuade her parents to accept Emile when they realised the depth of her devotion but inwardly she knew she was deluding herself. More than anything however she was determined to see him again by whatever means possible and when she'd almost lost hope fate stepped in the following week which looked promising in bringing this about.

Mary Perry, a long standing friend of the Smith family, had learned about the fearful row between Madeleine and her father during one of her weekly tête-à-têtes with Mrs. Smith, and after whispered confidences and feeling overbearing sympathy for a girl she had great affection for, she insisted on seeing her. Despite all that had been said, when they came face to face however, Madeleine felt torn between a dutiful respect for her father and a feeling of shame that she should have been the source of such an outrage and found it difficult to divulge all the details – until emotion got the upper hand.

'My parents urge that I seek a husband Mary,' she sobbed. 'Yet the one man I believe may be right for me is treated as an outcast!' Giving way to resentment she revealed how at one point she feared her father would strike her, which came as no surprise to Mary who knew by earlier confidences with her mother how she too had often been filled with dread.

After this tearful outburst, and surprising Mary by her swift recovery, Madeleine suddenly straightened and brushing a hand across her eyes looked at her appealingly and said that whatever it took to make it happen she was determined to meet Emile again. 'It's cruel to deny our friendship Mary,' she said with conviction, 'I love this man and I fail to see the reason for my father's behaviour when he wishes me to be wed so urgently.' Then following further blatant criticism of her father's unfair behaviour she suddenly jumped to her feet with eyes blazing and declared that she would refuse to comply with his demands.

Concerned by this unexpected attitude, and suspicious a request for a favour was about to follow, Mary immediately sought to calm the situation and retorted, 'I would fear vexing your father Madeleine if you are seeking my help. This is a very difficult family matter and I insist in any case that this confidence between us must remain as such.'

'All I want is for Emile to know how things are Mary,' she pleaded as though she had not heard. 'That's all. But what can I do?' Tears welled again as she hesitated and Mary gradually softened as Madeleine went on to explain that all she wanted was for a message to be sent to him, 'somehow, and by whatever means. He will be wondering what's happening after that dreadful meeting with my father. It was so rude to abandon him like that and I have no idea how to get in touch. I must at least apologise to the poor man Mary, but I don't even know where he lives.' With her face brightening as she lived it all over again, she mentioned his name, described what he looked like and enthused about his impeccable manners and charm. 'He's just recovering from the dreadful time he had in the war in France what's more,' she said with a pained expression, 'and now to be treated like this!'

In her enthusiasm Madeleine failed to notice Mary's

lips tighten when she mentioned Emile's name and she did all in her power to avoid any show of recognition as Madeleine rushed on to describe the disastrous meeting they'd had with her father. She knew well whom Madeleine was describing. She had met him herself only recently. Her good friend Mrs. Jenkins was his landlady and had introduced them when she'd called one evening, leaving them both in the drawing room where they had talked at great length. Secretly Mrs. Jenkins wished to get Mary wed and thus curb the neighbours' predictions about her destiny being that of an old maid – and as she listened to their chatter and laughter she saw her new elegant lodger as being a suitable husband.

'I do happen to know Emile,' Mary decided to say at last and managed a smile. 'My good friend happens to be his landlady. I met him only the other day.' At which Madeleine gripped Mary's hands with delight, pleading for help.

'So you could take a letter to him Mary! Please. Would you do this for me? It would be wonderful! I can write a letter now Mary to explain.'

'Or you could leave me to explain the situation if you wish,' Mary interrupted, as she secretly savoured the chance of a further meeting with Emile.

Madeleine gazed at her thoughtfully with half-closed eyes. 'A letter would be more appropriate I believe,' she said quietly. 'And if he understands, as I'm sure he will, and wishes to continue the friendship of course, he would surely reply.'

Mary had no need of Madeleine's persistence and non-stop urging as they each savoured reasons for contacting Emile and as their whisperings became more earnest so the plans gradually developed. Mary nevertheless began considering the dire consequences about acting as a go-between, with Mr. Smith as a formidable figure in the background, and repeatedly warned that this be a well-guarded secret between them. 'It must never be revealed that I am doing this Madeleine. Never! Even to your mother.'

'You have my promise Mary. With all my heart I vow,' Madeleine rushed on. 'How could I ever betray you when my father is being such a menacing threat?'

So with the prospect of Madeleine being able to communicate and hopefully see Emile again – and Mary relishing the chance of visiting him once more, the letter was written and delivered.

★ ★ ★

'I know of Madeleine's concern about her father refusing to acknowledge your friendship Emile. But beyond that, nothing further.' Mary had decided to choose her words carefully when asked whether she knew about the contents of the letter she had brought, although she noticed his face brighten when she explained the situation. Having enjoyed their previous conversations, and to his landlady's delight, he had again invited her to the house and they spent a pleasant hour talking before he opened the envelope. She watched his slow smile and raised eyebrows as he read and saw how his face lit up as he turned it over and the way he glanced up at her every now and then, as he contemplated it in silence. But there was no need for words with his feelings etched on his face and in the continuing hush she felt a tinge of disappointment and was ashamed to admit, jealousy – especially when he asked with undisguised enthusiasm if she would take a reply back to Madeleine.

And so began a spate of letters between Madeleine Smith and Emile L'Angelier – as also did his friendship develop with Mary Perry and the confidential chats he enjoyed so much with women older than himself.

Madeleine too welcomed Mary as her confidante in what promised to be a new love affair and told her with feeling that she would always be grateful for what she had done. She had already convinced herself to be head over heels in love again and yearned to see him again, hear his voice, to be near and feel his touch – and with her plans for bringing this about now looking more hopeful, she wrote another letter for Mary to deliver.

★ ★ ★

The large house where Madeleine lived offered everything she needed for clandestine meetings with the man she now regarded as her lover. Admittedly, it posed risks, but in keeping with her partiality for excitement, she had dwelt seriously on this daring tryst and after much thought decided to discuss it with Mary who had willingly shared their secret liaison.

'We could meet here, in the garden maybe,' she told her. 'When the family have retired for the night. It's the only way Mary and my parents would never know if we are quiet and choose the time well.'

Mary's visits to the Smith household had become more frequent since her involvement as a go-between for the lovers with everything going well until Madeleine made this astonishing announcement.

'There's just one problem,' she said, ignoring Mary's look of horror, 'I share my bedroom with Janet, although of course she does go to bed much earlier than myself and always sleeps very deeply Mary, so I'm sure she would never wake.'

'You mean you would invite this man into your bedroom?' Mary interrupted.

'Of course not! I dare not. It would be too dangerous. Imagine if my father should discover! How could I?' she said, throwing up a hand.

'Then what do you intend to do? You described waiting until your sister was sound asleep, and refusing to be intimidated, Madeleine enthused about meeting in the garden or the summer chalet. 'Well away from the house of course where no one could see or hear,' she went on, until Mary could stand it no longer and hurled in disgust, 'Think what you are doing Madeleine. Inviting a man to meet you alone. Late at night! In your parent's house! How could you even think about such an idea? It's unspeakable!' And to further endorse her outrage she told Madeleine she wanted nothing further to do with the arrangement and would not be taking any more letters to Emile. 'Or convey any back from him,' she snapped. 'I want no hand in this underhandedness. It's downright improper.'

As Mary flounced from the room, Madeleine watched unbelievably as she hurried away without a backward glance, and cursed herself for being foolish. She had talked too much again. It was one of her failings and, biting her lip as she paced the floor, wondered what to do next. At least her latest letter to Emile had already been delivered she contented herself so it was just a question of waiting. Emile will surely find a way of getting in touch she reasoned, particularly with the plans she had in mind. And her face settled into a satisfied smile.

★ ★ ★

Having made excuses for not being able to continue acting as a go-between any longer, Emile had shrugged nonchalantly when Mary called at his landlady's house that evening. She was quick to read his face after getting her message across however and although sensing his disappointment felt relieved that he still welcomed her company if she cared to call – and she certainly had no hesitation making it clear that she would!

For ulterior motives or otherwise nevertheless, Emile had been devastated by Mary's ultimatum having already set his sights on developing a relationship with Madeleine. There seemed little choice other than to accept the situation for the time being however and after Mary left that evening he sat for a long time pondering how he could make contact, or at least respond to her latest letter – until a new turn of events brought them together in a reckless plan.

Chapter Twelve

Regardless of his personal feelings being in disarray over a planned romance, Emile L'Angelier continued working industriously at the Seed Merchant's office in Glasgow. It was a long day he put in, which included the occasional Saturday in order to add a meagre amount to his wages. So there was little time left for any philandering after returning to his lodgings late in the evening and getting up at the crack of dawn the next morning to face another boring day. But as time dragged on with no foreseeable chance of meeting Madeline he began getting restless and, knowing his friend's contact with her family, again sought Robert Baker's help.

'Leave a letter with her sister. That's the best thing. She goes to a local school. You could intercept her on her way. It's near where you work,' and teasing, 'you know how she drooled over you. She'd do anything to help!'

Although Robert's scheme seemed outrageous at the time, particularly being in the warehouse working all day, the more Emile thought it through it seemed the only option. It meant some kind of an excuse for having an hour off, and losing money he could ill afford he thought irritably, but if it worked, he decided it would be worthwhile. So on the pretext of attending the funeral of a relation later that week, he found himself walking casually along the road one morning near the school Robert had described, trying to pick Bessie out from a streaming crowd of giggling schoolgirls.

Assuming a look of surprise when he caught sight of her, she willingly separated from her friends when he called her name and as Robert predicted came running towards him eagerly. 'What a delight seeing you,' he said in the grand manner reserved for such occasions – and carrying on to make small talk as he indulged her blushes and skittish behaviour, he seized an appropriate moment to lean forward with a worried expression and ask after her sister. 'Madeleine is her name I believe,' he enquired with his eyebrows lifting. He trusted she knew nothing about the exchange of letters between them – and when her bland expression confirmed this he continued, 'I was on my way to the post box but as this letter is rather urgent... perhaps... I wonder whether you would mind taking it. It's something we discussed in the bookshop, when you came along too you may remember. Some information your sister wanted,' he lied, 'I'd be so grateful if you could take it.'

After a moment's hesitation – and disappointment that his thoughts focussed on Madeleine rather than her – she tilted her chin provocatively as he turned on the charm again. She did not know anything about letters her sister had been writing as it happened. Emile had been right in that supposition. Nor did she have any knowledge about them meeting their father or the resulting flare up. She had also accepted, with Madeleine having a new chaperone, this had put an end to any further jaunts along Sauchiehall Street where she might possibly meet this charming young man again. So having waylaid her, and flirting with her she fancied, she satisfied herself this would be a fine opportunity for teasing her sister, and posturing petulantly, she plucked the letter from his fingers and promised to do as he asked. 'Just for your sake I'll do it,' she simpered.

The letter was the last thing on her mind however, when she reached home and rushed to Madeleine's room blabbering the news. 'He was waiting for me Madeleine. The Frenchman we met. Remember? He was there, waiting to see me. Just me – and we talked for ages. He is wonderful Madeleine. I'm sure he likes me and wants to see me again!' Then suddenly calling to mind the letter, she reached into her pocket and handed it over after Madeleine's barrage of questions.

It was an effort concealing her feelings as she snatched it away and for the time being she decided to ignore Bessie's silly nonsense and shooed her out of her room. His note was formal and scrawled carelessly – *so unlike his earlier romantic meanderings,* she thought, *or hers come to that!* However, it was the reply she needed.

> '*Should this be your desire,*' he wrote after a formal preamble. '*It will give me immense pleasure to see you and I shall await details of when we may meet.*'

With her father away from the house on business and her mother once more confined to her room, Madeleine managed to slip out of the house to post her hastily written reply in one of the new postboxes recently installed nearby. She had already described how they could meet in the garden of her house in her last letter and now suggested a suitable day and time – also explaining how she would place a lighted candle in the window when she knew it would be safe for him to approach. She concluded her letter:

> *You can then make your way round the side of the house.*
> *I shall leave the door unlocked and shall be waiting*
> *in the arbour at the end of the rose garden.*

★ ★ ★

After just a respectful exchange of letters following that disastrous meeting with her father, there was no polite conversation or shy reserve when Emile arrived for this daring new tryst. They fell into each other's arms like long lost lovers, embracing and caressing without embarrassment in the shadowy seclusion of the garden, until Madeleine tore herself away with her distressing news.

'Mary will no longer deliver our letters,' she said, 'and I can't think why.' She thought it unwise to mention everything Mary had said and added guardedly, 'Perhaps she disapproves of us being together – like my father?'

'Mary always speaks so well of you,' he said, 'and also as a friend to me, I see no reason for this.'

'But she does refuse. What can we do?'

'Post them,' he said without hesitation and with surprise added, 'you've already done this. Why not carry on like this. I received your letter in the evening of the day you posted it!'

'But I can't risk receiving any from you Emile – you don't understand,' and she went on to explain what had happened after they'd met her father on that fateful afternoon and how she'd been treated. 'I have the feeling I'm being watched all the time and any letters addressed to me are bound to come under suspicion – and most likely be opened.'

'Then I shall deliver mine personally,' he said stroking a finger across her cheek, 'all you have to do is tell me where I can leave them outside the house where they can't be discovered.'

And for the time being these clandestine meetings continued unobserved – until even this carefully arranged plan became yet a further challenge in their relationship.

Chapter Thirteen

Madeleine's parents were still persistent in their endeavours to find an acceptable suitor for their daughter – and with Bessie also approaching maturity, she was now included in their elaborate dinner parties and social functions in the hope of attracting eligible bachelors. This was a girl however, who had never wavered from coveting Emile L'Angelier as her own lover – dreaming endlessly of a romance since first setting eyes on him in Sauchiehall Street. So with fierce rivalry strengthening between the sisters, she had taken to tormenting Madeleine – even making up stories when she had a mind to about having met Emile again and rushing to her sister's room to tease unmercifully. Madeleine, in her inimitable way with her young siblings however, put this down to immature skittish behaviour, although she had to admit feeling increasingly irritated each time her sister charged in with yet another fantasy and often struggled to keep her temper. In any case, she had met Emile several times at night in the garden to dispute any underhand behaviour on his part and as their romantic encounters become more intense she told herself she had to see sense and dismissed any thought of disloyalty. She could not really believe Emile would flirt with her sister. It was insane to imagine. Only last night when they met in the garden they had been so close – and she blushed remembering! Nevertheless, when Bessie burst in with yet another preposterous story about having met him, she could not stop the suspicious thoughts and walking across to her table, just to keep her face turned away, she shuffled papers around – then flared like scolding a spoiled child as Bessie persisted.

'I do believe we could have an affair,' she said, edging across to Madeleine and ducking her head to gaze up at her. 'The way he looks at me Madeleine,' she went on dramatically, 'you would surely agree...' and to irritate further she concocted a story about him kissing her hand, 'and he even suggested meeting again,' she dared.

'For heaven's sake will you stop? Can you not see he is just being polite you silly girl.' It was like speaking to a child again and she strained to stay calm as she turned back to the window – but the irritating doubts would not go away.

'I can't think why you are so cross,' Bessie drawled on provocatively. 'You never even talk about him now and probably you have even forgotten all about him,' and sidling up to face her, 'Remember, it was me he sought the other day.'

Madeleine swung round at this, snatching up her bag and began hustling her sister out of the room, hating her – and herself – for having to behave this way. 'Come along you silly girl. There are things to do in the house,' she snapped. 'No more of this nonsense. You can help with the children,' and nothing further was said for the rest of the day as Madeleine bided her time. There is plenty of time to think about by Bessie's behaviour, she thought. Even so, it had to be resolved. She felt she could trust Emile – although trying to believe this more to convince herself than otherwise. He could not be flirting with Bessie. Could he? No! Never would he do that! Or would he? she wondered.

★ ★ ★

When her young sister Janet had been asleep for many hours, Madeleine parted the curtains in her downstairs bedroom as usual and placed a lighted candle on the sill signalling it would be safe for Emile to approach, but instead of looking forward to him arriving that evening, she felt unsettled. Bessie's stupid behaviour had put her in a bad mood and pacing up and down she dwelt on questions that demanded answers when he arrived. She glanced at the clock. He was later than usual and with no sign of him when she peered repeatedly through rain beating at the window, her petulance slowly turned to anxiety. Never had he been so late. Something must have happened she thought unless…, but hastily brushing aside Bessie's latest fantasy about meeting him, she decided to quell the candle and draw the curtains. She had already made up her mind to confront him about this flirting nonsense and his alleged behaviour – according to her sister at any rate – and staring miserably into the gloom as the night dragged on, her eyes slowly became heavy. Janet stirred restlessly when she eventually decided to climb into bed. He would not be coming now she told herself as she settled rigid and unmoving alongside her sister until she could hear her regular breathing again, although there was no sleep for her straight away. He had not come and something had gone very wrong.

★ ★ ★

The following morning started bright – which was a fine chance for Madeleine to rise early and secure the gate she had left unlatched for Emile the night before. Realising no one would be around so early she lowered the bar quietly into place – then instantly she was on guard when she heard footsteps approaching from the other side wondering what to do when she heard a call.

'Open this gate whoever is there.' It was her father, his voice unrecognisably gruff, and obeying immediately, she fumbled nervously pushing the gate as she confronted him with a fixed smile.

'Goodness, how you startled me father.' She tried to sound flippant. 'I had no idea you were there – and so early.'

'And what might you be doing out so early my girl, latching gates. This is unlike you to be up and about at this time.'

Fortunately, no further questions followed her excuse of needing a breath of air and remedying the situation when she had discovered the gate unlatched. And apparently satisfied with this explanation, he marched off towards the house, where the smell of frying bacon drifted from the kitchen, with her trailing behind. But with a further stab of alarm she was immediately on guard again when her father thrust open the door and she noticed him dangling a scarf in his other hand, muddied and wet from last night's rain. A scarf she recognised! *So he had been! He had come after all – when she had given up watching for him and she'd closed the blinds. Shutting him out!*

As they entered the dining room where the family were already tucking into their breakfast, James Smith plucked the scarf between his fingers holding it at arm's length for all to see.

'Does anyone own this?' he asked, looking at it with distaste. 'I found it on the forecourt outside – soaking wet and filthy.'

Nobody spoke while Madeleine's mother gazed enquiringly around the table as Mr. Smith dropped it into the coal scuttle like a piece of unwholesome rubbish. 'Just as well to burn it then,' he said to his wife. 'Never know who it belonged to. Might be infested.'

At that, Bessie jumped up. She too had recognised it and frowning thoughtfully, announced, 'I believe I know who it belongs to father. It's very similar to one a friend of mine has,' she started to say and Madeleine knew she was struggling how to continue. Moving across to the fireplace Bessie plucked at a corner of the scarf, examining it closely. She knew it belonged to Emile and she wondered what had been going on. He had obviously been to the house. 'Hmm, yes,' she said, thinking quickly. 'I'm pretty sure I know who it belongs to. I'll make enquiries today father.'

'A friend of yours you say?'

Bessie assured her father convincingly as she deposited the soaking scarf onto paper and bundled it up – and casting a meaningful glance in Madeleine's direction, she took her leave from the table.

Madeleine felt a surge of bitterness knowing she now faced having to deal with Bessie who she knew would move heaven and earth to see Emile – and as soon as she thought reasonable, left the table and hastened to her sister's room. Hesitating at the door, she stopped to collect her thoughts. She had to be careful. No one, above all Bessie, must know about her secret meetings with Emile so she had to watch what she said, but when she flung wide the door Bessie had already gone and the scarf was nowhere to be seen when she searched! *The bitch. She has done it again!*

★ ★ ★

Bessie had lost no time leaving the house. She knew Emile L'Angelier's route to work near her school and with the scarf carefully wrapped, and despite the atrocious rain having returned in torrents, she waited hopefully for sight of him. Fortunately, the weather was keeping people indoors so she could dodge unrecognised to wherever she could shelter on the way, until having waited cold and miserable for what seemed ages she was on the point of giving up. Then suddenly she noticed him approaching in the distance huddled against the wind and rain and ran to meet him, grabbing at his sleeve and urging him into a recess where she had been sheltering.

'I hoped to see you,' she said urgently. 'Something awful has happened,' and immediately fearing some kind of disaster had befallen Madeleine after his abortive visit the previous night, Emile waited speechlessly.

'My father discovered your scarf in the forecourt of our house this morning and started asking questions. Look!' she said, thrusting it at him.

'Did you say it was mine?'

'No. I thought it best not to do so. I told him it belonged to a friend. A friend of mine, but I knew it was yours. I recognised it. You were wearing it when I last saw you.' She met his gaze, puzzled by his expression and continuing silence, and then asked, 'Why were you at our house?'

There was no point denying the scarf belonged to him. Yet something had to be said and certainly something not involving Madeleine! Plucking at stupid thoughts as he scrabbled for excuses under her scrutiny, he suddenly laughed aloud. 'What a blessing he dropped it where he did,' he said, taking the scarf and running his hand down the length of it, he flicked the dirt from his fingers. He stared at it, feigning disbelief as he shook his head and embellishing the only stupid story coming to mind joked about a dog he had played with running off and disappearing with it – 'to your house of all places. Thought I would never see it again! I gave chase, but he was too fast for me,' and meeting Bessie's suspicious look with another roar of laughter went on, 'sounds bizarre I know,' he said. 'Unbelievable, but it's true!' – And as he relaxed as far as he dare into a further description of hopelessly chasing the animal, Bessie's naïvety appeared to be accepting his lame alibi. 'How can I thank you enough?' he continued without giving her a chance to speak. 'And you came out in this weather too!' He took her hand, holding it between his own as he smiled down at her, pandering to the spate of simpering he knew would follow and revelling further he leaned closer as he watched her blush, and then immediately spoiled it for her by enquiring after Madeleine!

'She is well,' Bessie answered tartly, beginning to wonder what was going on and whether she should really believe this incredible story. Emile began racking his brains further for what to say, watching her baffled expression, and more so how to get a message across to Madeleine. He had to say something after this and stumbled on.

'I know she detests the rain too,' he said trying to sound plausible. 'As we all do. But perhaps by this evening it will be better,' and with nothing more tangible coming to mind as he struggled, he leaned close to Bessie again, making her blush all over again as she felt his breath. 'Will you tell her that my dear?' he asked, straightening. 'Tell her I'm sure the weather will improve by tonight – shall we say for late night travellers at any rate,' and stupidly repeating himself, 'although I know how much she detests the rain at any time.' He touched her cheek pandering to her pleasure as she turned away shyly and allowing time for her to recover he bowed politely. 'It's been nice to see you again in any case Bessie,' he said, and thanking her once more for bringing his scarf he explained he was already late for work and had to rush, and realising he must have made a complete fool of himself with his ridiculous story, bid her a hasty farewell and hurried away.

★ ★ ★

Confronting Bessie was inappropriate when

Madeleine noticed her approaching the house as lunch was about to be served. Her father had decided to join the family for once instead of having his usual snack in his study and having settled down amiably to his meal he looked up surprised when Bessie arrived late – looking flustered and somewhat damp.

'Wherever have you been to get in that state my girl?'

Immediately Bessie reminded him about taking the scarf he had discovered that morning to her friend and hoping to avoid further interrogation busied herself handing vegetable dishes to the younger children.

'I asked you a question about arriving home, late for lunch as it happens,' he said eyeing the clock, 'And in that condition.'

Madeleine's heart lurched, praying her sister would not be foolish. She certainly looked uncomfortable and when her father again demanded an answer Bessie's voice faltered. 'Unfortunately my friend was not there father when I called,' she murmured. 'So I had to walk back to the school to make enquiries. That was how I became drenched, searching for her. There was no shelter anywhere.' She rambled on lost for further excuses and as her father's frown deepened, she flashed a glance at Madeleine who immediately dropped her gaze. Dumbstruck in the silence that followed, Bessie rambled on about meeting someone near the school who knew her friend and promised to take the scarf...

'And would that have been a man by any chance?' her father suddenly interrupted. 'You were undoubtedly unchaperoned?'

Caught unaware and completely out of her depth to dredge up anything tangible, she blurted out without thinking, 'Yes,' and believing it would help, rushed on, 'with really charming manners, father and so grateful to be able to help. I saw no harm...'

Madeleine saw the panic in Bessie's eyes as she faced her father, fumbling for words and by now looking bereft of her wits. *How could she be so naïve!* But the damage was done. Her father snatched up his serviette, wiped his moustache hurriedly and swept a long searching look in Madeleine's direction before further interrogating Bessie.

'And were you on your own when you met this man?' he demanded, narrowing his eyes.

'Well, y-yes,' she started, looking close to tears. 'I was in a hurry and the weather was so dreadful... It was early for my friends to be there.'

'Whatever the reason for leaving the house, you know I will not allow this,' he declared and the china rattled as he banged the table. 'You know the rules about being chaperoned when you leave the house. Both of you do.'

Madeleine rose from the table excusing herself with a headache and as she passed Bessie she asked flippantly, 'Why ever didn't you ask me to accompany you? I was here, as you must have known. In my room as you knew I would be.'

Bessie looked fearfully at her father as he got to his feet noisily, astonished he should confront Madeleine instead of her as he demanded, 'And does this happen to be the man I forbade you to see Madeleine?'

She turned in amazement. 'I've no idea who it was father. Whatever do you mean? How can I possibly say? Bessie was alone – as she said.'

'I will not have either of you seeing men outside this house. Do you hear?' The violence of his rage swamped all reasoning as he glowered at both girls expecting answers and receiving blank expressions – and Madeleine irritated him further by absolving herself with composure as she faced him with her eyes hardening.

'I have not seen anyone this morning as you seem to be implying father,' and with a tinge of exasperation, 'and

I have no idea whatsoever who Bessie met this morning. She was alone – as you heard her explain. It's for Bessie to explain father,' she said, spreading a hand towards her sister. 'Your questions should be directed at her. Not me.'

Alarmed by what was going on, the younger children were now cowering nervously – not really understanding and looking insecure, and sensing their concern, Madeleine quietly ushered them from the table, cupping their elbows as she led them from the room. Her mother, she noticed, had adopted her usual expression of intimidation and Madeleine offered the suggestion of a smile as she nodded in her direction, closing the door quietly as she left, contenting herself she had done everything possible to absolve herself from any further questioning. Nevertheless, she had to sort things out later with her sister to determine exactly what had happened when she left the house that morning. Had she been up to more of her tricks? Had she met Emile again and if so what had happened! But it was not Bessie she faced later that morning. It was her father who pounded up to her room and burst in after thumping on the door, throwing it wide, white with rage, and demanding an explanation about her continuing to see 'that common little Frenchman' when he had strictly forbidden it.

Chapter Fourteen

Bessie had absolutely no knowledge about Madeleine and Emile meeting in the garden at night and the possibility of him seeing her sister had been her own mischievous deduction as her father wrenched information and twisted facts. In terror, she told him the man she had met sounded like the person he described – although this was more to save her own neck! This was enough for James Smith however and satisfying himself with Bessie's side of the story, he gradually calmed.

Madeleine heard the heavy pounding of her father's approach long before he barged into her room, and alarmed by his thunderous expression, she immediately backed to the window.

'How dare you disobey when I give an order?' he roared.

The distance between them helped her to keep calm, although her innocent questioning about his unjustified attack further inflamed him as she continued quietly, 'What has Bessie been telling you?'

It was all Mr. Smith could do to stop himself hitting her as he charged towards her – for not only having disobeyed him so outrageously but more for her act of serene composure in the face of his accusation! *How dare she behave in this way. How dare she defy his authority with such impunity? Such rebelliousness he had never met – and now turning to ask him questions indeed!*

'What has Bessie told you,' Madeleine repeated quietly as she edged further away.

Mr. Smith glared at his daughter with increasing contempt. He'd prised information from Bessie –

unfairly maybe with the girl so upset he now considered, but false or otherwise in her confused state, and having discovered Madeleine latching the gate at an early hour that morning, then finding the wretched scarf, what else could he deduce other than suspecting her involvement.

'I'm asking the questions my girl! Are you seeing that man again?' he demanded between clenched teeth.

Madeleine paused, thinking hard. She felt positive they had not been seen in the garden. Nor been heard. They had only ever spoken in whispers and praying her expression would not betray guilt she gulped a breath and met her father's glare with confidence. 'No,' she lied. 'I have not seen Emile L'Angelier since you forbade me to do so father.'

'Then why should Bessie tell me otherwise?'

Hatred for her sister burned through her body and prevented an immediate answer, until her father angrily demanded she do so.

'I have absolutely no idea father,' she said bitterly. 'She is acting like a child. Making mischief. What has she said? Tell me.'

'Are you denying this then?'

'If you are implying that I am seeing Emile L'Angelier? Of course I deny it.'

'You had better be telling me the truth Madeleine. I will not be disobeyed,' and stalking back across the room he halted abruptly as though struck by a sudden thought and wheeled round with a look of disgust. 'I have very good reasons to know the truth Madeleine.' He was on the point of confronting her with his knowledge about the loss of her virginity, relishing the shocking impact this would have, but despite her arrogance and impudence, he could not bring himself to do so and turned away.

'Just don't question my authority Madeleine,' he said

in a low voice as he spun round prodding a finger. 'As long as you are under my roof you will behave in the way you have been brought up to behave,' and with his voice rising, 'furthermore, I will not be disobeyed when I have given an order,' and with that he turned on his heel and made for the door, slamming it with force.

Random thoughts tormented irrationally as Madeleine stared fixedly at the door listening to her father stomping along the passage. *Will I ever be free? Shall I always be watched? Shall I ever be able to live my life as I want?* and a further surge of hatred for her sister suddenly brought her to her senses and filled her with murderous rage. *One certain thing is, I have to see Emile to sort this out*, she breathed quietly *but first ... first I have to deal with Bessie!*

★ ★ ★

Madeleine practically dragged her sister to where they could talk, out of sight and out of hearing. Striving to check her temper, she towered over Bessie demanding an explanation, waiting in the growing silence as her sister cringed. She was content to wait.

'Father questioned me over and over,' Bessie whimpered at last. 'You know how cross he was when he forced me to say I had met a man. He must have suspected straight away.'

'Suspected what? I did not meet him! But you dared to involve me!'

'He went on and on Madeleine,' she grovelled, 'talking about you and Emile L'Angelier. You know what he's like.'

'So what did you say?'

Bessie reddened, wiping a hand across her eyes. 'Like I said, he went on and on, forcing me into saying it.'

'Saying what in heaven's name? Tell me you stupid girl.'

'That... well, that you were seeing him and that he must have come to see you that night when he dropped his scarf.'

Madeleine's intended slap missed as her sister jerked away and she grabbed her arm yanking her back as she tried to run from the room.

'I'm sorry Madeleine. I didn't mean...'

'Rubbish. You knew what you were doing. You're a jealous little cat because Emile happened to like me better when we met him – and sent me a rose for Valentine's Day.'

It was true and Bessie nodded as tears streamed. Just a short time ago she had entangled her sister in this suspicion as much to save her own neck, although secretly hoping that somehow there may be a chance for her with Emile. Now she felt afraid.

'Why did you tell father I was seeing him,' Madeleine persisted. 'What reason had you to say this? You know it isn't true.'

Bessie's gaze sharpened with envy. In temper, her sister looked prettier than ever. Her eyes sparkled and as the colour rose in her cheeks, her face shone and in that instant she realised she never really stood a chance with Emile. 'No reason Madeleine,' she answered quietly. 'No reason at all. And I'm truly sorry,' and looking down at her feet as her voice began trailing away she admitted making it all up when their father started shouting and demanding answers. 'I didn't know anything Madeleine but I felt I had to say something,' and pleading now, her face a picture of misery when she looked up, 'I felt frightened Madeleine. You know what he's like.'

At least it was a relief knowing that nobody knew what had really been happening when she'd met Emile at night Madeleine thought and then suddenly remembering, she clutched at her sister's hand, 'Did you tell him about the letter he asked you to give me last time you saw him?'

'No. I didn't say a word about that,' she said brightening. Actually, she had forgotten about it. She had been so afraid with her father shouting and losing his temper she had been unable to think properly.

Thank God, Madeleine thought. The girl had been foolish through sheer jealousy and for a split second, remembering her own interrogation by her father, she even began feeling protective towards her. It had not been as bad as she feared – although she vowed not to weaken.

Watching Bessie shrink back uncertainly in the growing silence, Madeleine suddenly felt exhausted and dropped into a chair, lowering her head in her hands. The past events had taken their toll and uncharacteristically she felt unable to cope any longer, and Bessie was instantly on her knees beside her. 'Please forgive me Madeleine. I am so sorry. You are right. I was jealous. I am jealous and I lied and teased about Emile. I have been beastly I know but it's not for either of us to do as we wish. From now on we shall both be watched – wherever we go and whatever we do, that is if we are ever allowed out again!'

'Of course we shall be allowed to leave the house you silly girl. We can't be kept indoors for ever.' She put out a friendly hand noticing a naïvety in her sister she had not recognised until now and there was nothing further to say. She wanted to be quiet. Everything would be that bit more difficult from now on, but she would get by. She managed a smile and told Bessie she wanted to be alone. She was not in the mood for any more talk. 'Just leave me,' she said. 'I've had enough,' and even though she still felt betrayed, she forced a kiss on her sister's damp cheek. More to the point, she needed time to think. She was determined to see Emile again and in the present circumstances the sooner the better – even running off with him she thought again as she had once before. She would do anything to be away from all this restriction! Then remembering with pride how she had survived before when the behaviour of others had intruded on her life she began feeling stronger. Her father had belittled her. Treated her like an outcast. His own daughter! She was made of sterner stuff though and with resentment growing decided there and then that she would carry on with her life as she intended. Already the rain had cleared with the sun now dodging out – and with a tingling of excitement she began pondering whether Emile would be turning up that evening. She could but hope, and with Bessie having forgotten to pass on Emile's guarded message about the weather improving for late night travellers, that's about all she could do.

★ ★ ★

Taking special care that evening, Madeleine slipped out of bed as soon as her young sister Janet was asleep. Quietly she opened the door listening for any sounds in the house – and to make absolutely certain, padded softly along the passage, even venturing a few steps up the stairs to make sure. Back in her room, she drew aside the curtains quietly, placed a lighted candle on the sill and pulling a shawl around her shoulders, stole outside to unlatch the side gate.

Although optimistic about his veiled message for Bessie to pass on to her sister, had she even understood it he now realised, Emile set out hopefully along the darkened streets – and when he saw the parted curtain and light in the window, he sprinted into the courtyard and quickly made his way to the garden.

'Whatever is it?' he whispered rushing up to her. He had heard her sobbing from a distance and stepping up his pace until he reached her she slid into his arms unburdening all that had happened.

'We must get married Emile,' she suddenly declared. 'It's the only way. They cannot keep us apart like this. We have to make plans. I've got to get away.'

At a loss what to say, he tightened his embrace and remained silent. Up to now, they had never discussed marriage and with the thought of the miserable pittance he earned any plans in that direction were out of the question. He drew her head down to rest on his shoulder, stroking her fingers as she quietened, turning over in his mind what to say with her in this state. A proposal was completely out of the question – at least yet! She would never understand he could not marry a girl of her standing on his meagre wage and with her father's attitude now, there was little chance of that happening anyway. More than likely, she would be shunned without a dowry, let alone a continuing allowance he realised, but in the circumstances pushed away these devious thoughts.

Between sobs, Madeleine explained about Bessie's mischief and teasing. 'She's making things bad for me Emile,' she said and turning to him, watched carefully for a reaction. 'She tells endless tales about meeting you. I believe she likes you Emile,' she said, facing him squarely. 'Flirts with you I understand,' she said with her voice rising, and if Madeleine expected an immediate denial, it did not come. Instead, he laughed and teased, drawing her close to him again.

'I do believe you are jealous my love,' he said quietly and she flicked another quick glance and wondered why he was still smiling. If he had denied this to be outrageous nonsense, or even regarded Bessie as a spoiled child she would have felt better but he made no such comment. She had to content herself about imaginary fears. He was an honest, good man she told herself clasping his hand tight as though making a rightful claim. She had been overwrought with the recent disastrous events and it was telling on her, but one thing now becoming clear in her mind was that she would never ever tolerate anyone interfering in her life with Emile again or with any of her plans that were already starting to take shape.

Chapter Fifteen

When Madeleine entered the drawing room one morning where her mother sat talking with Mary Perry, the conversation stopped abruptly. 'May I join you?' she asked with a smile, and as Mary glanced at her sheepishly, her mother looked away in stony silence.

Clearly, they had been discussing the events of the previous day when her father had lost his temper. Then like a bolt from the blue her mother suddenly announced plans about a forthcoming holiday, which Mary assumed Madeleine had full knowledge about until she saw her expression of surprise.

'Only the children and I shall be going,' her mother stated looking directly at Mary. 'My husband will be remaining here. 'A break before winter sets in will do us all good,' she continued. 'We shall be leaving in a day or so.'

With Mr. Smith's increasing wealth, he had acquired a country house known as Rowaleyn, surrounded by secluded woodland and situated on the Clyde. The family had spent many holidays there, although visits were generally in the summer and planned well in advance. Never had they left on the spur of a moment as seemed to be happening now, particularly with winter approaching. So with this startling news, and after an uneasy pause in the conversation, Madeleine faced her mother defiantly. 'If I am to be included in this sojourn, it would have been nice to have known,' she said indignantly – at which her mother shrugged irritably.

'You have nothing planned,' she said. 'At least that is what your father tells me. As I understand the situation you will not be going anywhere at the moment Madeleine - except to the children in the village for their reading lesson, and that can wait.'

So her father had planned this! She had been restrained against her will once more. As a precaution should she meet her lover no doubt! Madeleine decided to stay quiet however. Her quarrel was not with her mother and her fingers tightened on the letter in her pocket she intended slipping into the post box when she had a chance to escape from prying eyes. It needed changing now of course in view of the latest development she realised and politely excusing herself she returned to her room with another idea taking shape.

★ ★ ★

The more he thought about visiting Madeleine at Rowaleyn when Emile received her letter, the more it appealed - and do him some good into the bargain he thought! He could do with a break and from her description of the place there would certainly be no necessity for furtive arrangements with candles in the window and drawn curtains, or any risk of being discovered in compromising situations, so the chance was too good to ignore! The only problem was getting time off from work – *but for God's sake, he was due for a break and with a bit of luck he could get a lift to Clydebank and stay with a friend overnight to cut down on expenses.* Madeleine's urgent plea in her letter implying that they should become engaged and make plans for a wedding made less welcome reading however and this concerned him. He had already spoken to his manager about his pitifully low wages - and been put off yet again with the promising statement that, 'When things improve in the business young man, we can certainly think about it.' So it was useless deluding himself about becoming involved in any matrimonial plans - although still needing to keep his options open! For the time being however, he kept this to himself.

'It would be easy for you to visit me at Rowaleyn,' Madeleine suggested when they met in her garden later that night. 'My father will not be there so we shall only have my mother and brothers and sisters to be aware of.'

'Just let me know when you are going my dearest so I can make arrangements,' he replied hoarsely – and carried away by thoughts of unrestricted lovemaking as she nestled, he kissed her forcefully as he fondled her breasts.

'No, not here Emile,' she said, pulling away. 'It's not safe.' She'd also visualised their time together in the woods and felt a flutter deep in her belly each time she thought about it ... *but they must wait!* 'I'll write,' she said breathlessly, moving away. 'I can slip out to the post box secretly as I've been doing and as soon as I know when we shall be leaving, you will know too.'

Their parting that night was only a brief embrace but they were content to bide their time knowing what lay ahead and they crept back to the gate hand in hand, Madeleine remaining quietly a while after Emile had slipped away, breathing gulps of the cool night air to quell the excitement surging through her body. With the anticipation of being together soon, and well out of sight of her family where they could meet and love unhindered, she felt fulfilled at last. *This is how it should be between lovers. It's everything I've ever wanted* - and with her spirit of adventure tinged with revenge when she returned to her room, she relished that her clever planning had outwitted the stupid restrictions imposed by her father.

★ ★ ★

Many letters had passed between the lovers since their first meeting in the garden of Madeleine's home – hers usually long emotional missives written late at night sitting hunched up in bed as she fantasised romantically about their future. One written before leaving for Rowaleyn read:

My own darling,
I trust ere long to have a long, long time with you,
sweet one of my soul, my love, my all, my own best
beloved. My kindest love, fond embraces and kisses
from thy own true and ever devoted Mimi.

After these ardent outpourings, therefore, there was little wonder that their first meeting in the dead of night at Rowaleyn bordered on frenzied passion. With Madeleine's earlier sexual experiences in London, she had longed for this new coupling and gave vent to her feelings avidly. Emile on the other hand - who had nevertheless experienced many conquests himself with the opposite sex - felt deep concern. His earlier affairs had mostly been one-sided with the girl quietly complying with his desire in the fullness of time, so Madeleine's lack of restraint was something he had never experienced. And this was not all. Not only did the swift development of their torrid lovemaking disturb him. Also came the fear that, as a gentleman, he could be forcibly committed to marriage if Madeleine became pregnant - which would then dramatically expose his present circumstances and abysmal failure as an inadequate provider! Certainly, he revelled in their passionate romps, although up against her ardour he often feared his masquerade as a great lover was gradually coming under threat as night after night she told him she was 'burning with love.' She appeared to thrive on this unrestricted sexual indulgence, although strangely always adopting a shy attitude beforehand and remorsefully begging forgiveness for giving in to his advances so willingly afterwards! If only she could be more inhibited he thought - and not for the first time began questioning his diminishing stamina. He cursed the infections and constant colds he suffered of late - which their nightly romps in the damp grass did little to improve! - and fearful Madeleine may interpret any shortcoming in his sexual prowess as disinterest, he felt compelled to indulge more frequently in swigs of alcohol and doses of arsenic.

★ ★ ★

The night before the family were due to return to their home in Glasgow, Madeleine had waited for Emile in the shadow of the woods for nearly an hour - and as she was about to turn back to the house when he arrived, he ran quickly to stop her, puzzled by her usual lack of affection. Quick to realise something was very amiss, and suspecting this being his late arrival, he apologised profusely and drew her towards him as he begged forgiveness.

'Forgiveness for what? What are you sorry about?' she flashed, pulling away.

'Being so late my darling,' and he reached for her again. 'I couldn't get away and...'

'Is that all?' she interrupted.

Baffled by her mood, he caught her hand as they walked in silence past the spot where only a few nights before they had shed clothes and tumbled together.

'It'll be better tonight,' he whispered hoarsely and when she sobbed he stopped, drawing her to him gently and an eternity passed as he desperately wondered what to say. The previous night had been a disaster. He knew that! He had been tired and felt miserably cold. He had been unable to match her passionate demands, but if he told her this, and about his feeling of wretchedness, it would not have helped! So he said nothing. He could not tell her about having to rely more and more on stimulants to match her desire, which was the damned reason for being so late tonight – *traipsing around this Godforsaken place looking for a pharmacist prepared to supply him with what he wanted!*

Madeleine had lain awake for hours after she had returned to her room the night before. There had been something very wrong. Emile had not been the same and she wondered if it had been her fault. Then when he had arrived so late ... *their last night together and the last time to enjoy the freedom they'd had!* ... she feared their romance was over and that she would never see him again. Perhaps I expect too much, she fretted. Perhaps their lovemaking had been too intense. Perhaps he didn't really love her after all and was losing interest – and it certainly showed she thought. She had stopped sobbing now and he whispered again that it would be better tonight.

'But I felt your disappointment Emile, your reluctance and ... and you were different somehow, as though you were unwell.'

'Ah, yes that's it. I believe I have a cold just starting,' he interrupted, turning away, thankful for an acceptable excuse yet mortified she had noticed his poor performance! *Good God, I must have been dreadful!*

'There, I knew there was something', she said, sounding relieved. I wondered whether you were... well, if you were angry.'

'Angry?' he said in surprise. 'Why in heaven's name should I be angry?'

Madeleine wondered whether to continue and then decided to turn the blame on herself. 'It was my fault Emile,' she said earnestly. 'We should have waited until we were married. I should not have allowed... we did wrong,' she cried suddenly, drawing away and confronting him. 'And I've been stupid. You must think me absolutely stupid.'

'There was nothing wrong my love,' he lied as they continued picking their way into the woods and he tried to sound convincing despite his misgivings. 'How could loving one another be wrong? It's nonsense to suppose!' He had to say something - anything to placate her, but she had been right! Everything had happened too swiftly. She had hindered his dominance over her and he didn't like it. It was unladylike. Utterly out of character for a young Victorian girl - and even now she carried on provoking him with a complete change of heart as she stepped before him and draping her arms, kissed him full on the lips.

'But now that we have, sweetheart,' she went on, 'we can consider ourselves married can't we? I am your loving wife now my darling - and you my devoted husband.'

Emile cupped her face in his hands as she continued simpering and felt thankful for the fading light not betraying his feelings. There was nothing else to say - and thankfully, for him at least, there was no repetition of their previous passionate nights. She seemed content to sit quietly, continuing with her maudlin romanticism and fantasising about being husband and wife and her parents eventually accepting him when they realised the depth of their love.

'They can't keep us apart Emile,' she murmured dreamily as she eased closer. 'And we shall have a grand wedding and spend a honeymoon somewhere delightfully romantic.'

Thankful for the chance of a peaceful evening, he allowed her to dream on with her extravagant plans, but when she suddenly turned to him and demanded they set a date for their wedding, he decided it was time to bring some reality into the situation.

'I am not a rich man my love,' he announced, and shifting upright he placed his hand on hers as she looked enquiringly. 'You must understand Madeleine - I can't provide...'

'Hush, don't spoil it my love,' she interrupted, placing her fingers across his lips. 'Whatever we do my love, however humble our life may be, as long as we are together. It's all that matters.'

'The job I have pays badly,' he went on, 'very badly, Madeleine and it would indeed be a humble life. When I arrived here, it was the only job offered, and my prospects still look bleak. It's difficult to get work in Glasgow that pays well. Perhaps you don't realise.'

Madeleine's long silence left Emile in no doubt where he stood and failing any forthcoming words of encouragement, he compensated for his crumbling prestige by changing the subject. For a time his imagination went wild boosting his confidence with an imaginary description of his parents' successful business in Jersey.

'It's one of the finest market gardens on the Island,' he told her and embellishing further he described a home of luxury. 'The envy of many,' he went on. 'Overlooking rolling acres of fine gardens with produce supplied far and wide.' He had never revealed to Madeleine the truth of the miserable situation back home where his parents worked tirelessly to make a living, or how he had escaped these lamentable conditions by joining the army - just to get away and lead a more acceptable life! Then having given vent to this fanciful lifestyle back home to boost his ego, Madeleine threw him completely off balance with her next question.

'So why did you come here where it was difficult to get work after living in luxury and with the business doing so well in Jersey?'

Never being short of ideas he quickly recovered and with renewed vigour went on to declare how fate had led him, 'to where I've found the girl of my dreams! And having met you, my love, how could I ever leave?' he said, kissing her hand and fondling it between his own. He spoke quickly to prevent the chance of any further embarrassing questions. 'And this is more than any riches sweetheart,' he continued. 'You must understand that! More than anything in the world our love is richness indeed,' and feeling he should somehow return to the reality of his situation and let her down as gently as he could manage, he lowered his voice and mumbled, 'And my love for you my dear is all I have to offer at the moment. I know that things will change,' he went on, brightening. 'In the fullness of time Madeleine, things will change. I promise,' which seemed to appeal to Madeleine's whimsical nature for the time being and satisfied her that not all was lost.

Chapter Sixteen

After the unorthodox start to their intimate love affair at Rowaleyn, and with the weather quickly deteriorating for nightly trysts in the garden of her home as winter approached, Madeleine lost no time devising ways to be with her lover more comfortably when they returned to Glasgow. This came about by Madeleine's encouragement for Janet to sleep elsewhere in the house. She told her mother, 'She's growing up and is no longer nervous of being alone at night,' and Janet's delight in having her own room was unparalleled. 'As long as I can come down and sleep with you sometimes,' being her only proviso, to which Madeleine readily agreed and told her that there would be times when she would like this too.

Letters between the two lovers were also being exchanged more frequently by this time, with Madeleine's still being couched in her extravagantly romantic style, and when she returned to Glasgow she made a further arrangement to meet, but in a more intimate setting as she had planned. She wrote:

My own beloved husband,
Thank you, my love for coming so far to see your Mimi at Rowaleyn. And beloved, if we did wrong, it was in the excitement of our love.
But if only we could have remained my darling, never more to have parted. How I hated you having to leave.
Please come to me. We can be alone now in my room.
Things have changed.
Thy faithful wife.

So with Janet sleeping elsewhere in the house and their affair continuing unhindered in her bedroom, Madeleine now became obsessively fanciful about being Emile's wife and to his alarm even considered making plans for having a family. She wrote in a further letter:

Dearest, if we should have a child how I shall love
it for its father's sake. Your child I shall adore.
Emile, I shall feel happy when I am the mother of your
child, it shall be a binding pledge of our love.
Your Mimi.

Although Emile's letters were composed in a romantic vein, they tended to be more restrained compared with those from Madeleine. He still clung to his misgivings concerning her lack of restraint when they were together and his ongoing disquiet about their uninhibited lovemaking often came across in his letters.

'*My Dearest Mimi and beloved wife – since I saw you I have been wretchedly sad. Would to God we had not met last night. I would have been happier. I am sad at what we did. Why did you give way? My pet it is a pity...*'

A further bone of contention at this time - and an ongoing problem now Madeleine had drawn attention to it - was his humble job and pittance received at the end of the week. She continually questioned why he stayed in work that paid so poorly, 'for far less than a pound a week,' she had said with disgust at one time. 'You are worth much more than that Emile. You must ask for more, or at least get a job somewhere else.'

This he recalled unhappily, contrasted sharply with one of her earlier declarations that she would be 'happy to live on love in a tiny cottage,' although there was no escaping the fact that this constant criticism about his lack of money dented his pride. On the other hand, it nevertheless set him thinking seriously about improving his lot - despite taking decisions not being one of Emile's strong points! The prospect of him marrying into a wealthy family had not entirely vanished, but he now had to admit this was not the only reason for still courting Madeleine. By now, he had become completely besotted with her. He adored, needed and worshipped her, and had to accept that he had fallen hopelessly in love.

'What can I do then,' he told her in desperation after another altercation about his low paid job. 'I've asked for a rise many times and been refused - and searched frantically for better work elsewhere with no luck. And at least what I've got is better than no job at all!' he'd added miserably - and in her continuing silence he also said with a hint of irony, 'I know I'm not really good enough for you or your family the way I'm situated at the moment Madeleine - and your father has left me in no doubt about that!' But no words came from her. The only reaction was a penetrating glance from her piercing grey eyes.

★ ★ ★

In the background of Emile's life, Mary Perry remained staunchly loyal as a confidante to him at times such as this and always listened sympathetically whatever the problem - even endeavouring to strengthen the bond between the two lovers in spite of her own feelings about him.

'I have no future with her Mary,' Emile confided wretchedly. 'Can you imagine how I feel?' And pushing her own foolishly romantic thoughts aside, she was pleased at least to watch the worry lines disappear from his dear face as they talked.

'Perhaps you need a holiday Emile,' she suggested. 'Scotland is so drear at this time and soon the weather will be worsening. Why not go back to Jersey for some of that sunshine for a while?'

'But I can't,' he butted in, 'I've already had time off and what if I lose her if I go away!'

'That's nonsense! She loves you too much. You know that,' and Mary earnestly hoped for his sake she was right. Her heart ached as she watched him lower his head in distress and stifled an urge to rush across and offer a comforting hand. *If only it could be me. No matter how poor we would be. I would have him – as would my family. Now, this very instant she would have him, if only he needed her!*

Emile shifted uncomfortably. He knew what Mary said made sense and the suggestion of a spell back in Jersey sounded good, but the thought of parting from Madeleine terrified him. More than that, he had already had time off from this wretched job and risked losing money he could ill afford - and there was always the chance he may not be welcomed back! He needed to sort himself out though. The coughs and colds he'd suffered lately were getting him down and the thought of all that warmth back home in Jersey, and being cared for ... *and dare he think seriously about that job abroad he'd heard about from his friend recently and often pondered over?*

'There's a chance of working overseas, Mary,' he decided to confide to her as he looked up, and his brows lifted indecisively waiting for a reaction. 'I wondered about applying. It's an opportunity in Peru in a large market garden. A friend told me he'd recommended me to someone he knew back home who desperately needed someone to travel out there with him - and with the experience in my parents' business it would be ideal - and the wages are excellent. More than I could ever have dreamed of!' His face brightened as he talked about the challenge of having a worthwhile career. 'It's something I know I could do well Mary and something I would like to do anyway – to say nothing of the wonderful opportunity of going abroad and excitement of travelling,' he added. He paused a second, holding her gaze, his delight never fading. 'And I would be able to support Madeleine when I eventually go to her father for her hand!' he added skittishly. 'What a surprise that would be! And how could he possibly refuse?'

'Madeleine may like a break too if you go away,' Mary said and she tried to sound encouraging. 'It could be good for her. Good for both of you. Absence makes the heart grow fonder - you know that,' and she watched a smile spread across his face as he looked at her thoughtfully. She had brought solace into his troubled life once more she realised and knew it was time for her to fade into the background again and leave him to carry out his plans now he felt more able to think clearly.

'I must write a letter to Madeleine straight away,' he said, suddenly aware that Mary was preparing to leave, and for a wonderful moment he held her close and she felt his warm breath as he thanked her for being such a good friend as she bade him farewell. His soul is in torment she thought – and mine too she realised as she walked briskly up the road. The problems he faces may be resolved today, she realised, but what of the future? She feared that worse was to come - and her eyes misted over once she was safely out of sight.

★ ★ ★

Overcome with curiosity after receiving his latest letter, Madeleine awaited Emile's arrival that night with interest. He had written:

> *My Dearest Mimi, I have some important news.*
> *Exciting news. I must see you my darling and*
> *will come to you tonight. I will watch for a*
> *sign that it is safe.*
> *Your affectionate husband.'*

Perhaps anticipating a problem in their relationship as she had often feared - and unable to bear the thought of losing him she realised - she made careful preparations that evening. A candle had been placed on the windowsill as usual and to add a more romantic atmosphere, she had set others glowing elsewhere and sprayed lavender water liberally around the room. Looking around with satisfaction at the flickering shadows as she changed into a flowing chemise, she could hardly wait for him to arrive and when at last she heard him creeping along the passage she felt a thrill of excitement.

Smoothing her chemise demurely, she moved to greet him as he picked his way across to where she stood, and straightaway she detected a change! They embraced briefly, but it seemed different and she failed to understand why. He seemed excited and on edge and for some reason she felt totally excluded.

'What is it Emile?' she asked, and feeling even more rejected as he smiled broadly and shifted away, she went on, 'What is this important news you have for me?'

He kissed her fingers, each hand in turn, and holding her at arms length could barely contain his excitement as he told her in a voice barely above a whisper about his proposed plans to travel to Peru. 'I've decided I must go away my dearest Mimi,' he said. 'It's the only way. Then I shall be able to leave that paltry warehouse where I work for a pittance and earn big money. He drew her to him, nuzzling her head into his shoulder and caressing her. 'I intend returning to Jersey first Madeleine,' he breathed, 'to see my family and rest a while before making arrangements. I can make an absolute fortune abroad my love! Which means that we can...' but before he could finish, the atmosphere suddenly exploded into madness and wrenching away from him she began beating at his chest hysterically.

'You can't! What about me! What shall I do? And your health will get worse in a place like that. I know it will. It's stupid.' She beat her fists again, sobbing uncontrollably. 'You can't leave me. You said you loved me. You promised that was all you could offer,' and choking on sobs blubbered, 'I said I was happy with that Emile, you know I did, and now I'm beginning to wonder.'

Blind to her petulance and hysterics, Emile's continuing excitement about a new career carried him on unheeded and protesting furiously told her to calm down, 'It's for us that I go,' he stressed as loud as he dared. 'Don't you see that? It is for you that I do this! We can be married when I make more money.' He stood before her staring in amazement and in complete exasperation at her reaction. 'As things are it's hopeless that we can be together Madeleine. You know that.'

'You must stay in Scotland Emile,' she said slowly in a low controlled voice. 'Things are going well enough for you where you are. It's foolish to leave!'

'How can you say that when only recently you said just the opposite? You even suggested I find another job. Remember?'

She turned away, brushing a hand across her eyes and he grabbed her arms, forcing her round to face him.

'I never thought it would come to this,' she said pulling away.

'What do you mean?' he snapped.

'Don't raise your voice,' she warned slowly mouthing

each whispered word. 'Remember my family upstairs.'

'What are you saying then? Why the devil don't you understand? You know my dearest wish is for us to be together. You are being quite unreasonable. You know my financial circumstances are not good. Not good enough for you at any rate – or your father!' and taking a menacing step he grabbed at her arms again, 'You told me I was worth far more money in a week that I get now. Can't you even remember that?'

Suddenly he released his grip and strutted back to the door, prepared to leave as his enthusiasm plummeted. *God knows I need that holiday!* he thought irritably as he threw a scornful glance back at her. He knew that life would be better if he went overseas and felt convinced she would feel the same way. He could not understand for the life of him why she was behaving like this.

'Why have you changed?' he demanded angrily, swinging back to face her. 'We talked all this through. Remember? You know how things are.'

As Madeleine stood before him meekly, her eyes bright with tears, the memory of her yearning to be his wife and claiming she would be happy living in a mean cottage, flashed into his mind. He forced a smile. He had to be kind - and patient. 'Madeleine,' he said softly, 'Please don't be cross. We must not quarrel over this. We have to be sensible,' and like handling a child he guided her tenderly towards the bed, laying her down gently. 'You know I love you with all my heart,' he said thickly. 'Don't ever doubt that Madeleine. Never doubt that.' His breath became quick as he began unbuttoning her chemise and they spoke in whispers, Madeleine remonstrating quietly as he soothed - laying his fingers on her lips when she protested. He tugged away his own clothes, flinging them away as she slowly relaxed and with all her earlier yearning as he took her, she gripped him fiercely with arms and legs, drawing him tight to her with a fierce determination.

★ ★ ★

After a delicious eternity, Madeleine felt his perspiration cooling on her flesh as he raised himself on an elbow and traced a finger between her breasts, neither of them speaking. She wondered what their future held as she regarded him in the shadows, if indeed there was to be a future now she thought. Somewhere in the distance a clock chimed that claimed their attention and as one, they turned to listen to the hour as reality intruded.

'I must not stay,' he said hoarsely and she smiled as he moved away then immediately returned to kiss her - and suddenly shy she drew the sheet covering her breasts.

'Just go Emile,' she breathed quietly. 'Don't spoil this. Just leave - as always. Please,' and turning away from where he stood as he gazed down at her she closed her eyes and listened to him moving around, hearing the rustle of clothes and muffled sounds of doors opening and closing, and when at last it became deathly still, she drifted into a dreamless sleep.

Chapter Seventeen

Despite Madeleine's ongoing protests, Emile returned to his home in Jersey as planned and after a week of cosseting by his mother - who had been appalled by his unhealthy appearance when he arrived - she broached the idea of him returning to the family business. 'Even if you stay only for a short time,' she implored. 'Already you look better for being here. It would be good for you.' With her husband having died two years earlier - and struggling to keep the business going with her younger sons, it needed the strength and business sense she knew Emile possessed. As he gently explained his plan to go overseas however, where the money and prospects were too good to turn down he told her, she listened quietly without question. She knew nothing of Emile's affair with Madeleine and he had decided to keep this from her at present knowing how his ambition of marrying into a rich family had distressed her in the past. In turn, she also kept secret her disappointment about how much he had grown away from their simple family life since she last saw him – to say nothing of his newly acquired airs and graces! She gave her blessing nevertheless for this new venture abroad, albeit yearning for the return of her favourite son who had always been the one to make good in the family - and when well out of sight she prayed earnestly for his future.

★ ★ ★

Emile's enthusiasm for going abroad went hand in hand with his renewed energy, which was just as well for there was much to be done lending a hand in the family business, attending interviews, discussing travel arrangements and having health checks. Madeleine on the other hand, who had now seriously contemplated the situation in greater depth, failed to share his enthusiasm when she received a letter from him via Mary, who on this one occasion had agreed to pass it on to her after a desperate plea from Emile.

Considering their last disastrous meeting, he had taken care to point out in his letter the advantages of his venture overseas and particularly stressed his continuing devotion and desire for them to be married, and the speed of her upbraiding reply shocked him into disbelief when his mother handed him her brief reply when it arrived that morning. There were none of her usual endearments and flowery meanderings and in a few scanty lines, she had come straight to the point.

Dear Emile
I felt alarm when I received your letter and I hope you will have given up all idea of going to Peru by the time you receive this. I fancy you want to get quit of your Mimi. Madeleine.

With an immediate fear of losing her, his first thought was to return straight away. He had to go back to sort things out. There was no question. He loved her dearly. He knew that now with certainty and, more than anything, he wanted to spend the rest of his days with her as his wife and knew she felt the same way about him, so this disagreement over his future career had to be resolved. Face to face.

'I shall be returning to Scotland to finalise arrangements there and pick up the rest of my things,' he told his mother later that morning and his smile gave nothing away. She never asked questions about his life and what he was doing and he felt grateful. She nevertheless felt utterly bewildered by this swift decision to return north so soon after all his preparations, but once more decided to stay quiet. He appeared to be in command of everything, she reasoned and calmly accepting the situation told him she would keep everything as he had left it until his return, and without even staying to pack a bag, Emile set out immediately for his return to Glasgow.

Waiting patiently at home meanwhile, Madeleine was becoming increasingly furious. Since receiving his letter, and despite her earlier protests, their lovemaking and ongoing plans for the future, she felt betrayed by his determination to go ahead with this ridiculous idea. To her way of thinking, he had not given her any consideration whatever, and with no sensible reasoning about him enhancing his career to provide money for their much-discussed marriage, the only thing of importance at that moment was her injured pride. It cast a shadow over her romantic dream of a happily married life, which matched the mould of many Victorian girls of her age, except perhaps for one thing in her case. Madeleine was a girl not be trifled with - which seemed to be happening, she fancied - and this set her questioning whether she really did love Emile L'Angelier sufficiently to go along with plans he had in mind for providing an honourable marriage. She enjoyed their sexual encounters and thrived on his lavish attention. She enjoyed too the excitement of their secretive affair - particularly with it being carried out under the roof of her father's house of righteousness! So Emile's disappearance for God knows how long now brought all this into question and with her feelings hurt beyond any sensible reasoning, Madeleine awaited his response to her curt letter - which she hoped might perhaps bring him to his senses.

★ ★ ★

In the short time Emile had been away, life had nevertheless been far from dreary for Madeleine. The social visits with carefully selected young men of her parents' choice had continued and the arrival of someone who had taken up residence temporarily on the top floor of their home had stirred her interest. William Minnoch, although not handsome or particularly exciting, was an honourable, wealthy and charming gentleman who at thirty-four was regarded as one of the most eligible bachelors in Glasgow. Never one to miss an opportunity, Mr. Smith had considered all this carefully when hearing about the young man's urgent need of short-term accommodation - and with the upper floor of his house not currently needed by the family, viewed him as an excellent tenant until his own accommodation became available.

'He is a fine gentleman making a name for himself in the business circles of Glasgow,' Mr. Smith had bragged to his wife. 'I know his family well,' and, choosing his words carefully, went on to indicate his suitability 'and not only as a tenant, my dear,' he finally declared. As she looked up expectantly, he laid a firm hand on her shoulder as if a decision had been reached in a long contested plan. 'He has much to offer, both financially and with family status,' he continued pompously, 'and I do believe this will be the answer to our prayers Elizabeth and that before long we shall be planning a wedding.'

Madeleine was not particularly interested when first introduced to William Minnoch, although her vanity allowed a degree of pleasure when he began paying her attention. His shy manner, quiet demeanour and lack of experience occasionally rankled nevertheless and choosing to overlook this she tolerated rather than enjoyed his company. There was no doubting his interest in her however and despite his somewhat protracted advances, a friendship gradually developed. She accepted invitations to concerts, theatres and restaurants - and when the weather was fine at weekends they often walked out together, covering the same ground as she had with Emile many times she often thought with a smirk. It also has to be said that her conduct in his company always befitted that of a demure Victorian young lady. Never at any time did she display any of the wanton behaviour she had exposed to Emile!

From a practical viewpoint, Madeleine was fully aware of her new suitor's wealthy attributes, which compared more favourably with that of her more exciting French lover she realised, but for the time being she decided to bide her time. Her present life and the social occasions in the company of a successful businessman were very pleasurable - particularly as Emile had deserted her for his ridiculous plans she thought bitterly. Nevertheless, she had to admit missing the secretive meetings with him at night and often yearned to lie with him again, so until he responded to her letter, she made up her mind to keep her options open. *As long as William never found out about Emile!* she told herself, although fortunately there was little chance of this happening she reasoned as he was away from the house on business most of the time. *In any case Emile only called late at night. That's if their affair was destined to continue!*

Whether to tell Emile about William sharing the family house on the other hand was something she had to think seriously about. It could be a drawback - and she tapped her fingers thoughtfully mulling this over. Then gradually, as one idea followed another, she fancied the situation could be an advantage. Taunting him with this could make him so jealous it would certainly stop all this nonsense about going abroad for one thing! She knew he would crave for their affair to continue. She knew that! And it could actually be an enjoyable game! For a long time she sat wrestling with fanciful ideas, tormenting herself as she reasoned what would or would not work as she judged the two men. Life with William meant a good comfortable home with plenty of money, and even though he had never attempted to hold her hand so far, let alone kiss her, she contented herself that love would surely develop. 'But Emile,' she murmured and closing her eyes her loins ached as she breathed his name. She needed her French lover. *Damn it, I do want that man so desperately badly ...* and with warmth spreading like fire through her body, the dark thoughts already festering became realistic and she jumped up decisively. *I shall carry on affairs with both of them, I'll play them along at the same time, it'll be fun!* And when Emile's letter arrived about his immediate return to Glasgow, she made swift plans with no further misgivings.

He'd written,

My dearest Mimi,.
I received your letter and am distressed. I have to return to my dear wife.
We must talk. Let me know when we can meet. I shall come to you tonight in any case. I should be back in time.
All my love my dearest Mimi.
Your loving husband.

★ ★ ★

Madeleine made preparations for a romantic evening as she had on previous occasions with candles casting a soft glow and a strong scent of lavender wafting in the air, and as soon as she noticed Emile's shadow pass across the window she drew the curtains and awaited his arrival.

Although weary from his journey, he walked smartly to the side entrance and making his way quietly through the passage to the door left standing ajar pushed it open and threw wide his arms.

'You look wonderful!' she murmured as he strutted in. *She had never seen him looking so fit.*

'I've never felt better,' he said, seizing her by the waist and whirling her round. 'Everything is all but settled Madeleine,' and setting her down gently he fell to his knees and with outstretched arms again made a ridiculously dramatic proposal of marriage as she studied him suspiciously.

'Well?' he said, looking up - and carrying on his flippant mood continued, 'will you take this honourable gentleman as your loyal wedded husband?'

She kissed the top of his head, and then suddenly cross told him to stop playacting. 'Get up Emile' she commanded. 'Tell me what has happened,' she said, stomping away and immediately spinning round demanded, 'what is settled as you say? What have you done?'

Her tone warned of trouble. He had to be careful. Things were not going well. This was something he had not expected and recovering his composure he staggered to his feet.

'You already know of my intention about going overseas Madeleine,' he said as his voice trailed away in disbelief. 'I explained in my letter what I've done.'

'You told me you'd thought about it,' she said quickly. 'Not that you were going ahead with this... this ridiculous idea and making plans.'

'But you did know,' he said, 'we talked about it. You knew why I returned to Jersey. I've signed a contract. The money is superb Madeleine. Don't you realise this? We can be married in style when I return. It is what you wanted!'

She turned to meet his gaze wondering about his reaction should she challenge him about having another man in her life and backing away with downcast eyes she asked instead, quieter now, 'What about me then?'

'It is for you,' he said, and suddenly angry stepped before her demanding, 'do you not recognise that this is a fine opportunity for both of us you silly girl?'

'No!' she retorted, and her face was a mask of misery as she looked up. 'Actually I do not recognise it at all Emile,' and flouncing back hissed, 'What am I expected to do while you are away? Tell me that! What will happen to me?'

They stood tense, Emile fuming and Madeleine on the verge of tears, and when she wandered away he remained rooted to the spot, disbelieving. It was all going so wrong. Then like a spoiled child, she wheeled round suddenly, whining, 'Can I not come too? I've heard that women accompany their men, their husbands,' she corrected quickly.

'You are not my wife Madeleine!' and the words were out before thinking and he flustered, 'not yet anyway,' but it was too late and she flew at him screaming.

'How can you say that after all that has happened?'

'Peru is not a place for women,' he went on, ignoring her hysterics as he tried to make amends. 'The weather,' he hurried on. 'Food. Water. Just living there Madeleine. Everything is so different. You could become ill.'

'What about you? Will you not become ill? You're always getting ill anyway!'

There was no point arguing and he turned away angrily, torn with what to do. He feared losing her. Always had. He couldn't bear the thought of it, although at the same time recognising himself as a fool. 'Surely you would wait for me Madeleine,' he said, wheeling round. 'The time would pass.'

'I cannot wait,' she interrupted. 'It is ended Emile. We can't go on. We are finished.'

Lost for anything further to say, his confidence plummeted to rock bottom. It was unbelievable what was happening and he'd never felt so angry and helpless, although her frosty expression made him wonder whether he could tolerate losing her if she meant what she'd just said. A new job, particularly abroad, could compensate for the loss, but no, he would never cope with the rejection! He knew that, even feeling angry as he did.

He wanted to take her in his arms. Reassure her. Anything, to get back to how they were.

'Forgive me,' he started, sounding unsure. 'I didn't mean... it will only be a short time Madeleine.' He sounded uselessly weak and with shame knew that just about summed him up. Utterly spineless! He should have met her unreasonable demands and stood his ground. *What's wrong with me, for God's sake? I should have shown her up for her selfishness, at least!* But the shock of her threat had tipped the balance of his sanity and all he could do was stand there with his arms dangling, feeling a helpless wreck, until she suddenly flew at him with both hands flailing, screaming for him to go.

'Get out,' she shrieked. 'Leave me! And don't come back!' and unable to take any more as he mumbled futile excuses, he fled from the room.

Chapter Eighteen

What Madeleine had expected the night Emile arrived to explain about going overseas, even she could not fathom. She knew she had reasoned illogically and had not given a single thought to all that he had said about taking on a better job. All she cared about was feeling bitterly hurt and questioned repeatedly why he had not yielded as she'd expected. The only thing in her mind had been to prevent him leaving her and the more she thought about it she never shifted from this decision. Although having said their affair was over however, she knew deep in her heart that she did in fact need him and already felt twinges of regret. She had satisfied herself about managing two lovers at the same time – and with the relationship with William Minnoch now developing nicely, she remembered her earlier plan about taunting Emile with this choice piece of information - which will surely bring him to his senses pretty smartly she considered with a satisfied smirk. So deciding to leave matters for the time being, to see what developed, she waited patiently for the outcome.

Emile on the other hand quickly realised he had only one choice. The separation from Madeleine when he was away in Jersey had been enough to make him realise he could not live without her. If he chose the right approach he reasoned, the chance still existed of a life with the girl he adored. He would write he decided. Arrange to call. Do whatever it took to make her happy. Make love. Anything to please her! Above all, he must placate her - and quickly. First, however, he had to make sure of his job at the warehouse. Thankfully, he had made no mention to them about travelling abroad and decided when he returned he would lie about his absence being a recuperative break through a sudden illness with a promise to make up the lost time or have money deducted from his wages. God knows he needed that money, miserable as it was, and he had already lost a lot having time off before. That's how it had to be though. He felt convinced they would take him back, with no recrimination. They had always praised what he did - but he must lose no time getting in touch. Then he would make contact with Madeleine. Write a romantic letter. That would convince her - and if all went well they could get back to the way they were.

★ ★ ★

Mary Perry had the unenviable task of listening to both sides of the same story with Emile pouring his heart out over this latest upset and Madeleine confiding tearfully about their quarrel.

Madeleine's romantic whisperings to Mary about Emile had so far only touched on their affection for one another. Occasionally she had mentioned their tiffs, but after their last disastrous meeting, she expounded on this and between sobs said how she missed him and longed to see him again. Politely Mary reminded her that she no longer wished for any involvement - even though Madeleine did all in her power to persuade her to change her mind. More than this, having heard about William Minnoch moving into the Smith household and the developing friendship with Madeleine, she strongly voiced her disgust. She hated seeing Emile hurt and could detect trouble if Madeleine persisted in this association with another man, and in that instant Mary realised that she was beginning to detest Madeleine for the way she was behaving.

★ ★ ★

Pride, stubbornness - or maybe it was still fear of rejection - meant several weeks passing before Emile finally decided to write to Madeleine again. He had returned to his old job in the meantime and having had his pay docked for lost time, now worked longer hours and weekends to be able to pay his way. This however helped fill his miserable hours and gave him something else to think about, although he knew he was deluding himself and realised the only way out of his wretchedness was to write and somehow make contact.

Equally, Madeleine was also on the point of despair and despite becoming more involved with William Minnoch had to admit she missed the fun side of being with Emile. Although William had courted her diligently in his refined, dignified fashion, she cherished the thought of Emile visiting and making love to her again. So when his carefully worded letter arrived - which he'd laboured over in the knowledge of what would appeal to the romantic side of her nature - it lit up her life with such enthusiasm that she sat down straight away to reply.

She wrote:

My darling
There is a tie betwixt us neither God nor
man can cut asunder. I am your wife so you cannot free me.
No you cannot. I am glad there is such a tie. I love you, yes
love you for yourself alone. I adore you with my
heart and soul. Emile I swear to you I shall do all you
wish and ask me. I love you more than life. I am thine.
Thine own Mimi L'Angelier.

Before arriving at Madeleine's house after receiving this letter however, and suspecting their reunion would probably need an aphrodisiac, Emile took the precaution of imbibing a dose of arsenic, which he fortified liberally with a few gulps of alcohol. His main concern had been to disguise any sign of depression and maintain his vigour, knowing it would be unforgivable to disappoint her at this stage. He had to be sure of himself, and as he staggered uncertainly into the night, he began wondering whether he had overdone it! However, with no lights showing from other windows in the house when he arrived, and the usual flickering candle in Madeleine's window bidding him welcome, he saw this as a good start and taking several gulps of fresh air to clear his head, made his way along the passage.

The door to her room stood ajar – another good sign he thought as he felt his way - and with the scent of lavender wafting as he approached, he felt more in control. His head felt clearer and, thank God, the drug was working he thought as he braced up and swaggered into her room. But where was she? Was this some kind of a trick he wondered narrowing his eyes and squinting into the gloom? Then he noticed her day clothes piled high on a chair.

'Emile, my dear husband. I'm here.' Her voice drifted softly and she was hardly visible as he raised the candle. Her gown was opened almost to her navel revealing a generous cleavage he saw as she beckoned seductively, and backing away she made gentle cooing sounds, whispering for him to be quiet as he questioned and bidding him to undress.

Watching him all the while as he quietly replaced the candle, he stood willingly as she helped with buttons as he dropped his clothes where he stood.

'I'm burning with love,' she breathed, winding her arms around him, and as they moved towards the bed he kissed her fiercely as they writhed together delightfully in a tangled heap with his flesh burning against the coolness of hers as he thrust her gown up over her breasts. Never had they felt so relaxed and happy, loving and being loved. No arguing. No quarrels. No doubts, tears or hysterics. Just hours of sheer joy in that shadowy heaven which gradually descended into peaceful drowsiness and sleep until a faint shaft of light breaking through the curtains startled Madeleine wide-awake.

Instantly confused, she glanced across to where Emile still breathed heavily and began tugging at his shoulder. 'Wake up,' she whispered. 'Emile. We have slept. It's nearly morning. You must go.'

With the shadows already lifting, and knowing her father to be an early riser, Madeleine sprang out of bed, flinging back the covers as she urged him awake. She had no knowledge of the lasting effect of drugs and alcohol and watched horrified as her unrecognisable lover staggered out of bed, cursing under his breath all the while as he steadied himself with half-open eyes and reeled across the floor to climb into his clothes as best he could. She wondered whether he was ill as he stumbled and rushed to help, but he thrust her away clumsily and lurched through the door eager to get away from the house out into the courtyard where to her horror she heard him being violently sick in the gutter outside. Fortunately for him, the grey dawn concealed his humiliating indignity as he made his way unsteadily through the streets back to his digs - where he let himself in quietly without his landlady having had the slightest suspicion he had ever left the house! Madeleine however remained mortified for the rest of the day over this dreadful spectacle - which she could only believe was the onset of another illness and hurriedly posted a note later that day.

My Dearest Emile. My devoted husband.
Why were you so ill, my love? I am desperately worried darling. After our wonderful night of lovemaking I feel bereft without you and now wonder what to do. If only I could be with you to care for you. Come to me again soon. I need you.
Your affectionate wife, Mimi.'

Emile meantime had forced himself to take the breakfast tray his devoted landlady had brought when he'd not risen at the usual time that morning, explaining he felt slightly unwell when she enquired. She had no idea about the love affair that kept him out until the early hours of the morning on so many occasions and like Mary had no knowledge either about him being an arsenic eater - which he now wondered might be the reason for his frequent bouts of sickness.

'I'll soon be fine,' he told her. 'Don't worry,' and brushing off his malady with flippant excuses, and fearfully aware of losing more money if he didn't arrive at the warehouse on time, hastily prepared for work where his over-indulgences gradually wore off during the day.

On discovering Madeleine's letter waiting for him when he returned that evening though, he did feel concern. He tried to recall events as they had happened and could only remember her offering to help him dress that morning and pushing her away in sheer desperation to get out of that room before he threw up. He had felt so lousy and knew well that mixing drugs with alcohol had been stupid and wondered now why he'd done it! He should have known better! Had she seen him staggering when he left he wondered? Worse, had she seen, or heard him, vomiting outside? Just thinking about it made him cringe – and now this letter, worrying about him and wondering whether he was ill - inviting him to visit again what's more! It was unbelievable! She must have really believed he was ill! Did she know nothing about intoxication he thought? Was she that innocent? This was a shred of comfort though he thought and was all he could hope for to retrieve the humiliating situation - and when another letter arrived the following morning, reading:

> *I can't bear not seeing you and even as I write*
> *I grow excited. I long to be your wife so we may love*
> *like the last time we were together.*
> *Please do not forsake me Emile.*
> *I need you, my husband.*
> *Your Mimi'*

he immediately replied, telling her that he would visit her that very night and in the shadow of the shortening day, placed it carefully in the usual spot outside her house.

Chapter Nineteen

William Minnoch loved nothing better than springing surprises and even though it often meant Madeleine reorganising her life at the last minute, she had to admit she enjoyed it.

'William has a box for the theatre tonight. For the whole family,' Madeleine declared after bursting into her mother's room late one afternoon. 'It's a treat for us all. Yet another surprise,' she said raising her eyes dramatically – and preparing the children with hardly enough time to think, let alone get herself ready, Madeleine pitched straight into making arrangements for the event. And it was not until they all returned to the house later that night when she remembered Emile's promise to call.

'I'm sure I saw someone skulking just there in front of the house,' her father declared as he alighted from the carriage and Madeleine froze, terrified. Immediately William was striding up to the front of the house with her father following close behind and within seconds Madeleine made up her mind she had to join them. She assured her mother and the children they would be safe to remain in the carriage and securing the lock to make sure she moved swiftly to where William was now peering into every nook and cranny around the house. She tugged urgently at his arm.

'Come indoors,' she said desperately ... *anything to get him away from where she suspected Emile might be!* 'We can see from the upstairs windows if anyone is in the garden,' and seeing the logic of this William followed her into the house and made for the stairs.

Concerned about a break-in, her father was already inside rushing from room to room. 'Everything appears to be all right,' he called, breathing heavily. 'No windows broken. Nothing suspicious so far as I can see.'

'I'll go upstairs where I can see the entire garden,' Madeleine said, turning to William. 'You go and help father search the ground floor,' but irritatingly he followed and as she hurried along to one of the rooms, he caught up, surprising her by grabbing her hand and holding it tight.

'You didn't think I would allow you to go alone did you?' he said quietly and thrilled by William's first show of physical contact, Madeleine led him to the window where they stood gazing into the garden where clouds shrouded it one minute and unveiled it the next when the moon appeared.

'I wouldn't have missed this opportunity for the world,' William said in a low voice releasing her hand - and surprising her further encircled her in his arms and drew her towards him.

'Are you taking advantage of me in the gloom Mr. Minnoch?' she whispered as she delightedly melted into his arms.

'Of course,' he said thickly - and she shuddered as he traced a line of kisses on the curve of her neck until he reached her lips and she relaxed deliciously in this first show of real affection.

Her father calling breathlessly from the stairs and blustering into the room drove them apart like guilty adolescents as William uttered a gasp of exasperation and Madeleine moved closer to the window.

'Did you see anything?' her father asked, pushing between them.

'No. Nobody appears to be there.' Disappointment was clear in William's voice as he stepped aside, although this was due to hurriedly releasing Madeleine from their first embrace rather than not having seen a burglar, and he went on evenly, 'it all looks quiet. No one seems to be around.'

'I'm certain I saw someone when we arrived,' her father persisted. 'Damned sure of it.'

Madeleine began mumbling excuses. 'Perhaps it was a fox – or a cat against a shrub. There's certainly nobody out there father,' she insisted and anxiously hustling them out suggested they should return at once to where her mother and the children still waited. 'They are probably getting anxious. We must get everyone indoors. It's late for the children anyway.' She had to get her father and William away and distract them from any further searching. She had seen a branch twitch. She knew Emile was out there. Briefly, she had seen his outline and just before the moon moved behind a cloud, she'd caught a glimpse of his face.

★ ★ ★

It had been a close thing arriving just as the carriage had drawn up and at first Emile stayed out of sight as people started shouting and running all over the place. Eventually he had rushed into the garden, dropping to the ground and tearing his skin as he squeezed through brambles. Now, waiting until the house had darkened and everything became quiet, he had stayed hidden. He was soaking wet, miserable and covered in mud, but none of that mattered! Nothing mattered any more! The real pain had been watching those two at the window in a tight embrace. Madeleine, the girl he loved and vowed to marry - and responsible what's more for him giving up an excellent career - with a man he had never set eyes on! Mauling and kissing her and her enjoying it! And showing no resistance!

★ ★ ★

When Madeleine came looking for him later that night Emile had edged from where he had lurked out of sight, stiff now with the cold. She'd called softly, shushing all the while for him to stay quiet as she constantly glanced back at the house, and it was all he could do to contain his anger as he trudged to her room.

'Who was that man?'

'Not so loud Emile,' she whispered. 'The family are still not settled.'

'Answer me then. Who was it?' he demanded, grabbing Madeleine's wrist and wrenching her round.

'Be quiet,' she hissed as they hurried inside. She felt more frightened now than when she ventured into the garden after the family had returned to the house. She suggested bathing his face and hands, playing for time as she brushed at his clothes, but with a face like thunder he hurled her aside demanding over and over who it was he'd watched kissing her.

'Just be calm,' she whispered trying to conjure up excuses. Then knowing he would never let up she eventually admitted that it was their houseguest, 'I thought you knew about him,' she floundered inadequately and she attempted a smile. 'He's living temporarily at the top of the house which is unused. Just staying until his accommodation is ready Emile. His name is William Minnoch. He's a good friend of my father, works with him.'

'And a very good friend of yours too it would seem,' he sneered.

'He took advantage of me Emile. He had been drinking at the theatre. I couldn't stop his advances.'

'You encouraged him. I saw. There was no sign of a struggle keeping him away.'

'Keep your voice down,' she warned. 'And how could you see? It was so dark.'

'But not dark enough to see you not resisting!'

Her father calling along the corridor suddenly struck terror. Neither had heard his approach, and almost immediately he was rapping at the door. 'Is everything all right Madeleine? I thought I heard voices.'

Madeleine snuffed the candle and Emile scuttled behind a wardrobe door as she called out trying to sound dreamy. She dare not open the door. She was still in her outdoor clothes! 'I'm all right father,' she drawled, feigning a yawn. 'I must have been dreaming, talking in my sleep.'

'Are you sure Madeleine? Open the door.'

'No. No father. I'm in bed. I just want to sleep.' She held her breath praying he would go as footsteps shuffled. 'Thank you for coming father,' she called after another forced yawn. 'Don't worry. I'll see you in the morning.' More shuffling sounds and muffled rambling followed and after a gruff, 'Goodnight then,' his footsteps slowly faded away and she breathed a sigh of relief.

'I'll go,' Emile murmured.

'No. You can't. Not yet. Not after that. My father will be listening and watching from a window most likely. And for goodness sake keep your voice down.'

Emile sat on the bed hunched miserably with his head in his hands as she quietly undressed and slipped into her nightwear. She pretended settling to sleep after climbing into bed, drawing the covers high, not really knowing what to expect and secretly hoping he would eventually creep away. She wanted him out of her room while he was in this mood. And out of her life! She wished desperately that he would go!

'If ever a woman could make a man feel so utterly useless and unwanted, it's you Madeleine,' he said hoarsely as he turned to face her. She could just make him out in the gloom, a slumped shadow, and she didn't say anything. 'And after all we meant to each other before I went away,' he went on.

Still she failed to think of anything to say.

'So what's going to happen?' he persisted.

Pulling the covers tight to her chin, she sat up slowly. 'You must have faith in me Emile.'

'Faith?'

'Quiet!'

He was standing over her. She could feel his breath. 'Faith!' he repeated, 'after what I saw!'

'I told you what happened Emile. I could not stop it. If you refuse to believe me there's nothing more I can do.' She slid beneath the covers, pulling them tight, half expecting him to rip them back and hold her by the throat, but all she could hear was the thud of her heart until at last she sensed him moving away and heard shuffling noises and a door opening and closing quietly. Instantly she flew to the window - and as he loped by, stooping low as he usually did when he left the house to keep out of sight - and looking quite ridiculous she thought - she jumped back quickly, and her face twisted into a grin.

★ ★ ★

Madeleine had little faith of ever seeing Emile again and she had to admit to a feeling of enormous relief. A week had passed since he had seen her at the window with William Minnoch - a week during which William appeared to have gained confidence as a lover and, much to Madeleine's satisfaction, had become more demonstrative in his affection!

In contrast, Emile's confidence was fading fast. He had increasing spasms of melancholy and sleepless nights and making things worse was meeting Bessie in Sauchiehall Street one weekend to hear some devastating news. Whether her encounter had been contrived, he could not be sure, and he didn't really care one way or the other. He suffered her usual feigning of delight at meeting him as she went on to explain having slipped out to meet a friend - and as he forced himself to tease as she simpered and blushed she eventually blurted the news she hoped would increase her chance of a romance with him.

Although nothing had been announced officially, the relationship between Madeleine and William Minnoch had not escaped Bessie's notice and having overheard her parents discussing a possible romance, as well as picking up on the local gossip, she'd jumped to her own conclusions and decided it might further her own prospects if she informed Emile.

'There's soon to be a wedding in the family,' she declared, taking a deep breath. 'I believe Madeleine is about to become engaged,' and as her face settled into a satisfied smile he struggled with his feelings trying to get a grip on himself. Lost for words, he stood foolishly studying her pallid face, shrugging his shoulders and endeavouring a pleasant expression. What could he say? What did she expect him to say!

'Who is the lucky man?' he managed to force out.

Simpering irritatingly, Bessie's description matched that of Madeleine's ... *that bloody man kissing and fondling her at the window that night!*

'His name is William Minnoch,' she went on. 'He's staying with us temporarily until his own home is ready, and he and Madeleine have been going out together. For quite a while now,' she added, after a pause. 'Nothing has been settled about a wedding yet of course,' she prattled. She thought it wise not to be too specific. The important thing was letting Emile know what was going on - and if she could see him again, with some more flirting, well ...

He moistened his lips and flicked a finger nervously across his mouth. This confirmed his worst fears and as his world began collapsing, he asked thickly, 'When is this... er... wedding?'

'Oh nothing has been arranged yet, although my mother often discusses it with me, she lied. 'We're all thrilled - more than likely I'll be a bridesmaid and my younger sister - and of course my brothers will attend her.'

The stupid blathering went on incessantly and how he remained there listening to her ridiculous talk as his life became more and more unhinged was beyond him. He had to accept all this was true, despite what Madeleine had said, and as jealousy knifed through him he couldn't stand it any longer and plucked out his watch, feigning horror at the time, and politely excused himself inventing an appointment he had to rush to.

'Give my regards to your sister,' he said, forcing a smile that never reached his eyes. 'Tell her I'm delighted by the news,' and after a hasty bow he hurried away endeavouring to assume an attitude of complete disinterest as he strutted briskly. And when well out of her sight, and the people approaching had passed, he brushed away the tears beginning to smart.

Chapter Twenty

Since they first made love in the grounds of the Smith's country home in Rowaleyn, letters had continued to pass between Emile and Madeleine despite the occasional breaks when they had quarrelled. Most of these letters left little to the imagination about their lovemaking; particularly Madeleine's which concealed absolutely nothing about the extent of their affair. One section in such a letter read:

> *My own, my beloved husband.*
> *Tell me my pet, were you angry at me for allowing you to do what you did.*
> *Was it very bad of me? We should, I suppose have waited till we were married.*
> *Your loving wife, Mimi.*

Although Emile's letters to Madeleine were composed in a more restrained manner, they nevertheless exhibited the depth of feeling in their relationship. So in fear of them being discovered by her parents, or Bessie who had developed the habit of intruding into her room at the slightest opportunity - Madeleine had shied away from the romantic habit of tying love letters with ribbon as a keepsake and had always immediately destroyed them.

Those received by Emile on the other hand he stored meticulously in date order in a cardboard box and, to bolster his confidence since hearing about her infidelity, he often read them through trying to convince himself that all was not lost. Never did he suspect their romance would end like this he told himself, snatching out a letter.

He could not believe she would switch her affection to someone else after all that had happened between them, and he plucked out another letter, scanning it quickly, then another. How could she treat me like this he muttered, kicking the box in disgust. True they had quarrelled more often of late, and she had become more critical, particularly about him going overseas. Yes, their affair had been under threat. He knew that, but it was only since seeing that embrace at the window that he feared the relationship to be in real jeopardy.

He lifted the box again, placing it back on the table, folding the letters he had grabbed in anger and replacing them in order alongside the others and closing the lid. She had fooled him, the wretched girl. Set him up. Cheated on him, and - with his prospects for working overseas now in ruins - she had also wrecked his future career.

He sat for a long time staring into space wondering what the future held. He knew he was a fool for his persistence, but it would not go away! *Love like ours can't be discarded like this. It's too important* and he jumped up trying to calm himself and stop the tears he felt stinging. Whatever may happen, he thought as he paced miserably, he had to see her again. They had to meet and talk things over. Hear what was going on from her instead of listening to that stupid prattle from her sister. Just once more, they had to meet. That is all it would take to settle things. At least confront her with what Bessie had told him. Possibly, she had been making mischief. She had at one time and he brightened remembering this. He had stupidly accepted everything she told him about the marriage, but it could be untrue! Then the vision of Madeleine at the window that night flashed into his mind again ... *in that wretched man's arms, watching them kiss and her not resisting* ... and his confidence plummeted.

As one wretched day gave way to another, Emile dipped a pen in the inkpot several times and started a letter, tearing it up, starting again and destroying that one in exasperation. He became increasingly depressed. Lost his appetite. Depended more on drugs and failed to sleep peacefully at night any more. Since he left Madeleine the night he had slunk away dishevelled, cut and bleeding, he'd plunged to the depths of despair as never before in his life. The doctor listened sympathetically when he decided to seek his advice, albeit quite used to this young man by now who continually sought his advice and a possible cure for his many maladies.

'Take a few days rest,' he advised, believing this to be of more benefit than depending on yet more drugs or medicine - but in view of his recent respite in Jersey and the time spent with Madeleine at Rowaleyn this fell on deaf ears. In any case, having had so much time off, his job was now in jeopardy with his various excuses - and God knows he was entirely dependent on this pitiful work despite the niggardly wage.

His friends continued to be amazed how Emile persisted with this dwindling relationship and told him constantly it would lead to nothing. Repeatedly they advised he should end it once and for all when they'd listened to his ramblings about what was going on and were all of the same mind that the Smith family were totally beyond his integration into their midst when it came to marriage. They welcomed his company when Emile spent time with them at weekends, even though it meant more boring discussions about his problems - often well into the night - and even knowing he would ignore their advice and return to his useless pursuit they all listened patiently.

Following one of these weekend visits however, Emile's luck was in! Three letters were waiting for him, perched on the hall table where his landlady had placed them in order of arrival - the first one he noted with interest had been posted the day following his quarrel with Madeleine, which read:

> *My own, my beloved husband. You must be very*
> *disappointed with me. I wonder you like me at all. Please*
> *try. You must trust me. Please come to me. I want you so*
> *much.*
> *Your true and devoted wife, Mimi.*

The next letter was expressed in the same flowery way, but the third one set him thinking hard. It read:

> *I cannot sleep for worrying about this and can only*
> *dream of falling asleep on your bosom, dearest love.*
> *I cry constantly. I yearn to kiss and fondle you*
> *as I used to. What has happened to you my dearest?*
> *Where are you? My happiness is to be loved by my dear*
> *sweet husband. Please come to me.*

Delighted, puzzled and suspicious at the same time, he placed the letters alongside others in his cardboard box. She was anxious for another meeting - as he was but then began questioning her motives. Writing in this romantic fashion was her way. He knew that, but what lay behind it. Were some other artful plans afoot? Or was she playing another game? Perhaps the one positive thing about Emile was his awareness of the artfulness of women - and he'd had enough experience in that direction! He had also had a good chance of thinking everything through since visiting his doctor and talking to friends. Having reached rock bottom to a point of desperation, he made up his mind to be a match for her if she did happen to be playing games – and in the knowledge that their next meeting would be very interesting, he scribbled a brief note saying he would call to see her that night.

★ ★ ★

Prior to receiving Emile's reply, Madeleine had been at her wits end. His absence and lack of letters surprised her and she wondered what was going on. She had continually pestered Mary Perry about him and what he had been doing but apart from Mary passing on his landlady's comments about him looking unwell, she simply explained his absence as him being busy or having visited friends at weekends. In the presence of Mary nowadays however, particularly in view of her recent attitude about her philandering with William Minnoch, Madeleine felt she had to be on her guard when she expressed concern about Emile and always declared her ongoing affection. On this occasion, however there had been no need for her to give this impression. As Emile's confidante, Mary knew well what had been going on and having learned about an impending wedding during one of her confidential tête-à-têtes with Madeleine's mother, she decided it wise to say nothing more about Emile at this point and passed on to discussing more mundane matters.

With the arrival of Emile's brief note however, Madeleine's concern changed rapidly to one of foreboding. She knew something was very wrong by the abruptness of his hasty scribble on a scrappy slip of paper and hurrying to her room laid it aside. She wandered around the room, returning repeatedly to read it. Just two lines he had written. Cold and unemotional, stating he would call later that evening in the usual manner. There was not even the flourish of his signature ... *so unlike Emile* ... she thought as she continued pacing the floor.

Always he wrote with affection. Never had she received such a letter. It was totally out of character, and at a loss to understand this change of heart she was worried.

★ ★ ★

Come what may, Madeleine had made up her mind to prepare carefully for Emile's arrival that night. They had not met for a while and she wanted everything to go well. She placed candles around the room to create soft shadows and wandering about she sprayed lavender water to add a romantic touch. She also laid out a chemise in readiness on the bed – just in case! Until an unexpected situation suddenly arose which threw her into a blind panic.

The tap on her window startled her, believing it to be Emile at first, although knowing it was far too early with the family not yet having retired for the night. Rushing to the window she was amazed to be confronted by William Minnoch, tapping gently again and peering in. Something he had never done before!

'It's cold, but fine and dry with a full moon,' he said as she raised the window. 'Ideal for a walk and chat,' and fumbling for excuses, Madeleine forced a grateful smile. This was so uncharacteristic of William and she cursed under her breath. She had to put him off somehow. She must see Emile that night ... *and he would be arriving any time now!*

'I'm so tired,' she said not very convincingly and hurriedly went on with an explanation about needing an early night with contrived stories about the children having been tiresome and wearing her out, but William was not having any of it. This was completely out of character with the lively girl who always enjoyed his spontaneous arrangements and sudden plans – and he persisted, 'Just in case you happen to change your mind then, I'll call back later. We could even sit together quietly in your room if you still don't feel like going out,' he said encouragingly and with a wink added, 'I'm sure your parents would not object either as we are soon to become betrothed.' And as her excuses became less probable when he was more insistent, he promised to call back later, 'Just in case you change your mind, my dear.'

Madeleine stared at his retreating back with alarm as she lowered the window. This was something she had not bargained for when she decided to carry on with both men at the same time. There had never been any danger of them being here at the same time in the past, and she wondered how she was going to handle it!

★ ★ ★

After depositing his letter at Madeleine's house earlier that day, Emile looked forward to what promised to be an interesting reunion and set out from his lodgings swaggering with confidence. Not so with Madeleine however, who by now had become increasingly alarmed with the prospect of William calling back at any time. She dared not place a candle in the window. Not yet anyway! And as the time passed with no sign of William, her hopes began to rise that perhaps he had abandoned his plan.

Emile as it happened arrived a little earlier than usual and although puzzled by the absence of a candle on the sill, could just make out Madeleine at the window who appeared to be making urgent signs for him to stay out of sight. As far as he could make out no one was about and it appeared to be quiet at the house when he glanced back. Something was different though. No candle flickering in the window for a start and the room sparsely lit with only a few candles here and there. Something was going on beyond understanding though and he wondered whether he should burst in to find out. He had come for a specific purpose and certainly was not going to be put off. Another glance at the house confirmed it was still in darkness - bar a light in the top rooms and he knew who that was! There were no signs of lurking figures, or sounds coming from anywhere roundabout - and with his patience suddenly running out and furious for being at the mercy of her capricious behaviour once more, he rapped on the window.

She raised the window a little, crouching low to whisper, 'I'm worried my father may still be awake.'

'It's dark in the house. How can he be?'

'Shh. I can hear noises in the house. We must be careful Emile. You must stay hidden a while. Please.' Pushing the window a little higher she leaned out with a steaming cup of cocoa and a warning finger held to her lips. 'Drink this to warm you, my love. I'll call you soon. You must stay out of sight – just a while longer.' With that, she closed the window quietly.

There had been a tremble in her voice and he'd picked up a sign of nervousness he'd never detected before and knowing the fierce temper of her father thought better of making a fuss and sidled across to the shadows, positioning himself within easy sight of her window, leaning against the wall sipping his cocoa. There were still no lights in the house and straining to listen now and then, all seemed quiet. This new set of circumstances totally threw him though, skulking as he had once before he thought, irritably - hiding from God knows what - and this time with a cup of cocoa! He knew he had to get out of this ridiculous situation – *messing with my life again!* he thought, and tossing the drink away in disgust rushed to the window to demand an explanation. Then just as he prepared to knock he stopped, his hand in mid air. Footsteps, hurrying, were approaching from the back of the house in his direction and as they became louder, he shot back into the shadows. He just made out the slight figure of a man, not very tall, hesitating outside Madeleine's window - which he saw slowly opening.

'No Emile. It's not safe.' He heard Madeleine's voice and caught his name distinctly. Then followed confused whisperings he could not quite pick up - and the man suddenly laughed.

'It's me. William,' he heard plainly - also what sounded like questions being asked as the voices became louder. Madeleine was laughing now and it sounded like she was making excuses and as he shrugged back into the prickly bushes burning with rage, and shivering now as the frost hardened, he grew angry as never before in his life. So this is William! The houseguest! Her betrothed! This was the man who fondled the girl he had hoped to claim as his own when he had been lurking like a fugitive in the garden once before and his lip curled into a sneer. Idiot, he called himself as he crouched out of sight and it was all he could do not to rush across and raise a fist. Then commonsense began to dictate and with increasing rage, he began asking himself if she was really worth it. Should he see her anyway he wondered if she did invite him in later? He would be incapable of controlling his temper for one thing - or actions come to that if she taunted him and began flaunting herself! No! Their meeting could wait. He was in no hurry to find out what was going on and as soon as it was safe, he would be off! Then, *'Damn it,'* he muttered, straightening and striking out, *'why should I wait until it's safe! Let her take the bloody consequences if I'm seen,'* and edging out of the shadows he strutted away.

Chapter Twenty-One

Unsurprisingly, and as Emile suspected, a letter soon arrived from Madeleine full of remorse for what had happened the night William Minnoch appeared at her window. She wrote:

*'Whatever are you thinking my darling. I thought
it was you at my window – and called your name to
warn you. I must explain my darling lover. Please
let me. I want you so desperately. Please, please
come to your Mimi. Soon. Tonight if you can.*

Toughening up for once, he decided not to go. Who did she think she was messing about like this? As the day wore on however, jealousy got the upper hand. He could not get the image of that man at her window out of his mind, even though he cursed himself for being a fool. It was no use. He had no power to control the emotional side of his life any longer he realised, or his agitated mind. The only shred of comfort as he tried to shrug off his stupidity had been some straight thinking about a plan that had festered for some weeks. Which would mean a further confrontation, he realised. So swallowing what remained of his pride, yet still in two minds, he left the house twice that night - returning once having decided it would be a complete waste of time for any more talking, then in a mood that matched the heavy cloud and miserable outlook, strutting with malice in his heart along the deserted streets.

He arrived just before midnight, noted the dim light between the partially drawn curtains, and walking swiftly through the side entrance and passage leading to her room, threw the door wide and immediately jumped back, startled as she immediately flew to him.

'Not a word my darling,' she whispered, brushing her lips across his cheek. 'We must be quiet after what happened last night. I fear I trust no one now.'

Hesitating a second, he fixed her with a glare. 'And I no longer trust you.'

She shifted away, uncertainly. 'How can you say that Emile?' she murmured. Her voice sounded different. Uneasy he thought – but he had not come to quarrel. He had a different purpose for this visit and with resentment cutting like a knife it was all he could do not to strike her as he called to mind seeing her with that man.

'I hear you are about to become engaged to this... er, William, the man who stood at your window last night,' he went on.

'Lies,' she hissed. 'It's not true.'

'Why did he come to you? Answer me that!'

'You know why,' she said rounding on him. 'And keep your voice down for God's sake.'

'I don't know why. That's why I'm asking.'

'He's staying here. I told you. He said he heard noises and wondered if... if I was all right. I heard something too,' she rushed on. 'I thought it was my father. That's why I warned you to stay away.' Madeleine felt unsure what to say next and moved away. She had not expected this. She could hardly see his face, making it difficult to see his expression. 'Have you no sense of reason?' she said at last and simpering, 'you know I only love you. What more can I say?'

Emile knew she was struggling, pitying and hating her at the same time for what she was doing but determined not to give in he stood his ground. Remaining silent.

She realised it was pointless arguing. He was different.

Something had happened and in desperation, she rushed over to the bed throwing herself down, feigning distress as she played for time. For a wild moment, she wanted to rush to him and plead but she knew she had to take care with him in this strange mood - until the silence became a threat she could stand no longer and she sat up miserably, turning to face him. He was standing in the same spot. He had not moved a muscle, glaring at her like a stranger and she felt scared. She wondered what was going on in his mind and in a choked voice said meekly, 'I'm sorry Emile. I did not want this to happen. You know I only love you - my secret husband. You are my only one. You must know that.'

He continued to remain motionless. His face a mask, and in a flat monotone asked again, 'Why did he come to your window?'

She edged off the bed and sidled up to him, 'You must believe me Emile,' she said, her voice trailing away. 'How can you not my beloved?' He felt her wet cheeks as she reached up to kiss him but did not touch her. 'I so looked forward to us being together again tonight Emile. Why did this have to happen?' She took his hand to urge him across the room but he stood firm, dropping her fingers and staring embittered as she allowed her chemise to fall to the ground.

'I have made a decision Madeleine,' he said coldly. 'If you have a relationship with another man, then ours cannot continue. I have pledged my love. Over and over for heaven's sake,' he said, with his voice rising. 'We've both discussed being married and this is what I understand you always wanted.' He saw her eyes flash in the dim candlelight and his gaze fell to the statuesque grace of her naked body. 'I demand your promise of sincerity if our marriage is to go ahead Madeleine,' he continued, stepping away. 'Now! This minute I demand it!'

'And you have my promise,' she cried, snatching up her chemise and covering her body.

'I have not!' he said angrily, wheeling round. 'You are deceiving me and I can't stand it. I can't wait any longer.' Choosing his words carefully he went on firmly, informing her that their betrothal should be announced straight away and arrangements made for him to meet her parents as soon as possible. 'I am not a wealthy man as you know,' he said in an even tone, 'and there will be a certain amount of explaining to do. But I am honourable in my intentions and determined to wed you Madeleine and when you name a day - and time - I will be ready to meet your parents.'

Alarmed by the determination in his voice and noticing his hands curling into fists, her expression sharpened in terror. She could not do as he asked. It was impossible and struggling for excuses it was an effort to stay calm. More so, and thinking quickly, she realised she did not want to be married to Emile. He was her lover and that was different - but he could never be her husband. Never! Her father would never hear of it. It was ridiculous to suppose. He would cut her off financially if she insisted, and with this stupid thought, she swept a quick look around the shadowy room. Not luxurious by any means, but well furnished, with style. A fine assortment of clothes hung in the closet. There was good jewellery in the drawer. Emile had no money for such things! She had to be sensible. She could not marry him. He was a pauper!

'Well?' he demanded.

She needed more time and flustered, wandering away muttering, 'I can't say now Emile. I must consider what we tell my parents for one thing. Think about where we would live. How we would live! As you say, you are not wealthy. I know my father would disown me – and what would I do. What would we do?' she said, suddenly turning.

'So it is money,' he said coldly. 'I never doubted your love at one time Madeleine,' he went on. 'You've told me over and over, and you wrote as much - even calling yourself my wife in your letters. We have laid together Madeleine. We are as one. You thought that to be enough at one time rather than riches. What has happened? Why has it changed?'

She stared ahead as though not hearing - not wanting to hear. It was all true and she felt trapped.

'Let me know when you've decided on a date to meet your parents then,' he said resignedly and turned to go.

'But I can't,' she said, tugging at his arm. 'You know I can't Emile!'

'You can - and you will,' he said, and wheeling back abruptly and thrusting his face just inches away added, 'And I don't believe your parents would stand in the way of our getting wed when they read your letters.'

Her colour drained. Her body froze and she heard the thud of her heart. 'What are you saying? What... what do you mean?'

Emile faced her squarely. 'Exactly what I just said Madeleine. I propose showing your letters to your parents so they know exactly what has been going on. I imagine a pregnancy out of wedlock would be quite intolerable for a start.'

'But I'm not pregnant!'

'Then that is fortunate my dear, and I must say I'm surprised you're not.'

She rushed at him, eyes blazing. 'You know I'm not. For heaven's sake I would have said, and in any case there was never a risk.'

Emile turned away and her words hung in the air as

he savoured the memory of their time together. How could she forget it all and treat him like this? No other girl had made such audacious advances satisfying his advances and in a fleeting, stupid moment, he realised what he would be missing. He felt her hands around him, caressing, pleading and cheapening herself in desperation, and in disgust he spun round and thrust her away.

'I'll await your answer with a date and time,' he said coldly. 'And bear in mind I shall not wait long to carry out my intention,' and instead of striding out indignantly as fitted his mood he was forced into slinking away quietly in the usual manner, creeping like a footpad, hating having to behave as he had and hating himself for being duped by a girl he thought loved him.

Madeleine rushed to the window watching as he shuffled past, looking ridiculous again, she thought as he picked his way carefully in the shadows after this uncharacteristic outburst. *How dare he!* she said under her breath. *It's blackmail! How could he do this to me?* But something had to be done she realised - and quickly! She had been unable to break down his resistance by assuming distress or making sexual advances - which had always worked before she thought irritably. So there had to be another way and she paced the room thinking hard. Her letters were her property she reasoned and she had a right for them to be returned. *But how?*

★ ★ ★

After giving it great thought following many sleepless nights, Madeleine decided she had to see Emile again. She had to plead, deceive or do whatever she could imagine to stop this threat of exposing her, and clinging to this hope of retrieving the situation there began another exchange of letters - Madeleine's always politely worded, requesting the return her letters and Emile's continuing to refuse and adamantly standing firm by his decision.

Throughout this developing drama, William Minnoch had remained the perfect suitor. He accepted without question her fanciful reason for someone suddenly strutting out from her garden the night he had gone to her window.

'A tramp,' she'd told him, 'needing shelter, to which my father would have strongly objected and I saw no harm, poor man.' And after promising not to mention this to her parents, his pandering continued whenever he noticed her disquiet or deathly pallor, or when she excused herself as feeling unwell. Visits to the opera continued in the usual manner, as did the candle-lit dinners and strolls at the weekend, which she appeared to enjoy, and being seen together on these frequent jaunts in the locality, people began speculating about a blossoming romance and future wedding and Madeleine did nothing to dispute this when they met her in the street.

Inevitably, Emile picked up on this gossip, which served to strengthen his determination to expose Madeleine's promiscuous behaviour to her parents. New circumstances however were about to bring an abrupt halt to his threat when a letter arrived from Madeleine announcing that the only way out of the predicament he had placed her in would be her death. She wrote:

My Dearest Emile,
On my bended knees I implore you. Do not inform on
me. Do not make me a public shame. How can you hurt
someone you professed you fondly loved? I am so
miserable. The only way for me to escape this
torture is death – and I have the means...'

Unsurprisingly, Emile's immediate reaction was one of suspicion. She had played him along so many times and with this William Minnoch's intrusion into their lives, he no longer trusted her. He kicked at the box containing her earlier letters with disgust - nonsensical, romantic meanderings from a stupid girl that paled into insignificant tripe he told himself. How could he have been so stupid to get himself into this state! He had to end the affair once and for all as his friends told him and get on with his own life, and there could even be the chance of going abroad still if he stepped in quick, he thought. Fortunately, the people were still keen for him to go when he last enquired and he relished the idea of getting away from the bone-chilling cold and damp of Scotland anyway, and above all away from this conniving female who was wrecking his life.

Staring from the window for what seemed an eternity Emile's knuckles whitened gripping the ledge, and when he moved away he realised he was crying. They had made plans for the future. She suggested at one time they should marry secretly, 'We could then go to my father,' he remembered her saying in a sultry voice and she'd gone on to fantasise that once they were wed there would be nothing her parents could do about it. They had talked about this. Laughed and made plans, and he brushed a hand across his eyes irritably as he moved about the room remembering how she'd never wanted to talk about getting married recently when he mentioned it. There was always a stubbornness and he recalled how her face set into a blank expression when she refused to reply, and this generally brought about another quarrel.

His thoughts darted in another direction and, brightening, he felt in more control as he savoured the sweetness of revenge - kicking at the box where he had stored her letters. They were all incriminating. Every one of them damn it! In that box, he told himself with a sneer spreading, was clear evidence that she had willingly invited him to her parents' house at night, and that she had given him her body! And he couldn't help smiling when he considered the devastating effect that would have on this William Minnoch! He knew he'd been weak giving in to her precocious behaviour, tears and petulance in the past and once more felt ashamed of himself for having done so - particularly when he thought about the ridiculous humiliation of skulking out of sight in that garden! Twice for God's sake! He remembered too, shamefully when he thought about it, how he had relied on arsenic to reinforce his stamina on more occasions than he wished to admit - *just to match hers*! And with this thought, he suddenly recalled her letter and threat of suicide. He knew she had the means to do this. She used the bloody stuff as a cosmetic and realised how easy... *Oh no. If she killed herself...! If she really meant what she wrote, because of him!* No! He knew that would be the end of him too! More than anything, he feared losing her, but not like that!

He took up a pen writing quickly and urgently - warning her about the dangers of arsenic – then tore it up and started again. He had to include some loving endearments. She liked this he knew and it may even move their relationship onto a new level of understanding he thought. Stupid he knew. He could but hope! There had to be a warning though and, with more enthusiasm, he wrote with increasing frenzy, ending his letter,

> *I can only guess your intent when you say you have the means. Arsenic to make you beautiful is just for that my dear girl, although you have no need for it*

> *of course in my eyes. But in no circumstances whatever*
> *my sweet should you ever ingest it.*

★ ★ ★

By the time Madeleine received this letter she had recovered sufficiently to be enjoying herself once more. Her confidence had soared with Emile's concern about her threat of suicide and the touches of affection he had added strengthened her hope that she could play for a bit more time. She would have to end the affair with Emile pretty soon in any case however, having just received a proposal of marriage from William Minnoch, but this unsavoury business about the letters had to be settled, or perhaps - she considered with a smile curling – *maybe I could string them both along for a bit longer. I'll just have to be a bit more careful! After all, it would be my last fling before settling down!*

★ ★ ★

There had been no further passionate advances from William since they had embraced at the window overlooking the garden and he remained a severely reserved man. He had held her hand at the theatre and they kissed briefly when they met for an evening out, with a longer exchange of rubbery kisses when they returned. Bland indeed Madeleine often thought scornfully compared with Emile. Despite the disastrous development concerning her letters however, which terrified her alarmingly at night when she lay awake, she missed their exciting lovemaking, and her loins ached wretchedly at the thought.

She dipped a pen, staring thoughtfully out of the window considering her reply. He had shown concern about the veiled threat in her letter. This had brought him to his senses she realised and visualised his concern, and she dipped her pen again, writing in her usual flowery terms, urging him to visit her as quickly as possible as if nothing had gone wrong between them. She wrote,

> *My love, my pet, my sweet Emile,*
> *Please release me from the torture of not having*
> *seen you for so long. My body aches for you. We*
> *must meet as soon as possible to help me through*
> *the long empty days I'm suffering without you. It*
> *must be the same for you my darling. We are destined*
> *never to be apart ... and if I am no longer able to*
> *enjoy this should my destiny be otherwise...*
> *Your devoted wife, Mimi.*

She knew he would run back to her with his usual eagerness when he read this. She knew too that she would have to handle everything carefully when he did!

Life is getting very interesting, she mused as she sealed the letter slowly and placed it to one side thoughtfully, and taking her pen to paper once more, she stared out of the window allowing time to adjust her train of thought. Her next letter had to be worded differently she realised. Just a few lines would suffice, in a more restrained manner she considered, and choosing her words carefully, she began,

> *Dear William Minnoch,*
> *After fair consideration of your recent kind proposal*
> *of marriage, it gives me the greatest pleasure to accept.*
> *Yours, Madeleine Smith.*

Chapter Twenty-Two

Such was the relief on Emile's next visit to Madeleine, he had given little thought as to how he intended the evening should proceed as he hurried through dark streets shortly before midnight. He had imbibed his usual dose of arsenic to boost his stamina before leaving and, seeing a glimmer of light in the window as he approached the house, crept quietly through the side gate, along the passage and into a candle-lit room heavy with the scent of lavender. At first, they had stood awkwardly and when he did open his mouth to speak, she ran to him and quickly raised a finger to his lips. 'We must be quiet,' she breathed huskily, 'and love peacefully,' and as she tugged at his clothes they spoke in whispers.

Emile thought what he should do. He didn't want to spoil things. For the time being all seemed well and he decided to bide his time. There was no mention of suicide - or returning her letters. She was like her old self. Everything appeared to be back to normal. She had changed, and for the next hour or so, they gave in deliriously to their feelings.

'We must meet again. Come to me as often as you can,' she mouthed, stroking his face. 'Don't desert me Emile. Please don't,' she urged. 'Never ever leave me. I couldn't bear it.'

He regarded her with an expression of amusement as he shrugged into his clothes and without really thinking muttered, 'It's not worth it you know Madeleine,' and he watched her face change. The smile had gone as she looked away, but he felt no regret and went on, 'I know you are playing a game,' and he laughed. 'Nice game of course,' he said with a grin. 'I enjoyed it. I always do. Remember though my love,' he said softly, and with a quick stride back to the bed took her hands, kissing her fingers before he spoke, 'We still have a pact my darling.'

Her face darkened but no words came.

'Well?' he questioned, still smiling.

'I want my letters back Emile,' she said, after an uneasy pause. 'They are my property. They belong to me and you must return them. Legally they are mine.'

She flinched back alarmed when he released her hands and lunged at her - but it was only to take her in his arms, holding her tight and speaking firmly as to a child.

'There is no turning back Madeleine,' he whispered. 'I meant what I said the last time we met. Your letters were addressed to me and they are mine.' He stroked her hair, tilting her chin with his other hand, smiling down at her. 'I'm sorry my darling. But I am quite serious about this.'

Tearing away from him, angry and frightened, Madeleine felt torn. Tears were useless, as was pleading and further sexual advances. She had tried all that and it hadn't worked, and when she shuffled from the bed when he released her they stood quietly regarding each other like strangers, neither of them speaking.

'We can't part like this Emile,' she said in a small voice. 'I feel trapped. How can you do this to me?'

Only once in her life had Madeleine fainted and remembering how the overwhelming heat on that occasion caused her to sway and sink to the floor she did this now in sheer desperation, clutching at Emile before allowing herself to fall gracefully to the floor - and it did the trick! Immediately Emile was on his knees, cradling her head as she allowed it to loll, and faking slowly coming round as he lifted her in his arms she began breathing heavily as he carried her to a chair, holding her until she was steady.

'No,' she said weakly brushing a hand as she struggled to her feet. 'It's all right. I am feeling better. I'm sorry. I can manage now.' She stood unsteadily and with hands outstretched edged slowly over to a table, doubling over and leaning heavily, refusing his help when he followed. 'I'll rest for a while. I can't think what came over me,' she said, playing for time. 'Then... then...' she murmured weakly as she turned to face him, 'I'll make us a drink. I can't let you go on such a cold night without something to warm you.' Pausing briefly, she caught him watching her carefully and content there was no recognition of her insincerity scolded him gently when he again offered help. 'Just wait a while my love,' she simpered, barely audible. 'I'm feeling better already. I'll heat a kettle,' and confused by this new turn of events Emile shifted about uneasily not quite knowing what to do.

'You shouldn't be doing this,' he said, trying to intervene. 'It's unnecessary. There's no need to make drinks, or at least let me do it if you need one.'

'I'm feeling better,' she insisted with a wan smile, waving him away. 'Don't worry Emile. I cannot think what came over me. It must have been the shock,' and she gripped the table suddenly again pretending to steady herself as she turned to face him and he rushed over but once more she urged him away.

'There my love,' she said, indicating the steaming cups. 'You bring them across. You can do that, then come and sit beside me and we shall sip our drinks together. Then I must sleep.' Taking each step delicately, she moved falteringly towards the bed, patting a space for him to join her.

'It's very late,' she said wearily and fondling his head as he finished his drink, she watched quietly as he prepared to leave. She felt contented she had won him round ... *as long as things can stay like this everything will be fine. It had been like old times. As it used to be ...* and she began feeling more positive about the future.

★ ★ ★

As Emile made his way back to his lodgings he thought long and hard about what had happened. Having picked up more local gossip about a forthcoming wedding in the Smith family, he realised things were now taking a change for the worse. There was no doubting his own marriage to Madeleine was in jeopardy, whatever he did. It was foolish to think otherwise - but this fainting fit tonight, and her behaviour, had completely thrown him. Revealing the letters to her father had been his trump card. Still was! Would the disgrace of this change her mind about marrying William Minnoch when he learned about it he wondered? Certainly exposing her letters would have a devastating effect on this marriage and that was about all he could hope for, but how would it leave things for him? Could he carry on with his threat of going to her father, or even Minnoch, in the face of her threatened suicide? Two threats now, with the possibility of her death!

★ ★ ★

Mary Perry continued as a staunch confidante to Emile throughout this drama, listening sympathetically as she always had to his unhappy state of affairs. She had stepped up her visits in knowledge of the worsening situation and when she called the day following his latest encounter with Madeleine he was more than grateful. There was no need for her to be told what had been happening in the Smith household and in his present state of depression, she decided to keep her awareness of this to herself - until what he had to tell her next.

'This affair is spiralling out of control Mary. We're

both suffering now,' and without taking his eyes from her face went on to talk about Madeleine's threat of suicide, his fear of losing her this way and how wretchedly ill he'd also felt. 'It's getting to me as I never imagined! The very thought of her killing herself makes me want to cry and this is something I have never done in my life.'

Her stomach lurched as he dropped his gaze and turned away, wondering what to do if he did break down. Should she take his hand? Put her arms around him and hold him? What should she do? They had never touched. He looked up at last, talking incessantly about his guilt should she carry out this threat of killing herself and Mary listened patiently. She tried to balance the image of Madeleine's suicidal tendency with the girl who had talked about her wedding plans with such excitement she remembered. Going on and on about plans she had absolutely no interest hearing about! She knew also how the girl had been enjoying life with William Minnoch, but what was wrong with Emile she thought, suddenly remembering him talking about feeling ill? She felt more concerned about that than Madeleine's wedding, or anything else about the girl - and ignoring his talk about her suicide she cut across and began questioning him.

'Why are you unwell so often Emile? You constantly tell me this. You say you have pains. It's not right. There must be a good reason.'

Taken aback by her sudden intrusion he gave her a wry look and with a hint of irritation, 'Oh, there's a good reason all right. A very good reason!' *What more could he say?*

'But it's not being overwrought about this affair or what's going on now. It can't be. There must be something very wrong.'

He held back, not wanting to explain. Mary knew

nothing about his increasing indulgence in drugs and patent medicines he now suspected contributed to his ill health. He had never revealed this to anyone, apart from close friends. Never had and never would! She went on and on however - about his health, delving into causes of his problems. He knew she was trying to help - but there were too many other things on his mind at that moment and this talk didn't help! *Mary always fussed so ... she meant well ... but for God's sake not now!*

'I'll go to my friends again at the weekend,' he said, trying to look cheerful. 'That's what I need Mary. Get away from all this nonsense. Have a bit of fun.' He tried sounding positive. Forced a smile. Promised to take more care with his diet and get his life back into shape. He jumped up, thanking her for coming and for being a friend, telling her he had something to prepare for the following day. He had to be alone! This talking was not helping. He coped better on his own, and Mary, feeling hurt and trying desperately hard not to show it, promised she would call again. 'If you wish me to do so of course,' she said meekly. Which he readily agreed would be wonderful if she could spare the time, and that appeared to satisfy her. He gave her a hug and as she turned to leave, he felt she understood, to his way of thinking at any rate!

★ ★ ★

Having recovered from his temporary bout of sickness, and feeling more positive after another weekend away with his friends, Emile decided he had to go ahead with his threat of exposing Madeleine's letters to her father. He knew events were moving swiftly to a break up in their relationship but he was determined to put an end to all this nonsense. He made up his mind to investigate that job of working abroad again. And with advice from friends still ringing in his ears about Madeleine's despicable behaviour, he wrote a forceful letter informing her he would be calling to discuss something of great importance – and stressed she should be there to receive him, which terrified Madeleine when she read it and she instantly took to her bed in distress.

★ ★ ★

With arrangements for the wedding now getting seriously under way, Madeleine had begged her parents to postpone the announcement with an excuse about her increasing feeling of lassitude. They knew she had been unwell lately and putting it down to anxiety about the coming wedding, suggested she take a short holiday. Madeleine, needless to say, turned this down as being unnecessary as she did her mother's insistence about visiting the doctor for a check on her health! *She had to be around in case Emile approached her father with her letters! She could not go away now!*

James Smith constantly reminded his daughter she had nothing to worry about and was very lucky to be marrying such a fine young man as William and having people around who cared about her, which failed to boost her confidence however! Pressure from other sources also irritated, like William being overly concerned for her health and it was all she could do to stay in a good temper when he fussed. A further annoyance was her sister running into her room making futile excuses, albeit for a different reason. 'What will you do about Emile when you are married?' she asked, bursting in one day. And with more to think about than answering silly questions, Madeleine made an issue about her privacy being invaded and screamed for her to go, although her sister's parting shot that someone should let Emile know about her forthcoming marriage left Madeleine staring hopelessly at the door after Bessie had slammed it shut. He will know soon enough she mumbled to herself, if he doesn't know already, and shivering involuntarily she realised some serious thought had to be given to his latest letter, 'to talk about something of great importance,' he'd said! Whatever did he mean? *It had been fun stringing both men along at the same time. It was fun ... something she really enjoyed ... but now ... goodness knows what now ...*

When Emile arrived that evening however, it resulted in a complete disaster with both of them being determined to finalise the matter of the letters to their own satisfaction. Madeleine refused to enter into any sensible discussion and became petulant. Emile stood his ground and told her what he thought of her. And when she demanded the return of her letters like a child asking for the moon and he adamantly refused, she stamped her foot and screamed hysterically that if all he could do was argue he may just as well go! And after a heated argument when she feared at one point they might come to blows, he took her at her word and stormed off in a temper.

★ ★ ★

Although Madeleine was far from getting her life back together after yet another disastrous quarrel, she at least started to feel more in charge of her feelings when she decided to see Emile again. Just once more. She had to. If he was serious about going abroad as he had told her, what about any other plans he had in mind before he went she wondered and her mind skittered wildly. As a gentleman he couldn't possibly ignore her demand for returning the letters and she felt convinced he would surely be as concerned for her happiness as for his own. She knew he would never be able to stand up to her father in any case if he persisted with this stupid threat! But what if he did she wondered? Her fears came flooding back. She had no intention of backing down from marrying William. That was final. Furthermore, Emile was beginning to irritate with his threats and demands, to say nothing of his failing health which now bored her rather than evoking pity. And what kind of a future could she possibly have with a man like that she wondered? He had no money, or any prospects of improving himself, except for this stupid job overseas! *Whereas William...* she thought dreamily, and with a sudden shiver, along with a feeling of contempt, she realised she wanted Emile out of her life and immediately sat down to write another letter.

We must meet my dearest. Come tonight. We have
to talk about you going abroad as you said. And
I feel so distressed about our quarrel. I can't
bear losing you. I cannot let you go ... whatever
shall I do without you. I couldn't go on living.
Your loving wife Mimi.

Was this another threat of suicide he wondered! Was it another game? Although puzzled and concerned at the same time, Emile was determined to deal with this sensibly. If he did go it would probably be his last visit in any case, and with a quick glance at his box of letters, knew there was nothing to lose. All the same, the unexpected endearment in her letter threw him, particularly after that last display of temper! However, all this failed to deflate his determination and he sidled into the side entrance of her home later that night prepared for whatever lay ahead.

Neither of them spoke as they exchanged glances and as he waited to see what would happen, he felt uncertain. Madeleine was smiling but there were tears in her eyes he noticed as she edged towards him and put out a hand.

'I'm sorry,' she said breaking the silence. 'I've behaved badly Emile. Forgive me. I didn't mean...' She paused, blinking, brushing away the tears and still unsure he took her hand, but no words came.

He seemed tense and odd she thought as she met his gaze and hesitantly reached for his other hand. 'I've thought everything through,' she said softly and he noticed tears brimming again, glistening on her cheeks. 'I cannot say what kind of reaction we shall get from my parents,' she went on. 'But we shall go together as you suggest Emile and face them, whatever may happen.'

Emotions darted between confusion, delight and suspicion and he held on desperately to his earlier convictions as they threatened to fade. He blurted out, 'You mean that you... we... tell your parents we want to be married Madeleine? You've decided?'

'Of course,' she said with a look of surprise and she brushed a hand across her eyes. 'This is what you want?'

He felt unsure. This was unexpected. Was she playing a game again? He had to be careful. Choose his words. 'But... what about this, er, William Minnoch,' he started. His mouth felt dry, then as her face darkened he immediately checked himself, hating having spoiled it and trying to make amends by taking her in his arms, praying she wouldn't feel his heart thumping as he kissed away her protests. 'Of course we shall go my darling,' he went on quickly. 'Whenever you say, whenever you feel the time is right. Then we can make plans. I can't wait – you know that!'

For a wild moment, he wanted to sweep her up. Take her back with him straight away, for the night. They could then stay together until the time came for facing her parents - but nothing further was said as Madeleine reverted to her old delightful self, simpering and behaving coquettishly as they embraced and kissed.

Everything seemed to be back to how they were and although doubts still lingered at the back of his mind, he felt happier and more relaxed than he had for many months. Even if it turned out to be a lie, or a trick, he relished the relief of so much doubt and pain giving way to this blissful serenity. He had to believe her. He could not go on with this torment any longer and neither could she! He had to force away the past. They both had to move on. Look to the future. Relax. And he needed no encouragement as she slid into bed, breathless and trembling with desire as she submissively indulged him as they made love, staying quietly together long after the time for him to leave.

Despite all their earlier misgivings, an enormous sense of relief enveloped both lovers, and Madeleine lay back clasping her knees, glowing with satisfaction as she quietly watched Emile dress. Then easing off the bed she kissed her fingertips and drew them across his lips. 'I'll make our drinks,' she said dreamily and moved away. As they sat quietly side by side on the bed sipping their steaming cocoa, they watched the changing shadows cast by the candles until, one by one, they flickered down to nothing and left them as shadows just visible to one another in the light from the window.

'I'll leave now,' Emile said huskily, and cupping her face in his hands he kissed her lips as she traced a finger lightly over his brow and her sweet smile lingered, he noticed, as he eased away. The warmth of her love overwhelmed his whole being as he stole quietly across the room and as he turned for a last glance, he cast aside a doubt that rankled momentarily. Perhaps it was the hurdle of facing her parents. He could not be sure - but he would climb a mountain! Do anything! Nothing was impossible and he blew a kiss, which he knew she could not possibly have seen but knew she would be expecting.

For a long time Madeleine gazed at the closed door, still sensing the warmth of their love and touch of his hands as she stared into the darkness. It was quiet and completely at peace after a wonderful evening, her eyelids gradually became heavy as she relaxed, and drawing the covers high as she eased beneath them, she fell into a dreamless asleep.

Emile meanwhile trod lightly along the pavement, the frosty air heightening his senses as it tingled on his skin. The evening had been perfect, wonderful - and he tried pushing away the suspicion still lingering at the back of his mind. Perhaps he should have heeded caution. Females went to extraordinary lengths to get what they wanted he knew – and Madeleine was skilled in that direction! Even so, with this new turn of events, he felt more in charge. He would face her parents, alone perhaps he thought, with the letters in his pocket, just in case - and having made that decision he gulped in the cold air and began singing quietly. The houses were shrouded in shadow as he passed along the frozen streets and as the tranquil aura travelled with him with no sound from anywhere around, even a breath of wind, he felt wonderfully at peace with the world as he neared his lodgings.

For fear of waking his landlady he lightened his tread as he approached and quite suddenly a searing pain bored into the pit of his stomach, making him double over, and he pressed a hand hard against his body as he heaved over to a wall for support. This had happened once before he remembered, but never so bad and he pressed his hand harder into his belly. He remembered Mary being concerned about this. Perhaps she had been right, but he'd always recovered before and, panting, he waited, hoping it would go. His stomach was always out of order these days he cursed, but this pain ... *God!* Never had it been so bad, never! Intensely sharp, it felt and seemed to be spreading slowly ... *what for Christ's sake's happening? My guts are burning up!* Then it disappeared and gratefully he caught his breath, taking gulps of fresh cold air with relief, until it came again, worse this time, making him double up as he clutched at his belly and fell to his knees retching violently into the gutter.

Chapter Twenty-Three

Emile managed to drag himself to his lodgings and lunging at the doorbell hammered at it before collapsing in agony once more. Frightened by the pounding on the door at such an hour, and hearing an agonised cry, his landlady dashed from her bed flinging the door wide. Crying out in alarm she stared at him huddled on the ground and wondered whether he was drunk, but there was no smell of drink when she leaned close and saw his face twisted in pain. Often, he had been unwell, particularly of late. But never this bad. Panting between spasms, he told her, 'It's just bile. I've had it before,' and gasping heavily to get his words out he pleaded for a glass of water. 'I'm burning up inside Mrs. Jenkins. Water might clear it through. It often does.'

Using the wall as a support, he staggered to his feet and she put out a steadying hand trying to help him inside. Every effort seemed too much and she struggled to keep him steady when he hesitated to draw breath. 'I never thought I'd make it.' He sounded weak and between gasps described how he'd crawled on all fours and how sick he'd been.

'It must be something ye 'et to mek ye this bad,' she said and with renewed alarm as he clutched at his stomach she grabbed a pan and thrust it under him as he dropped to his knees and vomited.

'I'll fetch the dochter,' she said, hurrying down the dark passage, getting halfway and running back again wringing her hands. 'This isnae right. I must get the dochter.'

'No!' he moaned with effort. 'No need. Just ... just the

water, Mrs. Jenkins,' he managed to say, thrusting a hand to make the point. 'I must drink. It'll clear.'

She scuttled away again, returning quickly with a cup and a candle held askew dripping wax. He looked ghastly, unable to take the cup and she held it to his lips as he steadied himself against the door. Briefly, he straightened after taking a few sips, holding his head back gulping air, and with help managed to stand upright unsteadily.

'If I can get to bed,' he mumbled, 'I'll be better,' and supporting him as best she could they staggered one step at a time up to his room, stopping now and then when he doubled over. Faltering outside the door and leaning against the wall, he gasped again for air. 'If I can sleep, I'll be better,' he mouthed.

'Give me ye arm,' she said, and lurching together as they pitched into the room, he sprawled across the bed, crouching in agony as he clutched at his stomach and Mrs. Jenkins shrunk away wondering what on earth to do.

'Perhaps some tea...' he said between gasps '...some tea,' he managed to say, 'I must drink... this awful thirst.'

She put a match to a candle, trembling as she lifted it, placing it in a safe place well away from the bed, then covering him with a blanket she bustled about the room, first one way then another mumbling. *Wad ye believe! Asking for tea at a time like this! ... 'E needs a dochter, not tea! ... somethin' was vera wrang – an' why didna he want a dochter? ...* This was him though, she told herself as she hurried out and lumbered downstairs. Never wants to trouble anyone or make a fuss that one and she snatched up a kettle in the kitchen and thrust it on what remained of the glowing embers. Then alarmingly she heard a scraping noise across the floor upstairs followed by groaning and she rushed out, loping up the stairs clumsily side-to-side, to discover Emile stretched face down across the bed vomiting into his chamber pot.

Trembling, and capable only of making sympathetic noises, she watched as he gradually eased himself back. *This was bad. She had to get help, whatever he said! This man needed help. Och! I'll go for the doctor despite what he said.* It was late she realised glancing at the clock and he would be abed but she could knock him up, although staring out at the deserted street and black windows opposite drained her confidence. No matter, she thought pulling herself together, but first that tea and hastening as quickly as she could downstairs, she bustled about the kitchen banging cupboards and dropping things.

It looked like he was sleeping when she returned and placing the tea quietly beside the bed she tiptoed from the room, feeling bad at leaving him but knowing he needed help. Something had to be done, and something more than a cup of tea, she thought, pulling on a coat.

★ ★ ★

'Give him some laudanum and hot water to drink and put a mustard plaster on his stomach.' The doctor's voice sounded thick as he called down from a top window. She had shouted endlessly outside his house after knocking uselessly at the door and after tossing shingle at the top window in desperation, it had suddenly shot up when the doctor appeared holding aloft a candle and scowling with indignation. 'I've been ill myself,' he told her when she pleaded for him to call at once. 'I'm unable to turn out now anyway,' he said as an afterthought. Already he began lowering the window, then pushed it up a bit and added reluctantly, 'Let me know how he is in a few hours. Try the laudanum... er... and... er... the mustard plaster.' Staring at the closed window as it darkened almost immediately after he'd disappeared, Mrs. Jenkins shuffled away, anxious what else she could do and mortified at the thought of what she may find when she got back.

She had left the street door ajar and all appeared to be quiet as she crept up the stairs fearfully and pushed the door to his room. His eyes were closed but he was clearly still in pain she thought as she moved closer to the bed, watching him clutch at his belly every now and then. He seemed weaker too as he tried raising his head when he noticed her there. The room reeked of vomit and she hurried away to fetch another chamber pot, leaning her head away trying not to look as she removed the one he'd used.

'Try tae tek a drink of water,' she insisted when she returned after hastily preparing what the doctor had suggested. He had already brushed away the laudanum, refusing adamantly to even try! The mustard plaster was equally useless as he tore at it and writhed pitifully when she'd tried fixing it in place. An ah'm useless too, she thought to herself, distraught beyond words now and worrying what else to do as she watched him taking laboured breaths until he gradually quietened.

★ ★ ★

At first light Mrs. Jenkins made her way back to the doctor, knocking repeatedly and begging him to call. 'Ah'm vera worried noo,' she said wringing her hands. 'E's still nae right. Really suff'ring dochter.' She had returned to her bed earlier for a few hours when Emile had calmed and appeared to be sleeping, although there had been no sleep for her that night and whenever she'd heard a sound she had been out of bed in a flash, rushing into his room to stand alongside his bed feeling hopelessly witless. Once she just made out 'water' as his words ran together incoherently and pouring from a jug she'd filled a glass, adding a dash of the laudanum that he'd already refused but hoped he'd try this time and holding it to his lips some of it dribbled in. He was still deathly pale with beads of perspiration glistening on his face and she felt her heart pumping as he began writhing fitfully again.

'Can you do nothin' fer the puir man?' she pleaded urgently when the doctor arrived and hurried up the stairs, but he didn't reply and she took deep breaths trying to calm herself as they moved towards the bed. The room still smelled foul and she felt ashamed as the doctor began fumbling in his bag.

'Is he a heavy drinker Mrs. Jenkins?' he mumbled.

'Nae 'e isn't. Aye I ken that for sure dochter.'

'And has he been like this before?' he asked, still sorting in his bag and not looking up.

'Only noo and then, altho' never as bad. 'E allas put it doon to bile.'

The doctor straightened and peering over his spectacles looked at her searchingly. 'For what reason does he put it down to bile as you say. Do you know where he had been when he felt like this? And what he'd been doing?'

She could not answer that and shook her head. She knew so little about him and said as much. ''E worked long hours,' she said thoughtfully. 'I knew that. An' 'e went awa mony times an oot at nicht, getting back late. I don't know where'd been of course an' I widna ask. I know 'e had health wearys. A long time 'e'd been like that, an' took medicine sometimes. I saw it in his room.'

The doctor knew well about Emile's history of indulgence in medicine and his many ailments, but this was something he could not account for. The man was obviously in severe agony and he was unable to understand why. 'I'll give him some morphine to relieve his pain,' he said flicking a syringe, and promising to call back later, he advised giving him plenty of hot water to drink and to apply a mustard plaster to ease the pain. 'I'll return in a couple of hours,' he said, snapping his bag shut. 'There should be an improvement by then,' and as the drug slowly took effect, Emile did become quieter. His room still reeked of vomit and she flung the windows wide still feeling ashamed of the stench in her well-ordered house with the doctor having stood there noticing it. There was little she could do though, and walked about muttering to herself. The chamber pot had slopped. His bed was a mess - and Emile was too, she saw, as she stood over him.

More than that, rather than improving as the doctor predicted, things suddenly took a turn for the worst. She'd returned to her room briefly after he had grown quieter for a bit and, rushing back when she heard him first mumbling then shouting, she discovered him sitting bolt upright with his eyes staring wildly and as she approached he flopped back with a groan and weakly thrust out a hand.

Petrified, she leaned over the reeking bed, 'Wha' is it?' and she leaned closer. He was whispering something but nothing made sense and almost retching herself from the stench she watched his lips. He seemed to be trying to form a name. 'Mary?' she said, 'is that what ye saying? 'Mary? Mary Perry?' she questioned trying to understand his rambling. 'You wanae to see 'er?'

His head lolled, the morphine curbing his movements as he flung about. 'Fe... fetch her,' she made out. P... please Mrs. Jen... Mary...' and with his voice fading and his eyes rolling up, he fell into a fitful stupor.

She called to the house-girl who had shot straight up the stairs on arrival after hearing a disturbance in the bedroom and now stood wide-eyed at the door.

'Come in gerl. Danae stand gawping.' And together

they cleaned up as best they could, the girl wrinkling her nose as she was bid, wiping up the vomit. Mrs. Jenkins hovered over Emile every now and again to reassure him when he groaned and when he quietened she stole from the room, pushing the girl before her and bidding her to fetch Mary Perry quick as she could. 'Tell 'er aboot whit's happened. Tell 'er Emile wants to see 'er. Tell 'er to be quick,' she insisted. 'Whitever she's doing tell 'er she must stop and hurry here noo. Quickly,' she said, flapping her hands, 'Off wi' ye!'

She looked into his room every few minutes when the girl had gone. For some time he had been quiet and appeared to be sleeping, she thought and tiptoed from the room, thanking God the drama seemed to have passed. When the girl came racing back announcing breathlessly that Mary promised to be here as soon as possible, Mrs. Jenkins recovered her bossy attitude sufficiently to be able to threaten her to go about her jobs as usual. 'And quietly!' she ordered ... and as she continued to glance into Emile's room, hovering over him watching for any sign of improvement, she was unable to settle to doing anything herself.

When the doctor returned later that morning, Mrs. Jenkins noticed Mary Perry hurrying up the road in the distance and leaving the door ajar for her, led the doctor upstairs.

'Aye I think 'e's better,' she told him. 'E's bin quiet a bit noo. Sleeping I think, thank goodness.' The room still smelled foul as they entered and hastily she removed the chamber pot, covering it with a cloth and stepping back as the doctor approached the bed to take a closer look. He placed a hand on Emile's forehead for a second, searching for his watch in a pocket with his other hand and taking up Emile's wrist, felt for a pulse.

'Thank God. 'E's better at last,' Mrs. Jenkins said

breathing a sigh of relief. 'This 'as bin so awful. Juist dreadful!'

The doctor looked up, quietly regarding her over his glasses, and glancing down at the bed again he slowly lowered Emile's wrist. 'I'm afraid not madam,' he said, and taking up a corner of the sheet he drew it high to cover Emile's face as he announced that he was dead.

Chapter Twenty-Four

The enormous shock of Emile's death stunned Mrs. Jenkins into disbelief and her mouth gaped wide before she managed to stammer, 'I thought 'im being quieter meant...'

The doctor put out a reassuring hand and taking her elbow led her out of the room and down the stairs. Mary still waited in the hall, not knowing what had happened yet aware something was badly wrong by their expressions. Choking back a sob, Mrs. Jenkins faced her with the appalling news as the doctor left and unable to take it in at first Mary stared unbelievingly in the painful silence before making a dash upstairs.

'I've 'ad no time to freshen the room Mary. It's orful in there,' but Mary had already reached the landing insisting she had to see him as Mrs. Jenkins stumped clumsily up behind her protesting.

The smell of death mingled with the foulness of Emile's last agonising hours as Mary pushed open the door slowly, the silence foreboding as she moved across to the bed. Plucking a corner of the sheet she drew it back carefully and for what seemed an eternity gazed at the face she had loved for so long and had never admitted to anyone, or him. Then dropping to her knees she began weeping uncontrollably, unaware of Mrs. Jenkins standing close by with a hand on her shoulder.

'This is dretful Mary,' she said at last. 'You was so close...' she started and immediately jumped back, startled by Mary's sudden reaction as she swung round. 'We were just good friends Mrs. Jenkins,' she said flatly. 'Just friends.'

Mary's distress was disturbing, but more so was what she had just heard and without thinking blurted out, 'I thought ye were courting Mary. 'E asked for you me dear,' she said with her voice rising. 'On 'is deathbed 'e asked. Ye were the only one he wanted Mary. That's why I sent for ye.'

Mary moved over to the window, her shoulders rising and falling rapidly as she gasped deep breaths. 'I was a very good friend to Emile Mrs. Jenkins,' she said at last in a low voice, still facing the street. 'A very good friend,' and turning now to confront her, went on quietly, 'Just that Mrs. Jenkins. Nothing more. He confided in me at times and we talked - many times. But we were just friends.'

The bitter tone in Mary's voice came as a surprise and she felt unsure what to say as Mary went on to explain that Madeleine Smith was the woman he loved.

'It was never me Mrs. Jenkins,' she said fixing her with a look devoid of emotion. 'Madeleine Smith was the woman he adored, and he visited her frequently. Late at night generally. They were lovers Mrs. Jenkins.'

Further than that, Mary refused to be drawn, despite the barrage of questions following and turning to leave, she walked slowly back to the bed. Her lips had to remain sealed she decided. As she gazed down at Emile once more, her face softened and closing her eyes, she stooped to kiss his forehead and briefly laid her fingers on his lips. For a moment, she hesitated with her hands resting on the bed and before leaving, she lifted the sheet and folded it down clear of his face. She could not bear him not to be part of her world.

'Someone oughter tell this Madeleine Smith what's 'appened then don't you think?' Mrs. Jenkins said thickly as she followed Mary out of the room.

'It's no business of mine,' she said sharply hurrying

down the stairs and making for the door. Then suddenly she stopped and hesitated before wheeling round - and with an uncharacteristic look of spite said, 'Yes.' Nodding thoughtfully, she continued, 'I do believe you are right Mrs. Jenkins. Madeleine Smith should be informed about Emile's death,' and as she turned to leave announced that she would go straight to the Smith household to inform her.

★ ★ ★

Having changed her mind by the time she reached the Smith's house, Mary Perry abandoned the polite greetings when Madeleine opened the door and asked instead to see her mother. Her distress was patently obvious however, and barely able to conceal her bitterness, she waved aside Madeleine's concern and offer of refreshment.

'Are you sure? A cup of tea perhaps Mary?' Madeleine insisted. 'You are obviously very put out.'

'I wish to see Mrs. Smith alone,' was Mary's tight-lipped reply. 'My visit concerns your mother only. I want to make that clear,' and with a tilt of her chin, she turned to stroll into the drawing room at Madeleine's bidding to await Mrs. Smith's arrival.

Although curious, Madeleine's interest quickly vanished as she went in search of her mother. There was still much to occupy her mind preparing for her forthcoming wedding and when things like this got in the way, it had the effect of making her irritable. Her mother on the other hand immediately panicked. With her dwindling strength aggravating her nervous disposition, she had become increasingly dependent on Madeleine who managed such matters to a large extent. So fearful of facing something she may not be able to handle when informed that Mary Perry had arrived in some distress and wished to see her alone, she entered the drawing room with great trepidation.

Spite was unquestionably in Mary's mind when she had taken the responsibility of breaking the news about Emile's death and with a fixed expression informed Elizabeth Smith in blunt terms exactly what had happened.

'You may - or may not - perhaps,' she said after her lengthy account, 'have known about your daughter's association with Emile L'Angelier.' And with no comments forthcoming from Mrs. Smith, whose face had frozen into a mask of misery, continued, 'Unfortunately I was at one time instrumental in delivering letters between Madeleine and Emile – quite innocently you may be assured - although of late I refused to have any further dealings of the kind.' She went on to explain at some length about, as she put it, a suspected romance, albeit not revealing her knowledge of their secret meetings at night in the Smith's house, or about Emile's recent confidential chats to her about Madeleine's behaviour, which could obviously come later if need be she decided.

Mrs. Smith continued listening impassively, raising a hand every now and then and covering her lips in horror, until Mary mentioned that in view of Emile's sudden death, questions may be asked about her involvement with him, and Elizabeth's face transformed immediately.

'Why?' she asked in a voice pitched high in alarm.

'I cannot say. I don't know. It is as a friend that I am here. I wish you to be aware Mrs. Smith, for whatever may happen. As I say, Madeleine may be asked questions, but I cannot say anything further. I don't know any more!' This nevertheless had the effect she intended and hating herself for upsetting someone who had been a friend over many years, Mary apologised for being the bearer of such awful news and excused herself politely. It was towards Madeleine that her spite had been directed for bringing misery to a man she loved so dearly, although she had to admit that the satisfaction of exposing Madeleine did very little to relieve her pain.

Mrs. Smith, a tiny trembling figure on the point of losing control, remained on the same spot long after Mary had left, staring into space, nervously twitching at her gown. She knew her husband was at home but feared facing him with the news knowing there would be a violent reaction simply by mentioning the Frenchman's name. This news had drained what remained of the confidence she had summoned when told about Mary's distress and her desire to talk with her alone, yet she had to do something, and taking several deep breaths, she decided the right thing would be to confront Madeleine. She would seek the truth first-hand, but before getting any further than opening the door, there came a thunderous hammering at the front door that brought the maid rushing from the kitchen, her husband marching indignantly out of his study, and sent her scuttling back up the stairs and into her room where she huddled beneath the bedcovers.

★ ★ ★

The gentleman, who demanded in a loud voice to see Mr. Smith, was shown into the drawing room by the maid where he strutted about impatiently until Madeleine's father entered with thumbs thrust into his waistcoat, glaring at the stranger who'd had the audacity to thump at his door.

'Auguste de Mean, sir,' he announced, extending a hand. 'Chancellor to the French Consulate at Glasgow and a close friend of Emile L'Angelier. Without giving Mr. Smith a chance to speak, he launched straight into a graphic description of his friend's sudden death that morning and embellished this information with details about Emile's association with his daughter.

'I know nothing of this,' Mr. Smith blustered, shaking his head vigorously until his cheeks quivered. 'What are you saying?'

'The full implication of the situation is not known at the moment sir. I have merely come to warn you...'

'Warn me! What do you mean warn me? Warn me about what?'

De Mean put out a restraining hand, 'If you will allow me to continue Mr. Smith.'

Realising there was no point in a dispute with someone of this standing, Mr. Smith stood back, stiffening abruptly.

'I am sorry to be the bearer of this news Mr. Smith,' he apologised. 'I'm truly sorry in the circumstances. This has obviously come as a shock and you appear to have no knowledge about your daughter's association with my friend L'Angelier.'

'Indeed. I have not!'

'Again, I regret having to be your informant sir. You have my full sympathy, but I have to tell you - and I do this in all good faith before gossip or enquiries from other sources reaches you - that your daughter has written many letters. Intimate letters sir, I understand, and they are in Emile L'Angelier's room where he lies at this moment.' Hesitating briefly, he lowered his eyes and with a slight tremor in his voice when he glanced up, he continued in a voice edged with pity. 'My friend has been the victim of an untimely death Mr. Smith,' he continued. 'And I must emphasise, although I haven't seen the letters myself, I must point out, that they could be... ah... somewhat incriminating.'

'Incriminating! Whatever do you mean? Why should

they be incriminating? This is foolish female behaviour - writing letters!'

'It appears that my friend L'Angelier visited your daughter late at night - on many occasions sir. At your house, I understand, - and after his last visit, the night before he died, he became violently ill when he reached home.'

Mr. Smith's bulky stature appeared to droop and noting his sudden pallor of shock, de Mean decided he had said enough for the time being and chose to leave this unfortunate man to deal with the situation as best he could. For a considerable time, Emile had been his good friend - who despite his considerable counselling had foolishly allowed himself to become besotted with a girl who trifled abominably with his affection - and he felt compelled to stand by him. Nevertheless, with knowledge about Mr.Smith's status in society, he also felt it his duty to visit and inform him about his daughter's dalliance with Emile before the authorities became involved, which they undoubtedly would as things stood. In any case he was determined to find out for himself why his friend had died so tragically in mysterious circumstances. Having achieved his formidable task, Auguste de Mean extended a hand and bid an abrupt, 'Good-day.' And as both men reached the door, he stopped suddenly, announcing that he would like to return later that day to talk to Madeleine. 'I have to emphasise sir, my friend Emile L'Angelier has suffered a premature death in what appears to be unusual and very suspicious circumstances,' and as he turned to leave he added in sombre tones, 'and I fear the consequences.'

★ ★ ★

Similarly to his wife after Mary Perry had called earlier, Mr. Smith remained rooted to the spot long after his visitor had left. Initially he had felt utter relief learning about L'Angelier's death, until advised about his daughter's involvement with this wretched man. He had always feared this association may have continued and now knowing this to be the case ... *with written evidence for all to see for God's sake!* ... he felt his hands tightening into fists as his anger rose beyond reasonable thinking. His daughter had outrageously flouted his ban to see this philanderer and, what's more, indulged in an affair under his own roof, with a flow of seamy letters to prove it!

Madeleine had sorely tried him on many occasions in the past and he realised that dealing with this devastating situation would be a threat to his composure. He had to discover for himself nevertheless, what had been going on after hearing this appalling news and, struggling to keep his feelings under control, he stormed off to her room bellowing her name at the top of his voice.

'So you disobeyed!' he thundered. 'You lied. You betrayed your parents,' and Madeleine, who was so far unaware of the alarming news imparted to her parents, registered only mild concern when she'd heard her father stamping along the corridor. Panic shot through her however when he charged into her room after flinging the door wide and she shrunk back in alarm wondering what was about to happen. His eyes were cold and full of hatred, his face puce with anger and spittle collecting on his mouth. Never had she seen her father in such a temper.

'You have been with that Frenchman!' and his eyes narrowed menacingly as he sneered, 'that common little Frenchman I forbad you ever to see again, and intimately I understand!' Raising a fist as he approached, she thrust a protecting hand, fearful of being struck. 'I have just been informed about this my girl, by a complete stranger!'

Madeleine cringed away, thinking quickly. Was this

anything to do with Mary Perry being so distressed? Had Emile been to the house as he had threatened?

'Tell me father,' she said, trying to keep her voice steady. 'I don't understand. What is wrong?'

'Wrong? You tell me what is wrong my girl,' he said stabbing a finger. 'You tell me what's been going on behind my back.'

Madeleine's effort endeavouring to remain calm had the effect of infuriating her father to such an extent that she feared for her safety as he took a menacing step. Ridiculously, there was nothing she could say in defence of something she knew absolutely nothing about, and although still not understanding, she nevertheless decided it wise to keep a distance between them. She edged round the back of a table, trembling now, until her father suddenly called her a whore and at this she blazed.

'How dare you call me that? How can you say that about your own daughter?'

'Do you deny it?'

'What do you expect me to say? Have you no respect for your family?'

'Respect! Don't you talk to me about respect my girl when you have been cavorting with that common little Frenchman. Here. Under my roof, I understand. While the family have been asleep, and writing him letters.'

Madeleine flinched. So despite everything, Emile had taken her letters to the house after all. It was all out, her parents knew everything, and she was at their mercy.

'He wanted to marry me father,' she said clutching at excuses. 'I tried to stop him... kept telling him... and he threatened...'

'Marry! Marry you! How can he marry you? He's dead girl. And his room is stuffed full of letters from you about carrying on with him, and in my house!' He towered over her threateningly, lowering his voice. 'Do you deny it now?'

'Oh my God!' Madeleine clamped a hand over her mouth, fear clutching the pit of her stomach as she felt her father's hot breath.

He strutted away, then immediately wheeled round bringing his face within inches of hers again. 'You've got some explaining to do my girl,' he scorned in a low voice. 'There are questions that have to be answered. Your lover has been found dead, after visiting you apparently! People will be coming here, to the house. My house!' he roared. 'Asking questions and demanding answers. Someone has already called this morning to inform me about this. Someone I have never clapped eyes on before telling me what has been happening behind my back! And he is coming back later I understand, to see you. To ask questions. Do you understand now?' he bellowed.

Madeleine managed to pluck an iota of strength and in a steady voice said, 'I am sorry to learn about Emile L'Angelier's death. Yes, I admit having seen him father,' she continued hurriedly, 'but there has never been any illicit association between us. I can assure you of that.'

'I don't believe you!' he roared. 'You lie!'

As though she hadn't heard, Madeleine continued without flinching or changing her tone. 'Furthermore,' she went on, 'there have been no letters of which I am ashamed. How could there possibly be when we hardly knew one another?' With that, she managed to slip in front of her father who stood open-mouthed as she rushed for the door with her head held high. 'If you require me to talk to mother,' she said, turning briefly, 'I will do so now if you wish,' and struggling to keep her voice steady added, 'and certainly I will receive anyone else who may desire to see me, or to ask any questions.'

'Come back here,' he thundered making a lunge ...
Auguste de Mean had convinced him about this affair with

L'Angelier. So it must be true! A man like that would not do otherwise! ... Yet here she was denying it all. Proclaiming her innocence, and looking it bedamned!

'Don't you dare defy me about this!' he threatened, grabbing her arm. Although terrified, and trapped in something she couldn't immediately handle, Madeleine managed to wrench herself away. Never before had she needed to rely on physical strength to defy her father as she did now, or dared to flaunt her defiance when she screamed at him, 'I propose continuing with my marriage arrangements despite all this, she said, flinging a hand. 'I have not seen Emile L'Angelier for several weeks and the circumstances of his death are as big a mystery to me as to you, or anyone else you say you have seen.' And tearing her sleeve from his grip, she rushed from the room, picking her way carefully so as not to betray her trembling, and with her skirt billowing she raced along the corridor and fled up to her mother's room.

★ ★ ★

When Auguste de Mean called at the house later that day asking to see Madeleine, she was already in the drawing room with her mother and rose elegantly to meet him when he entered with her father. She had gathered confidence about her like a suit of armour and unflinchingly extended a hand in greeting. Auguste de Mean, however, was in no mood for pleasantries and after a swift exchange of hands launched straight into the attack.

'I understand my friend Emile L'Angelier visited you late in the evening on Sunday Miss Smith,' he started, and ignoring Madeleine's attempts at protesting otherwise, and without even looking at her, hurried on in a loud voice, 'According to the landlady at the premises, he left his room at 11pm, apparently quite well,' he emphasised, glancing at her quickly. 'And it was on his return early the following morning, when she discovered him on the doorstep in agony and where...' he paused momentarily here gazing at each person in turn in order to make a point, 'where, in his bed some hours later, he died in what the doctor described as rather strange circumstances.'

If Auguste de Mean had intended such a devastating blow to the group standing before him he had certainly achieved it. Mrs. Smith collapsed in tears and began looking around for a chair. For once, her husband was lost for words and for a split second Madeleine's face revealed panic. Noticing the latter, de Mean then launched into his next challenging statement.

'My friend Emile L'Angelier did visit you on Sunday night Miss Smith,' he said coldly, and not waiting for an answer went on to describe the consequences that would undoubtedly follow should she choose to dispute this. 'This man was a good friend, as I've already indicated to your father, and I want to know the truth about what happened that evening.'

Madeleine's gaze never wavered ... *how dare he! A complete stranger ... calling at her home ... interfering in her affairs ... demanding explanations!* She faced him defiantly having recovered from her initial shock, and answering in a similarly assertive manner demanded to know why he had come to ask such questions of her and on what authority.

At this Mr. Smith thrust himself between Madeleine and de Mean, first apologising profusely for her behaviour and turning to face her angrily protested, 'This gentleman is here to help you Madeleine. Answer!' And as he shifted away to join his wife who now sat snivelling in her chair Madeleine noticed the sweat heavy on his brow and veins protruding in his neck.

Taking her time as she shifted her position, Madeleine faced de Mean and in a voice clear of any emotion stated, 'I swear I have not seen Emile L'Angelier,' and turning in her father's direction nodded to reinforce her earlier statement to him.

'You must have seen him on that Sunday night,' de Mean persisted, 'and there are bound to be others who would have seen him on his journey if questions are subsequently asked. Of that you may be absolutely sure Miss Smith.' He pursed his lips as he looked at her speculatively before continuing. 'I know for a fact that my friend came back to Glasgow in order to meet you, and that cannot be disputed,' he said. 'We were together that weekend you see and he told me of his intention to visit you.'

Still without emotion, Madeleine went on to state vehemently that she could give no reason whatever to account for Emile's untimely death and still declaring her irreproachable behaviour she again pointed out that he had never at any time visited her home. This she did with a further nod at her father and went on to state that as she had been forbidden to indulge in this relationship she would never have dared invite him into her home!

De Mean knew she was lying but realised also that there was little further he could do. Despite his attempt to help her God-fearing parents - if help he could in these abominable circumstances he thought - it would now be down to the authorities to take whatever action was necessary. He said, 'There is nothing further to say or to be done then,' and turning his back to Madeleine he faced Mr. Smith as he prepared to leave. Like de Mean, Madeleine's father also felt his daughter was keeping information concealed, but not wishing to lose face at this point he shook the man's hand warmly, thanked him for coming and escorted him out of the room.

Madeleine felt she had disguised her feelings well and noting her mother's distress walked sedately across the room and placed a comforting arm around her shoulders, soothing and tut-tutting sympathy for all this nonsense over something that had nothing whatsoever to do with them. 'We'll go up to your room,' she said with feeling, and without even a fleeting glance at the two men now talking earnestly at the front door, Madeleine and her mother made their way slowly up the stairs.

Chapter Twenty-Five

Emile's sudden death brought a swift reaction in many directions. When he failed to arrive at his place of work, and with a strong rumour already circulating among the staff about a young man living nearby found dead in suspicious circumstances, one of the managers, Arthur Huggins, intervened immediately to stop the gossip. And taking it upon himself to investigate personally, he visited his employee's lodgings to confirm one way or the other.

Faced with the appalling truth after being shown to Emile's room where his body was now laid out in burying robes, and calling to mind the scandalous talk he'd heard from the staff, Arthur Huggins' immediate reaction was to insist on a post mortem examination being carried out. Earlier that day the doctor had decided against the necessity for this and faced with this demand from someone he neither knew nor respected, saw it as a downright intrusion by someone outside the medical circle to be so presumptuous. With a strong suspicion that some impropriety had taken place however, Huggins stood firm, and with his rhetoric about his employee's exemplary sober habits and fine lifestyle as far as he was aware, arrangements were made for this to be done.

Having been left alone for a while in his employee's room when Mrs. Jenkins hurried away to deal with another caller, Huggins also took the opportunity of a swift look round and noticing Emile's diary with letters tucked between pages, assumed full responsibility for its removal.

'Emile L'Angelier was a fine, upstanding gentleman

who served me well for a considerable time,' he told Mrs. Jenkins authoritatively when he left, 'and it is my duty to honour his service and do whatever I am able to in investigating his untimely death.'

Completely out of her depth with the constant stream of people calling at the house and removing all manner of items, she took the business card he handed over, showing where he could be contacted if needed and with a final woeful glance towards the bed he bade her 'Good-day' and made a quiet, respectful exit.

★ ★ ★

In this escalating drama, life went on much as usual in the Smith household as far as Madeleine was concerned. William Minnoch, who had no knowledge so far of the alarming events taking place, continued to court Madeleine in the same devoted manner and with her unremitting air of innocence about anything untoward having happened, she thought fit not to inform him otherwise. All this changed very rapidly however, the morning after the couple had spent a pleasant evening together and Mr. Smith sought William at an early hour to inform him that his daughter had mysteriously disappeared! As his account unfolded about Emile L'Angelier's sudden death, William listened with mild interest but never having heard of the man up to now it meant very little until Mr. Smith broke the news that Madeleine had been involved with him in some way.

'However can she be involved?' he asked in astonishment. 'I don't even know the man. Never heard of him - and I am sure she would have said.'

Amazed by his lack of knowledge with L'Angelier's name on everyone's lips - and the rumours circulating like wildfire - Mr. Smith thought better of enlightening him at that point. What had to be investigated straight away was Madeleine's sudden disappearance and the responsibility for that lay with the family, as it did also with William Minnoch as her intended husband he decided. Despite the seriousness of the situation, he continued to feel increasingly irritated by this stupid female behaviour, although with the finger of suspicion now aimed at his daughter in this sordid business - and with the whole family likely to be involved soon he realised - something had to be done, and quickly.

He had already thought through what action to take and without bothering to seek their opinions informed Madeleine's brother Jack and William they should set out on a search. After much arguing and suggestions, it was decided Rowaleyn to be the most likely place to start looking.

'It's the only place she knows well,' said her father, 'and the journey is familiar,' and with a glance at the clock he suggested the two of them set out straight away. 'It's still early,' he said, as he began hustling them into action, 'she could possibly be intercepted on the journey.'

'She could have gone in the middle of the night - in which case she may already be there!' Jack suggested, already shrugging into a coat.

'Quite impossible,' William interrupted, 'we were together until late last night and there was no suspicion about any of this when I left her, and how would she have reached the station on her own? More to the point would there have been a train then?'

Irritated by this useless talk, James Smith suggested she could have gone anywhere - at any time and by any means - and with her future husband within hearing kept to himself any further comments about stupid female behaviour!

'It could be a wild goose chase,' he said, trying to keep the exasperation out of his voice, 'and if it means going all the way to the house, then so be it! At least we will have tried. I'll take both of you to the station in any case,' he said, getting up, 'although I'll not accompany you. I'll get in touch with local people when I get back, people we know who may be able to throw some light on what's happened ... and in any case it's best for me to stay at the house should anyone call. With all this going on my wife is not in a fit state to be alone.'

On the way to the station nobody spoke. All three were wrapped in their own thoughts, William largely concerned for his bride-to-be, but at the same time puzzled about what was happening, Jack busily conjuring up many interesting situations he dared not voice and James Smith continuing to fume inwardly about his daughter's disgraceful behaviour in the face of his authority.

When they reached the station, however, everyone sprang into action. William dashed up to a barely awake porter to enquire whether a young lady of Madeleine's description was seen boarding the earlier train. Jack raced to the platform to check the time of the next train and Mr. Smith made his way to the ticket office.

Having confirmed, after a befuddled conversation with the porter, that someone resembling Madeleine had been seen boarding the early train, William and Jack contained their frustration for over an hour in a nearby pub until the next train for Greenock pulled in. One thing in their favour they realised once they got under way was a delay linking up with the onward boat journey to Rowaleyn. This would give them a chance, if they were quick, of intercepting her at the dock if she happened to be there - and both men were sharp on the lookout as the train slowly ground to a stop some time later.

'I believe she's over there,' Jack shouted, rushing from

the station, and William pounding after him had people flinching in all directions out of his way. It was difficult to pick out anyone in the crush of people waiting for the boat but Jack seemed to think he had spotted her in the distance and calling her name at the top of his voice as enquiring faces turned in his direction, he raced through the barrier. Sprinting close behind, William waved desperately. He had seen her he was sure and calling and waving, the waiting crowd now turned in her direction as she craned her neck to see what all the fuss was about, and when they reached her, hot, sweating profusely and breathing hard, she stared at them speechlessly in bewilderment.

There was a catch in her voice and they could see she was on the verge of tears. 'My family were in such distress over this awful business,' was all she could say following their barrage of questions. 'And with me being the cause of such an upset what more could I do than to get right away from everybody so as not to cause any further trouble.' She mumbled so quietly they could hardly hear, but neither of them said anything further.

Trying to ignore the interest when he noticed people easing in closer, William offered a protective arm and led her away. He saw her distress and suspecting she may break down at any time decided against further questioning and whispered, 'I just thank God that you are safe Madeleine and that I'm here to look after you,' and this was all he cared about anyway at that moment as people began turning away. 'If only you knew how worried we were though,' he went on once they were out of earshot, 'and without a word about where you were going! We were at our wits' end,' he said.

'I shouldn't have left,' she apologised, 'not when you have been so kind William...' and she could not go on as she choked back a sob.

He talked about his total ignorance about what had happened as they made their way back to the station, either deliberately to make it easier for her, or maybe it was for himself he thought. He was not sure. 'I'm certain it did not merit you fleeing like that in any case. Surely?' he said kindly.

Madeleine managed to hold back her tears. Having aroused so much interest in the commotion they had caused in the crowd, her one thought now was to get away. There was time enough to talk. Perhaps on the way back. She had to enlighten William some time anyway and he would understand she felt sure. Whether he would accept the situation, and fully understand as she supposed when they had all settled for the journey back home, he certainly did not commit himself. She talked ceaselessly about her involvement with L'Angelier and the visit to their home by his friend Auguste de Mean while he listened without comment – and in heavily embroidered terms to place her in a good light, she touched on her letters that had been discovered. 'He was just a friend, William,' she insisted, turning to him with a pained expression. 'He was an acquaintance. Someone I have known for some while - and I cannot think why everyone is so interested in my association with him,' she said with her eyes growing large in amazement.

William continued to remain silent however as he reflected on the situation. What could he say anyway, he thought - and even if he did know what had been happening, should he intervene anyway at this stage? He nevertheless felt disturbed and relied on Jack's animated conversation with Madeleine for the rest of the journey back to Glasgow as he dwelt on her predicament. *Why had she been corresponding with a man he knew nothing about? And what was in those letters causing such interest?*

★ ★ ★

Madeleine took straight to her bed when they arrived home in the late afternoon feigning exhaustion after the drama and travelling. More truthfully, she wished to escape another violent outburst from her father - or indeed cause any further anxiety to her mother who had not ventured from her room since Auguste de Mean had called the previous day.

Events outside the home however were moving fast. Following the post mortem examination, it was revealed that L'Angelier's body contained a quantity of arsenic large enough to kill at least forty men, and the police began stepping up their investigations. Checks were made on people who had purchased arsenic from druggists in the area and following the examination of several organs taken from his body, it was concluded that L'Angelier had either consumed a large quantity of arsenic with the intention of committing suicide, or had been murdered.

Despite the worsening situation, and his growing disquiet about what had been going on in this L'Angelier affair, William Minnoch continued his undivided loyalty to Madeleine. In turn, she feared that the malicious gossip circulating in the district might turn him against her and decided the time had come to divulge more information about her association with Emile. She also thought fit to put him in the picture about her use of arsenic as a cosmetic and depilatory in case her name happened to turn up on one of the poison registers!

'I understand that checks are being made on people who have bought arsenic at local druggists,' she told him – and simpering casually she explained how she had heard about its value as a cosmetic while she had been at the school in London. William listened impassively as she enlightened him where and how she had obtained the arsenic. 'One druggist even questioned me over and over,' she said indignantly. 'And I could hardly say I wanted it as a beauty aid could I? I would have been much too embarrassed! - and although I explained I wanted it for getting rid of the rats in the garden he still looked at me suspiciously!'

William Minnoch was no fool however and decided to keep an open mind; although he still found it difficult to allow any doubts about the girl he was to marry being linked with anything so gruesome as murder.

'So if my name appears on a poisons register, you may be sure I have an unblemished conscience,' Madeleine had continued, and laying a reassuring hand on his arm told him it was preposterous to suppose she was in any way involved with this ghastly affair. 'There is absolutely nothing for any of us to be concerned about, except of course to be sad for the family of this poor man ... whoever they may be,' she hurriedly added. 'I really can't stand these pointing fingers though and dreadful rumours that are circulating,' she said. 'It really is quite ridiculous – and so tiresome!'

Despite this protective cloak of innocence she had drawn around her, Madeleine nevertheless refrained from appearing outside the house if she could avoid it. There had always been a smile for her from neighbours who had been looking forward to a wedding before all this happened. Now people bowed their heads pretending not to notice when she passed by and women in groups stopped talking until she was well away from hearing. The whole family also hurried through the streets with downcast eyes whenever compelled to leave the house and Mrs. Smith never ventured out – or seldom out of her room nowadays! - and her husband had all but withdrawn from public life.

The biggest blow however, was when William announced that it would be prudent to postpone the forthcoming marriage a little longer 'Until all this nonsense has died down,' he reassured Madeleine's parents. 'For the time being I shall say nothing to her and I think it best she doesn't know. She has more than enough to contend with at the moment in any case,' he said with feeling. And this turned out to be a wise move when the finger of suspicion pointed more strongly towards Madeleine when her name showed up several times on poison registers in Glasgow.

Chapter Twenty-Six

With evidence accumulating about her involvement with Emile L'Angelier and his sudden death, Madeleine was summoned to attend an interview at the office of Archibald Smith, the Sheriff-Substitute of Lanarkshire where she was required to make a statement. In her usual fashion, she irritatingly dismissed this request as disgracefully wrong. She was nevertheless compelled to attend and her father, who by this time had resigned himself to a state of affairs over which he had no control, accompanied her to the interview in a state of depression. Despite her diminutive height alongside his usually imposing figure of authority however, his daughter's air of the unjustly accused carried them both into the office with dignity when they came face to face with officials.

The gloomy office, oppressive, dusty and smelling of stale tobacco smoke, offered little comfort as they were ushered in and the only shred of encouragement to Madeleine as she walked sedately towards the Sheriff-Substitute and stood before him with her head held high, was his apparent embarrassment. Having quickly picked up this discomposure to boost her confidence, Madeleine then afforded a charming smile and bowed her head becomingly as he peered over his spectacles - and after shifting about noisily and clearing his throat several times, he launched into the formalities.

'You are required to make a Declaration before me which will be recorded in writing,' he explained, indicating the clerk sitting alongside ready with pen and paper. 'You will of course have the opportunity of reading it through and making any comment before signing Miss Smith.' And speaking slowly and deliberately he made it clear that should a trial ensue following her statement, she would not be entitled, by law, to make any further comment, or to refute any evidence which may contrast with what she regarded as the truth. He fixed her with a penetrating glare as he hesitated and suddenly asked in a loud voice that made her flinch, 'Do you understand Madeleine Smith, having explained this to you, that what you are about to tell me will be your only chance to defend yourself concerning the circumstances you are currently facing?'

Quickly recovering, Madeleine confirmed in a confident voice that she understood perfectly well everything he had just said - and even managed another brilliant smile ... wasted as it happened as Archibald Smith immediately rapped out his first question.

'Where did you meet L'Angelier?' he asked, and barely allowing her time to reply, leaned forward to ask, 'And how often did you meet together? Why did you buy the arsenic mentioned? And for what purpose did you require this? And answer me this Miss Smith,' he continued relentlessly, 'did you at any time make drinks or give food to the deceased when he visited you?'

Her father's eyes never left his daughter, watching her growing indignation as the unceasing questions followed one after another and she began stumbling over her answers. He noticed her tightly clasped hands, her knuckles white from clenching - and the way she sat ramrod straight. A twitching muscle he also saw and a sudden quiver on her lip at one time when she felt unsure about a reply - and as Madeleine dug her nails into her hands to stop them trembling she was telling herself over and over ... *I must not give way. I must stay strong. I must not betray fear.*

The Sheriff-Substitute produced the box of letters taken from Emile's room, plucking out one marked with a tag and opening it with a flourish before handing it to her. It was the last letter she had written and scanning it quickly she handed it back as though it had no consequence whatever.

'This letter requests a visit from Emile L'Angelier to inform him about my forthcoming marriage to William Minnoch,' she said primly. And with no comment or show of having heard, Archibald Smith continued with his relentless questions about her affair with L'Angelier, voiced with a touch of irritation now and urging her to embellish everything in detail whenever she held back any relevant detail.

She mentioned Emile's proposal of marriage, although chose not to say anything about her refusal and how he had threatened emotional blackmail by going to her father with the letters. She replied to all the questions staccato fashion with at least no outward show of emotion, until the Sheriff-Substitute suddenly asked again whether she had given anything to Emile L'Angelier, either to eat or drink, that would cause him to become ill, and at this she rose instantly from her chair and faced him with scorn.

'Never did I do any such thing!' she exclaimed with disgust, and the man scribbling notes alongside the Sheriff-Substitute looked up unbelievably in the shocked silence. This unexpected reaction further infuriated Archibald Smith who now stood staring at her tight-lipped before continuing with his questions about refreshments - until with more reserve Madeleine was finally forced into admitting that she had prepared drinks of cocoa on various occasions, 'And just cocoa,' she pointed out with her voice rising. 'No food,' and believing she had satisfied him with this information went on to stress with some indignation, 'and I also drank the cocoa that I had prepared. We drank it together at the same time.'

Precise details were recorded of when she bought arsenic and where, with exact information extracted about how she intended using it, to which she replied slowly at one time, 'I'm not quite sure whether I was asked what it was for,' and then rambled on to say she couldn't remember if she had ever been asked to give a reason. 'But... oh yes,' she said, flourishing a hand in sudden recall, 'I believe on one occasion I did say it was for the gardener to destroy vermin,' and went on sheepishly to explain she did not wish the chemist to know she wanted to use it as a cosmetic.

Whether appropriate or not at this point, the Sheriff-Substitute repeated his earlier warning that the document to be prepared would represent the only statement she would be allowed to make, 'Whether summoned for trial or otherwise Miss Smith,' he told her again sourly as he frowned over his spectacles. And despite the incriminating information gradually building up, she continued to behave like the injured party - and to the embarrassment of her father protested her innocence whenever the occasion arose – even adding after an explanation at one time, in a voice bordering on exasperation, 'in this sordid affair!'

After the laboriously extensive interview, Madeleine and her father were ushered to a bench to await the preparation of the Declaration. Both were quietly contained in their own thoughts and neither spoke as they sat listening to the background of mumbling coming from another room. By this time, her father felt humbled beyond words and it showed. He was utterly out of his depth in this horrific situation and in contrast to his usual figure of authority, he sat hunched over his knees fearing what would happen next. Madeleine on the other hand continued to uphold her composure as the innocent victim as she had throughout the entire procedure and sitting erect - still of the opinion that all this was a ghastly mistake - she showed no outward emotion whatever as she stared unflinchingly into space.

When the Sheriff-Substitute, the clerk and other officials returned to the office, they watched Archibald Smith shuffling the papers into order and as he placed them carefully on the desk before him in a tidy pile, he looked across at them and requested they return to their seats before him. When invited to do so Madeleine read the Declaration and not a murmur was heard as she scanned the papers, flipping them back to read again at one point. After solemnly swearing that everything written there to be the truth, the whole truth and nothing but the truth, she then nodded her approval and signed her name in a flourishing style at the end of the document. The Sheriff-Substitute, his clerk and other officials then stood with downcast eyes as Madeleine rose from her chair with a smile and in her usual dignified way she bowed her head graciously and with her father ambling alongside, left the office at Archibald Smith's bidding in a formidable hush.

Everyone in that room knew that preparations were already in progress for her arrest and before she had even reached the door to the street she was approached by two police officers who told her that she was to be taken to the North Prison in Glasgow 'to await trial Madeleine Smith,' one of the officers announced in strident tones, 'on two charges of attempted murder by poisoning and one charge of murder by the poisoning of Pierre Emile L'Angelier'.

Her father following close behind ignored the police officers as they positioned themselves either side of his daughter, pushing through and shuffling between them, telling Madeleine in a trembling voice that there was nothing for her to worry about. 'I will arrange for legal advisers straight away,' he said in a voice she barely recognised and when she turned to him and held one of his hands briefly, she lowered her eyes when she saw the tears forming in his. Then with a fleeting smile at him, she allowed herself to be led away, a small, dignified and upright figure she looked as she walked between the two burly officers with their hands placed firmly on her arms.

★ ★ ★

The family waiting for James Smith's arrival at home were alarmed to see him arriving alone. He broke the news gently to his wife, whose hands worked nervously the whole time as he led her to a chair - and for what must have been the first time in his life he had never felt so helpless and lost for words when he faced her stricken expression. The younger children, although not really understanding, stood saucer-eyed - yet sensing the seriousness of the situation they remained silent - whilst Bessie and Jack plied continuous, unanswerable questions.

'Shall we be able to visit?' Jack asked; and Bessie, 'But will she be allowed to have visitors?' 'I'll go soon, if I can,' Jack went on – actually savouring the thought of seeing what it was like in a prison but daren't admit it - and all the while their father continued staring straight ahead as though he hadn't heard and with their questions remaining unanswered they all eventually fell silent. His eldest daughter had been committed to prison on a charge of murder and apart from what would happen to her in the future, James Smith realised that from that moment on their own lives would never be the same. The humiliation they had all suffered so far could only get worse. They would all be subject to public ridicule and however determined any of them were to hold their heads high, the scandal would eventually drag them all down to the same shameful level. Madeleine had protested her innocence, and in spite of his assurance that he would enlist the finest lawyers, James Smith feared the worst and decided there was no point in hiding this concern from the family.

'I have decided,' he said, looking at each one in turn, 'that until this matter is resolved you should all go to Rowaleyn where it will be possible for you to either stay in the house or within the confines of the gardens,' he announced solemnly. 'I shall have to remain here in Glasgow to continue with my business affairs,' ... *and thank God my friends and business associates are continuing to stand by me so far*, he thought with relief – 'but I feel it is my duty to send you all away until this unfortunate matter is settled.'

William Minnoch, still largely ignorant concerning Madeleine's outrageous flirting at the same time as he was courting her, had nevertheless gone along with her reasoning that all this was a dreadful misunderstanding that needed sorting out. Whatever he thought now, however, he kept well hidden when he met up with the Smith family later. Like them, he had also been at the mercy of humiliating treatment from people in the locality and felt the time had come to withdraw from public life as far as his business allowed.

'I would prefer to find accommodation elsewhere for the time being,' he explained to Mr. Smith with some embarrassment. 'I shall of course leave a forwarding address should you need to contact me at any time.' And within a few hours of talking this through, he had packed all his possessions, and with a polite farewell to Mrs. Smith and the rest of the family, made a hasty exit.

Chapter Twenty-Seven

Still convinced that the accusation of murder was a huge mistake, Madeleine settled down reasonably well to prison life despite the horrifying conditions, and considering the meagre rations of hard bread and gruel with occasional helpings of suspicious looking meat and under-cooked potatoes, she never lost weight. Other women in the gaol were prostitutes, thieves or those discovered drunk and disorderly in the street, and although largely outnumbered by the male prisoners they heard in the distance but never saw, they were considered by the warders to be an irritating nuisance that had to be endured.

There was no discrimination between rich or poor. They were all regarded as contemptible individuals and treated alike, except for one prison rule concerning clothes. On arrival, all prisoners received clothes regardless of size, condition or the time of the year, whether it happened to be stifling hot or freezing. If a prisoner had arrived wearing flannel underclothes however, she would be entitled to a similar set – although no regard was given to size or condition. So making the best of the disgusting set Madeleine received, she hugged the generous, foul-smelling folds of material around her body at night and by rubbing her feet and hands vigorously before rolling herself tight in the thin blanket, she managed to gain a few hours of sleep before the cold eventually crept through.

The biting cold affected everyone - especially at night - and even the warders who patrolled regularly, walked about with blankets wrapped around their heads and shoulders. For this reason most of the prisoners shivering in their cells rarely slept and spent hours crying and calling out until silenced by the warders who threatened them with the strap if they didn't stop. But the worst things were the cockroaches and rats scuttling about in the dark and Madeleine bit her lips trying not to scream when she heard claws scratching on the stone floor and felt the rats moving near her body as they tried to work their way through the blanket. With insufficient room to move away on the narrow bench that passed for a bed, she felt their lumpy bodies shifting about. Once she felt a snout prodding against her leg, then a claw, and she tried jabbing them away. Then stiffening with fear, she buried her head under the blanket, terrified they would jump and bite her face.

Determined not to give in or allow the grim-faced warders the satisfaction of seeing her break under the strain, Madeleine managed to hold on to her sanity. The days dragged by monotonously in a punishing routine and she spent many hours of drudgery in a laundry stinking of chemicals and sweat. The work using ancient equipment was backbreaking, scrubbing filthy, stained clothes and blankets and accidents occurred frequently when prisoners slipped and fell on stone floors awash with water and suds. And the cries of the women as their faces burned a blistering red when compelled to work close to the hot stoves were muffled by the clanking machinery.

A welcome relief from this torment was attending chapel each morning, and it was here the women sat ramrod straight on wooden benches as a parson lectured them about an eternity spent in the ravages of hell if they did not change their ways. It was here too, on particularly bad days when he scowled and threatened them, that Madeleine often wondered whether he owned a whip with which to endorse his theories for improving the prisoners' wayward souls!

With no warm clothing provided if it happened to be freezing outside, the women were marched around a yard outside for exercise every day under the watchful eye of warders. When Madeleine joined the other prisoners on her first morning, she was appalled as shrunken old women with withered faces and young girls with haunted expressions and skins yellow with jaundice, shuffled out. No communication took place between the women and if they so much as glanced at someone, the treatment was harsh. Even smiling was frowned upon and anyone caught doing this was instantly reprimanded. 'This is not a place for smiling!' they would be told and on one occasion Madeleine saw a young girl's grimace swiftly removed by a hard slap.

The enforced silence was worse still and this Madeleine could not stand. She yearned for conversation and was told to 'Shut up!' if she attempted to talk to warders approaching with food or when joining the other women when they washed together in the stone trough where warders patrolled with grim expressions and shouts of, 'Make haste and no talking.'

With Madeleine not as yet labelled guilty of a particular crime like the unfortunates around her however, the Governor was compelled to listen with some irritation when she dared to ask for books to read and some paper and a pen to write letters. He was not accustomed to dealing with women showing the slightest degree of good breeding or intelligence. The only women he had to tolerate in his job were those in charge of the prisoners, who were often as ignorant as the inmates! But as time passed, and Madeleine showed no sign of trouble-making, he told her in an offhand way that he might consider allowing suitable reading matter if her good conduct continued, although when this did eventually turn up the tiny grating in her cell prevented sufficient light to indulge in such a pleasure even on the brightest of days!

Despite this ghastly transformation in Madeleine's life, and her continuing persistence in not revealing any outward sign of her feelings, the Governor and warders were astonished by her composure. Moreover, throughout her long stay in prison, this attitude never changed. No one saw her cry or rock back and forth when she sat isolated in her cell as many of the other prisoners did. Nor did she ever complain - either by a grimace or by word - although had she dared to do so she would have been silenced or slapped!

'No one would believe she could be on a capital charge,' the warders often remarked whether she was within earshot or not. And with the intention of striking fear into this new prisoner who behaved like a paragon of virtue they crowed, 'Doesn't she realise she could be hanged in public before a crowd baying for her blood if she's found guilty!'

Madeleine had no need to be told what the future could hold however, as prying eyes waited for her self-control to fracture. She knew about hanging and remembered Neville wanting to take her to a public hanging when they were in London - and in the foul inky darkness of her cell at night, listening to the howls and cries of other prisoners and the rats darting, jumping, scratching and gnawing, her confidence drained and tears flowed unobserved. During the day, she forced herself to keep down the revolting greasy food and drove herself to cope with the endless hours of scrubbing in the laundry that made her hands sore and red raw - and as time passed she accepted the nauseating odours and gruesome sounds. Even the horror of slopping out buckets of her urine and stools she gradually accepted as an inevitable routine, but the thought of that rope, tightening and choking as she swung, tormented her unmercifully.

★ ★ ★

The majority of women imprisoned in the Glasgow gaol never had anyone to care about them in their everyday lives let alone visit them when they'd been locked up in prison for whatever their crime. So this was something that never happened. Visiting was nevertheless discouraged in any case if the Governor could possibly prevent it and if he had no choice, it generally turned out to be a miserable experience. At least Madeleine was fortunate having people who cared about her and she felt convinced someone in the family would want to come to see her at some time. So by her continued grovelling insistence that they be allowed to do so if they wished, the Governor's disapproval was eventually worn down, particularly when her father pressed endlessly to see her.

Visiting a prisoner however was a one-sided affair and they never knew about it until that person called. They were considered too unimportant to be given any such information and the only indication of someone arriving to see them would be a sudden demand to make themselves ready, and even then they wondered why. On the other hand, any person making a request to see someone in prison would be treated with a degree of respect, all the same having to undergo extensive enquiries regarding name, address, relationship to the prisoner and reason for the visit before being allowed anywhere near the cells. When these formalities were complete, and the Governor satisfied that everything appeared to be in order, visitors would then be accompanied by a warder and escorted to stand in a small compartment with a small aperture with bars for viewing the prisoner, who waited in a similar compartment about three or four feet away. And two warders were already in place either side of the two compartments to watch and monitor the conversation after escorting Madeleine from her cell when she had been told to make herself ready. When she heard footsteps approaching, she peered anxiously into the gloomy passage wondering who would be arriving.

Having already put enquiries in hand concerning her legal representation as promised, Madeleine's father had repeatedly requested to see his daughter as soon as allowed to do so. His primary intention nevertheless was to question her about her involvement in this sordid affair in order to liaise with the lawyer ... and always eager for details of a convict's earlier life and the reason for them being in prison, the warders leaned forward eagerly and pricked up their ears as James Smith settled in his compartment.

Although well prepared for what he had come to explore, it took a good five minutes before Madeleine's father could bring himself to say anything. He was disgusted by the repulsive conditions, the smell and the offhand manner of the warders, and having to be placed in something resembling a cell as though he was also regarded as a convict was unbelievable! Astonished to see his daughter smiling through the bars of her compartment when she called to him, he felt appalled by her complacent manner in such dreadful conditions, although he made no comment when he could bring himself to speak. Then concentrating on the purpose of his visit, he asked how long the affair with L'Angelier had gone on and asked how many times she had bought arsenic, and gaining confidence in the objectionable confines of his compartment, 'are you being absolutely truthful Madeleine about not giving some to...'

He hesitated, pursing his lips and floundering, but Madeleine knew what he was about to ask and immediately turned this scrutiny of her life with Emile into a travesty, telling her father light-heartedly there was nothing whatsoever to worry about.

'I can assure you father that I am innocent of any corrupt involvement here,' she said smugly. 'You heard my statement to Archibald Smith and there is nothing different that I can add. I am innocent!'

For a minute Mr. Smith forgot the eavesdroppers standing nearby and in exasperation thrust close to the aperture and murmured between clenched teeth, 'But you are not. How can you plead innocence when you have been carrying on with that Frenchman behind my back, and buying arsenic! You actually admitted doing that.'

'For my own use, father,' she interrupted, with her voice rising. 'I said that in my statement. You must have heard. You were there.'

He withdrew from the bars, brushing a hand across his eyes and Madeleine's heart ached.

'You have no idea what you have done to us,' he went on, his voice quieter with the hint of a tremble every now and then. 'I am ruined Madeleine. Do you understand that? No one in the family can walk through the streets without shame and your mother is on the verge of a breakdown.' He moved further back and all Madeleine could see was the top of his head, bowed low, and when he appeared again he told her in an emotional voice about the family staying at Rowaleyn. 'Away from it all,' he said. 'It was the least I could do.'

For a moment they stood shrouded in their shadowy compartments, neither talking, and Madeleine stifled a sob as she fought for reasons causing her mother's distress other than those inflicted by her own doing. She said at last, 'I'm sorry about mama. Really, I am very sorry about mama. But she has always been unwell father,' she placated. 'You know that,' and ready with another excuse went on, 'anything upsets her nowadays, poor dear, even the wedding began to worry...'

'Wedding?' he bellowed, forgetting the warders again. Then lowering his voice when he saw the wretched women straining their necks, went on quietly, 'You can forget about a wedding my girl. There'll be no wedding now... especially if you are...' and he stopped, casting a quick glance round, thinking about what he was about to say but dare not put into words. *She knew the outcome of this business if she was found guilty and what would happen to her for God's sake ... just as he knew what would happen to him if labelled the father of a murderess!*

In her cell at night, Madeleine had often pondered about William Minnoch and their wedding. It was the only thing keeping her sane and as her father's bitter recriminations went on she decided to drop any further discussion about the wedding and asked instead about William, how he was, what he was doing.

For what seemed an age James Smith looked at his daughter and felt ashamed, bewildered and lost for words. He even considered her sanity. Did she not care what was happening or was this feigning of innocence a cover up? He shuffled his position, desperate to leave the ghastly place and he left the question about William Minnoch unanswered. Then, suddenly changing his mind thrust his face up against the bars and speaking slowly and deliberately as though to a child blared, 'What do you expect to hear about William Minnoch? He has gone! William suffers as we do and he's gone to live elsewhere.'

'I am suffering too father,' she interrupted in a voice barely audible, but as though he had not heard, he carried on, 'William was at the mercy of local people – as we were - and he's gone. He has left our home to find accommodation somewhere else, away from the jibes and gossip. He has gone Madeleine. Do you hear?' and leaning closer he jabbed a finger at himself. 'Like me,' he said. 'He's trying to run a business that could be ruined by all this.'

She looked away. There was nothing further to say - and when she heard a movement in his compartment and the sound of a door, she glanced up quickly. He was peering at her through the bars for a last look, his eyes glistening. 'I have engaged the best lawyers,' he told her, his voice hoarse, 'but I shall not be in Court Madeleine. Don't expect to see me there. I have asked not to be called as a witness and I have been assured that this will not be necessary.'

She could look no longer and listened to his footsteps fading on the flagstones - a broken man endeavouring one last attempt in his paternal role she thought - and for the first time since she had arrived at the prison she felt that all the fight in her was sliding away.

★ ★ ★

Whether word reached William Minnoch after her father's visit, Madeleine never knew. Nor did she question him when he arrived some weeks later, such was her delight seeing him. His manner had changed however, perhaps due to the surroundings she supposed when he greeted her abruptly with great embarrassment as a disgruntled warder, eyeing him curiously, ushered him into his compartment.

'I'm so pleased to see you William,' Madeleine said at once and with a beaming smile raised her fingers to her lips to blow a kiss.

Even in the dim surroundings, she saw him flush with

embarrassment, staring quickly at the two warders either side as though willing them to go away.

'Can we not talk privately Madeleine?' he said brusquely, which only resulted in the warders gaping indignantly as they moved closer. 'If only it were not here Madeleine,' he said in a broken voice. 'What a dreadful place this is. It's so awful seeing you here and I still don't understand...'

'Neither do I William,' she interrupted. 'It's absurd. A dreadful mistake. I've always said...' and she picked up a snigger from one of the warders.

William had never shifted from believing Madeleine was anything other than innocent, which was strange with the newspapers now full of the story and newsvendors shouting from every corner. He still refused to believe the girl he'd chosen to be his wife could be capable of committing such a dastardly crime, although with the authorities now indicating that his presence in Court as a witness would be necessary, reality was catching up fast ... *and this sordid, stinking place didn't help much either!*

Having to appear in Court was something William secretly dreaded, and feared! So far, he had kept this to himself, unable to discuss the shame of being involved in a murder trial. It was a disgrace! ... a*nd he knew so damned little about what had been going on anyway and didn't even know this man she was suspected of poisoning! So what did they expect of him? What was he expected to say in Court?*

Madeleine began to feel inhibited by William's nervous hesitation and reluctance to talk. He had changed so drastically since she had last seen him and was scarcely recognisable as the same man. He peered anxiously from the grille with despair in his eyes she had never known and appeared to be fidgeting nervously the whole time. He never asked questions as she had expected and talked hesitatingly all the while about stupid inconsequential matters, which she found herself answering in the same way, but even this talk was limited and the long silences between them grew longer and embarrassing. More than that, there had been no display of affection at any time, even when she had blown him a kiss. He had turned away in shame and shifted away from the bars! ... *and he certainly had made no mention about their wedding, and in view of her father's statement she daren't mention it! It might be true!*

'Time's up!' one of the warders suddenly shouted. And with barely time to have said anything sensible after such a short time Madeleine felt she should remonstrate, uselessly of course as they ignored her with a look of disgust and moved towards William's cubicle ... *all they're doing is glaring at one another and 'im looking so helpless, we're wasting our time,* one of them thought. Inwardly however, Madeleine felt relieved. She had been facing a different man. It seemed they had nothing in common any more, and dared she wonder about any affection that might be left?

Locked in her cell for the night as the shadows swallowed her up, Madeleine felt more desperately abandoned than ever. Up until William's visit, the thought of her future life as the wife of a successful businessman and raising a family in his image had kept up her spirits. As the weeks dragged on though - and visits from William became less frequent and more harrowing - it was a struggle to maintain her composure without constant doubts clouding her mind.

Jack, her brother, came to visit as often as allowed, as did her father who now offered strong support despite his earlier misgivings on his first visit. Her mother never came, or was ever encouraged to do so, and Bessie, still nursing her grievance over the death of her adored Emile, came only very reluctantly and then not at all as time passed. One prominent visitor nevertheless was the lawyer her father had engaged for her defence, the Dean of Faculty, John Inglis, a highly respected and outstanding member of the Scottish Bar, and the Governor of the prison took it upon himself to escort this distinguished visitor directly to Madeleine's cell rather than placing him in an interviewing cubicle.

John Inglis retained his youthful appearance, striking good looks and soft persuasive voice although now well into middle age. It had been said of him in the past - and an observation not escaping James Smith's notice when considering Madeleine's defence - that he was a lawyer who would never defend a client unless he was totally convinced of their innocence. Many people however were already predicting the outcome of this trial and were now disputing this long held claim. Furthermore, some were saying that he would surely regret having taken the case on.

Why Inglis visited Madeleine in prison however remained a mystery and many people speculated over his motive – if indeed there was one! He had never done such a thing before and in some circles, people wondered why such an eminent lawyer should even consider defending a loose young woman well known for telling lies, let alone visit her. Perhaps he needed to get to know the unusual young girl who so stubbornly protested her innocence in the face of such incriminating evidence many wondered, and others concocted their own theories.

'Was she insane?' they said. 'Surely nobody facing what the future held for such a woman could be in their right mind!'

Then there were the more compassionate critics who suggested the frequent visits were purely out of sympathy for a young girl of good standing dragged down by a rogue committing suicide deliberately. More so, a girl compelled by law to remain silent during a trial for his murder as witnesses gave evidence, whether accurate or not!

It appeared everyone had an opinion about the outcome of this trial, although the majority were in no doubt that it would result in a public hanging. By now the papers were full of stories about the young woman from a middle class family living cheek by jowl with the scum of society in gaol and every day something featured about the suspected murder with glaring headlines in bold letters whenever new information became known. Madeline Smith's name was on everybody's lips both countrywide and throughout the world and people from all walks of life could be heard discussing the case. Furthermore, they were generally of one mind, that her life would be in jeopardy once she entered the dock, and who could have been more aware of this than John Inglis when he visited her in prison for the last time.

Chapter Twenty-Eight

The trial was fixed for the 30th of June and a week before; Madeleine was transferred to a prison in Edinburgh and placed in the care of the matron, a Miss Aitken. This move not only meant more amenable conditions, but also brought Madeleine the joy of having long conversations with someone who was under strict orders to maintain a constant surveillance. She knew her life was doomed from now on, but at least the relief of being able to talk to someone in the prison offered a shred of comfort. Her transfer to Edinburgh also brought about an even greater degree of composure and Miss Aitken even detected an air of relief when Madeleine told her she was glad that, 'this sordid affair would soon be over!' So within the space of a week there had been constant chatter between them, in particular about Madeleine's marriage to William Minnoch when she walked free from the court. She had never wavered from believing that her wedding would still take place, even to a point of discussing details of the dress she would wear!

'Already ordered,' she announced, 'and in the process of being made, although temporarily abandoned of course in view of the circumstances I understand,' she thought fit to add.

Meanwhile, all evidence for the trial was in place by this time with two hundred exhibits ready for scrutiny. Letters written by Madeleine had been copied in a clear hand for easy reading at the appropriate time. Medical reports were available, as were notebooks and papers taken from L'Angelier's and Madeleine's rooms, as well as an assortment of bottles and jars containing various substances for investigation by the lawyers, one of which was the contents of L'Angelier's stomach!

Fifty-seven people were due to be called as witnesses for the prosecution and thirty-one for the defence. Madeleine's father was not to be called, as he'd already explained to his daughter, and despite William Minnoch's protests about being summoned as a witness and his earnest enquiries whether his appearance would in fact be necessary, he had been warned it could detrimental to her case for him not to be present. The only member chosen from Madeleine's immediate family was her young sister Janet who, having shared a bedroom with Madeleine at one time, was required to give evidence concerning the nightly visits from L'Angelier - something she rarely talked about to her parents so as not to worry her mother - but which she secretly dreaded.

★ ★ ★

Having suggested an early night to be fresh for the trial the following day, 'with a sedative to make sure of a good sleep,' Miss Aitken felt astonished by Madeleine's cool attitude when she refused.

'Only the dreadful cold and roaming rats ever prevented me from sleeping when I was in that place in Glasgow,' she said. 'Nothing else! My clear conscience has never restricted me from sleeping well, and still doesn't!' At a loss to understand her composure, the matron had placed a sympathetic hand on Madeleine's shoulder, not really believing and expecting some kind of reaction - tears, an outburst of remorse or even a confession. But Madeleine had merely covered her hand, thanked her for being a good friend and told her she would always remember her kindness. Then more amazingly she suddenly clapped a hand over her mouth when realising she'd given no thought to what she should wear for her court appearance!

'I must look my best,' she exclaimed, jumping to her feet, and with continuing astonishment Miss Aitken spent the rest of the evening with Madeleine riffling through clothes brought in as a special concession and discussing between them what would be the most appropriate outfit to wear!

★ ★ ★

By dawn on the first day of the trial, a huge crowd had already gathered outside the court. Many hours were yet to pass before Madeleine's arrival and as time passed, the rowdy throng grew larger. Never had there been so much excitement at a trial in the city and the police had their hands full keeping people in order. A major proportion of the crowd were men jostling for sight of this beautiful young girl facing a public hanging for the murder of someone they considered an unworthy rapscallion. Whilst the few women in the crowd were more than likely there to see a scarlet woman with loose morals and murder in her heart get her just reward! Whatever their reasoning, the atmosphere was gradually turning into something resembling a festival rather than awaiting the outcome of a trial for murder, and police were ready with sticks and truncheons to prevent the crowd barging forward when the main door opened a fraction to admit anyone connected with the proceedings.

Madeleine arrived in a cab under heavy guard. She was hustled in through a side door to the sound of rousing cheers from those who happened to spot her, and for the first time since her committal to prison three months ago, Madeleine's nerves got the better of her as grim-faced officials manhandled her down through the murky passages beneath the court. Her dark thoughts haunting her at night in the Glasgow gaol returned manifold when she heard the shouts and yelling outside and she wondered whether they were for sympathy or lust for her blood! And with her confidence sinking fast as she waited in the damp corridor leading to the dock, she drew on what little remained of her resources of strength and gained a shred of comfort from the protective shell she'd managed to gather around her.

When a distant signal filtered down from the court that the prisoner should enter the dock, Madeleine felt hands tighten on her arms and taking a deep breath she began shuffling along the uneven flagstones between the matron and police officer. Despite the warmth outside, it felt cold, damp and smelled strongly of urine at one point as they made their way, although it was not this that struck fear. It was the pounding of feet above, the chairs scraping and the mumble of voices as people settled into position, and the noise penetrating from the unruly crowd outside seemed to be getting louder.

Moistening her lips as they entered the narrow corridor leading to the dock, Madeleine felt a reassuring squeeze on her arm but she dare not look at Miss Aitken as she struggled with her feelings. She kept her eyes fixed straight ahead, holding her head high and breathing hard now she realised that in a matter of minutes she would be entirely at the mercy of strangers. People, unknown yet, would be giving evidence and saying things true or otherwise. Strangers would soon be determining her fate, and deciding whether she should live or die!

Chapter Twenty-Nine

By ten o'clock, every space on wooden benches in the small courtroom was occupied by legal representatives, court officials in their high black top hats, businessmen, clergymen and reporters who had come from all over the world. The team for the prosecution, the Lord Advocate, James Moncrieff, the Solicitor-General, Edward Maitland and the Advocate-Depute, Donald MacKenzie took their places, followed by the defending counsel, the Dean of Faculty, John Inglis, and his attendant advocates, George Young and Alexander Moncrieff, all names widely known and respected in legal circles throughout Scotland.

At 10:30 the judges appeared, led by the The Lord Justice-Clerk, the Right Honourable John Hope in his magnificent scarlet robe and hood and followed by Lord Ivory and Lord Handyside, all men of high integrity and great experience, who settled themselves on chairs placed high on a platform beneath a canopy bearing the Royal Coat of Arms.

Already the courtroom was hot and stuffy with any windows that could be opened now tightly shut to keep out the increasing pandemonium outside. The police force keeping the crowd in check had now increased to 50 and as Madeleine exchanged a swift glance with the matron, she visibly shuddered when she heard the yells and raucous shouts. Heavy footsteps approaching the dock brought a further shudder and smarting tears of panic as the trap-door lifted, and the commotion of scraping chairs, shuffling and the sound of voices in the court immediately stopped.

'Madeleine Smith, your presence is requested in court.'

This disembodied command struck further terror and with a lurch in her stomach as hands tightening either side urged her forward, Madeleine placed a foot on the first step of the narrow staircase leading to the dock, resolutely resigned to her destiny.

She had dressed with care that morning from clothes selected the night before. The brown silk dress with a large brooch pinned high on her breast suited her pale complexion well, as did the white straw bonnet trimmed with ribbon, which she'd felt appropriate at the last minute to be draped with a fine black veil. And as she stepped daintily into the dock, gasps resounded round the court, a reaction which incredibly checked her trembling.

With an instruction to remain standing, Madeleine forced a smile. Her nerves were settling she thought and steadying herself with one hand on the bar, she raised the veil of her bonnet. Still clutched firmly, as had been recommended by Miss Aitken, was a small bottle of smelling salts and tiny handkerchief, and by her outward appearance to everyone in the court her inner turmoil was well disguised.

All eyes were fixed in her direction when she had taken a quick glance round the court and when she looked at the 15 members of the jury who were to judge her destiny, all grim-faced as they sat motionless in their high wooden stall, she raised her chin in an attitude of defiance. She recognised it as an act of defence coming into play to quell her nerves, but it helped to maintain her composure. Everything was so formal and frightening, she thought. Something she had never expected. It looked so important and imposing. Men in white wigs wearing elaborate scarlet cloaks adorned with white fur. The court packed full, all of them men, crammed together. Every space was taken, and quite suddenly, it then became ominously quiet with every face looking in her direction.

'Madeleine Smith you are indicted and accused, that you wickedly administered arsenic or other poison, with intent to murder, and are guilty of the said crime.'

The boring voice droned on relentlessly as the lengthy indictment interspersed with legal jargon, was read out.

'And that you, the said Madeleine Smith should be punished within the law to deter others from committing like crimes.'

Without a twitch of a muscle Madeleine managed to remain ramrod straight with her chin still thrust out defiantly as the charges were read. When requested to do so she leaned forward and answered in a clear steady voice, 'Not guilty', and having uttered these words publicly, the dauntless faith in her innocence returned manifold! ... *This unsavoury business is a complete waste of time!* ... And the momentary flash of impatience etched on her face did not go unnoticed by some in the court who shifted in their seats and exchanged glances.

★ ★ ★

When Madeleine was instructed to sit, the first witnesses were called for the prosecution. They came from all walks of life, some recognised by Madeleine as they were summoned to the box and others complete strangers who had been called to give evidence against a woman they had never known or seen yet believed to have maliciously ended the life of Emile L'Angelier. They declared their full knowledge of all the circumstances leading to L'Angelier's death, which infuriated Madeleine as she stared dumbfounded at people she had never known about or even seen. She was not allowed to speak however. Archibald Smith had made this clear when she made her statement in his office. She had to remain mute. Contain her feelings as best she could, and turning her attention to the lengthy examination of these witnesses by James Moncrieff, followed by the cross-examining by the Dean of Faculty for the defence, she endeavoured to clear her mind of resentment.

The process was long, laborious and often emotional and some witnesses crumpled under the strain. Not once however did Madeleine look ruffled. She had resolved to remain passive, outwardly at least, even in the face of unfair criticism or outrageous lies. She faced each person squarely as they entered the witness box and took the oath and only allowed a hostile stare if they dared look her way when stating facts she disagreed with.

A druggist in Glasgow who knew Emile well spoke glowingly about the deceased and confirmed his knowledge about his frequent requests for medicines to alleviate various ailments. 'And he often bought medicine I myself had recommended,' he announced confidently.

A grocer who shared accommodation with Emile when he first arrived in Glasgow followed, a Robert Baker, looking travel-worn and dishevelled after his journey from St. Helen's in Jersey as he made his way nervously to the witness box to speak in his friend's favour. 'I knew Emile visited the accused at night, which was quite often,' he whined and Madeleine looked in disgust at a man she had never seen or knew anything about and felt an instant dislike for the stupid, ignorant little man with pig-like eyes and wispy moustache. He shuffled nervously, gripping the front bar each time he had to reply to a question. He described himself as a good friend and said he had known Emile for a number of years when they both lived in Jersey.

'How close was your friendship during this time and did he ever confide in you?' the Lord Advocate asked in his quiet forceful manner that had the effect of dragging information out of the most reluctant of witnesses.

'At first I knew very little about his personal life sir, but as time passed he started confiding in me. Many times he confided your honour,' and he went on to describe how he had also met the accused on many occasions, at which Madeleine's mouth dropped open in astonishment.

'And what did he tell you on these occasions when he, er, confided in you?'

'That he wanted to marry the accused sir. He had been visiting her. I knew that - and that he feared losing her to another man.'

The Lord Advocate stepped up his questioning at this point, which further unnerved the witness, making him shuffle about and stammer when he replied.

'You said L'Angelier visited the accused. Where did these visits take place? Did you know?' he asked.

'At the accu-cused's house, sir. In her b-bedroom I understand - at night, late at night when her f-family were in bed.'

Madeleine dropped her gaze, hating this mealy-mouthed man she had never seen in her life as gasps echoed throughout the court and faces turned in her direction at this disgraceful revelation

'Where he could also have had refreshment by way of a drink, or food had it been offered do you suppose? Did you know anything about that?' the Lord Advocate continued in an even tone.

'I know nothing about that, sir, but he may have done. I don't know.'

'So L'Angelier did not tell you everything when he confided in you?'

'No, I s'pose he didn't your honour.'

Madeleine recognised John Inglis, the man now rising

to take his turn in questioning this witness for the defence. She remembered his kind, if somewhat brusque, manner when he had visited her in prison and took some comfort as she recalled his assurance that despite the incriminating circumstances that he would do his utmost within the scope of the law as her defending counsel. He had glanced in her direction several times before rising to interrogate Robert Baker and when he moved towards the witness box immediately went in for the attack.

'So your friend did not tell you everything – particularly about him having accepted food or a drink from the accused?'

'No sir. I don't think he told me everything,' he said hesitatingly.

'Yet you knew about his fear of losing the accused to another man you say?'

'Yes sir, he did tell me about that.'

'About which he must have been very upset - and perhaps depressed would you say?'

'He did become very depressed at times sir. Yes. Many times, particularly of late your honour - and it worried me.'

'Why were you worried when he became depressed? Did you think he would possibly harm himself in any way for instance when he felt this misery of depression?'

Robert Baker's anxiety was apparent as he faltered and he shifted about again, moistening his lips before speaking. 'Yes sir. I was worried about that at times,' he said quietly.

'Did anything ever happen - at any time when you knew him, which made you suspect that he was capable of harming himself in order to escape from this misery?'

Here followed a long description from Robert Baker of L'Angelier's bouts of suicidal tendencies whenever crossed in love and still stammering nervously as John

Inglis pressed for more information, he became carried away.

'I pulled him back from a window once sir, in Jersey, I remember, when a girl had just jilted him. He threatened to throw himself out.'

Inglis pursed his lips, regarding him speculatively for a moment, then went on to questioning about arsenic and whether he knew about his friend's possession of this drug - 'which could easily have been used to end his misery of depression if he so desired.' And Baker vehemently denied this.

'And you had no knowledge either, you say, about him consuming anything that would have caused his death when he went to the house of the accused?'

Baker shuffled uncertainly again, seemingly unwilling to answer, and completely out of context he suddenly blurted out the choice piece of information he had been waiting to reveal as he grasped the rail before him and drew himself up to his full height.

'I know that they were intimate sir,' he stated in a loud voice, 'and that they slept together!' And a shared intake of breath resounded throughout the court.

Madeleine hardened her gaze at this detestable man and met his furtive glance with scorn, noticing him shudder as he looked away, and lowering her head she prayed her heated face was obscured.

'Answer the question put to you,' John Inglis said with irritation. 'Did you or did you not know whether the deceased consumed any liquid or partook of any food which could cause his death when he visited the accused, particularly in view of the allegation made that he died the day following his visit to the accused the night before?'

'No sir,' he answered morosely. 'I don't know anything about that your honour.'

★ ★ ★

The relentless questioning continued as the day wore on and under Miss Aitken's watchful eye Madeleine did not demonstrate any weariness or have any need of the smelling salts she had recommended, or the handkerchief still clutched tight in her hand. Nothing appeared to affect her as witnesses held her gaze when they passed before her. It was like people entering for a performance on stage she thought more than once; those knowing her well glancing at her briefly, with a hint of a smile occasionally, and others, knowing they would soon be testifying against her, slinking by sheepishly. Despite this outward appearance of serenity nevertheless, she felt her stomach lurch when she came under attack and the protective shield she had gathered about her often wavered. At one such time when Emile's landlady Mrs. Jenkins described her as a 'loose woman,' she tightened her hands and had to force herself not to cry out that this woman had never even known of her existence or had any idea what she even looked like until entering this court! *How could she say such things ... hateful woman, standing there brazenly dabbing her eyes!*

This witness however was considered as significant in the trial. She had been the last person to see L'Angelier alive and her evidence about circumstances leading to his death was crucial.

'Tormented wi' pain sir. Ah hae nae doot aboot that,' she said when questioned about discovering him lying outside the house in agony. 'An' the puir man came straight frae that woman,' she went on, turning to Madeleine with tears in her eyes and a face darkened in rage.

The Prosecuting Counsel allowed a short pause for her to recover, then requested her to resume.

'Ah ken he was courten,' she went on. 'An' sometimes he seemed tae be vera upset, altho he never talked aboot it. Ah never ken who it was he saw, sir. He went oot late at nicht and ah dinna hear him come home, but he wasnae late for breakfast in the morning afore going to work, and ah ken there were letters,' she rushed on, raising a hand as she suddenly remembered. 'Watched tae get the letters frae the postman, an looked maist unhappy sometimes.'

Mrs. Jenkins was examined and cross-examined for more than two hours. She talked about L'Angelier's eating habits, his health, the medicines he took, his work and the occasions she had mentioned when he went out at night - with a further long description of his suffering when he arrived at her house and his agony when she'd managed to get him up to his room - and eventual death. And this turned out to be the longest interrogation of a witness so far.

With an account in all the newspapers about Emile L'Angelier being a seducer of women and a sex-raved arsenic eater, people possibly began speculating at this point about this beautiful young girl in the dock facing a murder charge. Could she really be responsible for his death after this lurid account by his landlady they probably wondered? As they listened to her grisly account of how he suffered unmercifully before he died however, the fact remained that he had just returned from a visit to this hussy! So mingling with earlier expressions of compassion in the court for this serene young woman not allowed to defend herself, there were now many looks of scorn on faces. Furthermore, the occasional hostile glances had not escaped the notice of Madeleine when members of the jury looked her way following Mrs. Jenkins' scathing testimony. John Inglis also caught her eye once or twice, as had the judges ...

What were they expecting to see? she wondered as she lowered her head each time she caught a scowl or stare ... *Did they expect tears of remorse as this dreadful woman described Emile's last tortuous moments in this world, and how do they expect me to react to all this drama ...* Yet as she continued to struggle with her composure, not a muscle betrayed any of this emotion.

★ ★ ★

Throughout the recess for lunch, Madeleine adamantly refused to leave the dock where she had sat for the last three hours. She refused all offers of refreshment, even a glass of water from which Miss Aitken suggested she should at least take a few sips.

'There will be many more hours of questioning yet,' she said quietly and went on to advise that she should at least take a walk. To no avail, however. Madeleine replied that she was content to remain where she was and to reinforce her decision even managed a smile for the only friend she felt existed in her world at that moment. So in the full gaze of people in the court and public gallery, now busily munching sandwiches and drinking, she appeared to be indifferent to the inquisitive stares that came from all directions in a stifling atmosphere that became more oppressive as the day wore on.

At the end of the day, she sank gratefully into the vehicle taking her back to prison and when at last away from prying eyes, Miss Aitken placed a reassuring hand on hers, which Madeleine clasped feebly between her own.

'I had no idea how tiring it would be,' she said, straightening and arching her back. 'I'm utterly exhausted and my body aches like it never has before.'

'You should have walked at least, or taken refreshment. It is too much. You must heed my advice tomorrow Madeleine. There are many more days yet before this is over and you must preserve your strength.' Overlooking the appalling circumstances this girl faced - and whether innocent or otherwise - the matron felt genuinely sorry for her. Many women she had accompanied in similar situations in the past had broken under the strain in far less gruelling circumstances and Madeleine's stamina was nothing short of amazing. Further beyond her understanding was Madeleine's ability to be able to sleep peacefully throughout the night when she returned to her cell, as though she hadn't a care in the world!

Chapter Thirty

Day two of the trial concentrated entirely on evidence given by doctors and forensic experts who had studied the case over many months and called to give their professional opinion concerning the use and misuse of arsenic. Also questioned were several druggists about the supply of arsenic to the deceased and the accused and all were under pressure by both the Prosecuting and the Defence Counsels to describe in detail when the poison was bought and how it had been recorded in the poisons register.

L'Angelier's physician, Dr. Thomson, described how his patient had consulted him on many occasions for various complaints and went on to talk about his attendance on him the day he died when his landlady arrived at his house in the early hours of the morning asking him to call.

'He was far from a healthy man in any case,' he blustered, shifting from side to side pompously. 'Often he would talk about having pains and bouts of sickness and I formed the opinion that these were bilious attacks which could have been brought about for any number of reasons, although at one time he did show signs of jaundice,' he said, stroking his chin thoughtfully.

He discussed in more detail L'Angelier having to resort to medicine he prescribed when he called at the surgery and spoke about how he had occasionally sought an opinion about remedies he had purchased himself from the apothecary.

'Although I had no knowledge about him procuring arsenic at any time for his own use,' he said, with jowls quivering as he shook his head. 'Certainly he never discussed this with me. I knew nothing about that.'

The next witness called was a Professor of Chemistry at the University in Glasgow, a Dr. Penny. He was required to discuss arsenic in more detail, particularly when used as a stimulant and the resulting effect it would have if ingested. He talked laboriously, describing at length the technicalities of colouring matter - such as indigo or soot - which by law had to be added to prevent the poison being mistaken for any other white substances such as sugar, salt or flour. 'So if mixed into a drink, such as cocoa or chocolate,' he explained, 'arsenic containing this colouring matter could possibly be ingested without any suspicion, depending of course on the individual,' he added with a shrug, 'although obviously there would be a certain grittiness in the drink which would be unpleasant and difficult to ignore.'

Seizing this statement as an opportune moment for further interrogation, the Prosecuting Counsel questioned, 'It is known from statements made by other witnesses that the deceased often partook of a drink of cocoa when he visited the accused. Would you therefore suggest that arsenic could have been administered in this way without the deceased noticing?'

Apparently considering the question Dr. Penny hesitated briefly and then answered confidently, 'Quite possibly sir. As I said, it depends on the individual of course and it's difficult to be specific.' He went on to describe in detail about the chemical properties peculiar to arsenic and referred back to his earlier statement about colouring matter having to be added in order to comply with the law.

Turning to the exhibits, he indicated the jar containing the contents of L'Angelier's stomach, and peering over the top of his spectacles continued, 'The deposit in the contents of the deceased's stomach when examined however, was discovered to be indicative of a white powder. I have to make it clear however that in cases of severe vomiting - which apparently happened in the case of the deceased prior to his death, the colouring matter added to the arsenic could have been removed.'

Gasps of disgust were heard as he described cutting pieces of L'Angelier's stomach into small pieces and boiling them for some time in water containing hydrochloric acid, and lowering his voice as he concluded he announced, 'My analysis, determined that the quantity of arsenic ingested by the deceased would have been capable of killing at least 40 men.'

When John Inglis rose to cross-examine Dr. Penny for the defence, he decided to refer to the earlier evidence given by the druggist who supplied arsenic to Madeleine for killing rats. 'He confirmed, did he not' he asked unhurriedly, 'that colour had been added to the arsenic bought by the accused in accordance with having to comply with the law, as you have also stated?' Then barely waiting for a reply and narrowing his eyes as he leaned towards the witness box, he demanded, 'And you stated that the poison in the stomach of the deceased was white and that the act of vomiting could - 'could' you said, and I emphasise that word - have had the effect of separating this colour from the arsenic.'

'That is correct.'

Drawing himself to his full height with thumbs thrust into his waistcoat John Inglis continued dourly, 'Surely in a trial for murder it is vital that all information given in this court is factual and not open to speculation?'

Unmoved by this reflection on his expertise, Dr. Penny repeated his earlier statement about the possibility of colour separation in arsenic by the act of vomiting, emphasising clearly the word 'possibility'. He further explained that colouring matter could also be physically removed from arsenic before being used. He also endorsed his earlier statement about large doses of arsenic being gritty to the taste when stirred into a drink such as chocolate or cocoa, with or without the colouring agent,' he stressed. 'On the other hand', he continued, with an air of irritation, 'a more acceptable drink made with a similar quantity of arsenic – and say boiled with the chocolate or cocoa - would make the drink more agreeable to the taste, and even more so if made slightly sweeter.'

'Is it correct to assume therefore that arsenic may be disguised in chocolate or cocoa, boiled or otherwise, but could not be concealed in a drink of tea or coffee for instance?' This came from the Prosecuting Counsel when he rose to face the witness for questioning.

'That is correct.'

'And could it also be assumed that with a large quantity of arsenic being used without detection in cocoa or chocolate that this was the reason for L'Angelier being offered these beverages when he visited the accused rather than - as you say - coffee, tea or any other beverage?'

'It could be.'

Members of the jury who were closely following this evidence and obviously endeavouring to absorb the technical details within their understanding, were noticed to be glancing occasionally in Madeleine's direction. Quite clearly, the proceedings were not turning in her favour and as news of how the trial was progressing trickled to the crowds waiting outside, bets were now being set up concerning whether or not she would escape the gallows.

Madeleine nevertheless managed to remain unemotional, at least outwardly! Her appearance continued to assume the air of a young innocent girl wronged by her lover and unjustly accused of causing his death, but the way things were going there were not many people in that court who went along with the theory Madeleine clung to, particularly after listening to the gruesome details about the contents of L'Angelier's stomach! Despite this external show of impeccable virtue, however, Madeleine's inner turmoil was now chaotic and she struggled to stay calm. On countless occasions in the past she had managed to suppress fear or block out threatening waves of emotion by assuming a different personality when things got tough - like acting in a play she recalled from her schooldays - but even flaunting this ability did not come easy. All the same, she managed to keep a tight hold on this theatrical flair and using it as prop, now gathered strength by placing faith in friends and family she knew would soon be taking their turn in the witness box. For a start she knew her dear husband-to-be would be a wonderful pillar of support and warmth flooded through her body as she dwelt on his protective affection in the past ... *he could deal with that dreadful man for the prosecution with his horrid twitching whiskers and menacing voice!* So even as her confidence faltered and her throat constricted with fear every now and then, her faith remained steadfast as she summoned all the courage she could muster, and this was just as well. For worse was to come.

Chapter Thirty-One

Madeleine recognised the man now making his way to the witness box as the person who had called at the Smith's family home when this drama first started. Emile L'Angelier's good friend, Auguste de Mean, entered the box with great poise, glancing round the court confidently before taking the Oath and facing John Inglis. He spoke impressively of a friend that he had known for a number of years. 'A man with an exemplary character,' he said. 'A fine fellow who had splendid principles and held strong religious beliefs.' When asked about his health and lifestyle however, he shifted about uncertainly before replying and giving a less glowing account of his friend by admitting he had often complained to him about his bad health, commented further about his habit of taking pills and drugs on many occasions.

'And what about his military career, in the Army in France I believe. What knowledge do you have about that stage in his life?'

'I know very little actually. It was never discussed in detail and I did not ask questions about this at any time.

'But he talked freely to the accused on many occasions - apparently about his exploits on the battlefields and told her that at one time he was wounded I understand.'

De Mean appeared to lose some of his grandeur at this point, somewhat reluctantly admitting that his friend could at times be rather imaginative, and sometimes made extravagant claims about his exploits in the Army. 'But I think he understood I was not interested in such talk,' he said nonchalantly, 'and we never pursued any lengthy conversations about this,' he stressed.

'And would you say he was also inclined to set his sights rather high in society, having, as I understand, come from a somewhat humble background?'

Still loath to imply any insincerity by criticising his friend overmuch, de Mean reluctantly agreed under pressure that this was so and when questioned repeatedly about Emile's personality he admitted feeling personally distressed concerning his bouts of depression and occasional outbursts of emotion, and went on to describe how he'd supported him many times when he'd invited him to his home.

'And were you aware of him resorting to any kind of stimulant or any similar drug when he was suffering from these, as you say, emotional outbursts?' John Inglis questioned.

De'Mean pursed his lips, looking vulnerable again by the possible implication of his friend's self-harm. Then firmly he announced, 'I know he occasionally carried a bottle of laudanum in his bag when he visited me,' and throwing up his hands, 'which I would never have questioned as being harmful,' and then added hastily, 'but I know nothing about stimulants or any other drugs.'

'What about arsenic? Were you aware of your friend's habit for imbibing arsenic?'

With his voice trailing away, de Mean admitted discussing this with the deceased at one time, and with a touch of irritation Inglis asked him to speak up and repeat what he had just said and followed up by asking him to elaborate on this.

'What did he discuss with you? - and tell me also if you would, why he found it necessary to use arsenic and when he felt it was necessary to use it.'

Taking a deep breath and thrusting his chin as if seeking inspiration, Auguste de Mean shifted uneasily as he contemplated his reply. 'I was aware he kept a supply of arsenic for his personal use,' he said guardedly. 'And I would imagine he used it when he felt in need of it. I cannot give any specific reason for his use of this, and I certainly never questioned.'

Gazing down thoughtfully as he strolled before the witness box, John Inglis went on quietly, 'You said, Mr. de Mean, did you not, that he discussed with you at one time this unfortunate habit he had for imbibing arsenic - and having imparted this information - made you aware of the fact that he found it necessary to take this when, as you said, he felt he needed it. What do you suppose his needs were when arsenic would have been necessary?

'As I said, I never questioned him about this.'

'Even when, as you also described earlier, you counselled your support for him when he visited your home and he became emotionally distressed?'

De Mean looked uneasy, shifting about again as he weighed up his response, which as the time lengthened prompted John Inglis to a swift riposte urging a reply. 'You must answer my question.'

'He discussed... erm... well... he told me he needed this when he visited the accused at night, more so I understand at the time leading up to his death when things were becoming, shall we say, difficult for him.' Then shrugging and fluttering his hands he added in a throwaway manner, 'It was used as an aphrodisiac I understand.'

Madeleine kept her eyes fixed on de Mean to avoid the glances she knew would be focussed on her following this remark.

'So Emile L'Angelier's need for arsenic increased towards the end of his life you would say, when, as you said, things became more difficult for him. And in his unfortunate circumstances, when he found it necessary to depend on such a drug, presumably larger quantities of this became inevitable to suit his requirements?'

'I have no information whatsoever about quantities and how much he took on these occasions. I am unable to give an opinion here.'

With the suggestion now arising about the possible suicide of an inadequate lover suffering increasing bouts of melancholy, John Inglis at last saw a chink in his favour for the first time in the proceedings. On the negative side however he was also well aware of this witness's glowing report of L'Angelier by setting him up as a virtuous citizen who at times indulged in the harmless embellishment of his earlier achievements in the Army, and equally harmless, a desire to better himself by involving himself with well-to-do friends. But coupled with this, John Inglis was also aware that this fine reputation Auguste de Mean had portrayed about his friend clashed abysmally with the local criticism of L'Angelier, which had not escaped his notice - or the reports published recently in various newspapers which were more revealing:

'A Frenchman with unpleasant habits,' it had been reported. 'Highly sexed,' they described him 'and a lecher known by many to have seduced young girls, and known to have taken arsenic as an aphrodisiac.'

For the time being however, John Inglis reserved judgement in building up on the evidence given by this witness. Up to now, the evidence from other witnesses had weighed heavily against the young girl whose life depended on his responsibility and when he had glanced her way, it was hard to tell from her expression whether she still upheld her claim of innocence as she had when he'd visited her in the Glasgow prison. She still appeared to be quietly impassive as she awaited her fate he thought, although he had to admit at that moment that the future looked bleak.

★ ★ ★

Back at the Smith's home in Glasgow - where Madeleine's parents had now returned from their country home in Rowaleyn - few of the family dared to venture out. They kept abreast with events in Madeleine's trial by newspapers delivered to the house or when they heard the newsvendor shouting at the end of the road when anything startling had been revealed. Mrs. Smith, who now spent more time in her bedroom than out of it, shuddered whenever she heard the boy calling, 'Read all about it,' at the top of his voice and on more than one occasion couldn't stop herself rushing to the window and opening it a fraction to listen. Once, a passer-by noticed her behind the curtain and shook a fist, calling, 'Murdering little whore you've got. You should all be ashamed,' and she had slunk back out of sight vowing never to show her face outside again.

Little was seen or heard of William Minnoch, although he had been forced to return to Glasgow where he'd found lodgings well away from where the Smiths lived. They knew he was to be called as a witness in the trial at some time but never sought him out and likewise he saw fit to distance himself from them. He still felt disturbed that he had to appear as a witness in a murder trial and more than anything feared the possibility of being tricked into making an unintentional statement that may be harmful to Madeleine. So much had happened beyond his understanding of the true situation, although with events about Madeleine's association with L'Angelier reported liberally in the press, he now began doubting his own trust in her innocence. As her future husband, he had convinced himself it was in her best interest when he decided to leave Glasgow, but in reality it had been to escape the cat-calls and vicious remarks of the local people. Then to his alarm, when he learned that his non-appearance in court could be detrimental in her defence, he had been forced to scurry back with great reluctance to his new digs in Glasgow where he was once again in the public eye.

Madeleine's father managed to carry on with his business as best he could despite his respectability being called into question by some colleagues, and learning that prospective clients had sought business elsewhere. Madeleine's young siblings, better able to take the knocks meted out by the public if recognised in the street, carried on with their lives almost unaffected. Janet had yet to appear in court, which she still awaited with dread but never voiced for fear of upsetting her mother. And Bessie, who was not to appear as a witness, carried on with her frivolous flirtations whenever an opportunity arose, despite them often being clouded by her sister's trial and she grew angry when continually questioned for details. Jack remained a staunch ally having visited his sister in prison as often as allowed and during the trial wrote her many letters of encouragement and support. Madeleine warmed to his generous show of affection and gained strength from his dedicated efforts to maintain her stamina and outwardly, this show of fortitude never wavered. In the same way as the governor and warders at the Glasgow prison were amazed by her calm attitude, so did the people in charge at the Edinburgh prison wonder at her composure. She ate everything provided by them, such as it was, and slept peacefully in her cell every night, even following days when witnesses testified against her and drained her confidence.

Miss Aitken's undivided loyalty also offered Madeleine encouragement as their friendship developed, and regarding herself as her only ally in the prison she increasingly took on a maternal role - which Madeleine secretly welcomed but for some reason never openly admitted. Her life by this time was in fact taking on an unreal existence as the trial progressed and her ability of being able to block out emotion took more and more hold. She still likened the circumstances to taking part in a drama where each day people performed a role in changing scenes with emotional outbursts erupting every now and then, and the fact whether she was deluding herself never occurred to her. It all helped to keep her on an even keel, as did the considerable time devoted each evening deciding what she should wear the following day! Clothes laid out meticulously in the evening were fussed over, matched against something else and then after changing it all for a different colour or style she often abandoned the whole lot for something worn the previous day before creeping beneath the coarse blankets to sleep peacefully until dawn the next day!

During her continuing surveillance by the matron, they also talked about what might be happening the following day in court with Madeleine speculating who might be there and what questions might be asked, 'and lies told!' she often exclaimed. As an excellent mimic she impersonated some of the witnesses as she picked out colourful events of the day and they often found themselves laughing helplessly, with the matron immediately checking herself when she thought about her position! But like the play-acting Madeleine often resorted to for consolation, so too did this escape from reality maintain her equilibrium when the most incriminating evidence weighed heavily against her. She relied repeatedly on this escapism, particularly when intimate details of her affair with L'Angelier were revealed in court and faces turned to her with interest or disgust. This was the worst time during the proceedings, having to listen to her sexual behaviour discussed openly by these ... *dreadful nosey people prying into my affairs who most likely did the same thing!*

As a further mainstay in keeping a hold on herself, Madeleine cherished the thought about her forthcoming marriage when the awfulness of this ordeal had been resolved and often she felt it to be the only thing keeping her sane. She knew deep in her heart there was no fear of losing William's continuing affection despite his appalling change when he'd visited her in prison or what her father had said - and regardless of the fact that she'd not had a single reply to the many letters she had written to him. He had promised to come to court to speak in her favour as her prospective husband, she told herself and sought comfort in that, totally ignorant of course that he had been summoned by law to do so!

With his appearance in court now looming ominously, William Minnoch had no such glowing attributes as a devoted future husband and could only cope in what he now regarded as a disastrous affair by putting on a bold front. Unlike the Smith family when he moved back to Glasgow nevertheless, he refused to remain indoors any more than he could help and met any remarks levelled at him from passers-by with contempt. 'Marrying a murderer are yer?' he was faced with once. And, 'Don't worry, she'll swing first, but watch out for yerself if she don't! You might be the next to get a dose!' At heart, William Minnoch was a sensitive man who up to now had led a reserved existence and although it needed a good deal of effort coming to terms with the humiliation he now faced, he managed with as much confidence as he could muster, until the time came for him to appear as a witness in court.

Chapter Thirty-Two

On the third day of the trial, crowds outside the court had lessened to some extent, as had the commotion. After the initial excitement, men had been compelled to go about their work. And with young children to care for, fewer women appeared. So it was only the roughnecks and people with time on their hands who turned up regularly each day, although there were enough of them to indulge in the shouts and boos when court officials arrived or to raise a cheer when Madeleine was hastened through the side door.

If witnesses happened to be recognised by the crowds, they were met either by shouts of abuse or encouragement and after they had been hustled into court noisy discussions often followed about their importance in the trial or otherwise. Newspapers were still selling hot off the press every day with vendors shouting themselves hoarse if journalists happened to divulge an interesting snippet of information when they slipped out of court, and this is when the tipsters taking bets in the crowd became at their busiest.

When William Minnoch arrived at the court, he cringed at the abusive remarks hurled from the crowd and as police cleared a way for him, he kept his head well down until he reached the door with fear clearly etched on his face. Looking around anxiously once inside and with no inkling of what to do or where to go, Madeleine watched unbelievingly as he stumbled and had to be escorted to the witness box where he stood looking dejected and bewildered. Worse, as proceedings got underway, both the prosecuting and defending counsels questioned him relentlessly.

'How long did you know Madeleine Smith? When did you propose marriage? Did you know about her association with L'Angelier while you were courting her?'

The barrage of questions was rapped out in quick succession and as the interrogation stepped up, he answered in a timid voice Madeleine failed to recognise. There were constant demands for him to speak up, which had the effect of making him falter and stammer when he was compelled to repeat what he had said.

'Did you really have no knowledge of the accused having an affair with Emile L'Angelier when you were courting her?' There was a hint of irritation in the voice of the Prosecuting Counsel.

'N-no, none whatsoever.'

'Even when you say you were living in the same house as the accused?'

'I had n-no reason t-to suspect this.'

The questions went on, and on, and often with a tinge of surprise he was repeatedly asked about the duration of his association with the accused when she was having an affair with L'Angelier at the same time. 'During which time it is now known that the accused was entertaining the deceased in her bedroom and in the house where you also had a room! Did you not have the slightest idea this was happening when you were living so near to her?'

'N..no. Not at all.'

'And arrangements for your wedding went ahead despite all this going on?'

'That is correct.'

Not once did William glance in Madeleine's direction and when he finished giving evidence his relief was palpable as he stumbled clumsily from the box with downcast eyes and made an awkward exit from the courtroom as swiftly as possible. Madeleine had followed his every move closely, willing him to look her way and desperately urging his support. Just a brief glance would have been sufficient and she felt mortified, not only by his appalling performance, but also by his not offering her any shred of encouragement. And as if this was not enough, she was plunged into further despair by the next witness who was someone she'd regarded as a good friend and had relied on to be a pillar of support.

'I was with the accused and felt appalled when she bought arsenic on one occasion. We were just out walking one day and when we passed a chemist Madeleine casually mentioned she had to buy something and we both went in.'

This was a friend Madeleine had grown up with, shared secrets with since childhood, and chosen to be a bridesmaid at her forthcoming wedding. She gave her testimony in a bright, self-assured manner when asked by the Counsel whether she had any knowledge of her friend using arsenic, for whatever reason.

'I thought it odd at the time,' she went on confidently, 'and I did question why she needed it.' She hesitated at this point, swivelling her eyes in Madeleine's direction before going on. Then more subdued, she went on to describe how her friend had explained that it was for killing rats, 'Although I did think it was rather strange and couldn't help wondering why she was doing this anyway rather than the gardener who should have been dealing with such things.'

The girl prattled on as she gained confidence, throwing her hands up at one point with a pained look when she said, 'I really could not believe what I was hearing when she asked for arsenic, quite light-heartedly too I remember. I was quite shocked to hear it. Something quite unexpected. We both bought some other things in the shop I remember, but it was the arsenic she asked for that stuck in my mind.'

Viewing the testimony from this witness as vital evidence, she was allowed to carry on talking about this casual purchase of arsenic in case any other crucial information came to light. And Madeleine hated her for what she was doing. Loathed her! ... *inferring indeed that she'd had murder in her heart when they had both entered that shop so innocently!* ... and when the lawyers were satisfied she could not provide any further useful information, they thanked her for what had been important evidence and called for the druggist whose shop the two girls had entered to appear in the witness box.

'Call Hugh Hart!'

Walking to the witness box confidently this man left no doubt in anyone's mind about the flippant attitude of the accused when he challenged her reason for requesting arsenic. 'Both the girls appeared to be in a somewhat skittish mood that day I would say sir,' and he further commented on the casual attitude adopted by the accused when he had requested her to sign his register for the poison. 'She told me that she would sign anything I liked! Those were her very words sir and I had to explain to her that this was a requirement instigated by law and that it would also be necessary for her to indicate the reason for buying it and how it was intended to be used.' He shifted about pompously at this point and added, 'I must say I felt rather indignant about her behaviour at the time.'

Conflicting with Madeleine's statement about needing this poison for killing rats, the next witness - a gardener in the employ of the Smith family - denied ever having been given any arsenic for this purpose. 'Although I must admit there were many of them beasts needing to be destroyed at the Smith's country 'ome,' he said. 'But I generally used a phosphorous paste to get rid of them things sir,' he went on, 'An' I wouldn't 'ave expected a young girl like Madeleine to be buying such a thing 'ad it bin wanted anyway.'

The prison matron cast a quick glance in Madeleine's direction, expecting to see a reaction of some kind under this escalating criticism of her behaviour but there was no indication whatsoever of emotion or distress. Only once had she noticed a show of interest that day when she had suddenly brightened and raised a hand when William Minnoch entered the box and then became aware of her body slumping slightly when he left.

If she felt drained by the way things were going, Madeleine still managed to disguise her feelings. At least during the lunch recess she decided to accept a drink of water, although she still chose to remain in the dock during the recession and not once during this time did her eyes ever wander around the court.

When they returned to prison at the end of the day the only consideration and support the matron showed was allowing Madeleine to speak her mind, and she listened patiently. It went beyond her responsibility to discuss the way things were going during the trial and despite the gloomy outlook Madeleine continued to sleep peacefully throughout the night and woke looking refreshed in the morning and ready for another day in court. But things were looking bad as one witness after another testified against her, even those she'd put her faith in as friends and felt in no doubt would be speaking in her favour. So whatever was passing through Madeleine's mind at this point in the trial when Miss Aitken glimpsed through the bars long after she had settled down for the night, she could only speculate.

★ ★ ★

In contrast to Madeleine's continuing air of serenity, William Minnoch all but went to pieces after leaving the court. Regarding him as an important witness, the crowd had swelled to several hundred and having greeted him with raucous cries when they saw him hastened into court earlier, now hurled catcalls as police struggled to get him away.

Having faced jeers and ridicule from the local people in Glasgow, this humiliation had been the last straw and with his appearance in the witness box now over his one object was to escape as quickly as he could from this grisly affair. He knew it meant breaking completely from Madeleine. That was uppermost in his mind, and with this realisation, his first visit had to be to the Smith's home to make his intentions clear. He knew they were also plagued by despair and shame, but having asked for their daughter's hand in marriage he felt it right to finalise the matter in a courteous manner. As it turned out however, he had no need for such concern when Madeleine's father greeted him warmly after such a long absence - even managing a smile, which temporarily lightened his haggard appearance, apart from relieving the delicate situation.

After a polite exchange of greetings and commiseration for the present circumstances, William totally ignored mentioning his appearance in the witness box and came straight to the point about his withdrawal from the marriage. 'I shall be moving away from the area as soon as possible,' he announced firmly, 'and should the court need to contact me again I intend leaving an address with my solicitor for that purpose only.' He met Mr. Smith's haunted expression with what he hoped was a look of determination and continued in a low voice, 'Whatever the outcome of the case however, we shall regretfully never meet again and I will be writing to Madeleine advising her of this.'

Hovering in the background, William noticed

Elizabeth Smith standing with her head lowered uncertainly, although as he raised a hand in recognition she instantly backed away and disappeared from sight. Mr. Smith, nodding his understanding of the situation, escorted him to the door and it must have been at the back of both their minds whether Madeleine would live long enough to read this promised letter from William. With as much dignity as he could muster, William removed himself speedily from the house that had caused such havoc in his life, as had the malicious tongues of Glasgow. He transferred his business to a distant place where he was totally unknown and vanished to a secret location never to be seen or heard of again by anyone in the Smith family. In truth, not only did he want to escape from what had turned into a nightmare existence, he also wanted to be well away from further humiliation when he learned that the letters written by Madeleine to her lover were due to be read out in court the following day. Already he'd felt ridiculed as a witness when questioned about his courtship with her at the same time as her being so intimately involved with L'Angelier, but to actually hear what she had written during the affair would have been unbearable. So with everyone eagerly awaiting the choice information that would reveal details about the lovers' intimate relationship, William Minnoch swiftly disappeared from sight and James and Elizabeth Smith shrunk further into obscurity as they also fearfully anticipated the grim revelation of their daughter's correspondence.

Chapter Thirty-Three

On Friday, the fourth day of the trial, the Prosecuting Counsel rose early in the proceedings with the announcement that the Clerk of court would be reading letters Emile L'Angelier had received from the accused.

'Written by the accused,' he announced slowly in a grave voice as he scanned the court, 'which depicts her as a woman totally without morals who enticed a man in an outrageous manner to her parents' home where they slept innocently unaware of what was going on.'

Madeleine lowered her eyes as the Prosecuting Counsel, James Moncrieff made this announcement, then fixed her gaze on the Clerk of the court as he produced the letters and read from an itemised list in an unemotional dreary tone before launching into reading each letter in turn. She appeared not to turn a hair when she took a swift glance around the court at one point, but inquisitive eyes were not on her now. Totally absorbed, every person in that court concentrated on the monotonous voice of the Clerk of the court for the information many of them had been waiting for, and not a sound was heard as they listened.

For reasons not disclosed to the court by the authorities, certain sexually explicit passages had been removed from some letters - maybe for the protection of any puritanical Victorian minds that happened to be in the court. The lawyers however, who needed to grasp every shred of evidence on which to base their judgement, were nonetheless put out as were the sensation-seeking journalists who wished to impress and shock their readers. Even so, judging by the gasps and outraged expressions, many people were still embarrassed by what was revealed and anything not fully disclosed journalists made it their business to embellish with their own ideas when they returned to their offices, which once more sent newspaper sales rocketing and queues forming before vendors had even arrived at their stands.

This development in the trial had also drawn a larger crowd than ever outside the court and people jostled noisily with the police when any snippet of news came from witnesses or the journalists coming and going. Money was also changing hands like wildfire with bets placed whether Madeleine would soon be led away to the gallows, and the way things were going this now looked like a distinct possibility.

Somehow, Madeleine still managed to hold on to her aloof appearance. Inwardly however, she was beginning to crumble. Helpful were the encouraging glances from John Inglis when she caught his eye, although with the appalling end to her life now hovering as a threat, she found it more and more of an effort to remain calm. Her friends were letting her down. William Minnoch had completely forsaken her, and the hostility in that court was getting to her. There had been no time in her life before when she had fought so desperately for composure and it was only when she was back in the seclusion of her cell at the end of the day that she betrayed any emotion.

'I feel the whole world has turned against me,' she murmured miserably and not for the first time the matron detected a look of fear. There was little she could say, and in her position dared to! She could only convey comfort by offering a sympathetic hand, feeling Madeleine shudder under her touch as she gave way to sobs. *How can I offer any words of comfort or reassurance to someone sliding into the shadow of the* hangman, she thought, and when their eyes met, she hoped at least that there would be some recognition of understanding.

★ ★ ★

One of the last witnesses to appear for the Prosecution was Mary Perry and as she approached the witness box in a confident manner and pledged her Oath, Madeleine's so far well-concealed feelings were in for a severe test.

For such a diminutive little figure, Mary spoke in a clear, loud voice about her friendship with the deceased, and how he had confided in her on many occasions concerning his affair with the accused. When encouraged and questioned fastidiously by James Moncrieff, she left nothing open to speculation and her testimony turned out to be the most damaging so far.

'There were occasions when Emile told me how ill he'd been after drinking coffee or chocolate that the accused had prepared,' she said with confidence and went on to describe how he had once wondered whether the drink could have been poisoned. 'He treated this lightly,' she said, 'almost as a joke I remember. But I felt concerned at the time and indicated this to him.'

Not a cough, whisper or rustle in the court interrupted her evidence and people leaned forward in their seats so as not to miss a word of her condemning statement.

'When he talked to me about whether the drink had been poisoned, I recalled him also saying that he said he would forgive the accused, even if she were to poison him,' and she darted a penetrating look at Madeleine.

'And did you question him about making such a statement?'

'I rebuked him for saying such an outrageous thing about someone claiming to love him and I asked why he should suspect that the accused should even think of doing such a thing.'

'And did he offer any explanation concerning his thoughts about the accused, perhaps that she was poisoning him?'

'Just that he felt she... the accused may not be sorry to be rid of him.'

Mary went on to describe L'Angelier's impeccable character and with a choke in her voice defined him as a strictly moral and religious young man. 'But he was completely besotted by the accused,' she said suddenly, shaking her head with irritation as she looked directly at Madeleine and held her glance with scorn. 'I know that he loved her to distraction and feared terribly about losing her affection.'

★ ★ ★

When Mary stepped down from the witness box, John Inglis for the defence knew that the way ahead spelt disaster in the face of this damning evidence and looking swiftly at Madeleine, who had not shifted her position or aura of control, certainly did not share her attitude of serenity. He nevertheless decided to set the scene in another direction by recalling evidence given earlier by another close friend of L'Angelier. Up to then many witnesses had spoken glowingly in favour of the deceased and his excellent character and loyalty, which Inglis now realised made it difficult for him to blacken as a scoundrel, blackmailer and a seducer of women. Whilst still upholding this embellished side of his character however, he considered there could be the possibility of throwing a new slant on his personality, which might perhaps persuade the jury along another course.

Robert Baker from Jersey, who had professed earlier about having a close friendship with the deceased, had described how L'Angelier contemplated suicide at one time after he'd been jilted by a girl. He had also given evidence about his friend's bizarre behaviour on other such occasions and when questioned in more detail about this had described further suicidal tendencies when up against difficulties of this kind.

Prior to recalling this witness nevertheless, John Inglis took the unusual approach of approaching the jury first, and standing before them with his hands resting on the bar, he informed them in a quiet confidential manner that he may be forced to refer to some rather unfortunate incidents concerning L'Angelier that had occurred before he had even met the accused. Then turning to the Prosecuting Counsel, and continuing in this quietly composed manner, he politely requested his assistance in this matter should it become necessary.

This gentle approach and courteous request to the Prosecution Counsel for co-operation may well have influenced all the members of the jury that here was a man with a dispassionate mind appraising the appalling responsibility that eventually rested with them, and this could well have caused the foreman of the jury to wrestle with his conscience. Being a fair-minded man with a family of his own, he may even have offered a prayer for guidance when he glanced at the beautiful young girl in the dock awaiting his judgement. And with John Inglis realising he needed all his strength, persuasion and legal expertise to proceed with his defence after Mary Perry's condemning evidence, he possibly also offered up a prayer at this juncture when he announced, 'Recall Robert Baker,' and launched into an appraisal of L'Angelier's state of mind.

★ ★ ★

In his soft persuasive manner, John Inglis encouraged

Robert Baker to talk freely about his friendship with L'Angelier, 'And you shared accommodation with him did you not when he first arrived in Scotland?' he concluded.

'That is correct your honour.'

'And did he discuss personal details of his life with you? Perhaps the association with girls he knew and any affairs he may have had.'

'On occasions we talked sir. Usually when he was feeling low, we'd have a drink together and got talking.'

Robert Baker's ongoing account concerning his friend - which he'd already given earlier he realised and now had to repeat - left no doubt that L'Angelier had suffered severe bouts of depression, particularly when crossed in love. Furthermore, that he had often turned to friends and talked in confidence concerning his depressive state and fear of being spurned by women.

'Would you say that he was suicidal when he had these bouts of depression - and maybe talked about doing something drastic?' John Inglis enquired quietly.

'Yes sir and it worried me,' Robert Baker answered readily. 'When he felt really bad once he told me he wished himself out of this world. I remember that well.'

'So he had talked to you about ending his life?'

Baker hesitated, seemingly lost for words as he stared vacantly, trying to collect his thoughts. He knew he had already said something similar when summoned to the witness box before and possibly began wondering where all this was leading and whether he could be doing his friend a disservice. With gentle persuasion from John Inglis however, that 'In this court of Law, Robert Baker you must answer all questions put to you,' his witness felt under pressure to answer and continued in a barely audible voice.

'Once sir,' he began in a faltering voice, 'like I said

before your honour, on one occasion it was... he began climbing out of the window. High up we were in that building sir and he would have killed himself if he had fallen. I pulled him back and shut the window. I was that frightened.' Robert Baker looked relieved as he declared this heroic gesture, absolving any guilt he may have had about betraying his friend, and this information was just what John Inglis needed at this point. Pondering in speculation for a few seconds before continuing, he walked slowly towards the witness box - many thought with a look of understanding.

'And what about ending his life by taking poison? Did he ever talk to you about that?' he asked gently.

'No never sir. At least I never got to know about that.'

'Did you at any time know that he had arsenic in his possession?'

'No sir. He never told me anything about arsenic.'

★ ★ ★

Having steered questioning in the direction of suicidal tendencies, John Inglis then recalled other witnesses who had claimed to be a friend of the deceased and knew him well enough for confidences to be exchanged.

'I remember him taking up a knife on one occasion and threatening to stab himself,' a friend from Jersey revealed after John Inglis had persuaded him at length that any information he could provide was of the utmost importance and should not be withheld. And urged in the same fashion, this suicidal tendency was further corroborated by another acquaintance who went on to state that Emile had confided to him once about his habit of taking arsenic.

Employees from the warehouse where L'Angelier worked were recalled to the witness box and added to this growing account about Emile's morbid turn of mind.

Many of them knew he hoped to be married in the near future and said they were puzzled by his behaviour at times. 'He was always very quiet at work,' one witness stated. 'He hardly spoke to anyone and then, just before his death,' he said, lowering his voice with the news he was about to impart, 'he suddenly became very depressed. Utterly miserable he looked and when people asked what was wrong he talked about killing himself and we all tried to cheer him up and told him not to talk like that.'

With another side of L'Angelier's personality now becoming known as John Inglis intended, he nevertheless responded sympathetically when further witnesses, perhaps through guilt about betraying a colleague's unfortunate side of life, also upheld his fine morals and regular attendance in church and praised his good work. And having given time for them to recover from their feelings of remorse, if indeed this was the case, Inglis then turned to the use of arsenic which some witnesses had mentioned when questioned before and now endorsed again.

Several druggists were recalled concerning the supply of arsenic and walking across to the table containing exhibits, John Inglis extracted a photograph of L'Angelier, holding it before them in turn and asking whether they recognised the man, which many of them did.

'I remember this gentleman calling in late one evening,' said one. 'Clutching his stomach he was and asking for laudanum to cure his pain.'

'Such as the severe griping pains the deceased apparently experienced just prior to his death would you say?'

'Yes. That was more than likely sir. Although I must make it clear I didn't supply this person with arsenic on that occasion, or on any occasions. I concluded he had purchased it elsewhere, if that had been the cause of his pain of course.'

All the druggists confirmed the mystery and shame people had when requesting arsenic and being asked to sign the poison register. All agreed too that when questioned about its use, they never admitted needing it for their own consumption. 'They generally gave another reason for buying it rather than the real purpose, and the most common reason given was for destroying vermin,' one witness stated.

'As happened when the accused requested it on one occasion for killing rats, when in point of fact she needed this for her personal use as a cosmetic but felt reluctant to say so through sheer embarrassment?' John Inglis retorted.

With this observation steering evidence away from any criminal intent when Madeleine bought arsenic and John Inglis thanking all the witnesses it had been necessary to recall to corroborate their earlier statements to make the situation clear, he then turned to the last witness for questioning - Madeleine's young sister, Janet, with whom she had shared a bed on many occasions.

In the company of a court official, Janet walked uncertainly to the witness box and her pretty, young face, not too unlike that of her sister, clearly betrayed her anxiety. Similarly to the witnesses recently recalled, John Inglis realised that everything this young lady said would also be of vital importance in the defence. She had been present in Madeleine's room during the time of her alleged association with L'Angelier and as a child just short of thirteen years old he also realised she would have to be treated with care. He allowed time to make certain she had settled comfortably, and as she peered anxiously just a fraction higher than the top of the witness box, he smiled kindly as he put his questions in an easy way for her to understand.

'I often saw my sister drinking cocoa,' she answered timidly when questioned about any drinks that were made in her room. 'Although I didn't like it myself so I never had any and no one else in the family liked cocoa either but Madeleine seemed to like it and often made it.' Her voice trailed away nervously as she shrunk back into the witness box so that just the top of her head was visible and John Inglis smiled reassuringly again, waiting a while before she appeared, her eyes large and curious, wondering what would happen next.

'And did you ever watch her make this cocoa at any time in the room Janet?'

'No, I never actually did, ever,' she said peering over the top of the bar. 'I always went to sleep early you see. My sister always went to sleep much later.'

'Was there always a kettle in the room to make this drink,' he asked gently, 'and cups?'

'Yes there was a kettle, and some cups.'

'And when you shared the bedroom with your sister did you ever wake at any time and notice that your sister was not lying beside you or perhaps was not in the room?'

Janet pulled at her lip nervously and looked worried and John Inglis gently reassured her to take her time until she felt ready with her reply.

'I'm certain Madeleine was with me all the time when we slept together,' she murmured softly. 'Sometimes she went to bed early I remember and I am sure there were times when we went to sleep at about the same time.' With her voice fading and coughing nervously, she peeked a quick glimpse at her sister and encouraged by Madeleine's smile went on quietly, 'She was always lying next to me when I woke up in the morning though. I do know that. And she was generally awake as well when I woke up.'

It was on this gentle note of two sisters innocently sleeping throughout the night therefore that John Inglis decided it was the right moment to end his questioning for the day. And the court rose.

Chapter Thirty-Four

There had been no relaxation for the judges and barristers that weekend as they continued to weigh up evidence by witnesses so far and to reflect on the outcome, and facing the sixth day of the trial, Madeleine began wondering how much longer she could go on. She thanked God for being able to keep up her pretence of calm so far, but as time dragged on, frustration and fear was beginning to take a hold. Her obstinacy about remaining in the dock all day without a break however never weakened and although not wanting to put pressure on her by mentioning this, it was also having an effect on Miss Aitken, who twice her age was beginning to stiffen up after sitting still for hours on end! Their evenings back at the prison had altered too. No longer did the friendly talks take place. Neither did the long discussions about the happenings of the day. Nor was there any further mimicry of witnesses, or even the dithering over clothes chosen for the following day. The only constant routine was Madeleine's ability to sleep throughout the night, which continued to astound the matron and prison staff when she turned in each evening and approaching the hard bench that passed for a bed, immediately fell into a deep sleep! To a large extent this put her in good stead for the gruelling day ahead, although with the end of the trial now in sight she probably needed more than sleep to maintain her strength during the summing up.

★ ★ ★

In a court now overbearingly hot and stuffy despite

the small hours of the day, the tension was electric. People had arrived early on Tuesday, the seventh day of the trial, to make sure of the most advantageous positions and as the judges and lawyers were led into the court, the silence was awesome. All witnesses had now been interrogated and cross-examined and with the jury now looking less than comfortable with their onerous obligation in sight, they were not the only ones in that court still speculating on the previous day when John Inglis had thrown a new slant on the proceedings. The situation nevertheless still looked ominous for Madeleine, particularly when the Counsel for the Prosecution rose to begin his summing up.

James Moncrieff spoke of what he described as his distasteful responsibility of possibly condemning a young girl to die on the scaffold. On the other hand, and surprisingly so considering his earlier statements, he had little to say and showed no compassion in favour of Emile L'Angelier, even going as far as to condemn him as a practised seducer! His address continued hour after hour in much the same vein, swinging only occasionally to L'Angelier's good qualities as described by friends, to highlighting the statements made by many witnesses who had confirmed L'Angelier buying and using arsenic. However, as he moved on to the appalling end to his life, he then raised the question of Madeleine's motives and subsequent behaviour and stressed to the jury the importance of keeping this in mind at all times when making an assessment. 'Furthermore,' he said, as he looked at them severely over the top of his spectacles, 'justice in itself would be defeated if you were to say, or even think, that you should not convict someone unless you found a person who actually *saw* the crime committed, and I emphasise here the word '*saw*'. In the case of administration of poison, that remark applies with peculiar force. In truth, administering poison *before* witnesses, and again I feel I must emphasise the word '*before*'; this is so far from affording a presumption of guilt that it is sometimes the strongest proof of innocence.'

The jury were most probably endeavouring at this point to put this advice into some kind of logical reasoning more suited to their understanding – which also possibly applied to many others looking confused in the court.

He went on to point out that a criminal did not have to *look* like a criminal in order to be convicted, or indeed to *behave* like a criminal to be convicted. He also denied that an innocent face was proof of an innocent mind, and looking directly at Madeleine, whose calm composure was maintained throughout his laborious summing up, this remark also undoubtedly held the court's attention as they too looked in her direction.

'It is impossible to prove that L'Angelier did visit Madeleine Smith the night before he died,' he continued, as he paced slowly before the jury. 'No one saw him, and investigations concerning anyone who may have had sight of him has never revealed any information at any time,' he said stopping abruptly before them. 'And when he returned to his lodgings in agony, dying in dreadful agony from poisoning by arsenic,' he emphasised with a pained look, 'he gave no indication to his landlady about where he had been, who he had seen, or what had happened to him.'

Madeleine concentrated on everything he had to say and even though much of it was repetitive and boring, her attention never wavered. Just once she dropped her gaze when he held one of her letters at arm's length and selected a passage that revealed her passion.

'*How do you keep yourself warm in bed my darling?*' he read slowly, allowing time for this statement to be absorbed. *'I have Janet with me sometimes, but I often wish you were with me. Would you not put your arms around your Mimi, and fondly embrace her and keep her warm?'*

'This is the romantic outpouring of a love-sick young girl,' he exclaimed as he flicked it with his other hand. 'It's a desire to mate! Not to murder! And there were many other similar such letters. But,' he cautioned, speaking quietly now as he looked at each member of the jury in turn, 'this does not prove anything gentlemen. Only passion may be read into this letter, as it can with many of the others written by the accused which were read out here in this court.' And here he once again reminded the jury that their verdict must be based on the facts of the case. 'Pure facts!' he stressed, pursing his lips. 'Nothing else! The accused had grown tired of her lover remember, as mistresses often do! And she had taken another suitor in the meantime and accepted his proposal of marriage remember,' he said shaking a finger, 'and with wedding arrangements having been put in hand, what's more at a time when she was still seeing this unfortunate man!'

He regarded each member of the jury in turn again as he paced slowly, biding his time in speculation. 'This unfortunate young man who had been her lover over many months,' he began quietly, 'refused to be cast aside at her bidding, understandably so in the circumstances you must agree? But what else could he do? And more importantly for you to consider gentlemen, what could she do?' He spoke convincingly of passionate feelings and motives that would rise to the surface when someone has to be removed from what had become an inconvenient arrangement. 'And you must remember at all times that the person the accused wished to be rid of died in very suspicious circumstances after visiting her the evening before and died in agony the following morning.'

Only a slight shuffling was heard in the court as the Lord Advocate allowed a short time before issuing his customary words of admonition to the jury when he told them he was convinced of the guilt of the accused and invited them to share his assumption that Madeleine Smith was guilty of murder. This at least indicated that his long speech - which had been wearisome at times and intensely boring when evidence already etched in their minds was repeated over and over - had come to an end and many must have sighed with relief. All eyes however focussed immediately as he stood squarely before the jury and announced solemnly in a loud voice, 'Gentlemen. I now leave the case in your hands. I see no outlet whatsoever for this unhappy person and if you come to the same result as I have done, there is but one course open to you and that is to return a verdict of guilty of this charge.'

Madeleine too had her eyes fixed on the man who had both praised and maligned her character and in the stunned silence following, some jurors turned to look long and hard in her direction. When the court rose for the day, she stepped delicately down the steps for her return journey to prison – and outside the court in the increasing mêlée, more bets were being placed on the outcome of the trial.

★ ★ ★

For most of the journey back to the prison, Madeleine remained silent, just acknowledging Miss Aitken once when she placed a hand briefly over hers. When they arrived, and hesitated at the gate as officials wrestled with bolts and locks, she asked to be left entirely alone that evening with the excuse of being completely exhausted. Madeleine's real need however was to reflect on the events of the day and come to terms with what was happening, or would be happening very soon. Up to this point, she had felt in control. Now she was afraid. The hostility of witnesses, even those she'd placed her faith in, had completely unnerved her and when James Moncreiff had recommended that the jury should return a verdict of guilty, it had been like facing wolves baying for her death. So far, and ever since she had been arrested, she had managed to absolve herself from what had been determined by others as a crime. Her innocence was a belief she'd desperately clung to in order to stay sane, but as witnesses had passed through the court over the past days, even her own little sister who had been so nervous and tried so hard, she now recognised that her show of pretence was crumbling at last and her despair plummeted to rock bottom. She really believed at this point that there was no one left in the world who could offer any encouragement, support or love - even Miss Aitken who had been so kind, or the man she'd hoped to marry, and she still couldn't believe or even understand why he had let her down so badly.

Not at any time during the proceedings however had Madeleine reflected on the hurt she had caused to her loved ones by exposing them to shame and humiliation - although she had questioned once whether she was deserving of receiving the love for which she now yearned. The matron of the prison had become her only source of the affection she so desperately needed now and having turned to her at times as a daughter would to a mother, she knew she could never have survived without this undemanding devotion.

Whether Madeleine's thoughts ever turned to Emile and his agonising death will never be known. She had not mentioned his name or talked about him since her arrest, even to Miss Aitken. And if anyone ever questioned her about him she'd simply smiled and turned away. Now he was dead, he was no longer part of her life. It was as though he had never existed. And despite her traumatic existence in both the Glasgow and Edinburgh prisons and her ordeal in court, she'd continued to delude herself this was an episode in her life she had unfortunately been involved in that had to be endured. Now things were different however. The final days of her trial had changed all that and were taking their toll, and as the night closed in she felt grateful for being able to remove her brave face and indulge in the welcome release it brought. She was still not free from the torment though as her thoughts flittered. She wondered about the rope and her heart thudded. It haunted her, worse than it had in the Glasgow gaol. She could not rid herself of the fear. She wondered how long it would take to die. What would it be like? Would she be allowed to wear a silk scarf around her neck if she asked? The rope was bound to be rough. Would she choke slowly? Or would it be quick? She remembered learning from her first lover in London how people screamed and kicked their legs out when they swung. He had wanted to take her to a public hanging and recalled her horror as she had once before. She had not wanted to know about that side of life then. *And still didn't! They can't find me guilty ... they can't! How could they? They can't let me die! ... it's so wrong! I don't want to die!*

As the light outside dimmed and the cell gradually darkened, Madeleine clasped her arms tight round her body. She knew the violent trembling would come and told herself this was purely a release of emotion. And she straightened out. Tensing up rigidly. Gripping her hands and forcing herself to take a hold ... *the strain of the past days has been enormous and my reserves have taken a pasting ... but I shall be all right. It will be better tomorrow* ... and she struggled, fighting for control, praying quietly and earnestly as never before in her life ... and when the matron looked at her later that night, sleeping peacefully as she always had, she had no idea of the torment that Madeleine had suffered.

Chapter Thirty-Five

On Wednesday the 8th of July, Madeleine climbed into the dock dressed attractively as on previous days. Miss Aitken had ventured a consoling influence regarding the most appropriate outfit to wear and despite Madeleine's spirits lagging so despairingly the previous night, it had not affected her vanity when encouraged to select something suitable. Together they chose a dress in the new purple shade, displeasing to some in the world of fashion as being too garish, but most likely finally selected by Madeleine in defiance as she endeavoured to boost her confidence! She still clutched in her hand the smelling salts, unused so far, recommended by the matron, and in the other hand she now held a silk square matching her outfit which she took time to arrange carefully in her lap when invited to be seated in the dock.

The judges were already in position beneath the canopy when she entered the court and looking confidently at the man who held her life in his hands, she offered up a silent prayer. With John Inglis most likely having done likewise earlier, he now rose to present his case for the defence to a court that had suddenly been plunged into silence. Nobody in that court however, or the boisterous crowd outside, felt the tension as keenly as Madeleine. Nor had any man held her attention or urgent desire for help as the man who would soon be appealing to the jury for a conviction in keeping with his own. She looked at each member of the jury, all strangers to her with the responsibility of allowing her life to continue or not and she tightened her hands in her lap, resolving to preserve her dignity at all cost. Whatever the outcome and whatever her fate she told herself over and over, she would force herself to remain calm while she was in the full glare of the public, and as the opening statement by John Inglis sent a shudder down her spine, she clutched her hands tight to stop the trembling.

'Gentlemen of the jury,' he began. 'The charge against the accused is murder, and the punishment of murder is death.'

She felt the stares. There was no need to look. She knew all eyes would be in her direction. It happened each time after a dramatic statement. Her face felt hot and she looked down at her feet desperately trying to think about something else, but nothing came into her mind as John Inglis continued speaking in his quiet dignified manner.

He likened the circumstances of the trial to a heavily endorsed drama when an attractive young girl besotted by a man demonstrating his power over women, had fallen victim to his intimidation. And as he moved closer to the jury, leaning towards them as though intending to divulge a confidence, he placed his hands on the rail and said quietly, 'Gentlemen. There are certain peculiarities in this case of so singular a kind that there is almost an air of romance and mystery invested in it from beginning to end.' Straightening as he waited for the murmuring in the court to subside, he walked the length of the jury stall and back in a relaxed manner, and as he turned to face them, continued in a restrained tone. 'There is something so touching and exciting even, in the age and the sex and social standing of the accused,' he said. 'Ay, and I must add that with the public attention so directed to this trial that they watch our proceedings and hang on our words with such anxiety and eagerness of expectation, I feel almost bowed down and overwhelmed by the magnitude of the task that is imposed on me.' This remark undoubtedly related to the unquenchable thirst of journalists for knowledge on the day Madeleine's letters were read, some of which were ready for referral at his request on the exhibits table.

Standing to his full height now with thumbs thrust in the lapels of his waistcoat, he went on more aggressively. 'You are being invited gentlemen, and ay, encouraged by the Prosecuting Counsel, to snap the thread of this young girl's life and to consign her to an ignominious death on the scaffold!' Pursing his lips, he looked directly at Madeleine, lingering as he held her glance. And when he turned to face the jury his face set into an expression of indignation. 'A girl known to her family and friends as a gentle, confiding and affectionate girl,' he said firmly, 'who has been an ornament in her happy home what's more, and has taken pride of place there.'

Hanging on every word of this dramatic discourse, the jury gave their full attention, as did the judges, and by the continuing silence the entire court. Madeleine's eyes were also riveted in his direction and never having shifted in her seat since entering the dock that morning, her appearance was statuesque.

★ ★ ★

Continuing in a similarly strident tone, John Inglis tipped the balance further in Madeleine's favour by referring to L'Angelier's shortcomings, emphasising the facts gathered from witnesses who had described him as a character eager to marry into a wealthy family. 'And considering his standing in life and career so far,' he said, shaking his head in contempt, 'certainly not worthy of a girl such as the accused.'

He went on to describe the instability of the deceased. His alleged melancholy. His fits of depression as described by close friends. 'And whether intending to carry out his objective or not,' he stressed, 'he threatened suicide on many occasions as you have heard.'

Stepping towards the exhibits table, he selected a letter and feeling in a pocket for his pince-nez returned slowly to face the jury again, pointing out as he approached that what some of the witnesses may have mistaken as a sign of virtue in the deceased could have been more aptly described as a vice. 'And furthermore, laying the blame for this on his victim!' he said, turning to jab a finger at Madeleine in the dock.

Holding the letter at arm's length with a look of distaste, he said, 'The implication in a letter written by L'Angelier criticised her of bad habits and lack of restraint.' And as his face creased into a frown, 'This clearly describes his cunning if you listen carefully gentlemen,' and adjusting his pince-nez into position he selected a passage from a letter written by L'Angelier in the early days of the relationship.

*'I am trying to break myself of all of my very bad
habits. It is you I have to thank for this, which
I do sincerely from my heart.'*

'For what other reason would he make such a statement I ask you other than having a clear intention of ingratiating himself with his victim?' he exclaimed.

Repeatedly John Inglis quoted earlier accusations made against Madeleine and instantly turned them around in her favour. He flourished another letter plucked from the table that concerned the night of her deflowering when L'Angelier visited her at Rowaleyn. The Lord Advocate had read this previously when he addressed the jury on behalf of the Prosecution when the court had been so shocked by the brazen behaviour of the accused. Now Inglis placed the blame wholeheartedly on L'Angelier!

*We should indeed have waited till we were married,
Mimi. It was very bad indeed. I shall look with
regret on that night.. You are my wife,
and I have the right to expect from you the
behaviour of a married woman, or else I have no
honour in you.*

'How corrupting that influence must have been!' he thundered. 'How vile the depths to which that man resorted for accomplishing his nefarious purpose!'

He paced measurably before the jury still scowling, hesitating momentarily to look at each one in turn - some of them flinching in embarrassment. 'Gentlemen,' he said with contempt, 'whose fault was that? I ask you. Whose doing was that? Without temptation and without evil teaching, would such a girl fall into depths of degradation? No!' he exclaimed indignantly, throwing wide his hands. 'Influence from without - and a most corrupting influence at that - can alone account for such a fall. And yet,' he said, quieter now, 'through the midst of this frightful correspondence, and I wish to God it could have been concealed from you, and indeed from the world,' he flustered, 'and I am sure the Lord Advocate would have spared us this had he not felt it had been necessary for justice in this trial. However, I say to you again Gentlemen, that through the midst of this correspondence there breathes a spirit of devoted affection from the accused towards a man who had destroyed her. And this strikes me as most touching.'

John Inglis, shrewd and experienced as a lawyer, was also a born actor and the bigger the part he played, the more he excelled himself with his power of speech. He also knew how to manage people and knowing the fifteen men before him would soon to be facing the most important decision in their lives, allowed time for the facts he'd given so far to be absorbed. He knew what he had said had been heavily endorsed with his own viewpoint, also that he had relaxed and increased the pace as he considered necessary to further a point. And having achieved what appeared to be a favourable reaction as he regarded the expressions of the jury, he now proceeded in a quieter manner as he continued to analyse the affair between the deceased and accused, albeit still upholding Madeleine's character and presenting justice heavily in her favour.

Having already mentioned the letters that had had such a crucial impact on the court earlier by their erotic content – at the same time as recognising that they had damned the accused - he referred to them again but with a different slant and a further reproach against L'Angelier.

'Whatever else could have been expected of a young girl when her lover constantly derided her for being cold and unemotional?' he asked, and went on to suggest that the accused could even have been encouraged to write such explicit letters so that they may be used by the deceased when the opportunity arose. He scrutinised the jury as he allowed this to be absorbed and - placing faith in an anticipated reaction - drew himself up to his full height and jabbing a finger roared, 'He not only preserved these letters gentlemen, he kept them! He kept them as an engine of power so he might carry out his cold-blooded intent. And not only content to possess himself of her person, he intended using them for raising himself on the social scale by marriage. He blackmailed her, gentlemen. He used blackmail to achieve these ends!'

For a second John Inglis turned aside, closing his eyes, and in a voice bordering on distress leaned towards the men seated before him, shaking his head as he stressed,

'She repeatedly asked for the return of her letters gentlemen. Which were rightfully hers. She pleaded for their return, over and over, but Angelier's object had been blackmail from the very beginning, and that object he pursued constantly and unflinchingly to the very end,' he said, emphasising each word. 'He wished to expose this young girl to her friends and family, indeed to the world at large! He wanted to drive her to destruction, or to suicide as she threatened at one time you will remember, rather than let her out of his power.'

★ ★ ★

All members of the jury remained unmoving on their bench following this emotional outburst and silence filled the court like a fog descending. Madeleine remained unflinchingly calm and not once had her eyes left the man fighting for her life. Such was the concentration that even the oppressive heat and stuffy atmosphere had no apparent effect in that court as John Inglis, indomitable in his oratory and power of persuasion, continued relentlessly to defend her innocence.

Having mentioned Madeleine's threatened suicide, he now turned to evidence given earlier by a witness concerning L'Angelier's threat of suicide when thwarted in earlier love affairs - and at this point he offered counsel for the jury's judgement whether he had met his death by suicide or by accident. 'Whatever way he met his death,' he advised measurably, 'the question for you to consider gentlemen has to be whether murder, as has been suggested here, is actually proved. You are not bound in any way to account for his death,' he said advisedly. 'You are not in the slightest degree bound to account for the death of L'Angelier. You must remember that. The question you have to ask yourselves gentlemen is whether his death was caused by his own hand or by the hand of the accused?'

Returning to information given earlier by a doctor and one of the druggists concerning the embarrassment of people when purchasing arsenic, he referred to their obvious dilemma when asking for this. 'Often the genuine reason for its use would be cast aside through shame, even to the extent of suffering intense pain prior to death, or submitting to medical assistance if it was intended for self-destruction,' he exclaimed, 'as happened when L'Angelier told his landlady there was no need to send for a doctor.'

Switching to Madeleine's purchase of arsenic, he emphasised the puritanical state of her mind rather than any cunning guile when she required this for use as a cosmetic and said she needed it for ridding her home of rats. 'She did not wish to be ridiculed, which understandably as a young girl, she suspected could happen. She bought it quite innocently gentlemen when she walked into that druggist's shop. Quite openly she asked for it,' he said as a throwaway remark, and then went on questionably, 'and would such a girl enter a druggist's shop to buy arsenic with the specific intent of murder would you suppose? Is it conceivable that a young girl like that would even be capable of such devious cunning for the purpose of throwing her accusers off the scent if there had been any intent of using this arsenic to kill her lover?'

Inglis similarly argued about the quantity of arsenic consumed by the deceased. 'Half an ounce!' he said with a look of amazement. 'Two hundred and forty grains! Enough to kill forty men it has been established! How could anyone – anyone - have persuaded L'Angelier to take such an enormous quantity of this poison in a drink of cocoa or chocolate - or anything else - without his objection? It would have been gritty and ridiculously unpalatable to say the very least. Utterly undrinkable! So is it possible to believe that he – or anyone for that matter – would have accepted and actually consumed such a beverage?' He turned abruptly towards the jury again after walking away with his mouth clenched in contempt and threw at them, 'It's preposterous! Unthinkable!'

John Inglis paused as his expression settled and - assessing the jury's reaction from the bland expressions he observed - decided to continue championing the blameless character of the accused. 'Having been brought up within the sanctity of a fine upstanding family,' he said proudly, as though discussing his own daughter, 'how could she even contemplate murder? There was no motive here for her to do so in any case. No reason at all. In fact, she had every reason for wishing this man to remain alive. As long as L'Angelier lived,' he stressed flourishing a hand, 'there was a chance of being able to persuade him to return her letters, which he so obstinately refused to do. And the moment he was dead, with events cascading alarmingly to the situation she finds herself in today, she knew that this possibility had been lost and everything written about events taking place between them would be made public knowledge,' and observing the reaction, John Inglis knew that this statement had made an impression.

Three hours had passed since he had risen to speak. Three hours of splendid oratory during which he had never wavered from praising his client's character and criticising that of the deceased. Then seeking further to prove Madeleine's innocence rather than guilt at this point, he went on to examine the reason for her sudden disappearance when she heard about L'Angelier's death which had prompted suspicion and led to her arrest for his murder.

'This was clearly, and overwhelmingly so, evidence of her innocence rather than guilt. When she realised her letters were to be exposed, she feared the embarrassment it would cause her family. This was probably her first thought! And knowing how much they had already suffered from this dreadful affair so far, what more could she have done?' However, many in that court were yet to be convinced that Madeleine Smith's flight from Glasgow was entirely an act of innocently escaping from the public eye.

Chapter Thirty-Six

As the proceedings continued, the hushed court assured John Inglis of concentrated observation as they awaited his judgement concerning Madeleine's decision to flee from her home, and as he walked towards the fifteen men with concern etched on their faces, he stood before them with renewed energy.

'The accused knew she would be totally exposed when these letters were discovered by people investigating L'Angelier's death,' he flared suddenly. 'Of course she knew! And understandably, she ran away. She was terrified at the prospect of everything that had happened being revealed to her family, nay, the whole community, and the world as it happened,' he said with disgust. 'And what else could have been expected of a young girl I ask, who grieved for the distress it would cause her family and, worried out of her mind, could only think about removing herself from them?'

He rested his hands on the rail before the jury, speaking again in a confidential manner. 'And she returned almost straight away to her home, did she not, gentlemen? Her distraught family discovered her after their frantic searching. And encouraged by them she returned to her home. Quite willingly she returned gentlemen, where they consoled her and assured her of the love and support she so desperately needed.' With his face transformed into a mask of pity he went on, 'The state of that young mind is unimaginable after first being subjected to blackmail by L'Angelier concerning the return of her letters, then learning that he had died. And following that, her alarming realisation that all her letters, which she had so innocently written for L'Angelier's eyes only, were about to be snatched by strangers! What more could she have done I say to you again gentleman, other than to remove herself from her home in order to prevent any further misery to her family?'

Whether the jury was influenced by this was not obvious. He judged them to be moved emotionally however. They had remained motionless the whole time, watching his every movement, some still refusing to meet his challenging stare. However, satisfied so far that all augured well, he turned towards them with a sorrowful expression saying he would like to read to them another letter. 'This is written by the accused,' he said pacing slowly. 'It is a letter she wrote to L'Angelier gentlemen in sheer desperation after he threatened to expose her by sending her letters to her father.'

On my bended knees, I write you and ask you, as you hope for mercy at the Day of Judgement, do not inform on me. Do not make me a public shame. Emile, my life has been one of bitter disappointment. You and only you can make the rest of my life peaceful. My own conscience will be a punishment that I shall carry to my grave. I have deceived the best of men. You may forgive me, but God never will.

'Picture the moral temperament here,' he said forcefully. 'Paint the feelings if you can, of a human being who could even contemplate preserving letters such as you've heard read in this court from a girl described so innocently.'

He replaced the letter on the table before him, smoothing it flat and taking his time before returning to face them. Then suddenly glancing up at the jury with tears in his eyes he held their attention in a voice close to breaking and demanded in exasperation, 'Is that the state of mind of a murderess? I beg you. How can anyone assume such a frame of mind by reading those pleas in a letter written by a young girl?' Hesitating a moment to compose himself, he went on, 'Or do you believe a suggestion that was made in this court that this letter actually covers a piece of deceit?'

Fully recovered now, John Inglis stood to his full height, breathing deeply, and as he backed away he thundered, 'No! Certainly not! The finest actress that ever lived could never have written those words unless she had been genuinely driven by despair!'

The jury, and the rest of the court, were undoubtedly influenced by the compassion of this man and his emotional outburst. It had certainly been a plausible argument in favour of the innocence of the accused ... and gaining confidence by this assumption as the silence continued, Inglis went on adamantly. 'My learned friend, the Lord Advocate, suggested that the accused prepared for L'Angelier's deliberate murder whilst still writing these letters, needing him to be out of her life, it was implied, when William Minnoch had proposed marriage.' With a shrug, he shook his head disparagingly and, with a swift glance around the court before facing the jury again, he went on, 'I must dismiss this observation gentleman. Completely out of hand I must reject it as being too ridiculous to even consider. How could a young Victorian girl of such refinement and good breeding possibly be capable of such wickedness? Think, gentleman, I implore you, and consider how foul and how unnatural this murder has been suggested. The murder of a person, who over a period of time was the object of love by the accused, and an unworthy object and unholy love as it happened to be,' he said as he flourished a hand. 'But, while it lasted, it was a deep, absorbing and unselfish devoted passion for that person who the accused is now suspected of murdering!'

Grasping the bar he lowered his voice as he leaned confidentially again towards the jury, 'Are you content with that conjecture gentlemen?' he asked. 'And will you be content with the suspicion levied against the accused however repugnant it must appear?' Adopting a firmer attitude now he further enquired, 'Or will you be so unreasonable as to assume that, with the man having died of poisoning, that the theory of the Prosecution is the most probable?'

His face darkened as he strutted back and forth several times with his hands clutched tight behind his back, then halting suddenly he demanded, 'Gentlemen, is that the manner in which a jury should treat such a case? Is that the kind of proof on which you would convict a young girl on a capital offence, and furthermore, be content to commit her to death on the gallows?'

★ ★ ★

Clearly the jury was moved, in particular William Moffat, the foreman, a teacher from the High School, who would soon be called upon to announce the verdict. As a family man with two teenage daughters, he had considered his own feelings had he been in the position of facing similar circumstances during the trial, and whoever the people were, he realised - and whatever they'd done - deciding the fate of another person would be an onerous task he knew would haunt him to the end of his days. Each time he had glanced at the young girl in the dock, the image of his own daughters sprang into his mind and more than anything he wished to be away from this place and stripped of the responsibility for this burden.

Other men in the jury undoubtedly had similar

thoughts. A farmer with a young family, a grocer with a newly-born daughter, a farrier with a son about to be married. What would his feelings have been about Angelier had his boy died in the same way?

None of the men in that jury relished their duty, whatever their calling in life happened to be. However, they had been chosen, all of them selected at random, and they knew they had had no choice to refuse this responsibility. What's more, they knew that whatever course of action they decided, they would be bound to face the scorn of others who had opposing convictions, possibly for the rest of their life! But they had a duty to perform, and with all of them undoubtedly praying for guidance, there cannot have been many people in that court who envied them!

John Inglis meantime, was still immersed in his unstoppable oratory. He had been talking for nearly four hours and although his voice still rang clear, the strain was beginning to show. Facts from witnesses had been put in excellent order and by observing facial expressions and watching for reactions, he had either endorsed a point or glossed over anything suspected to be unfavourable for the defence of the accused. He had injected emotion into his rhetoric quite deliberately and with satisfaction he now took heed of the jury's apparent absorption, which he considered, reflected a similar mood throughout the court. He had given his all, and having swung from indignation, scorn and compassion as he took the jury through all the well-substantiated events and on to emotional issues, he now wound up his speech for the Defence with a passionate appeal.

Silent for a few seconds as though drawing strength - and badly needing it most likely - John Inglis looked at each member of the jury long and hard. Then straightening abruptly, revitalised it appeared by his changed expression, he took a deep breath. 'I am deeply conscious of a personal interest in your verdict gentlemen,' he began in a quiet manner, 'for if there should be any failure of justice, I would attribute it to no other reason than my inability to conduct this defence. And I feel persuaded that - if this were the case - the recollection of this day when this young girl faced execution, would haunt me as a dismal and blighting spectre which I would carry to the end of my life.' Pausing here, he again regarded every man on that jury, some quivering again under his scrutiny, and continuing almost as though uttering a prayer, he announced firmly, 'May the Spirit of all Truth guide you to an honest, a just and a true verdict! But no verdict will be either honest, or just, or true unless it satisfies the reasonable scruples of the severest judgement, and yet leaves undisturbed and unvexed the tender conscience among you.'

With these closing words, he appeared to droop both mentally and physically. He was burned out. He had given every ounce of his being. Then struggling to retain composure just as he had turned to sit down, he forced himself to wheel round almost immediately, standing erect again to bow for the standing ovation that reverberated throughout the court, which was immediately silenced by the objecting officials!

Chapter Thirty-Seven

Madeleine showed no outward sign of emotion when John Inglis returned to his seat. Her hands were still tightly clasped in her lap and her face continued to retain a mask of serenity. Having mastered the art of self-control throughout her short life, she had used it now as never before, although the effort in needing to do so was wearing thin. Her defending counsel had fought her corner wonderfully with great dignity and superb eloquence and watching him staring ahead without once glancing in her direction, she realised how much her fate rested heavily in his hands. She knew her life still remained uncertain with other opinions yet to be voiced, which could easily twist everything in a different direction - and after the short break as people shuffled and mumbled, silence fell once more in the court as the Lord Justice-Clerk entered for the final summing-up.

Undoubtedly, all members of the jury, and likewise many others in court, were still impressed by the Defence Counsel's dramatic speech and as though sensing this mood the Lord Justice-Clerk launched straight into rhetoric of a different tone by presenting a down-to-earth summary of the case. It was nearing the end of an exhausting day with the hot stuffy atmosphere in the court matching that of the rising emotions arguing for and against evidence given by witnesses, and with the verdict now approaching rapidly, there was an aura of heightened expectancy.

'Gentlemen of the Jury,' he began evenly, 'the contest of evidence and of argument is now closed and the time has come for deliberation and decision.'

Unlike John Inglis, the Right Honourable John Hope seldom shifted from his imposing stance before the jury and his summing up conveyed careful reasoning and scrupulous fairness. He held everyone's attention, particularly that of the jury, to whom he now looked with intense concentration.

'You must remember that the case is to be tried and decided solely on the evidence. Solely on the evidence,' he repeated slowly as he looked at each man in turn. 'You are not to give the slightest weight to the personal opinion concerning the guilt of the accused which, I regret, my learned friend the Lord Advocate allowed himself to express. Nor must you be weighed in favour of the accused by the moving and earnest declaration made by her counsel the Dean of Faculty regarding his own conviction of her innocence. Still looking fixedly at the jury, he furthered this point by making it clear that such expressions of opinion ought never to have been brought before a jury. 'Neither of them are good judges of the truth as all of you are,' he explained. 'You, the jury, are here to judge the guilt or the innocence of the accused from the evidence given by witnesses and not from the speeches of the counsel, however able or eloquent those speeches may be,' he added soberly.

He stressed that his duty was to go over the details of the evidence and to comment as he thought fit in order that members of the jury might be guided fairly in their verdict. 'And I must impress upon you that whatever doubt there may be in your minds in the defence of the accused, you must also rely on evidence given against her.'

From the anxious expressions, the jury were looking decidedly uncomfortable. They had never doubted at any time their responsibility; although it would be true to say that the emotional outpouring by John Inglis in arriving at a conclusion had possibly swayed many of them. How could they not have been? Now however, with the Lord Justice-Clerk placing all the facts and evidence in a logical order and - indicating clearly that in his opinion the accused was a woman utterly devoid of any morals - they were now being challenged in a different direction.

He examined the evidence dispassionately, criticising at one time John Inglis's claim that his client was an innocent girl, 'and indeed a heroine!' he exclaimed. He also propounded his own theory about Madeleine's sudden disappearance after learning about L'Angelier's death, suggesting it could even have been a plan to elicit support from the gardener about arsenic being needed to kill rats when she had reached the family's country home, which plausible reason then threw the jury into further despair. And when the Lord Justice-Clerk announced that the summing-up would continue the following morning, and the court rose for the day, it was more than likely that the jury were grateful for a break to refresh their minds and reassess the situation.

★ ★ ★

The matron decided not to invite conversation on their journey back to prison that evening and just returned a smile when a doleful looking Madeleine happened to glance her way. Her appetite never suffered however and after a substantial meal, she announced she would prefer to be alone for the rest of the evening and retire early to be fresh for the final day in court.

Having already considered how to treat Madeleine the night before either being acquitted or removed to the condemned cell in preparation for execution, Miss Aitken purposely kept her conversation light-hearted as she locked her cell for the night, although aware of her fastidious heed of fashion she tentatively broached the subject of what she would wear the following day. However, she need not have bothered. 'I have already decided,' Madeleine told her somewhat glumly. 'I must look my best and I've decided on something colourful.' Pausing speculatively, she glanced up at the tiny grating in her cell where the last rays of the day entered in shafts loaded with dust-mites. 'The weather is still so hot,' she said, 'and it's bound to be unbearable sitting in that court. So I think my lace-trimmed lawn dress with the sprigged flowers will be absolutely ideal,' and confirming with the matron that proceedings were due to start at 9a.m. sharp the following day, Madeleine laid everything ready for her early departure and bid her goodnight. It was only later that night that her true feelings were revealed when Miss Aitken heard the soft sobbing filling that darkened cell, and with a heavy heart she whispered a silent prayer.

Chapter Thirty-Eight

At nine o'clock on the morning of Thursday, the 9th July, the last day of the trial, the Lord Justice-Clerk resumed his summing-up. Earlier, Madeleine had stepped briskly into the dock looking more glamorous than she ever had on previous days, wearing a lace-trimmed lawn dress and straw bonnet decorated with flowers, and if anything, she looked brighter and more self-assured than on earlier occasions as she smiled down at people she knew and believed to be her friends.

The Right Honourable John Hope opened the proceedings with the implied theory concerning L'Angelier's possible suicide - albeit discounting it as wholly untenable that he should have poisoned himself in the street with such a large amount of arsenic secreted on his person. 'The defence would have been better advised to have concentrated on the point that the guilt could not be brought home to the accused, which was really the matter on which the case turned,' he said. And returning to whether the jury could believe that the accused was the type of person who would kill her lover, he referred to the Lord Advocate's theory and statement that after meeting with her lover the evening before he died, the accused did administer that dose of arsenic. 'On the other hand,' he continued, 'the counsel for the defence saw this as an incredible supposition and it was stated that she could not have had such a purpose and that it was too monstrous to believe, or even enquire into!'

He hesitated here as he moved closer to the jury. 'Gentlemen,' he said, 'it is very difficult to say what might not occur to the exasperated feelings of a female who had been placed in a situation such as this woman was placed, and it is here where the letters written by her are so important in assessing her feelings. What was the state of her mind? Was any trace of moral sense or propriety found in her letters? Or do they not exhibit such a degree of licentious feelings as to show that this is a person capable of cherishing any object to avoid disgrace and exposure - and indeed to take any revenge which came to mind when driven nearly to madness as she says she was?'

He referred then to phrases from her letters read out earlier...

'*Fond embraces and kisses*', he said, flourishing a hand, and went on to suggest that this was evidence of the passion of the accused before any sexual intercourse took place.

'*Oh to be in thy embrace, sweet Emile,*' he read, and looking up said, 'It may well be asked what else did she intend or wish for other than sexual intercourse after provoking and inviting it?'

In pointing out that the letters showed an extraordinary frame of mind and passion, 'as perhaps had ever appeared in a court of Justice,' he then asked, 'Can you be surprised therefore gentlemen, after receiving such letters, that he got possession of her person?'

With responsibility weighing heavily on their shoulders as the trial drew to a close, and possibly still turning over in their minds the emotional speech by John Inglis, the members of the jury were by now most likely wrestling with their conscience, and although well meaning, the final words of the Lord Justice-Clerk did little to inspire confidence.

'There are three charges on the indictment and three possible verdicts available,' he advised, 'Guilty, Not

Guilty and Not Proven. I am quite satisfied that whatever verdict you may give will be the best approximation to the truth at which we could arrive,' he said. 'But let me say also - as I said at the outset of my summing up of the case - you are the best judges. Not only in point of law, but in point of fact, and you may be perfectly confident that if you return a verdict satisfactory to yourselves that is against the accused, you need not fear any consequences from any future imagined or fancied discovery which may take place.'

Fine words and well-intended reassurance this may have been, but it did little to relieve the jury of their enormous burden as they considered these closing observations, and several of the men were noticed to be looking long and hard in the direction of the dock and obviously weighing up the situation.

'You have done your duty under your Oaths,' John Hope continued brusquely. 'Under God, and to your country, and you may feel satisfied that remorse you never can have.'

All eyes were fixed on the jury as they shuffled out to consider their verdict, except for Madeleine who stared straight ahead avoiding eye contact in any direction. She appeared to be lost in a world of her own with no betrayal of emotion, and in that hushed atmosphere, tense now with anticipation, the burden of her fate weighed heavily.

Chapter Thirty-Nine

Two bells were due to be rung after the jury had retired, one to summon the judges back to court and another that would announce the return of the jury. When a loud bell rang only a few minutes after they had disappeared, people began turning to one another in bewilderment. What had happened? With nothing apparently taking place, the whispering and fidgeting gradually died down but undoubtedly leaving everyone feeling uneasy and curious.

Madeleine's immediate thought was that the jurors had reached a swift decision and she braced herself for the worst. Her confidence had already weakened watching the changing expressions of the jury during the summing up and with the spectre of death now hovering closer, waves of fear quivered throughout her body.

As it turned out, the bell had been a false alarm and it was a further fifteen minutes before another bell sounded and the judges filed in to take their places. Not a murmur or movement stirred the court. The atmosphere was heavy, and when the second bell sounded ten minutes later, the tension heightened. It had taken twenty-five minutes for the jury to decide their verdict and as their names were called, they filed in solemnly one by one and took their places in the stall. William Moffat stood to attention when summoned by the Clerk of the court to deliver the verdict and with tears in his eyes as he faced the court he read from the paper held shakily in his hand.

'The jury find the panel not guilty on the first charge in the indictment by a majority,' he read. 'Of the second charge, not proven, and by a majority we find the third charge also not proven.'

Madeleine stared at Moffat unbelievingly in the hushed court as all eyes turned in her direction, and this was the lull before the storm! Within seconds, there was absolute pandemonium and the court went wild. Thunderous clapping and cheering drowned the cries of the purple-faced officers of the court who struggled to keep order and angry judges endeavoured uselessly to quieten the commotion as some stood to cheer the slight figure standing motionless in the dock. Raucous cheering filtered into the court as people rushed from their seats and flung doors wide to carry the news to the crowd. Friends with tears in their eyes ran to the dock grasping Madeleine's hands, congratulating her on her escape from the gallows, whilst others overcome with emotion just stood staring and speechless.

John Inglis remained in his chair with his head bowed, apparently impervious to the uproar around him and not once did he glance up at the court or in Madeleine's direction. She looked at him desperately urging his attention as she waited for a reaction, but with no response she was eventually obliged to leave the dock and bowing to the judges and jury, she gathered up her skirts and turned away as the trap door was lifted. Just once she glanced back before disappearing from the court, her face alight with expectancy as she once more urged John Inglis to look her way, but his head remained bowed and she moved away, making her way down the steps to leave the court a free woman.

★ ★ ★

In the dingy passages below, the surprise outcome of the trial had come as a shock. The condemned cell had already been prepared with the gate standing slightly ajar, and out of sight, a coffin was in place. Outside the prison, notices were ready for issuing to officials who would precede the cart conveying Madeleine to the gallows and undoubtedly money had already changed hands for those seeking the most advantageous points to view the execution. However, with this unexpected turn of events, fresh plans had to be made, and swiftly!

Fortunately, Madeleine had brought a change of clothes that morning at the suggestion of Miss Aitken. 'Whatever the outcome, you'll need a change most likely,' she had explained, although nearer the truth she had expected Madeleine to go straight to the condemned cell where the clothes she wore would have sufficed until her execution. In the circumstances now, they were vital for the hastily contrived plans officials had in mind for her safe exit from the court where crowds were now going wild for sight of her.

'Find a girl we can use as a decoy to lead the crowds away,' the police cried to court attendants as the cheers and shouts outside grew louder, and a young girl resembling the slight figure of Madeleine was eventually brought from the few women employed there and hastily dressed in the clothes Madeleine had been wearing in court. Confused and protesting loudly she was hustled along passages, the poor girl believing all the while that she was either involved in some criminal activity or in trouble with her employers. Pacified by the officials however as they helped her change into Madeleine's clothes, she was eventually led away from the court by the police with crowds following on a false trail. And as the pandemonium died down hasty arrangements were made for Madeleine to slip away via another exit, and then it was her turn to protest, arguing vehemently that she'd had no time to say good-bye to Miss Aitken or John Inglis!

'I can't leave without seeing either of them,' she

insisted frantically. 'The least I can do is to thank them. I must see them!'

'Time enough for that in the future,' her brother Jack snapped as he grabbed her arms and hustled her into a waiting cab. He had been summoned by court officials to get her away as quickly as possible and as they both unceremoniously tumbled in, he flung a blanket he'd been handed over her head as the cab pulled away. At the railway station, where no one yet knew about the outcome of the trial, he managed to keep her out of sight in an unoccupied carriage for the journey to Greenock where they boarded another train, still incognito, and travelled on to Rowaleyn where he told her the family waited.

Mixed emotions stunted conversation on that journey. Madeleine was still in shock following the startling events in court and the drama involved in rushing her away and Jack felt equally shaken. As they neared their destination however, he felt it his duty to prepare his sister for the reality of the situation when it came to facing the family.

'Mother has been very unwell,' he told her and he watched his sister's expression change from one of bewilderment to anguish. 'She has changed Madeleine. She has lost a lot of weight, and father... well, you will notice a change in him too.'

What could she say? She was still coming to terms with being free. Time had stood still since she had last seen them and she tormented herself trying to see them as Jack described, not as she remembered them. Her parents had suffered, like her. Of course they had, and the whole family.

'I've brought nothing but unhappiness,' she murmured at last and with her voice rising in panic, 'what can I do then? I'll have to get away Jack. I can't go back home to face them. I really can't,' and she fidgeted from her seat as Jack immediately jumped up, imagining in his concern she may jump from the clattering train. 'You can't get off Madeleine. Stay still!' he said tugging at her arm.

With a look of outrage, she flared, 'You think I'm mad don't you? Do you think I want to kill myself after all I've been through?' And then quietening as they settled, 'But I can't face them Jack. It's not right for them to suffer any more. I should go away. Be on my own.'

'How can you? You don't understand. There's nowhere you can go now without being recognised. Your face has been in all the papers. You must remain hidden, for a time anyway.'

'Go into hiding? What do you mean?' Horrified, she stared at her brother, unable to speak. In the past she'd enjoyed being the centre of attention, but... No, she could never hide!

'Don't you realise what it's been like Madeleine? Papers up and down the country have carried the news. Even abroad, I've heard. You're notorious!'

She burned with shame, still unable to say anything and shrinking back into her seat the years fell away as she remembered once before watching trees, houses, bridges and fields flashing by as they had on her way to the London school. So long ago now, she thought. But is it she wondered? So much has happened.

'I didn't know Jack,' she said in a small voice. 'I've heard nothing since I was first taken to...' and she could not finish. It was all behind her now and she desperately wanted to forget.

Jack looked away; his shoulders slumped as he stared from the window. 'But you must have realised,' he said, still glancing away. 'None of us could go anywhere without people glaring and making remarks. They were people we knew well too. People we thought were our friends, saying dreadful things, spiteful! That's why everyone is at Rowaleyn Madeleine. Although how long people will stay away from us there goodness knows.'

Jack had supported his sister while she had been in prison. He had been present in court whenever allowed to do so, and certainly was there for the verdict. Fortunately so, he reflected. He loved his sister despite everything that had happened and secretly admired the way she had coped. But she had to know how all this had affected the family and how this nightmare would probably continue for all of them, perhaps for ever, until he saw her tortured expression.

'I know it must have been dreadful for you too,' and he touched her arm with concern. 'Of course it was,' he said quietly, 'But it never showed Madeleine. Ever!' he said encouragingly. 'When I saw you in court you hardly moved and you always looked the same! It was amazing. Despite all that was being said about you – and all lies more than likely - you looked so composed!'

What could she say? she thought, gazing at her young brother through tears, and moments passed. 'I can't talk Jack,' she said at last. 'There's nothing I can say just now. It's too soon,' and as the train clattered on, both lost in their own thoughts, no one spoke, until Madeleine suddenly announced again in a firm voice that she could not stay at the family home. 'I've decided it would be right for me to get away, as far as possible Jack, perhaps immediately after reaching Rowaleyn and I have seen...'

'You'll need to rest Madeleine,' he interrupted. 'Settle a bit, after all this,' and he caught her look of resentment.

'Of course,' she said in a while. 'Perhaps a short rest, but then I must make plans.'

Jack also had plans to leave Scotland, unspoken yet to his parents in the circumstances, but firmly established in his own mind for some time. He wanted to travel to

London where he had friends. See a bit of life. Seek a career. Perhaps they could go together he thought. It would be unwise for Madeleine to travel alone in any case. However, for the time being - yes, for the time being, when the dust had settled - that would be something to consider for the future.

Chapter Forty

Elizabeth Smith was inconsolable when Madeleine entered the room with Jack at Rowaleyn and for a brief minute, she hesitated, wondering whether to rush to her, take her in her arms and console her. Despite always being the stronger of the two, Madeleine had never taken the lead in affection for either of her parents and they had always been equally cool but now she waived that aside and for what seemed a lifetime, they clasped each other when Madeleine ran to her and sobbed without a word being spoken.

The whole family had gathered to await her arrival, lining up and facing her silently as her mother continued to sob quietly in the background. John and Janet stood with eyes downcast and Bessie, dressed attractively as always, regarded her with mild interest. Her father, pale, drawn and shrunken, looked gangly she thought; his eyes rheumy like those of an old man. This was worse than she had ever imagined and wished more than anything she could turn away and leave now, this very minute.

Her father walked towards her, guiding her mother gently until they both stood before her and Madeleine lowered her eyes hating the accusing scrutiny.

'It's been so dreadful for all of you,' she said at last, her mouth so dry she could hardly form the words. 'I'm mortified and so very sorry,' she said in a broken voice, and when her mother collapsed once more in tears she held her again, shocked as she felt her frail shoulders.

'I would like to go to my room if I may,' she said in a while. She didn't know what else to do – or say - and yearned desperately to be alone. This was not as she supposed it would be. But could it be any other way? Her mother had quietened and as she drew away, she apologised again for the distress she had caused. 'They are feeble words I use,' she said thickly. 'But what more can I say?'

She detected an expression remembered from the past as she glanced at her father who was now turning to leave and she placed herself directly before him. 'I can only beg forgiveness for what you have suffered,' she implored. 'Please,' she added, but it was as though she had not spoken. Her mother smiled uncertainly through her tears as her father led her away and they left the room, followed by the rest of the family.

★ ★ ★

Madeleine's room had been prepared to be as comfortable as possible although now barely recognisable from how she remembered it. The bed looked familiar, but most of her personal things were no longer there. They had been removed many months ago when evidence was needed for her trial. The dressing table was cleared of trinkets and nothing remained on her table. No papers were in evidence anywhere and empty trays were piled together. Indignantly Madeleine strutted about opening drawers and cupboards, angry at the intrusion and meddling with her personal things, even at their holiday home where she seldom came anyway.

'How dare they,' she murmured under her breath and with a mix of emotion as she crossed to the window overlooking the garden, she stopped suddenly as memories of Emile triggered fleetingly. Just beyond the trees, they had made love, deliciously sweet she recalled, then turning away bitterly she drove the thoughts away. It has all finished now she regarded, even a life with William whom she had half-expected to see waiting for her with open arms along with her family. Even Jack or any of her family had not mentioned him, and she did not like to enquire. However, if that is how he wants to behave, she thought with contempt, then so be it!

A knock at the door startled her back to reality and she moved across the room uncertainly.

'Madeleine? Just a word.' It was her father and as she opened the door, she again felt appalled by his gaunt appearance as he stooped before her.

'We must talk,' he said. 'There is so much to say, yet I hardly know where to begin.'

This was unlike her father, always so positive and now a broken man and with an onrush of humility or guilt, she knew not what, she wrestled with a desire to embrace him as she had her mother earlier, but it would have been an embarrassment. They had never touched.

'You ask for forgiveness Madeleine,' he said feebly. 'And it is difficult, as you may imagine. But you are our daughter and much as I dislike the expression, our responsibility.' He moved across to a chair, brushing imaginary dust before sitting. 'I must sit. I tire easily nowadays.'

She had to take a hold. She was the stronger of the two now she realised and fighting back emotion told him she understood how difficult it had been for them all. 'I disobeyed you father,' she said quietly, 'and I am filled with remorse for all that has happened. Saying sorry is so meaningless but I know not what else to say.'

He sat silently, his eyes watery and she could hardly bear it as he struggled to clear his throat to speak and not allowing him time, rushed on, talking about her plans to go away. 'I cannot stay here father. I know that now. It will make it easier for everyone if I go. I have to find a new life, away from here where no one knows me. It's the only way.'

'But you will never escape from this,' he protested with a trace of his old pomposity returning. 'Don't you understand Madeleine? Every day the papers were full of what happened. Even in other parts of the world. The news has reached far.'

'So I understand from Jack,' she said sharply. 'He has told me. But whatever may happen and whatever I encounter, it will be for me to face. Alone father. Entirely alone. I no longer wish to subject you, or any of the family, to what has been a dreadful time for us all,' and as she rushed on she incredibly regained her earlier indignity about her innocence being questioned and added vehemently, 'It has been an unfortunate circumstance totally without reason!' And strengthening her conviction that it had all been a mistake, and viewing her escape from the gallows as being wholly justified in proving her innocence, she faced her father with a challenging glare. 'In time,' she said forcibly, 'people will realise what they have done to me father,' and touching him on the shoulder added gently, 'and to you and the whole family.'

His mouth sagged as he started to speak and once more he appeared haggard and old as he rose from his chair.

'Do you really believe that we shall also escape from the humiliation we have already endured Madeleine? There is nowhere for us to go any more. We are recognised everywhere. And what of our friends? Can we expect them to forget and return to enjoy our company again?' He sank back onto the chair but the bitterness remained in his eyes and Madeleine fought against her rising despair.

'Yes, Madeleine. You are right. You must go,' he went on. 'And perhaps you may escape into obscurity and I hope this may be so for your sake, although I very much doubt it. Our sins tend to follow...'

'But I am innocent father,' she interrupted stepping before him indignantly. 'I was acquitted. You were not there but you must have heard!'

'Yes, I heard everything Madeleine,' and he put out a feeble hand. 'We were told and as I said, the papers reported it all.'

Was that a look of doubt, she wondered as their eyes met? Does he really suspect that they should have returned a verdict of guilty? Did he expect that by now she would be hanging from a rope? And her mother – and the rest of the family - for they must have discussed it. What did they think? But she cast the thoughts aside, hurrying on when he looked ready to speak again. 'I will rest here a while father if I may,' she said. 'Then I must leave.'

Suddenly drained of energy and bereft of anything further to say, she gave in to her feelings and dropped to her knees, closing her eyes to hide the tears she could feel smarting as she rested her head on his knees. And she felt his hand, light on her shoulder.

- End -

Epilogue

Madeleine left Rowaleyn after a short time, leaving her family to live out their lives as best they could after such harsh treatment from friends, business colleagues and people they knew. Mr. Smith provided well for his daughter, as he had at her trial in engaging the finest barrister he could afford. He was nevertheless a broken man and died six years later while still in his fifties. Elizabeth, his wife, died soon after.

The verdict of 'Not Proven' at Madeleine's trial however persecuted her as her father had predicted. She never escaped from the gossip and as time passed, rumours of uncertainty concerning the verdict haunted her wherever she went, and indeed for the rest of her very long life.

She received countless proposals of marriage following her acquittal and refused them all, although she did eventually get married to an artist by whom she had two children, a boy named Tom and a girl named Kitten. The marriage did not last however and when her husband suddenly deserted her, mischief-makers - who were aware of her past - commented that he had detected a glint in her eyes! She had led a very happy life with him before he left her nevertheless, and was a popular figure living in a bohemian life-style with other artists who chose to ignore her past and the countless stories about her that continued to be written in popular magazines and books.

Her vivacity and love of life was inexhaustible and at the age of seventy she decided she wanted to be near her son in the United States where he was now working and, selling up her home in London, she booked a passage to New York.

She never lost her good looks and refusing to look her age, she always dressed in the pre-Raphaelite style and wore a henna wig to cover her greying hair.

In 1910 she learned about the death of her husband in England, which then allowed her to marry an American man she had fallen in love with, a man much younger than herself, who adored her femininity and ability to command attention wherever she went, particularly in male company! It was a happy marriage and in 1926 when he died suddenly she all but went to pieces, particularly when she was told to leave America within a month in her then straitened circumstances so as not to become a charge on the public funds! This was when she was ninety-two, and even at this age her stamina still served her well, as did her friends and son who supported her claim to remain in America. Up to her death on the 12th of April, 1928 at the age of ninety-three, she continued to live in New York.

Wherever Madeleine settled throughout her colourful life however, news of her identity always leaked out, even in America where reporters often pestered her. Her father had been right. People never forgot, but despite this, she persistently refused to talk about her earlier life. She never returned to Scotland. 'It holds such bitter memories,' she is known to have said at one time. And whether she murdered Emile L'Angelier has been open to speculation ever since her sensational trial. Only two people knew the truth - Madeleine herself, who within the Scottish law ruling at the time, was required to remain silent in the dock throughout her trial - and the other, Emile, who was in his grave.

One interesting observation came to light after her death however. Since Madeleine Smith left Glasgow following her trial for murder, it was discovered that she had paid for Masses to be said in church for the repose of the soul of her dead lover, and this led on to further speculation and more published writings about her trial, as it will undoubtedly continue to do.